MYSTERY WRITERS OF AMERICA
*presents*

# THE
# MYSTERY
# BOX

MYSTERY WRITERS OF AMERICA
*presents*

# THE
# MYSTERY
# BOX

---

EDITED BY

# BRAD MELTZER

**GRAND CENTRAL**
PUBLISHING

New York    Boston

Compilation copyright © 2013 by Mystery Writers of America, Inc.
Introduction copyright © 2013 by Brad Meltzer

"The Amiable Miss Edith Montague," copyright © 2013 by Jan Burke
"Waco 1982," copyright © 2013 by Laura Lippman
"War Secrets," copyright © 2013 by Libby Fischer Hellmann
"The Vly," copyright © 2013 by C. E. Lawrence
"Heirloom," copyright © 2013 by Joseph Finder
"The Boca Box," copyright © 2013 by James O. Born
"Mad Blood," copyright © 2013 by S. W. Hubbard
"Dear Mr. Queen," copyright © 2013 by Joseph Goodrich
"The Delivery," copyright © 2013 by R. T. Lawton
"Mokume Gane," copyright © 2013 by Tom Rob Smith
"Angelina," copyright © 2013 by Mary Anne Kelly
"The Remaining Unknowns," copyright © 2013 by Tony Broadbent
"Double Jeopardy," copyright © 2013 by Steve Berry
"The Secret Life of Books," copyright © 2013 by Angela Gerst
"The Very Private Detectress," copyright © 2013 by Catherine Mambretti
"The Birdhouse," copyright © 2013 by Stephen Ross
"The Honour of Dundee," copyright © 2013 by Charles Todd
"Hedge," copyright © 2013 by Jonathan Stone
"The Lunar Society," copyright © 2013 by Katherine Neville
"High Stakes," copyright © 2013 by R. L. Stine
"Remmy Rothstein Toes the Line (annotated)," copyright © 2013 by Karin Slaughter

Grand Central Publishing
Hachette Book Group
237 Park Avenue
New York, NY 10017

www.HachetteBookGroup.com

Printed in the United States of America

RRD-C

First Edition: April 2013
10  9  8  7  6  5  4  3  2  1

Grand Central Publishing is a division of Hachette Book Group, Inc.
The Grand Central Publishing name and logo is a trademark of Hachette Book Group, Inc.

The Hachette Speakers Bureau provides a wide range of authors for speaking events. To find out more, go to www.hachettespeakersbureau.com or call (866) 376-6591.

The publisher is not responsible for websites (or their content) that are not owned by the publisher.

Library of Congress Cataloging-in-Publication Data

Mystery Writers of America presents the mystery box / edited by Brad Meltzer.
    p. cm.
    ISBN 978-1-4555-1235-5 (hardcover)—ISBN 978-1-4555-1234-8 (trade pbk.)—
ISBN 978-1-4555-2267-5 (ebook)    1. Detective and mystery stories, American.
I. Meltzer, Brad.    II. Mystery Writers of America.    III. Title: Mystery box.
    PS648.D4M98 2013
    813'.08720806—dc23
                2012025862

# CONTENTS

# CONTENTS

# INTRODUCTION
## BY BRAD MELTZER

I t won't hurt," they told me.

Right there, I was skeptical. Sure, the folks at the Mystery Writers of America seem like nice people. And they like mysteries (which is extra nice). But when they walked in with those nice smiles and asked me to be the editor of this year's MWA anthology, I knew I was in for some pain—especially when they said it'd be easy.

But then the MWA folks added that one key phrase that every writer longs to hear: "We'll do all the work for you."

See how tricky these bastards are?

My reaction was instantaneous: "I'm in."

Then, in a bit of verbal fine print, they delivered the final piece of news: "You have to invite ten of your friends to write stories."

Wait. So beyond all this heavy lifting I don't have to do, I also get to work with ten dear friends, all of whom will use their gorgeous talents to make me look good?

"Count me in. I'll do your next thirty anthologies."

And so, this book was born. The theme would be a mystery box. What's in the box? That was for our writers to decide: a long-lost gun, a personal secret, or Gwyneth Paltrow's head (just like in

*Seven*). The box could be real (like the gun), or metaphoric (like their heart). But they had to use a box.

All I needed after that were friends—the real secret ingredient— whose talents I have admired for years. Let me say it as clearly as I can: I love every writer in this book. And I owe every writer in this book. They are the ones who solved and then shared their secrets. But what I appreciate most is simply their friendship and generosity.

So thank you to my dear friends Steve Berry, Jim Born, Jan Burke, Joe Finder, Laura Lippman, Katherine Neville, Karin Slaughter, Tom Rob Smith, R. L. Stine, and Charles Todd for volunteering and for sharing. I feel truly honored that each of you said yes. I'm thrilled to have each of you in my life. And I know every editor of these anthologies thinks they have the best group of writers. They are all wrong. We have the best. And that's not even all.

A huge thanks also goes to Tony Broadbent, Angela Gerst, Joseph Goodrich, Libby Fischer Hellmann, S. W. Hubbard, Mary Anne Kelly, C. E. Lawrence, R. T. Lawton, Catherine Mambretti, Stephen Ross, and Jonathan Stone for doing the hardest things of all: putting themselves out there and sharing their own secrets. To everyone reading this: Go buy all their books. Please.

A special thank-you also goes to incredible miracle workers Barry Zeman of MWA and Larry Segriff of Tekno Books, who kept true to their promises and did all the real work. They are the reasons this book exists, and I thank them for their never-ending patience with me. And yes, it truly was painless.

Special thanks also to all the judges who helped read the volumes of submissions: Peter Blauner, Wendy Hornsby, Annette Meyers, Kris Montee, and T. Jefferson Parker, all of them wonderful writers themselves. Thank you to my secret weapons in publishing: Mitch Hoffman, Lindsey Rose, Jamie Raab, and all my dear friends at Grand Central Publishing. Thank you to Noah Kuttler, who is the best. And finally, thank you to Cori, Jonas, Lila, and Theo, for being the secret in my own mystery box, and for always having faith.

MYSTERY WRITERS OF AMERICA
*presents*

# THE MYSTERY BOX

# THE AMIABLE MISS EDITH MONTAGUE

## BY JAN BURKE

The murder of my beloved great-aunt, Miss Edith Montague, always known in our small but enterprising town as a most amiable woman, came as a tremendous shock to her nearest and dearest.

Since I am her only surviving heir, I suppose her nearest and dearest would be me. She was one of two children of the founder of Montague Manufacturing, my great-grandfather, the inventor Marcus Montague, for whom I was named in a shameless attempt by my parents to curry her favor. The other child, the ne'er-do-well from whom I am descended, squandered his portion of his inheritance and died destitute. An annual allotment from Aunt Edith allowed my parents to live fairly comfortably during their brief lives.

The woman I called Aunt Edith (from the start, she gently told me she preferred this to "great-aunt") was in complete control of the sizable Montague fortune.

As her sole heir, I might have been placed in the awkward position of being suspect number one, if I hadn't had an undisputed alibi on the night of her murder. At the time of her death, you see, I was having dinner with the chief of police.

Occasionally fate makes up for all its cruel tricks by actually doing one a good turn. That one, however, was hardly enough to make up for the loss of Aunt Edith.

She had taken me in after my parents died of typhoid fever—the illness apparently the result of hiring a rather unsanitary cook. Had my parents not sent me to boarding school, I probably would have met the same destiny. This was perhaps the only reason I ever had to be grateful for being sent to the Billingsfield Academy, although at the time I probably would have chosen typhoid fever over the torments meted out by the headmaster and my classmates. Aunt Edith, nearly the only relative who showed any concern for my welfare, rescued me from them.

Another unmarried, wealthy lady of a certain age might have found the unexpected responsibility of raising a ten-year-old boy daunting, but Aunt Edith seemed overjoyed at the prospect. She brought me to live with her. Indeed, over the next fifteen years she gave me more kindness and attention than I had received from my own fun-loving but rather negligent parents.

I said she was nearly the only relative, because I suppose I must give some credit to my somewhat misguided uncle Gilbert, whom I had never met. He was not actually my uncle, but some sort of cousin of my father. Aunt Edith told me he was her favorite relative, a salesman who traveled a great deal, and said it with a kind of twinkle in her eye that made me wonder things I dared not ask. He occasionally sent odd packages—never twice from the same address—with terse notes. In general, the contents were designed to ensure that although I was being raised by a maiden aunt, I was exposed to masculine entertainments. As I aged, they grew increasingly risqué.

He should have known that Aunt Edith was not the type to tie a boy to her apron strings, and indeed, she made sure I met and made friends with other males. If it was Uncle Gilbert who sent the pair of stilts, it was Aunt Edith who encouraged me to give them a try and, as in other areas of my life, cheered my successes and patched me up after my failures. Uncle Gilbert might send me packets of French postcards, but it was she who arranged for a male friend to discuss the facts of life with me in a no-nonsense fashion. I always had the suspicion she would have done so herself, but she rightly assumed I would have been mortified to hear of such things from her.

In almost every other sort of life lesson, she was my guiding light, an example I tried to emulate. She was someone whose confidence in me steadied me enough to leave the past behind and look forward. I knew that in the natural course of things, she would most likely predecease me, but not this soon. And not in this horrible way.

Jenksville is normally a peaceful community. Our entire police force consists of fifteen individuals. So the evening of Wednesday, May third, the night she was murdered, it did not take the officer sent by our single detective very long to locate the detective's uncle, Chief Irons, who was enjoying a good cigar and a fine brandy at Jenksville's best restaurant. The other fourteen members of the force knew where we were, because throughout the day, they had been hopeful that at some point during that dinner, I would hand the chief a check from my aunt, a donation large enough to help the department buy its first automobile. As usual, she did not seek publicity for her generosity. I'm sure Chief Irons was secretly relieved to have the check in hand before events took our minds away from dinner.

Some hours later I stood motionless in the center of the room in which Aunt Edith had died, staring at disorder that was entirely foreign to it, trying not to look at the bloodstained carpet. It was a room she had used as a study, the place where she kept her business records, wrote correspondence, made telephone calls, held committee meetings, and read quietly before the fireplace.

One end of the room was lined in bookshelves, now in some disarray. Detective Mortimer Osburn was at the opposite side, leaning his ample posterior against the handsome tiger maple desk where Aunt Edith had spent part of each day.

The clock over the elaborately carved mantel had run down, and so had I, although Detective Osburn seemed as oblivious of this fact as he was of any possible clues.

"So, to review," he said, not for the first time, "your cook and housekeeper, Mrs. McCray, who does not reside on the premises, has worked here for some time?"

"She has spent nearly twenty years working for my aunt, and is entirely trustworthy. She is so distraught that I have given her the week off, but she and her husband live nearby—in a home my aunt bought for her as a wedding present—and I'm sure she would be happy to answer any questions you may have for her."

"No, no, that's all right—known her all my life. In fact, I helped her when she fell and broke her arm a few months ago."

"Yes, my aunt told me about that. She was grateful for your assistance. And I'm sure you know Mrs. McCray has recovered."

He shifted his weight. "As for Mrs. McCray, officially, you see, I have to ask these questions."

I stared at him in disbelief. "Surely only once?"

His ears grew red, and he consulted his notes again, muttering something about never knowing "what might occur to a person on reexamination." He cleared his throat and said, "Yes, well, Mrs. McCray, who does not reside on the premises, admitted four individuals into the home at seven this evening."

I took out my pocket watch. "As of an hour ago, yesterday evening."

"Yes, well, I apologize, Mr. Montague, I do realize it is very late, but I want to make sure I have all of this straight before I leave. Last time, I promise, then I'll be on my way. I wouldn't want you to feel it necessary to hire outside help."

At last I saw what this dithering and delay was all about. Clorinda.

For a moment I considered reassuring Osburn that the odds of Clorinda Ainsbury's involving herself in this case were remote indeed. Instead I wound my watch, returned it to my vest, and waited for the fourth recitation of the few facts at Osburn's disposal.

Osburn went back to his notes.

"Mrs. McCray left not long after she admitted Mrs. Wainwright, Mr. Dillon, Miss Freedman, and Mrs. Conrad. All were expected as visitors today."

"It was a meeting of the Jenksville Opera Society."

"I've been meaning to ask—just the four of them. Executive committee?"

"The entire society."

Osburn raised his brows.

"My aunt did not intend to perform. If you heard the other four sing, you'd understand why it has been of limited interest to their fellow citizens."

Osburn snorted a laugh, but I regretted the words as soon as they were out of my mouth. Aunt Edith would never have said anything cutting about anyone of her acquaintance, a forbearance I found infinitely admirable and impossible to imitate. Whenever I had said as much to her, a sparkle would come into her eyes and she would smile sweetly. Then she would say that someday she would tell me the secret of her ability to hold her tongue, but in the meantime, she found my observations so amusing, she begged me not to withhold them from her. I don't know if she really did find them amusing, but it was like Aunt Edith to never make one feel as if one were at fault.

"Perhaps I haven't a proper appreciation for their art," I said to Osburn. "In any case, I cannot believe any of them would want to harm their patron."

"My unc—er, Chief Irons will find out soon enough."

Wisely, his uncle had decided to ask additional questions of the witnesses himself at the station. "My deepest sympathies, Marcus," the chief said to me as he prepared to take his leave. "Your aunt was a fine woman who will be deeply missed." He unthinkingly reached to pat the pocket in which he had placed the check, caught himself at it, then offered his condolences again. He left the house just after the coroner removed Aunt Edith's body.

Now, several hours later, Osburn scratched his head. "Truth is, sir, I can't think of anyone in Jenksville who'd want to harm her. That's why I'm sure it had to be a stranger. Some thief!"

"There are many valuable items in this room. Why would a thief leave them behind?"

"Something or someone scared him off."

I made no comment.

"You left the house at seven-thirty?"

"Yes, and as I've said, drove to the police station, where I met Chief Irons. I took him to dinner."

"Yes, of course. And you heard no arguing or anything of that sort?"

"No. But the garage is at the back of the property, where the stables once were. I left through the back door, and didn't walk past this room or interrupt the meeting to say good-bye."

I felt my throat tighten, then chided myself for wishing for something that could not change. I did not stop to say good-bye. I did not know . . . could not have known . . .

"The Opera Society meeting lasted until eight-thirty," Osburn said. "Then all four left together. Mr. Dillon drove the ladies home, then realized that he had left his notebook here and returned. That was at some time after nine, he said, and he was considering not disturbing your aunt at such an hour, until he saw the lights were still on. Then he noticed the front door was ajar and came in, and found—"

"Yes. I heard him tell Chief Irons what happened after that." I couldn't bear another recitation of the story of Mr. Dillon's discovery of my aunt's body, lying before the hearth. She had apparently received a single, mighty blow to the back of her head as she stood in front of the fireplace. The police had arrived quickly, but she was already dead. The coroner believed she was killed instantly. She had not suffered, but that fact alone is not the healing comfort some seem to think it will be to the bereaved. A death in the family will teach you that people are capable of saying the damnedest things.

"So the only thing that's missing is a wooden box?" Osburn asked again.

"I can't be sure. I will need to put the room in order again, and attempt to do a complete survey, but so far, it seems to be the only thing that is gone. Whoever was in here apparently searched for it until he or she discovered the false bottom of that desk drawer."

Again I confirmed to him that the only thing missing was the large, locked wooden box in which my aunt had stored receipts, canceled checks, and old bills. The bank would be notified in the morning to be especially vigilant regarding forgeries or other problems with my aunt's account, but I still could not see why someone alone in the house would overlook items in the other rooms, such as expensive jewelry, priceless works of art, and the silver pieces in the dining room. Even here in the study, in the very desk he had rooted through, a large sum of cash had been left behind. Why leave that and other valuable items in the desk and take only that box?

Osburn hinted that it might be best if he remained to guard me, but this service I quickly declined. Eventually he left.

Although it was the very thing I had been hoping he would do for several hours, I found myself wanting even his obnoxious company not long after he was gone. Alone, I began to realize that his dull conversation had distanced me from my own thoughts and feelings.

I was still in a state of shock, wishing I could find relief in tears but not really able to believe that my aunt was dead, let alone that someone had murdered her.

I decided I could not face spending another moment in the study. I locked the front and back doors and ensured that the windows were latched. It was a warm evening, but I decided I would rather suffer heat than a return of the intruder.

I reached my bedroom and was debating whether I should close my window, which was, after all, upstairs and at the back of the house, when I heard someone in the alley.

I was frightened, but I have a pistol and have practiced with it faithfully. I took it and a flashlight from my nightstand and hurried outside.

Someone was rummaging around near the garage.

"Who's there?" I called. "Come out now—I'm armed and won't hesitate to shoot."

"Don't shoot!" an all-too-familiar voice said.

"Detective Osburn," I said, lowering my weapon.

"I was just making sure your back gate is secure."

"Detective Osburn, it is now after two in the morning. Go home. Now. I don't mean to be rude, but really, if I see you around the house again, I will be forced to report to your uncle that you have been pestering me."

He left.

I went back into the house, relocked the doors, went upstairs, put the gun and flashlight away, and undressed.

I finally wept—of all the stupid things to set me off, it was donning an old pair of pajamas she had given me—and lay awake until exhaustion finally blessed me with a dreamless sleep.

I awakened at dawn to find a body in my bed.

This one was alive, warm, and naked.

"Clorinda?" I said drowsily, thinking I must still be asleep and dreaming.

"Hush, darling," she said, and sealed my lips with a kiss.

For once I wasn't going to argue with her.

Clorinda is willowy, stronger than she looks, and wears her dark brown hair bobbed. She is not quite a beauty—if forced to name her best feature, I suppose I would mention her large, dark eyes. Or perhaps her slightly husky voice. Or the curve of her lips—something about them always makes her look as if she has a delightful secret you want to know, without making her look smug about it. But it is the sum total of her Clorinda-ness that draws me to her. If I were blind, I would still love her.

She is intelligent, independent, and strong-willed. She has her own private investigations agency and is an avid suffragist. She does not suffer fools, which is why what I thought of as a romance and she thought of as experimentation went awry three months ago.

We had slept together, I had offered marriage, and she had told me she never wanted to speak to me again. And proved she meant it.

But she had just now said, "Hush, darling." I told myself not to be a fool. And made mad if not quite silent love to her.

I know what you are thinking, some of you. You are thinking that this was disrespectful of my aunt. In the interest of proving you wrong, I will continue my tale.

When we had caught our breath, I humiliated myself by weeping again, although I had not wanted to do so in front of her. She didn't ridicule me for it, merely held me until I quieted. "I'm so sorry, Marcus."

I couldn't speak for some time, but finally managed to say, "How did you get in?"

"Lockpicks. It has taken me months to get the hang of it."

"I would have let you in."

"I wasn't sure."

Clorinda, unsure? A new experience. I decided this was not the moment to say so.

"I know you weren't expecting me," she went on, demonstrating a mastery of understatement, "but I loved Edith, and her death has made me reconsider a number of things. I thought you might need a friend."

That last, distancing word might have been crushing under other circumstances, but I was too wrung out to worry about my failed love life. I merely nodded.

"I hurried over as soon as I read the newspaper," she said.

"Oh God. The newspaper. Reporters. Gaaagh!" I pulled the covers over my head. Clorinda had bribed someone at the paper to ensure that she received one of the first copies off the press, but it was only a matter of time before its later readers would demand sordid details that could not have made the morning edition.

"Don't worry, Irons is distracting them with a lot of nonsense about hobos."

I emerged from my bed-linen lair. "Hobos?"

"Marcus, of course a stranger will be blamed! No one in Jenksville will want to believe that the murderer of a respected and beloved elderly lady might be living next door, shopping at the same shops they do, sitting next to them in the pew at church. Chief Irons has already sent officers down to the hobo camp just outside of town, near the railroad tracks."

"Oh dear."

"Yes. It's a pity. The men there are already facing hard times."

"I hope no one suffers too much in the chief's quest to find a suspect."

"He knows he needs to make some sort of arrest soon or face an angry citizenry, but perhaps he'll do so without using the very tactics your aunt tried to persuade him are ineffective."

"I suppose it will now be my job to keep bribing him into better behavior."

"One of the best possible uses of your money," she agreed, rising and beginning to dress.

I couldn't help myself. "You aren't leaving?"

"Of course not. But I think it would be best if we wore clothing downstairs. You're bound to have loads of callers."

I groaned.

"Irons can put that idiot nephew of his out front to turn them away. It would be a better use of his time than his so-called investigating. Ring him up and ask him to do it."

"It seems cruel to turn away those who want to grieve for her."

"You'll see them later. You don't want a lot of rubbernecking buzzards poking their beaks in here."

"True."

"Get dressed. I'll make breakfast."

"You are giving a lot of orders this morning."

She smiled. "So I am. You can take a turn at it later if you'd like, but just now you probably need a little help to get going."

I couldn't deny it.

We eventually ended up exactly where I knew she most wanted to be, and if asked, I would have readily included my bed among the places that ranked much lower in interest to her. She observed the study and I observed her doing so. She moved slowly, stood at different places in the room, even climbed onto a chair at one point to get something like a bird's-eye view of the scene of the crime. There was one brief moment when I saw sadness cross her face as she looked down at the bloodstain on the carpet—then she shocked me by lowering herself next to it and asking me to position her as my aunt had been found. I complied.

She rose to her feet again and studied the mantel. My great-grandfather had commissioned the work of a master woodcarver to cover the columns, front piece, and sides with lions in various poses—some roaring, some springing upon prey, some in stately repose. The mantel had terrified me when I was a child.

Clorinda asked a few questions—most of them quite different in nature from the ones Osburn had asked.

"The intruder searched this room after he or she struck Edith down. Do you agree?"

"Yes. Aunt Edith wouldn't have allowed someone to search while she was here, and there was no sign that she had been anywhere else in the house after the meeting."

"And you agree she was given no opportunity to struggle? That this disarray was the result of the search, not a fight?"

"Yes."

"Why?"

I frowned. "The way things are left. The lamp is not knocked over. Nothing breakable is smashed, the desk is the only piece of furniture out of place. She...she had no marks on her, other than the single blow, so all that adds up to a surprise attack rather than a fight."

"Excellent. I agree."

"And even the search—the desk is a mess, and things have been pulled forward on shelves, books tossed down, and so on, but the cushions are on the chairs, and not ripped open. Perhaps it's because I know the box was taken, but I think the intruder found what he was looking for."

"Perhaps so. The grate is clean—no fire last night?"

"No. It was too warm for a fire."

"For you or me, but older women sometimes experience temperature differently."

"Yes, I understand," I said, "but there was no fire."

"So why was your aunt staring at the fireplace?"

"I don't know that she was. She was just— No, wait. The clock!" I said, suddenly seeing what Clorinda was trying to determine.

She frowned at it. "It stopped at eleven-fourteen."

"I noticed last night that it had run down. Even the clock couldn't outlast Osburn. Aunt Edith always wound them on Wednesday."

"Winding, Wednesday. All right. Does she—did she do that in the morning?"

"No, in the evening, usually after dinner. But she would have put it off last night until after the meeting."

"Hmm. Would she have locked the front door after her guests left?"

"No. I don't think half the people in town do."

"They will now. Fearing hobos, I'm sure." She opened the slender pocket watch I had given her to commemorate the day New York fully enfranchised women, a milestone reached, in part, because of her work.

I moved to the clock and opened the ornately painted glass door of its case. I was surprised to see not one but two brass clock keys, then decided that Aunt Edith might have kept the clock keys together as she made her rounds.

Clorinda distracted me by saying, "I detest people who disguise their nosiness as sympathy, and I believe you will soon be inundated by such. Make the call to the chief, please."

"Right." I put the clock keys in my vest pocket and moved toward the telephone on the desk.

"Ah, the telephone! Another sign that she was away from the desk and probably never saw the intruder," Clorinda said. "She might have used the telephone otherwise."

"Unless he threatened her with a pistol."

"A possibility, but I think he would have forced her to reveal the location of the wooden box to him, then, and spared himself the effort of searching for it."

"True."

I asked the operator to connect me with the police, and within minutes a patrol officer was dispatched to my aunt's home. Although the chief had not sent his nephew, Clorinda agreed with me that this was for the best—satisfying her thirst for petty revenge on Osburn was not worth dealing with his paranoia about her investigative abilities. "Besides, I know Duffy. He's the best of that lot over there. The chief wants you to be pleased."

Officer Duffy was equally gratified to see her. "Now we'll get somewhere, sir," he confided to me. "Miss Ainsbury's worth a hundred of Osburn. Smart of you to call her in."

He then seated himself in the foyer. As Clorinda had predicted, a steady flow of visitors began to arrive on the doorstep soon after. I overheard Duffy saying that they must not disturb the master of the house and that he was sure an announcement of arrangements would be made before long.

Master of the house. Arrangements. I resolutely turned back to the study and Clorinda. The master of the house didn't want to be such and had no stomach for arrangements.

I was brought up short by the sight of Clorinda standing on a chair, looking down on the mantel clock.

She heard me enter, and when she turned toward me I saw that her eyes were bright with excitement. "Close the door, please," she said just above a whisper. "And lock it, in case someone should get past Duffy."

"Unlikely, I would think." But I locked it. "What are you doing?"

"Come here, Marcus!"

"All right, but I don't think that chair will support our combined weight."

"Don't be silly. And please keep your voice low. I'd prefer not to be overheard." She stepped down and pointed to the still-open clock case.

"Have you ever tried to move this clock?"

"No, why should I?"

"Try it now."

I did. It wouldn't budge. "What in blazes—?"

"It's attached to the wall. It has a door—"

"What? Into the flue?"

"No. Look," she said, stooping before the fireplace. "The fireplace is deep, and the chimney is set back."

She was right. "Yes, I see what you mean, but what does that have to do with that clock being there?"

"Take the pendulum off."

"I assume you have already done this once?"

She nodded, not looking the least bit guilty. "I was going to try to move the clock. One should never move a pendulum clock with the pendulum attached."

I removed it and saw that the back panel, behind the pendulum, had a keyhole in it.

"You found two keys," she said. "Will one of them fit that slot?"

I tried the larger of the two keys. "I hope this won't cause some harm to the works." But as I turned it, we heard the muffled sound of a gear turning, and then something sliding. To our left, one of the lion's heads now stood out a good six inches away from the rest of his body, at the end of a smooth metal cylinder.

"Looks as if your great-grandfather the inventor included a few innovations when he built the place."

She encouraged me to try turning the lion's head, which I did, and was nearly knocked flat by a bookcase swinging out from the wall.

We stared at each other in wide-eyed amazement. I peered inside the opening and saw a small room lined with shelves. I brought the chair over to block the door open—my first concern was that we not be trapped inside. Clorinda approved but said she was certain there would be a mechanism to get out from the other side. First she found a flashlight on a small table just inside the door, and turned it on.

"The batteries seem fresh. The room doesn't smell musty. I'd say your aunt has been in here quite recently."

Next she found the lever that worked from this side.

"All the years I've lived here, I never imagined such a place."

We explored the shelves. Most appeared to hold treasures from Great-grandfather Montague's day. Some items were sentimental—a sword he carried in the Civil War, an embroidered handkerchief, and a miniature of his wife, who had died giving birth to Aunt Edith. Others were less so—a tray of jewelry, another of gold coins, a stack of stock certificates.

A final set of shelves held nine large boxes, each identical to the one stolen from my aunt's desk. They were made of black walnut and polished to a dark sheen. Five were open and empty. Four were closed and locked.

"I'll bet her father made these for her," Clorinda said. "Or had them made for her."

I lifted one. It wasn't heavy.

"Try the passage key again," Clorinda said.

I did, and it worked. I heard the lock turn, and hesitated. "Let's do this where there's more light."

I carried the newly unlocked box out to the study and placed it on the desk.

"Would you like me to leave?" she asked.

I shook my head.

"I'll sit on the sofa," she said. "You can have a little privacy, and I'll be near if you need me."

I felt ill at ease. Aunt Edith and I had always respected each other. She had never opened the cigar box full of boy's treasures I had kept as a child, nor rummaged through my belongings when I became an adult. I had extended the same courtesy to her—I had as much curiosity as the next child, but at first because I did not want to be sent back to Billingsfield Academy and later because I never wanted to betray her trust in me, I did not snoop through her possessions.

Clorinda, watching me, said, "She is dead, Marcus, and you were more important to her than anyone on this earth. Don't be afraid—she had faith in you."

I opened the box.

It was half-full of slips of paper of varying sizes. The handwriting, I knew at a glance, was Aunt Edith's own. Her handwriting and hers only on every note. I picked up a small stack of them and began to read.

> *If Phineas Carmichael believes that no one can identify the deadliest farter in the congregation, he is the biggest self-deceiver on earth. I am convinced the church is vermin-free because he gasses it once a week.*

I burst out laughing, startling Clorinda.

> *What cruel devil is telling Maud Blemsey she looks good in pink?*

> *Caught Mr. Diggs placing his thumb on the scale—again! Very difficult to be diplomatic about it. Shall drive to the market in Kerrick Corners for the next few weeks.*

> *Thought I heard Hortense Wainwright in a duet with Ulysses Dillon. It was only two cats fornicating in the alley. Is there anyone so deluded as an amateur musician?*

*Herbert Rushworth asked me to read his poetry. I believe I have found the answer to my question about amateur musicians.*

"So this was her secret," I said, which Clorinda rightly took to be permission to come closer. "This box is loaded with undelivered insults. She told me that one day she would let me know the secret of her amiability. This must be it."

"Public amiability, anyway. My, my."

"Go ahead—read some of them. You know I can't keep secrets from you."

"Do you wish you could?"

I thought before answering, and said, "No."

She smiled. "Perhaps we can figure out why her murderer wanted to get his hands on these." She chose a slip of paper and laughed. "Obidiah Pilsy."

"Picks his nose."

"Observant man."

"Not really. Obie is quite blatant about it."

As we looked through the notes together, we soon saw that some were not simply a way for Aunt Edith to express anger or loathing. Though never one to carry tittle-tattle among the townspeople, when confiding to the box of secrets, she had much to say about her neighbors. Many of her notes were full of gossip and innuendo.

*Stella Osburn's second and third sons bear a striking resemblance to George Horvath's boy. Am I the only one who sees it? I wonder if the chief would continue to blindly support his incompetent "nephew" if he knew?*

"Is she saying Detective Osburn and his brother are—"

Clorinda ruffled my hair. "You know that's exactly what she's saying."

*Estelle Freedman would like us to believe she came here from Boston, yet has not the least trace of a Boston accent. I would swear I hear a bit of the South in her vowels when she's not paying attention.*

*I've discovered what happened to my stolen bracelet, I'm glad I didn't report it missing. Lizzy Conrad took it, and frankly, now that I've figured that out, I don't care. It wasn't worth much to me, and it will help her to get her youngest daughter away from Lizzy's horrible second husband. Lizzy's secret is safe with me.*

It was then that I came across the first note that mentioned my own name.

*Marcus has still not figured out that I am "Uncle Gilbert." Marcus is so dear to me, and I am afraid that if—no, when— I reveal to him that his aunt is the one who has been sending him all these naughty items, he won't forgive me for deceiving him so. What a fix!*

"You know, Clorinda, I'm beginning to wonder if I knew Aunt Edith at all."

When I didn't hear a reply, I looked over to see that she was biting down on one of the sofa cushions, trying to restrain her laughter. Tears were streaming down her face. I realized then that I had been a bit too open with Clorinda about some matters—before we slept together, I had bashfully confided to her that my uncle Gilbert had sent me condoms.

"It's not funny!" I said, then saw that it was.

When we were able to breathe normally again, I said, "Duffy will think I'm the worst sort of person, laughing in here."

"Marcus, Duffy has been with more bereaved families than you can begin to imagine. He won't judge you, and neither will I."

"You'll just wonder why I didn't figure out that good old Uncle Gilbert was no more real than Santa Claus. Good God."

"Not at all. Your aunt was a master at keeping secrets, and you were very young when she established the idea of his existence with you. Had she done so later, I think you would have questioned it. You can't blame her for not knowing how best to handle such matters. As my father used to say, every infant is born into an experiment in child-rearing."

"She did a much better job of it than my parents did, Uncle Gilbert or no."

"I'm impressed with her ability to purchase such items for you."

"Like you, she could afford to hire discreet intermediaries. I shudder to think how many households in Jenksville and surrounding communities rely on you for additional income."

"Not enough to strain my coffers, if that's what you're worried about."

"I have never had need of your coffers, as you damn well know."

She smiled. "One of your attractions, Marcus. You've never been after my money. Another is that you'll swear in front of me."

"The feeling is mutual. On both counts."

I went back to work, somewhat mollified.

Not many minutes later, I came across a note that made me wish it had been cold enough for a fire, for I would have burned it immediately.

> *I believe Marcus has finally lost his virginity. This would make me happier if it made him happier.*
>
> *I can't understand what has gone wrong.*
>
> *I know there was mutual regard and, on his part at least, deep affection, if not love.*
>
> *He can't be worried about an unwanted pregnancy. Even if he failed to take the condoms with him, I know that Clorinda*

*has read Mrs. Sanger's "Family Limitation" pamphlet (illegal though it may be) and would be prepared.*

*Did it not go well? Apparently not.*

*I suppose even his own mother would not be able to discuss this with him, but how I wish I could. He seems so heartbroken.*

*I, too, am fond of Clorinda, and could not resist having such hopes for their happiness. I know Clorinda is quite fierce—I admire her for it—but I have not previously suspected her of cruelty.*

"And I never suspected you of the same, Edith."

At that moment, if I could have locked myself in the secret room and never reemerged, I would have made a dash for it. Clorinda had been reading over my shoulder. I opened my mouth, then shut it again.

"What were you going to say?" she asked.

"I was going to apologize for her. But that's not my place. And I do think, in the privacy of her own home, she was entitled to her own thoughts, however mistaken her opinions might have been. I've had a mistaken opinion or two myself."

There was a long silence; then I felt Clorinda's arms come about me, and she gently pulled me back against her. I have never been able to figure out how one person could be both so firm and so soft in such perfect proportion.

She rested her face between my shoulder blades, and I placed my hands over hers. It took me a while to realize she was crying. In five years of courting her, I had only seen Clorinda tear up three times. Once when I gave her the pocket watch. Once when she told me how much she missed her father. And when we had first made love. But she had never out-and-out cried.

I turned around and held her. "Did her words hurt you, Clorinda? If so, I am so sorry—"

"No, I'm just thinking of how much I've missed your—your Marcus-ness."

I held her even closer. "I was thinking something very similar about you a little earlier today." This brought on more tears. When at last they abated, I found a handkerchief for her.

"I had better lock this box away and close up the secret room," I said. "I know I should probably hand the entire collection of notes over to the police and let them sort out who might have been insulted to the point of murder, but when I think of the potential harm . . ."

"We need to think this through, but yes, for now, let's straighten the room."

As we worked to restore order, I answered some additional questions from Clorinda about my interview with Detective Osburn.

"What did he mean about your housekeeper's broken arm?"

"Mrs. McCray fell and landed badly on her arm, just out front. Osburn happened to be nearby, and helped her into the house. He assisted quite ably. Aunt Edith was grateful to him—I was with you that day, so I wasn't here to help."

"Oh. *That* day?"

"Yes."

"I was a damned fool," she said.

"So was I," I said. "Something we had in common." I closed the clock case, making sure only one key remained in the clock. The other I kept in my vest.

I had no sooner done so than a knock sounded and we heard Duffy call through the door.

"Pardon me, sir, but I stepped outside to have a smoke and noticed Osburn walking up the street, headed this way. He's got a lady and a gent with him. Just thought you might not want to be found—well, in a position that might compromise Miss Ainsbury."

I opened the door. "Thank you, Duffy."

He nodded, looked past me at Clorinda, and seemed shocked. "Miss Ainsbury?"

"It's quite all right, Duffy. Contrary to popular opinion, I am capable of crying, swooning, screaming, and a multitude of other so-called feminine activities."

He grinned. "You'll do, but you'd better get your beau to comb his hair. He looks a fright." He winked. "Wouldn't want any swooning."

As I quickly combed my hair, Clorinda called police headquarters and put in a request for Chief Irons's presence.

"Is that necessary?" I asked.

"He can control Osburn better than anyone."

"We have Duffy—"

"Duffy's going to run an errand for me."

"Clorinda—"

"A very quick errand. Trust me?"

Her face was tearstained, and she is not one of those women who looks gorgeous after a bout of crying. In fact, what she looked was—dear to me. And a little more vulnerable than usual. "Yes, of course," I said, causing her to reach for my handkerchief again as she ran out of the room to talk to Duffy.

The two people with Osburn were Ulysses Dillon and Lizzy Conrad. Lizzy was handcuffed to the detective. She appeared to have been weeping, with no more beautifying results than those on Clorinda. Dillon looked extremely unhappy.

"Well, Mr. Montague! I think we've solved the case," Osburn said.

"Is Ulysses going to accuse a hobo?"

"A hobo!"

"Never mind. Go on—I'm all ears."

At that moment, Clorinda came back into the room. Osburn scowled at her.

"Detective Osburn," she said sweetly.

"You've been crying," he said.

"I've lost the woman I had hoped would be, in essence, my mother-in-law. Of course I've been crying."

Detective Osburn caught me looking surprised—I'm to acting what the Opera Society is to singing. "Clorinda, I thought we agreed—"

"To let a decent period of mourning pass before announcing our news? Yes, of course. But none of these people will say anything to anyone, will they?" As she looked at each member of the stunned trio, she received pledges of secrecy.

It would be all over town ten minutes after they left.

"Clorinda," I said, "you'll be happy to know that Detective Osburn has solved the case."

She looked about. "Where's the hobo?"

Osburn was infuriated. "What hobo?"

"Oh. Surely it wasn't one of these people?"

"I'm afraid so. Dillon?"

"A few weeks ago, I saw Mrs. Conrad steal a bracelet from your aunt's desk," he mumbled.

"And said nothing?" Clorinda asked, earning more dark looks from Osburn.

"I felt sorry for her. Her husband's a brute. If I hadn't told him that two other ladies would ride with us to the Opera Society, and that being in it would put Lizzy in Miss Montague's good graces, I don't think he would have given permission for her to come with us to the meetings. As it was, I had to tell him that being in Miss Montague's good graces would lead to fat contracts for him for building sets, or he never would have let her out of the house."

"She stole from your aunt," Osburn said to me. "She's done nothing but cry since I arrested her, but I'll get the story out of her. It's obvious—she slipped back here after the meeting last night to see what else she could steal, killed your aunt."

"And forgot to take anything but a box of receipts," Clorinda said.

"Dillon showed up unexpectedly, and that scared her off."

"Does she have powers of invisibility?"

"What is that supposed to mean?"

"How did she get past him?"

"She went out the back, out to the alley, and away. Simple."

"But there has been a misunderstanding," I said. "My aunt gave the bracelet to Lizzy."

Lizzy, who had stood with head bent, looked up at me.

"I saw her take it from the desk," Dillon said, on the defensive.

"Of course you did. She did just as my aunt asked. Dear me, my aunt had hoped no one had noticed, because she feared the other two ladies in the society might expect similar gifts."

"Why not just give it to her some other time, then?" Osburn asked.

"As Mr. Dillon has explained, Lizzy was unable to leave the house much. This would be the only opportunity to bestow a gift on her without her husband's knowledge."

"Why in God's name would your aunt give an expensive bracelet to a nobody like Lizzy Conrad?"

"As I know from personal experience, my aunt didn't believe any human being was a 'nobody'—man, woman, or child. As for why, that was a delicate and private matter between the two of them, but let me just hint that my aunt had the welfare of Lizzy's daughter in mind."

"Is this true, Lizzy?"

Clorinda asked it before Osburn could, and she looked into Lizzy's eyes in such a compelling way, I was unsurprised when Lizzy said, "Yes, yes it is."

Chief Irons arrived just in time to hear Clorinda say, "Unless you are accusing my fiancé and Mrs. Conrad of lying, Detective Osburn, perhaps you would be so good as to free Lizzy from those handcuffs?"

With an uneasy glance at his uncle, Osburn said, "No, of course, if that was the way it was . . ." He freed Lizzy from the cuffs.

Clorinda walked Lizzy to the door, interrupting Dillon's profuse apologies to Lizzy by saying, "Mr. Dillon, I know Marcus has questions for you," damn her fine eyes, and then telling Lizzy that she would hire her to work in a place where she would be safe from Mr. Conrad if she should decide to leave him.

Dillon was looking at me expectantly, as were the chief and Osburn, when Duffy saved the day, or at least the moment, by arriving with Mrs. McCray. I smiled and said, "Mrs. McCray! Perfect timing. And Duffy!" I was about to continue in this inane fashion when I noticed that Duffy had donned gloves and was carefully carrying a black walnut box. Osburn noticed the box, too, and made a grab for it, but Duffy dodged the effort and stood out of Osburn's reach.

Clorinda came back just then. "Let's all move to the study, shall we?"

"Oh, please, miss," Mrs. McCray said feebly. "The blood and all. I can't bear it."

"Poor dear, then we'll begin here. Tell us about the day you fell and broke your arm."

Mrs. McCray glanced at me. I smiled and nodded.

"I was coming back from the market, and tripped on the sidewalk out front and fell and broke my arm...."

As we stood together in the hallway, she told of Detective Osburn's finding her and helping her up, and bringing her into the house.

"And where did he take you in, the front or the back?"

"The front, miss, and probably because I was screeching from the pain."

"And where was Miss Edith?"

"In her study, working on her bills and such. She come runnin' out, and was plumb distracted when she saw the bone stickin' out and all. Well, I thought I'd faint myself, but I didn't, did I? Then Mr. Osburn asks her to please get some clean towels and a bit of brandy for me, and when she goes off to do that, he asks me where's the telephone, and I points to the study. And he goes in and calls Dr. Willis, and that seems to take forever—you know how it is when you're in pain—and when he comes back out Miss Edith gives him the towels, and—forgive me, but he hardly seemed to know what to do. But luckily, the doc was not but the next street over and he was able to stop by and patch me up. Whooeee, that hurt like the devil, but all's right now, isn't it, Detective Osburn?"

"I'm glad you are recovered," he said mechanically. He was staring at the box in Duffy's gloved hands.

"Is this the missing box?" Chief Irons asked. "Where did you find it, Duffy?"

"Behind the house, sir. In a patch of grass between the garage and the fence."

"Thank you, Mrs. McCray," I said. "You may go on back home now. I appreciate your coming over here on such short notice and during your time off."

She was disappointed, I could tell, but I didn't want to have a bigger audience than necessary. Mrs. McCray spoke with me about my aunt, and how much she would be missed. I thanked her again and assured her that an arrest would be made before the end of the day.

She left, clearly brimming with curiosity. We adjourned to the study.

Chief Irons had grown quiet, as had we all.

We did not keep Dillon for long, although he must have wondered what would take place after—in answer to Clorinda's questions—he described how quickly Osburn had arrived after he had called for the police. Faster, he was sure, than Osburn could have arrived from the station. Clorinda thanked him, and he left.

She then outlined events. She told Chief Irons that we had found notes among Miss Edith's effects, notes that Detective Osburn had undoubtedly seen out on the desk the day Mrs. McCray broke her arm. Notes in Miss Edith's own hand, usually hidden, locked away, and never intended to be seen by any eyes but her own.

Clorinda paused, then said, "What I have to say next—perhaps you would prefer to have Officer Duffy wait in another room?"

"Duffy," the chief said, "you are now officially deaf."

"What's that you say, Chief?"

"Good man. Go on, Miss Ainsbury."

So she told him that one of those notes raised questions about the paternity of two of the Osburn brothers—the chief shook his head slowly as Clorinda recited it from memory:

*Stella Osburn's second and third sons bear a striking resemblance to George Horvath's boy. Am I the only one who sees it?*

"That's a damned lie!" Osburn shouted.

Chief Irons sighed. "Mort, I've long known that you two are George Horvath's sons. You and Clarence both."

"But—but—"

"My sister-in-law—your mother—is dead, and I don't like to speak ill of the dead, but facts are facts. Your older brother, Raymond, was the only real Osburn in the whole nest full of cuckoo's eggs."

"But then—then I'm not your nephew!"

Chief Irons sighed again. "Not by blood, no. Your mother and my wife were sisters, so you were never going to be my nephew except through marriage, and yet—"

"But we were Osburns! And since Raymond died in France—"

"You're beginning to get the picture, Mort. You've lost both parents and a brother. I've lost my wife. So right now, when it comes to family, I have only two living nephews. You were raised by a man who loved you and turned a blind eye to his wife's unfaithfulness. I have followed his lead. Up until now, anyway. You turned your back on the law, Mort. The law that I have worked my entire adult life to uphold. You killed Miss Edith, didn't you? And you were going to blame poor Lizzy Conrad for it? Well, the Devil and his right-hand man Horvath can have the responsibility of you now, for all I care, but maybe something can be made of Clarence yet."

"I asked Officer Duffy to use gloves, sir," Clorinda said. "I believe you'll find Detective Osburn's prints on the box. I suspect he knew—as did everyone in the police department—that Marcus would be dining with you last night, and therefore out of the house, unable to defend his aunt. Detective Osburn may not have known about the Opera Society, but it would be an easy thing to come into the house after they left. He killed her, and then looked for the box. Having Dillon return unexpectedly probably frightened him into grabbing the box and running out the back door with it. I suspect the murder weapon—perhaps his nightstick?—is either in the area where Duffy found the box, or perhaps by now is among the ashes in Detective Osburn's fireplace."

"Well, Mort?" the chief asked. "If you want any help at all from me, you had better tell me where to find your nightstick."

"Somewhere out by the garage," Osburn said miserably.

Chief Irons ordered Duffy to handcuff him. Then he sighed and said to us, "If it's all the same to you two, we'll work out a story that won't cause his brother Clarence any more shame and heartbreak than he's already bound to suffer. There will be no mention of any note."

We agreed.

Clorinda stayed with me that night, and asked me to marry her. I didn't hesitate to say yes. She said she knew her timing was bad, and I told her it was perfect.

Eventually we sorted through all the boxes. Aunt Edith had apparently been encouraged by her father to pen the notes from an early age. We immediately burned the worst of the notes, and used others as the basis of a book we wrote together, although we changed the names of those mentioned in them. Once the book was written, we kept only a few of the notes that were just about us, and consigned the rest to the fire.

The book became a bestseller and still provides us with a little extra money, which we use to help women like Lizzy to start new lives away from their spouses.

I know some of you think we probably wrote a colorful history of Jenksville, but no, it was *Aunt Edith's Giant Book of Insults*.

Now that I know both sides of Aunt Edith, I think she would have laughed heartily over that one.

Still, when the last scrap had been burned, I felt a great relief. Clorinda asked me if Pandora's box was now empty. I reminded her that no, there was always going to be one last item in any Pandora's box, which was a good thing, or I might have given up on her.

She's a smart woman, but it took her a few minutes to remember that the gods left Pandora hope.

# WACO 1982

## BY LAURA LIPPMAN

They called them black beans, although no one in the *Waco Times* newsroom could explain the origin of the term. They were just "Lou's Black Beans," dreaded equally by one and all. They appeared in the form of memos typed on scanner paper, the coded sheets that were threaded through IBM Selectrics when there were not enough computers to go around—and there were never enough computers, not in the crunch of afternoon deadline, not when one was the low woman on the totem pole. Forced to use a typewriter to file her copy, Marissa belonged to one of the last generation of journalists to type -30- to denote the end, but of course she could not know this in the summer of 1982. She also couldn't know that she would give up on newspapers by year's end, although the briefness of her tenure would not keep her from bragging, many years in the future, that she had once typed her copy and put -30- at the end.

Black beans arrived in one's mailbox cubby, innocuous slips of paper until unfolded. Then they became the black plague. Death to advancement, death to career, death to ambition.

> *Marissa, Go down to the park and write up a little something on the groundbreaking ceremony for the new public restrooms (no big deal). Best, Lou*

*Marissa, There's a program over at Baylor for young entrepreneurs, in which kiddos learn the ins and outs of business. But please—don't give us a lot of cute stories about kids. Focus on the business basics. Best, Lou*

*Marissa, Where does navel lint come from? And why do I have so much of it? Best, Lou*

The last one never happened. But it could, it might. Marissa came to believe that she would spend an eternity chasing down every idle thought that rolled through the mind of Lou Baker, lonely as a tumbleweed, something Marissa had believed she would find in Waco, Texas, knowing very little about the state's topography before she arrived there for a job interview on a sweltering April day. She feared that she would spend the rest of her life in Waco, Texas, because she had graduated in the middle of a recession and all the good newspapers insisted that applicants have at least five years' experience and she was never, ever going to have five years' experience.

Marissa was twenty-one years old.

The day she turned twenty-two, in late August, she found another black bean in her mailbox:

*Marissa, Wouldn't it be interesting, as summer comes to an end, to find out what is in the various lost-and-found boxes at motels, restaurants, the Texas Ranger Hall of Fame, et cetera? Best, Lou*

*No*, she thought reflexively, as if the question were not rhetorical. She made a dutiful effort to shoot it down. First rule of a Lou Baker Black Bean: Shoot it down. She called the motels. Mostly clothing. She called the restaurants. Clothing, a pair of binoculars. She called the Texas Ranger Hall of Fame and they seemed strangely proud of having nothing—nothing!—in the lost and found, as if part of being a Texas Ranger were making sure that a person was never, ever, separated from a beloved hat, fanny pack, or billfold.

But when she dutifully reported back to Lou that there really didn't seem to be much in the various lost and founds, the city editor asked for a list of the places she had called and scanned it with a puckered frown.

"I don't see the Waco Inn on here," Lou said.

That place. "I thought you wanted me to focus on the tourist destinations, along the interstate. The Waco Inn is pretty far off the beaten track."

"But Tatum Buford, who owns the Waco Inn, was the person who gave me this idea. At the Rotary Club luncheon. He said, 'Wouldn't it be interesting if someone looked to see what was in the local lost and founds at summer's end? I think it would be.'"

"Oh, it was a great idea in concept. But sometimes even good ideas don't pan out."

"Sure, if you just sit at your desk, making phone calls. You should go and ask to see the contents. Feet on the street, Marissa, feet on the street." It was one of Lou's favorite expressions, as mysterious in origin as the black beans.

"At every motel?"

"At every motel."

"What if they won't show me?"

"They have to, by law. Freedom of speech. Look, don't forget the five W's—they work, Marissa. You know what they say—no stupid questions!"

Marissa was pretty sure that the First Amendment did not apply in this situation and that there were plenty of stupid questions. But she resigned herself to spending a day or two visiting every motel in Waco and asking to see the lost-and-found boxes.

Lou tottered off, smoothing her too-tight skirt down over her hips. Lou was Louisa Busbee Baker, the first female city editor at the Waco paper. She had worked there her entire career, as she frequently reminded Marissa, starting in 1967 as a clerk in the features section—it was called Brazos Living, after the river that ran through town. She had moved up from taking paid wedding announcements to reporter, then to editor of Brazos Living and, for five years now, city editor. She was the only woman in management on the news side, a fact she frequently referred to. "As the only woman…" She favored tight skirts and high heels, although she always seemed uncertain in the latter. The general impression was of someone who used to be a knockout and didn't realize that her knockout days were behind her. Lou was, by Marissa's calculations, at least thirty-eight.

Marissa started on the interstate frontage road, where the motels were close together and she could cover a lot of ground. She had already interviewed clerks at almost every one, but no one seemed to remember her or the conversation, so she had to go through her spiel all over again. Perhaps they were as bored as she was on this despairingly hot August day. At any rate, they either brought out the box of left-behind clothing immediately or asked the manager for permission to do so, in which case the manager, also bored, did the honors.

The boxes themselves were remarkably the same from motel to motel, almost as if they had a single supplier, or as if there were state regulations stipulating what could be used as a lost-and-found box at a motel. Plain cardboard, beginning to sag and soften in that way that cardboard does over time.

The contents, too, were similar. Clothes and more clothes, an occasional paperback, usually a romance.

The young clerk at the Motel 6 said: "Off the record?"

Marissa thought that hilarious. *Off the record.* As if this were Watergate, which was part of the reason she was a journalist. It was the reason that almost everyone in her generation had become a journalist. *Follow the money, bring down a president.* That was what she should be doing, not staring into a cardboard box of dirty clothes.

"Sure."

"You're not going to find anything good."

*Tell me something I don't know.* "That's what I've been trying to explain to my boss. She seems to think I'm going to find, like, bowling balls or a live alligator if I ask the right questions."

"No, I mean—the valuable stuff, jewelry and the like, it's not going to be in the lost and found, not for long. It may never even get to the box. The maids get first crack, and you can't blame them for taking what they find. People are pigs. The nicest-looking people will do things you can't believe to a motel room." Actually, Marissa could believe it. "But even if someone does do the right thing and brings an item in, the boss lets them keep it if no one calls within a week. That's why it's all crap clothes and pantyhose. No one wants this stuff, not even the people who once owned it."

Marissa wondered if there was a story in this. *Rampant thievery at Waco motels.* But given that Lou had gotten this hot tip from a motel guy at the Rotary Club, that idea probably wouldn't be met with much favor.

Lou got most of her ideas from lunches and associates and neighbors. She didn't seem to have a life outside the paper. She didn't seem to read the paper, either, and often assigned stories that had already been published. On the rare occasions she had ideas of her own, it was because she had been jostled by a pothole or seen a billboard on the way to work. Many of Lou's black beans began: *Saw a sign on the way to work today, which got me to thinking...*

The most frequent supplier of Lou's ideas, if one could call them ideas, was the man who owned the Mexican restaurant on the traffic circle, where Lou went every Friday and had the taco salad with exactly one frozen margarita. She was very proud of that frozen margarita, which was why her staff knew about it. She seemed to think it signaled a wild streak, a *Front Page/His Girl Friday* type of devil-may-care shenanigans. Drinking! At lunch! But the frozen margarita at that restaurant was about as potent as a Slurpee.

The young reporters liked to drink beer and shots at a bar near the newspaper, a dive-y place called Pat's Idle Hour. Even as they sat there, drinking cheap beer and complaining about their bosses, they knew that one day they would enjoy telling people about Pat's

Idle Hour, where the clientele ran to VA patients and the jukebox played Glenn Miller's "String of Pearls." The young reporters were hyperconscious of the camp factor in their lives, the dives and the aptly named diners, the hilarious items at the flea market on the traffic circle, the bowling shirts and vintage dresses discovered at yard sales, although the elderly widows of Waco were surprisingly savvy about the value of their Depression-era china.

"She hates me," Marissa said that afternoon, as the young staffers closed out the week at Pat's Idle Hour, drinking the cheapest and best beers of their lives. To her horror, no one contradicted her.

"She doesn't have any reason to hate me," she tried again.

"Well," Beth said, "you *are* cute."

"So are you," Marissa said with automatic courtesy. Beth was cute. Cute was exactly what Beth was. She was the kind of girl who never lacked for a boyfriend. In fact, her boyfriends usually overlapped by a little. Marissa was attractive in a different way, sultry and exotic. Most of the men she met here thought she was Mexican, but she was a quarter Lebanese, on her mother's side.

"You're totally cute," she repeated to Beth for emphasis. "And so is Veronica. So how can that be the problem?"

"Hey—thanks," Veronica said, caught off-guard by the compliment. She was a pretty girl, if slightly overweight and in need of better clothes.

The two guys in their group, John and Jonathan, wisely kept their own counsel.

"Lou doesn't have the intellectual discipline to hate more than one person. She has a favorite"—Beth indicated Jonathan, who, not being a girl, simply nodded, acknowledging the truth. "And she has an unfavorite. That's you, for now. But it will change. I think it's just her personality. Which is to say, her lack of personality. She doesn't know who she is, so she fixates on the person she envies. You're cute, you went to a really good college back east, you drive that amazing car that your parents gave you for graduation."

"That amazing car," Marissa reminded Beth, "doesn't have

air-conditioning. Because my parents never thought I'd end up in Texas and neither did I. Especially not Waco, Texas, for God's sake. My parents thought I was going to Yale Law School, which I turned down to go into journalism."

John nodded. "Yes, we know. You went to Williams, you got into Yale, you have parents who will pay the full freight if you decide to abandon journalism and go to law school. We all know. And Lou knows. Lou knows that you have complete and utter disdain for the place where she has spent her entire adult life, since arriving at Baylor when she was eighteen. Lou grew up in Rosebud, Texas. Waco is the big city to her."

"We all want out," Marissa said. "Not a single person sitting here wants to work for this paper one more goddamn day than necessary."

"True," Jonathan said. "But the rest of us are a little more diplomatic about that fact."

Easy for Jonathan to be so lofty. The cop reporter, he had the best story of the summer so far, a suspected homicide, juicy by local standards. A Baylor coed had been found in a ditch off Robinson Road about a month ago. Although there were strange markings on her—the sheriff's office was being deliberately vague about just what they were—the cause of death had not yet been determined and was awaiting a more thorough autopsy down in Austin. But the death of a Baylor student was a big deal, under any circumstance, even a drunk-driving accident.

"That's so *unfair*," Marissa said, even as she hoped Jonathan was right about the source of her disfavor. Because she could change her attitude, if that was all Lou held against her. She could be kinder, sweeter. She could pretend wild enthusiasm for Lou's black beans. She could stop mentioning that she had given up Yale Law School for "all of this," waving her hand at the small newsroom, the town beyond. She had, come to think of it, said that more than once.

On Monday, newly energized, she attacked her list of remaining motels, the drives longer now that the motels were farther apart. By 11 a.m., her seat belt had left a wet stripe across her dress and her hair looked a wreck from driving with the windows open. It was the penultimate day of August and Lou wanted the story for next weekend, which would be Labor Day. Back at school, the days would already be pleasant, the nights verging on cool. Marissa had arrived in Waco with fifteen Fair Isle sweaters, sweaters that remained in boxes of mothballs. With only one motel to go by lunchtime, she decided to reward herself for her thoroughness with a coconut milk shake at the ironically named Health Camp, a burger place on the traffic circle. It wasn't far from Lou's beloved Mexican restaurant, but it was a Monday. Lou would never drink a frozen margarita on a Monday.

Marissa preferred her margaritas on the rocks, at a bar on the river that thought it was cool. She was having what her friends back home called a *Looking for Mr. Goodbar* phase, which made her something of a throwback, but then—Waco was something of a throwback. Her friends in Waco didn't know what she did on weekday nights after work. Beth, who had never been without a boyfriend, would have been shocked, Veronica worried, John and Jonathan tantalized. Besides, what could be safer than picking up men in Waco? The men that Marissa allowed to take her home for a night were, for the most part, wildly grateful. Almost every one said he wanted to see her again, but she gave them fake names and numbers, cut them dead if she encountered them again. Her pickups were Baylor boys and cowboys and Rotarians. They made her feel sophisticated, in her vintage black sundress and high-heeled sandals, her sunglasses up on her head. It was a heady sensation for someone like Marissa, who until arriving in Waco had had sex with exactly two men, both long-term college boyfriends, the second of whom had broken her heart when he made it clear, rather late in the game, that he didn't want her to follow him to Columbia's j-school, or even to New York.

But it was surprisingly hard work, getting these men to take her home. Most of them had to get drunk first, really drunk. After the first encounter, Marissa decided never to get into a man's car again, that the drive was the real risk. She followed them to shitty off-campus apartments and depressing duplexes and apartments that looked like cheap motel rooms and sometimes actual motel rooms. "Are you on the Pill?" every single one asked, usually just seconds before, hovering above her. "Are you on the Pill?"

She was.

One man had not asked, had not said much of anything. He'd also needed the least persuasion, instructing her after one drink to follow him to a motel room. Once there, he posed her, he told her what to do, still using as few words as possible. She found herself doing whatever he wanted, and he wanted some unusual things. Of all the men she had been with, he was the one she would have liked to see again. But no matter how many times she went to the bar along the river, he never showed up again. He said his name was Charlie, but that wasn't how he signed the register when they pretended, for the benefit of the night clerk, to be newlyweds who had driven up I-35 from Nuevo Laredo.

Fortified by a coconut milk shake and an order of onion rings, Marissa headed to the last motel on her list, the Waco Inn. A dull panic began to set in as she drove, because she had now spent two days on this assignment and had established only that she was right and Lou was wrong, which Lou would find particularly unforgivable.

At the Waco Inn, the manager showed her the usual collection of abandoned clothes, stained and torn and smelly clothes so awful that it was possible to imagine someone checking into a motel just to get rid of them.

"There's one more item, but the owner keeps it in his office safe."

"It must be valuable," Marissa said.

"Oh, it is. I'll ask Tatum if he wants to show it to you."

Ah, yes, Tatum, the Rotarian who had suggested the story to Lou, probably inspired by this very item, thinking it would bring publicity to his not-very-nice motel, whose customers were seldom tourists.

"I can't imagine someone leaving a beauty like this behind," Tatum said, lifting a black leather belt with a heavy silver-and-turquoise buckle from his safe. It was the first item of value that Marissa had seen in all her travels. Not to her taste, not at all, but clearly expensive.

"How long have you had it?"

"About four weeks."

"I'm surprised you haven't let someone on staff take it."

Marissa expected the owner to deny the practice of divvying up the lost-and-found spoils. Instead, he said: "No one on the staff has the initials CB."

She took the belt in her hands. It was the first time she had touched it, but not the first time it had touched her. She remembered it around her wrists, her throat, and, later, its brisk strokes on her back and ass, stinging but not hurting. "You are a very bad girl," the man she knew as Charlie told her in a low, strangely dispassionate voice. He didn't really hurt her. That was his gift. That was why she wanted to see him again. He knew how to take a girl right up to the edge, how to make sex scary, but not too scary. He had very dark hair and lots of it—on his head, on his forearms, on his muscled legs, on his chest, but not on his back. He had tightened that belt around her neck and she had let him, never the least bit tempted to tell him to stop, trusting him to anticipate the perfect moment. No, she couldn't be wrong. It was the same belt. But then—it was the same motel. Four weeks. It had been five weeks since Marissa had been here with him. Five weeks and five days. Five weeks and five days of going back to the bar by the river, but he was never there. She traced the initials on the buckle. CB.

"They call us the buckle on the Bible Belt." That was what one editor after another said to Marissa the day she interviewed for the job at the *Waco Times*. The executive editor, the managing editor, the assistant managing editor, and, finally, Lou. They seemed to be warning her, or at least challenging her commitment. But Marissa needed a job and she had started the hunt late, given that she'd thought she would be at Columbia in the fall, getting a master's in journalism alongside her boyfriend, with whom she had worked on the college paper. But he didn't want her there. And Columbia didn't want her there, which was almost as hurtful. Marissa decided to get a real newspaper job, show her ex that she was ready to do what he was only *studying*.

"They call us the buckle on the Bible Belt, Marissa. A little sleepy for young people, but it's a great place to raise a family."

The male editors all had families. Only Lou, married to her high school sweetheart, did not. The gossip was that Lou had the steady job in her household, that her husband called himself a developer but was just a man with a lot of raw land south of town.

The Waco Inn's owner, Tatum Buford, father of this bastard black bean, reached for the buckle, but Marissa did not surrender it. "I'm surprised you didn't try to find the owner."

"We did," Tatum said. "But he paid cash, and the name in the register, it wasn't with these initials."

"And when did you say this was?" Marissa asked.

"Four weeks ago. Maybe three. But no more than a month."

Five weeks and five days. When he was done, he stood up and she watched from the bed as he dressed, fastening the buckle, tucking in his shirt. "See you around," he said, and she had taken those words to heart. She didn't care that he had ripped her dress under the armhole; the seams in old dresses gave way sometimes. She didn't care that he spoke so little. She didn't care if he was married, raising a family in this town that was so good for families. She assumed he was married. But she couldn't imagine why he didn't want her again. Had she been too compliant, too eager? Should she have fought more, pretended fear? If she could find him again, she'd do it however he wanted.

"You should let me photograph this for my story," Marissa told Tatum Buford.

"Shouldn't I pose with it? A photo of a belt is awful plain."

"Oh, yes. But we'll need a studio shot, too, and that has to be done at the office, with proper lighting."

"You'll bring it back? After it's photographed?"

"Of course," Marissa said.

She often made such blithe promises, only three months into what she thought would be her career. She promised to give back photographs, scrapbooks, any and all artifacts that were beloved by their owners, of no consequence to her. She promised to inquire how someone might buy a photograph once it was in the paper. Sometimes she did, and sometimes she didn't, but it never worried her. It was just something she said, in order to get what she wanted. That was what reporters did. They said whatever it took, to get what they wanted.

In this case, she knew she wouldn't bring the belt back. Because in this case, the man who owned the belt would call her and she would give it to him, face to face. *Face to face.*

"The silver has tarnished. You ought to shine it up for the photograph," Buford said.

"I will," Marissa said. "I will."

She took it back to the newspaper, excited to have found a way into the story she had been trying to kill. When Lou came out of the afternoon meeting, Marissa was waiting at her office door, a puppy dog who had finally learned to play fetch. *Here's the stick! Love me! Pet me! Say I'm your favorite!*

Lou just looked at the belt and said, "Come on in."

Her office was small, windowless, without much in the way of personal touches, quite unlike the offices of her male colleagues, which were filled with evidence of the families that thrived in Waco. The young women who worked for Lou surmised that she believed she was not entitled to a private life, or even photographs of one. Lou had to prove, every day, that her head was in the game.

Lou turned the buckle over and over in her hand while Marissa talked about how it was the only interesting thing she had uncovered, that it would be better to focus on the discovery of this one beautiful object, that the owner might come forward and then they would have another story.

"From the Waco Inn?" Lou asked. "And the belt's owner never called and the motel didn't call him?"

"No, he never called and there's been—some screwup. They're not sure who left it there. The maid forgot to write down the room number. Or she didn't turn it in right away. I'll have to check my notes on that one detail."

"And they couldn't match it to the initials in the register?"

"No, but it could be an heirloom. The man might not even have those initials."

"It's tarnished," Lou said, tapping it with a manicured finger.

It was. "I need to shine it, I guess."

"Yes, you do that."

Marissa did. She polished the belt, she polished her story and turned it in, structuring it like a mystery, a safe one, the kind of breathless tale that the Happy Hollisters might take on. The assistant city editor thought it was good, for what it was. But the story didn't run and it didn't run and it didn't run. September continued hot; it felt like summer to her. Suddenly it was October, which was hot, too. When she finally asked Lou when they were going to run her story, Lou said: "Oh, it doesn't feel timely anymore."

"What?"

"Summer's over. We don't have a hook."

"It's really not so much about the lost-and-found boxes, the end of summer, not anymore. It's about this beautiful belt left at a seedy motel, whether it will be reunited with the owner."

"The Waco Inn isn't seedy. It's just—fighting a tough location. Tatum's doing what he can to bring it along. He's even going to add a Continental breakfast."

"Still, if we could reunite this buckle with its owner—"

"That's another thing. How are we going to evaluate the claims that come in? Any man with the initials CB could say he owned this and how would we prove he didn't? I don't know, Marissa, you did a good job, but I was wrong. It's not a story."

"What should I do with the belt?"

"Tell photo to send it back." But photo had lost the belt, as it turned out.

Unexpectedly, Marissa stopped being Lou's unfavorite about this time. The steady diet of black beans went to Veronica now, poor thing. Marissa even got to share a byline on Jonathan's story, when the state police lab determined that the girl in the ditch had a blood alcohol level of .02 but death had been caused by strangulation. The rape kit had been ambiguous—evidence of sex, but not force.

One day, an almost autumnal Friday, Marissa had a hankering for taco salad and talked Beth into going to the Mexican place, despite knowing that Lou would be there with her one frozen margarita. Veronica, firmly entrenched as the unfavorite, wanted no part of the escapade, but Beth agreed. The taco salad was a good one, the bottom of the shell-bowl giving way at just the right moment, the perfect combination of crunch and moisture.

Lou was alone with her margarita and they waved at her warily, fearful she would summon them for company, but she didn't seem at all interested in them. A few minutes later, a man joined her. A dark-haired man, very thick hair combed straight back from a widow's peak.

"Damn," Beth said, "I'd be the breadwinner, too, if I could go home to that. Even with that werewolf hair."

Marissa watched as Lou drank *three* margaritas that day, then led her companion out of the restaurant, giggling girlishly. She stopped by their table on the way out. Bumped it, actually, with her hip, miscalculating how much space she took up.

"Girls, I don't think I've ever met my husband. I mean"—another fit of giggles—"I don't think y'all have ever met my husband. Charlie, this is Beth and Ma—Ma—"

"Marissa," she supplied, staring at the man's midsection. At his belt.

"Weekenders due by two, girls, to make the bulldog," Lou said. "Hank is editing, though. I'm going to take the afternoon off. I don't feel so good."

She winked at them. Beth would regale the others for weeks about that wink, but Marissa never joined in the laughter.

Charlie Baker nodded at Marissa and Beth, courtly and regal. "You be good to my wife, girls. Treat her right. She's very precious to me."

Lou wobbled out of the restaurant, Charlie steady in her wake.

A few weeks later, a black bean appeared in Marissa's mailbox.

*Marissa, Tatum Buford has done such a good job fixing up the Waco Inn. How about a little profile on him for the Sunday paper? Don't forget to mention the Continental breakfast. Best, Lou.*

On her way to the Waco Inn, Marissa took a detour down Robinson Road, finding the spot where the Baylor girl's body had been dumped. The road, also known as US-Texas 77, eventually led to Rosebud, home of Lou Busbee Baker. And, by inference, home of her husband, Charlie Baker, her high school sweetheart, a man who took girls to the Waco Inn and wrapped a belt around their necks until they told him to stop.

Maybe he didn't always stop.

Marissa turned around, but instead of driving to the Waco Inn, she went to her apartment, a dowdy duplex full of secondhand furniture. She put everything she owned into her car, just piled it in willy-nilly, and began driving north, then east. Five hours later, she called her notice in to the night assistant editor, Hank, from Texarkana, making sure she was on the Arkansas side of the line. She then called her parents in Philadelphia and said she wanted to start law school that January, if possible. And if she had to defer until next fall, then she wanted to work at her father's office, doing whatever she could to be useful.

She sat in her motel room, hugging her knees, shivering despite the chugging space heater beneath the window. *Follow the money.* Follow the belt buckle. A motel owner finds a belt with a distinctive buckle, one that he recognizes, evidence of nothing more than an indiscretion. He makes sure that an editor at the newspaper knows that he has it. But he couldn't know what had happened, why a man might leave a room in such haste that he would forget his belt. *And Lou can't know, either. Can she? The husband, reunited with his belt, forgiven by his wife, will be more careful in the future. Won't he? It was an accident. Wasn't it?* There are no stupid questions, Lou had told her. But there are terrifying ones.

When Marissa checked out the next morning, she left some of her clothes behind. Not the ones she had been wearing the day before, but a vintage black sundress with a ripped seam and a pair of high-heeled sandals. Let them end up in the lost and found, in a sagging cardboard box, where they could keep company with all the other things that were torn and stained and shameful.

# WAR SECRETS

## BY LIBBY FISCHER HELLMANN

The chill that ran through Davood Sarand had little to do with the frigid winter air. Where was Julia? He had been knocking so long his knuckles were raw. He was to have tea with her parents at four. It was half past the hour now, a gloomy dusk settling over the city of Leipzig, stealing its colors and shapes.

The Goldblums lived on the third floor of a stone-facade building just west of the city, not far from Rosental Park. Once an elegant example of *Jugendstil* architecture, the building was silent and worn, as if the weight of time, and now the war, had crushed its Art Nouveau pretensions. Davood peered over the landing at the staircase below. He was about to go hunt for her when the outer door squeaked open.

Julia.

Davood smiled, the way he always did when he saw her. A few fat snowflakes had settled on her brown hair and coat. She was carrying a small cardboard box tied with string. Her cheeks were flushed, her blue eyes luminous. Was that because of him? Or merely the result of the cold? He let out a relieved breath. "Where were you?"

"At the bakery, my love." She held up the box. "Herr Bruchner wasn't supposed to, but he gave me some wonderful pastries. You won't find anything better—even in Vienna." She studied his

45

face, then ran the back of her hand down his cheek. "Davood," she crooned, rising to her toes. "Please do not worry. I am fine."

He kissed her lightly on the lips. "Yes, well, what about your parents?"

"They won't open the door if they do not know who's there." She shrugged.

Davood's smile faded. "I want to tell them, Julia. Today."

"No. Not yet." She shook her head.

"Why not? You know, I know. The times…you can't…we might…"

"Today is not the right time. They are just meeting you."

"But if they know—it may put their minds at ease."

"*Cheri,*" she said—the French term made him feel sophisticated and worldly, and she knew it—"It's enough that you're Persian. They won't be able to take in the rest."

"I'm Kurdish."

"Yes, of course, *mon chien*. But they are old. One step at a time."

Inside, Julia made introductions. "This is the man I've been telling you about."

Davood shook their hands and offered Frau Goldblum the bouquet of flowers he'd brought. Although they were nearly frozen, her mother seemed pleased and put them in a vase. They sat in a parlor crowded with dark, overstuffed furniture.

Julia was right. The Goldblums were old. Herr Goldblum was stooped with arthritis, his skin pasty, and his shaggy white eyebrows reminded Davood of his grandfather. Her father had been a successful furrier, Julia had said, until the Nuremberg Laws in '35. He'd tried to save his business, first by turning its management over to a Gentile friend, then watching his "friend" steal it at a rigged auction. They would have left in '36, and again after *Kristallnacht*, but for Julia's mother. A frail wisp of a woman, she'd had scarlet fever as a child and never completely recovered. She'd married late, had Julia even later, and always seemed to be ill from one thing or another.

Julia poured tea and passed around the pastries, chatting about the bakery and the wonderful aromas emanating from the shop. Davood let her finish, then turned to Herr Goldblum.

"Please don't think I'm being rude, sir, but given what you've suffered these past years, why do you stay in Germany?"

Julia's eyes flashed a warning.

Goldblum eyed Davood with suspicion. "Why do you want to know? Who are you?"

"It's all right, Papa," Julia said. "He is a friend."

Her father stirred his tea, then set the cup and saucer on the tray. He sniffed. "Where would we go? We have no connections in England, America, or Shanghai." Palestine wasn't an option, either, he went on. "We are Reform Jews and have no special allegiance to the Homeland." Goldblum paused. Then his spine stiffened and his eyes narrowed. "Why do you care? What do you know about our lives? You"—he sniffed again—"are a scientist for a Nazi. And you're Muslim. I must confess, young man, that the only reason we agreed to this—this meeting is because our daughter insisted." Goldblum swiveled away from Davood, effectively cutting him out of the conversation.

Davood felt the heat on his cheeks. He'd just been put in his place. Julia pursed her lips and changed the subject to a Beethoven symphony she'd heard on the radio. Her parents chattered as if they'd heard it, too. Davood's frustration grew. They should be talking about important matters. It was 1939. War had been declared, although so far people were calling it *der Sitzkrieg*, the Sitting War, or as the English said, the phony war. There had been little fighting and no major attacks, but the sense of impending doom was as real as the snow blanketing the city. It was difficult to be in Germany. More difficult to be a Jew. They should be talking about how to escape, not Beethoven's Fifth.

But Herr Goldblum hadn't finished. "A Persian . . ." he mumbled.

"And a Muslim." He shook his head. "You know, of course, where the shah got the name for Iran."

Davood looked down.

"Yes," Herr Goldblum hissed. "You know. *Aryan*. Iran. He and Hitler have a 'special relationship.'"

Davood looked up and met his eyes. "Not everyone in my country feels that way, sir. Most Persians have tolerance and respect for all. For example, I myself am a Kurd. But I have never felt excluded because of it."

"You may think that way now," Goldblum huffed. "But you are young, and young people have dreams. They won't last."

Davood thought about Herr Goldblum's words as he made his way to the lab the next morning. Just six months ago he had come to Leipzig as full of hope as the summer flowers that flanked the dusty roads outside the city. He, the star physics student at the University of Tehran, invited to work with the famous physicist Erich Schröder in Leipzig. The first Kurdish student to achieve such an honor. His parents were, of course, elated, but threaded through their joy was a note of warning.

"Are you sure you know what you're getting into, Davood?" his father asked. "There is going to be another war."

"Yes, but this time we are not the targets." Davood smiled. "I can do this, Papa. We have survived worse."

"Germany is a universe away from Persia."

"I am ready." Davood's voice rang with what he hoped was confidence.

Once he'd arrived in Leipzig and met Dr. Schröder, though, Davood felt less assured. Schröder wasn't military, but with his erect bearing, blond hair, and starched collar, which bore an insignia with the rank of SS *Hauptsturmführer*, he might as well have been. And when the man gazed at him with his steely blue eyes, Davood realized he was of no more importance to Schröder than the boy who brought in biscuits and tea.

Schröder had more important things with which to occupy his mind. He and his team had been asked to take part in the *Uranverein*, the Uranium Club. The club's members were prominent German physicists trying to develop nuclear weapons to use against the Allies before the Allies did the same to them.

This morning the lab, usually a quiet, placid place, was on edge. When Davood came in, the other assistants rolled their eyes toward Schröder's closed door. Schröder was arguing with someone. Davood heard the sharp exchange as he went to his desk. He pulled out his equipment and picked up his work from the day before. He'd been studying the way uranium atoms behave under pressure.

The argument persisted. Davood had studied German before coming to Europe, and he practiced with Julia when he could, but the quarrel was too fast and furious for him to understand. Schröder was agitated and spoke in a loud, raspy voice. The other man—whoever he was—talked in an urgent but incomprehensible mumble.

There was an abrupt silence; then the door was flung open. A man in an SS uniform—Davood couldn't see his rank—emerged, his cheeks crimson, his eyes tiny pools of rage. He stormed out the door of the lab and let it slam behind him. A moment later, Schröder came out, arms folded across his chest. He was breathing hard, his hair was out of place, and he looked as if he'd run a mile. He glanced around, flicking his eyes over his assistants. Each assistant looked down, suddenly absorbed in his work, but Davood wasn't fast enough.

Schröder's glare settled on him, as if Davood were the cause of the argument. Davood froze, and his heart leaped into his throat. Then Schröder turned and stomped out.

Over lunch, Friedrich, the chief lab assistant, explained. "The powers that be want us to move the lab to Berlin. Schröder doesn't want to. He accused them of not trusting him. Of wanting to keep an eye on him."

"That's what they were arguing about?"

Friedrich tilted his head. "I keep forgetting your German is not fluent."

The knot of tension inside Davood began to loosen. "Why doesn't Schröder want to go?"

"Who knows?" Friedrich took a bite of sausage pie. "Maybe his mistress is here."

Davood flashed to the time he'd first met Julia. He had been in Leipzig about a month, and he was homesick. He'd decided to take a tour around the city as a distraction. European buildings, with their intricate stonework, spires, and formal facades, were so very different from the graceful arches, tiles, and bright colors of Persia. He'd ended up in Rosental Park on a bench, when the vision that was Julia passed by. Her brown hair swirled in waves, her blue eyes sparkled, and her skin looked as soft and pink as rose petals. Dressed in a plain white blouse and dark skirt, her body swayed in just the right way. Davood watched her as if in a trance. Most Persian women were veiled, and, though they could be beautiful, there was something about *this* woman—her poise, her air of freedom, perhaps—that made Davood drunk with desire. He remembered the first lines of a famous poem by Rumi:

> If anyone asks you
> how the perfect satisfaction
> of all our sexual wanting
> will look, lift your face
> and say,
> *Like this.*

Still, he feared such a beauty would never notice him. He was acceptable, even handsome. But he was Persian. And a Kurd. He was an outsider. He didn't have a chance. For some reason, though, she stopped, turned around, and studied him. The smile that slowly broke across her face was all he needed. They spent the rest of the afternoon on the swings, ignoring the frustrated cries of children who thought *they* were kings of the park. By the end of the day, he and Julia were in love. It was that simple. Rumi was right.

But Schröder? Davood couldn't imagine Erich Schröder ever feeling that way about a woman.

"You have to be careful when you have a girlfriend, you know," Friedrich said.

Davood snapped back to the present. Was Friedrich talking about Schröder? Or him?

"Of course, it might be something else." Friedrich casually took another bite of his pie.

"Such as?"

"Have you heard of *Deutsche Physik*?"

Davood frowned and shook his head.

"The race for nuclear weapons makes strange bedfellows," Friedrich said. "Years ago a movement emerged. Its goal was to practice science the German way. The *Deutsche* way. When the Nazis took over, it became the *Aryan* way. It started with a general suspicion of Einstein's theory of relativity, which they called Jewish Physics. Over the years it became a way to discredit any scientist who didn't go along. Many scientists left the country. The few who stayed realized it was utter nonsense, of course, and ultimately came to the defense of relativity and quantum mechanics. And now, since war has been declared, we are all friends, united in our work to develop nuclear weapons. Still, it is an uneasy truce."

Davood nodded. "Wasn't Heisenberg one of the targets?"

"Indeed." Friedrich looked surprised that Davood knew.

Werner Heisenberg had become a target when he wouldn't denounce Einstein. *Deutsche Physik* advocates tried to strip him of his academic stature and called him the White Jew. Himmler himself had to step in, Davood recalled. Apparently, their mothers were friends.

Friedrich smiled. "Now, of course, Heisenberg is Schröder's superior."

Davood shifted. "But Schröder joined the SS. You can't be more loyal than that."

"True." Friedrich gazed at Davood. "By the way, have *you* joined the party?"

"Me?" Davood straightened. "I'm Persian. They wouldn't take me, would they? Despite the führer's 'special relationship' with the shah."

"You might try anyway." Friedrich chewed the last of his pie. "Being Persian won't protect you forever."

A week later, Davood walked to the bakery where he and Julia had arranged to meet. Snow was falling, and every so often he spotted Christmas decorations in the windows, although the *Tannenbaums* and lights disappeared as he neared the Jewish section. It had been a week since he'd last seen Julia, and he needed to touch her, kiss her, run his hands through her hair. He waited at one of two wrought iron tables in the shop. He asked the time. Half past four. Julia was late. She was to have been there by four. He tapped his foot impatiently. He asked the proprietor if she'd been in. Perhaps left him a note. The man shook his head.

Davood waited another ten minutes, then got up and walked around the corner. As Julia's building came into view, he picked up his pace. He stopped when he reached the front door. It was open. His stomach lurched. The door was never open, especially in this cold. Davood looked up to see if the lights were on upstairs in their apartment. He couldn't tell, but most of the residents had thick curtains on the windows, including the Goldblums.

He deliberated for a moment, then went up to the third floor and knocked. There was no response. He remembered what Julia had said about her parents not opening the door. "Herr Goldblum," he said softly. "It is Davood Sarand, Julia's... friend. Are you there?"

He knocked again. No response. It felt like the first time all over again. He peered over the banister. No door squeaked. No Julia rushed in with snowflakes in her hair. A sense of foreboding came over him. He sat on the top step. Maybe she had been called away. Frau Goldblum was frail. Maybe they were at the doctor's. Maybe they'd been detained trying to come home.

But the premonition wouldn't go away. Fear swept through him and twisted his gut. He stood up and knocked again. Nothing. He cried out. "Julia! Herr Goldblum. Please. Open the door!"

He knew he sounded desperate. He didn't care. He threw himself against the door. Nothing. Then again. A door opened on the landing above, and a quavering female voice called down. "Stop your infernal noise. They are gone."

"Where?" His voice was hoarse with fear.

"Where do you think?"

"When?" he managed to croak.

"Last night. About two. They won't be coming back."

"How do you know?" Davood rushed up the stairs. An old woman in a threadbare bathrobe stood at her door. He could see bald spots between tufts of white hair.

The old woman squinted. "I've seen you before. You were courting Julia."

"You must tell me where she is!"

"She is gone. And if you have any brains, you will disappear, too. People are watching this building. They have been for months. They know who you are." She sniffed. "Even an Aryan like you."

Davood spent the evening crying, cursing, and pacing his small room. He had heard about the knocks in the middle of the night. The arrests, mostly Jews, but other enemies of the state, too. Homosexuals, Gypsies, Catholics, anyone who strayed from the Aryan path. Sometimes they were shot on sight. Sometimes they were sent to camps. Julia was young and strong. They would probably let her live. But her parents? He shivered, unable to finish the thought.

It was late when Davood rose from his bed. He made sure the curtains were closed and locked his door. He knelt beside the bed and pulled out a bag that had been stowed under his mattress. He rummaged through an extra blanket, two towels, and the box of handkerchiefs his mother had made him pack and fished out a book. Leather-bound with faded gold lettering on the front, it had been used often at one time, but Davood hadn't looked at it for months. Now he gazed around his room. No prying eyes were watching. Still, he opened the book cautiously and thumbed through its pages until he found the right passage. He started to read aloud. The rhythms and lilt of his childhood language came back as though he'd recited it only yesterday.

> *Yis-gadal v'yis-kadash sh'may raba b'alma dee-v'ra che-ru-say, ve'yam-lich mal-chsay ... ve'imru amen.*

He had barely finished when there was a sharp knock at his door. Davood jerked his head up. He snapped the siddur shut and shoved it underneath his coat on the bed. The knock was repeated. Insistent. Who was there? Had they heard him reciting Kaddish? Did they know his secret?

A storm of thoughts thundered through his head. No one was supposed to know Davood was a Jew. Not even in Persia. Five years earlier, after his acceptance at Tehran University, his family had moved with him to the city. Given the times, they had left their religion in their remote Kurdish village. It was safer not to draw attention to themselves. Safer to behave like Muslims.

The only person, aside from his family, who knew was Julia. He'd had to tell her. She would never have let him court her otherwise. He knew she would keep his secret. But he had never anticipated that she would be arrested. What if the Gestapo tortured her? Forced her to tell them about other Jews in Germany? He'd heard the stories. He was in danger. Now he understood why his parents hadn't wanted him to go to Germany. Herr Goldblum was right. So was the old lady. He had been a fool. A young, arrogant fool.

The knocking on the door persisted. Davood considered not answering. Pretending no one was there. But the light seeping under the door frame would give him away. He sat on his hands. Then he heard his name.

"Sarand ... Sarand ... are you there?" a raspy voice called out.

Schröder. Erich Schröder was at the door to his room. Panic lodged in Davood's throat. What did his superior want? He moved to the door and opened it a crack. In the dimly lit hall Schröder stood hunched in a dark wool overcoat. His starched white shirt with the SS insignia poked over the collar. In one hand he clutched a pair of leather gloves; in the other, a briefcase. He peered at Davood with a curious expression.

"I was beginning to think you were not at home. Are you ill?"

Davood shook his head. He didn't trust his voice.

"I am not disturbing you..." Schröder said.

Davood shook his head again. "Of—of course not," he stammered.

Schröder flicked his gloves toward the room. "May I—come in?"

Davood swallowed and opened the door wider. "I apologize, sir," he croaked. "My room is but a simple affair. Certainly not up to the standards of the Reich's top physicist."

Schröder waved his gloves. "No need."

There was only one chair in the room, and it was covered with clothes. Davood wished now he had laundered them. The only other spot was the bed. Schröder sat on it, very close to Davood's coat. If Schröder stretched out his arm on the bed, he would feel the siddur.

"I want to talk about your work at the lab."

Davood tensed, immediately on the defensive. "Have I displeased you? How can I improve? Just tell me, and—"

Again Schröder raised the gloves. "No. In fact, it's the opposite. I have seen your records. And the recommendations of your professors. I think they—my assistants—are not using you to your capacity."

Davood unclenched his fists. His stomach started to settle.

"You studied physics, with an emphasis on classical field theory—"

"Yes, sir. I know it was not specifically nuclear fission, or relativity, but—"

"Stop interrupting," Schröder ordered.

Davood shrank back.

"You are familiar, of course, with Werner Heisenberg?"

"Of course." Davood felt a flush creeping across his face.

"He is also a theoretician, you know. It is an honorable pursuit."

Davood kept his mouth shut. Where was Schröder going?

"I saw your latest report. You mention the theoretical possibility of producing a chain reaction. Tell me what you have discovered."

Davood shrugged. "I am not sure, but I believe Leo Szilard was working with the wrong elements."

"The Hungarian scientist? He used beryllium and indium."

Davood nodded. "As you know, I have been working with uranium. And I believe the interactions between neutrons and fissile isotopes such as uranium 235 might be a better choice. At least, I believe there is a theoretical basis for doing so. It needs testing, of course. But it looks promising."

Schröder's mouth twitched. "What would we need to test it?"

"Probably as pure a sample of uranium as we can get, so we can study the release of the neutrons, their reabsorption into fissile materials, and whether—or when—it becomes self-sustaining."

Schröder rubbed his thumb and forefinger along his jaw.

Davood frowned. Something was off. The leading physicist in Germany does not come to a student's room—at night—alone— to quiz him on his work.

"You are wondering why I came here to ask you about your work."

Could Schröder read his mind? Davood swallowed.

"There is always such—competition at the assistants' level. Even jealousy, given that we have been wrestling with the issue for years. It would be better if the others did not know exactly what you have deduced. We will keep this our secret for the present, yes?"

Davood, still trying to figure out what was going on, nonetheless said, "Of course."

Schröder nodded as if he'd expected it and gathered his things. He had dropped his briefcase on the blanket only a few inches away from the hidden siddur. As he scooped the briefcase up, Davood held his breath. Schröder didn't seem to notice.

"Good. I want you to write up your analysis. I want to know what you suggest as next steps. In fact, this should be your priority."

"Yes, sir."

Schröder stood. "Good. That is all."

It was a sleepless night. A sharp pain knifed through Davood when he thought about Julia, her parents, and the probability that he would never see them again. But he was plagued, too, by the chance that he had been identified by whoever was watching their apartment. And then there was the strange visit by Erich Schröder, just after he'd said Kaddish.

He tried to make sense of the events, to weave together a pattern. Schröder's visit was clearly a pretext. Why hadn't he asked Davood about his work at the lab? Why make a special visit at night? Unless. Davood sucked in a breath. Schröder was SS. Did he somehow know Davood was Jewish? Or did he suspect it? What if he had heard Davood chanting Kaddish? Davood picked up the siddur and clasped it to his chest. He felt lost.

The next morning Davood crept to his desk an hour late, hoping no one would notice. But when the same SS officer who had argued with Schröder last week returned, Davood knew he was in trouble.

They knew.

The officer went into Schröder's office but after a brief moment came out and headed to Davood's desk. Davood's insides turned liquid. Schröder had been working with them all along. The same thing that had happened to the Goldblums would happen to him.

The SS officer extended his arm. *"Heil Hitler."*

*"Heil Hitler,"* Davood replied.

The officer looked him over. "You are from Iran."

Davood nodded shakily.

"You studied at Tehran University?"

He nodded again.

The officer sniffed. "Your academic record...how would I find it?"

"I can give you names. References."

The officer grunted and folded his arms. "Why would an Arab...a Muslim like you...be wandering around a Jewish neighborhood, eh?"

I am Persian, not Arab, Davood wanted to say. There is a huge difference. But he would be no better than a Nazi to make that distinction. He cast around for an answer. "I—I like the architecture. Art Nouveau. Especially in that area of the city. It—it is so different than my homeland."

The officer stared. "Part of that architecture wouldn't include a Jewish girl, would it?"

Davood pretended he hadn't heard. "There is a bakery on one corner. The owner makes pastries that are better than Vienna's."

"Oh, so that's the way you want to play it. What is his name, this baker?"

What was his name? Oh, God, Julia had told him. After a long pause, he said, "Bruchner."

Suddenly Schröder flew out of his office, looked around, and locked eyes with the SS officer.

Davood swallowed. What was happening?

"Enough, *Standartenführer*," Schröder barked, his expression one of fury. "You are disrupting my staff. Keeping my people from their work. Please do this another time."

The officer looked angrily at Davood, then Schröder. It felt like forever. "We are not finished, *Hauptsturmführer*," he muttered. He turned on his heel and left.

Schröder gazed at Davood, then went back into his office. Friedrich and the other assistants refused to make eye contact.

Back in his room that night, Davood made a decision. Last week when the SS officer had argued with Schröder, Friedrich had said it was over *Deutsche Physik*. But what if Friedrich was lying? What if the officer had been targeting Davood and no one had the nerve to tell him? Friedrich *had* made that odd comment about girlfriends. Did he know? Whom should Davood trust? He worried a hand through his hair. Everything was coming apart. It was time for him to flee.

A knock on the door interrupted him as he was packing his bag. He crept to the door and ran his hands over it, as if he could divine who was there by touch. A raspy voice called out. "Sarand. Open."

Schröder. This was the end. There was no escape. Davood decided to ask Schröder to kill him here and now. It would reunite him with Julia. He took a deep breath and opened the door.

Schröder was in the same coat. But his gloves were on this time, and he wore a fedora pulled low on his brow. "Come. Hurry."

Davood shook his head. "No, Herr Doktor. I want to end it here."

"What are you talking about?"

Davood straightened. "You heard me. I wish to face my death now. You were my superior. You owe me that much."

"Sarand, get your things. We must leave. Right away."

"But I want—"

Schröder cut him off. "Are you crazy?" He went to Davood's bag, closed it, picked it up. "Let's get going."

Davood was confused. "Where are you taking me?"

"You will see."

Davood trembled. He thought about Julia. His parents. His brother back in Persia. He thought about the village where he'd grown up. The family had uprooted themselves; hidden their identity because of him. He wanted to tell them it had all been wasted. The disease of anti-Semitism had claimed them after all.

He followed Schröder down the stairs and out the door. He thought about sprinting as fast as he could down the street. That way he would be shot from behind. At least he wouldn't see it coming. He was about to take off when a dark car screeched to a stop outside the *Pension* and two Gestapo officers climbed out.

"Thank you, *Hauptsturmführer* Schröder. We will take over now." One of the officers moved toward Davood. "You are under arrest, Sarand. You will come with us."

Davood stared at the men, but before he could register what was happening, Schröder dropped Davood's bag, pulled out a gun, and shot both men. They fell to the ground.

"Quickly. In my car." Schröder pointed to a Mercedes across the street.

Davood scrambled into the car. So did Schröder. He threw Davood's bag in back and keyed the engine, and the Mercedes roared down the street.

"What is happening? Where are we going?" Davood asked.

Schröder headed north and west, out of the city.

"Are we going to Berlin?"

"That would be east. We are heading west."

"Where?"

"To Amsterdam."

"Amsterdam?" Davood's voice cracked.

"From there we will be met by people who will take us to America to continue our work."

Davood was astonished. "*Our* work?" When Schröder nodded, he asked, "Why me?"

Schröder looked over. "Why do you think?"

"How long have you known?"

"You were seen in a Jewish neighborhood. With a Jewish girl."

"Yes, but—"

"And when I came to your room and heard you speaking *Aramaic*, I was certain."

"You heard me recite Kaddish."

"Is that what it was?"

"You didn't know?"

"There are only a few Kurds who speak *Aramaic* rather than Farsi. Those who do are usually Jews from isolated villages high in the mountains."

"Why didn't you turn me in? You are a captain with the SS."

Schröder let out an unhappy laugh. "Who says I didn't?"

"Is that why the SS officer came back to the lab?"

Schröder pursed his lips. He wouldn't answer. Which was an answer in itself.

Davood sat back in his seat, trying to piece together the events. Schröder was escaping Germany. He had carefully orchestrated his defection. And yet he had been a loyal Nazi. He'd even informed on Davood. But in the end, the man had saved him. And shot two Gestapo officers in the process.

"Why did you do it?" Davood asked.

Schröder's answer surprised him. "If I had a gifted son, I would want him to have the opportunity to prove himself. Since the Reich will not allow it, I feel obligated to find people who will."

"What about you? Why are you leaving?"

"For much the same reason." Schröder was quiet for a moment. "And because you have stumbled across a tantalizing possibility. What you have come up with inside your brain is remarkable."

"The chain reaction…" Davood murmured.

"If it is correct, it could become an astonishing weapon. A weapon that will change the world—forever."

Schröder stopped talking then, and stared through the windshield, as if intent on his driving.

After a while, Davood looked out as well. The grim winter night rushed past, the wind whipping tears of freezing rain across the glass. The Nazi and the Jew, bound together by war secrets, headed north toward the future.

# THE VLY

## BY C. E. LAWRENCE

The tale I am about to tell has, over the years, acquired the aspect of a murky, half-forgotten dream. At times I fear my memory of that fateful night is a product of my own fevered consciousness. But I have carried secrets far too long. Now that I am old and broken, close to the shore to which we must all return, I take up pen in trembling hand to record long-ago events which have haunted me ever since.

The Kaatskil Mountains (or Catskills, as they are now called) lie on the western banks of the Hudson River—bony protrusions stretching deep into Ulster, Greene, and Sullivan Counties. Seen from the gently rolling hills of Dutchess County across the river, they are serene and majestic. Up close, they can be forbidding. Some of the peaks have fanciful names, like Big Rosy Bone Knob, Peekamoose Mountain, and Thunder Hill, while others reassure the observer with their promise of splendor: Guardian, Eagle, and Overlook Mountains.

Legends chase these hills like the summer storms that come and go in the blink of an eye—one minute there is not a cloud in sight, and the next cascades of rain pour from the heavens. The mountains are moody and unpredictable, even to those of us who have lived here all our lives. But no part of this landscape strikes more fear into the heart of its inhabitants than the low-lying marsh between Krumville and Lomontville.

The Dutch call it the Vly.

I say "the Dutch" even though I am Dutch on my mother's side. On my father's I am English, and so I was raised. After the British conquest of 1664, Dutch ways persisted for some time. But just over a century later, little was left here of a once-thriving culture. My mother spoke only a few scattered phrases of that language, having taken most of my father's Anglo-Saxon customs. It was she who told me that Vly is an old Dutch word for "valley."

I grew up with stern warnings to avoid this evil place. The sandy soil, too poor to support crops, flooded in early spring, often staying soggy until October. Some said spirits inhabited the marshes and bogs at its center; others claimed travelers could lose their way, caught up in the mists and fogs that descended quickly on warm nights. There were stories of poor souls who wandered into the center of the marshland, to be sucked underneath it, trapped in the soft quicksand. I heard snippets of still darker tales—of a great, gaunt hound that roamed the Vly at night, a ghostly creature with an insatiable appetite for living flesh. The Indians had lived in this area for generations, and it was said the Vly was a place even they avoided.

None of this was on my mind one fine Sunday in late April when I ventured out hunting with my cousin Jacob. He was a robust blond fellow, tall and strong and lively, afraid of neither man nor spirit. His family lived not far from us, just off the road that passes through Krumville. Like so many of us this side of the river, his father was a tenant farmer on lands owned by Robert Livingston. It was said the Chancellor could sit on the porch of his mansion, Clermont, and gaze across the river from Columbia County, knowing that whatever lands he saw belonged to him. Those of us whose families worked those lands didn't own so much as a single stone or piece of straw.

Though I was the type to lie awake at night seething at such inequality, my cousin Jacob was of a carefree disposition. He would much rather be off hunting grouse with his black retriever, Dragen—*dragen* being the Dutch word for "bear."

On that day Jacob and I were roaming the hills around Krumville, uncocked rifles hanging loosely at our sides, listening for the rustle of grouse in the blackberry bushes. I had just turned twelve, and Jacob was sixteen. My mother had finally agreed to let me go hunting with him—no small decision on her part, since my father had died in a hunting accident just a year before. It took pleading and bribery on my part—in the end, I agreed to help her with the washing as well as doing my share of the chores the following day.

My stomach knotted with anticipation as I strode beside my cousin, stretching my legs to keep up with his long strides. Dragen trotted at our heels, his pink tongue lolling happily from his mouth. The bees buzzed lazily in the pink and white trillium, the fields still covered with dew from the night before, glistening like teardrops in the morning sun. Lost in the beauty of the day, we wandered for some time without much thought as to where we were headed. Jacob led the way, following deer tracks along a narrow woodland trail as it turned and twisted through forest and meadow.

We lingered beside a cool spring, to eat some jerky and biscuits from our pouches and fill our bellies with clear mountain water. We stretched out beneath the shade of a chestnut tree just coming into bloom. Dragen splashed happily in the creek, lapping up water and snapping at minnows and tadpoles.

Our conversation meandered from dogs and horses to the mysteries of the fairer sex—and finally, to family. Though every clan in our little community had its share of misfortune, ours had suffered the most recent and devastating tragedy with the loss of my father. It was almost exactly a year before, to the day, that the hunting accident had claimed his life.

My cousin tore off a piece of jerky and chewed on it thoughtfully.

"What do you suppose really happened to your father?" he asked, leaning back against the chestnut's broad trunk.

I felt my face go hot. "Why do you speak such a question? They said—"

"I know very well what they claimed," he replied impatiently. "That he tripped and his gun discharged in his face."

My forehead buzzed with confusion and my line of sight seemed to narrow. "What are you saying, Cousin?"

He gave me a searching look. "Consider it, Slade. Did you ever know your father to have a clumsy moment in his life?"

"Well, no, but Hugh Turner said he tripped—"

Hugh Turner had been my father's hunting companion that day.

"A shotgun does not easily go off in a man's face!" Jacob declared. He leapt to his feet and demonstrated with his own rifle, pretending to trip. The gun, instead of aiming at his head, fell harmlessly to one side. "There!" he said triumphantly. "That is what would happen—at least ninety-nine times out of a hundred, I'll wager."

A nameless dread slithered like a tapeworm through my gut. "What are you saying, Cousin?"

He flung himself on the ground beside me. "I never saw his body—did you?"

"No. But my mother told me it was too—"

"Too horrible to look at; I know," Jacob replied. "But my father carried the casket at the funeral and he said it was awful light to be the body of a full-grown man."

"Perhaps people shrink when they die," I offered.

Jacob shook his head, his corn silk–blond hair catching the rays of the late-morning sun. "Something else happened, Slade. Look at what became of Hugh Turner."

I shuddered. Hugh Turner had gone stark mad a few nights later, running through the streets naked, babbling incoherently about witches and goblins. He now lived with his daughter and her family, who tended to him as though he was a simple child. He could occasionally be seen on the village green, flailing his arms and muttering to himself.

"Do you believe my father is still alive?" I asked.

Jacob frowned. "I do not believe he perished in a hunting accident."

At that moment swarms of gnats descended upon us and we heaved ourselves to our feet.

"We must be on our way," said Jacob. Waving away the cloud of insects, he slung his rucksack over his shoulder. "The day is not growing any younger."

I spat a gnat from my mouth, grabbed my own pack, and looked up at the sky. He was right—the sun, having reached its zenith, was descending.

"Come along, Dragen!" Jacob called.

The dog bounded up the bank and shook his coat mightily, spraying us with water. He grinned up at us, evidently much pleased with himself.

We returned to our path, crossing the stream, whereupon we entered a birch grove. As we emerged from the woods into a wild field of winter wheat, we heard growling behind us. We turned to see Dragen baring his teeth, ears flattened behind his head.

"What is it, boy?" Jacob said, but the dog continued to growl. Saliva dripped from his jaws, and his eyes narrowed with fear.

I followed the dog's gaze. He seemed to be peering at a copse of scrub oaks, on the other side of a patch of blackberry bushes.

"What is he frightened of?" I asked my cousin.

"We must be near it," Jacob replied cryptically. "Have we really come that far?"

"Near what?" I said.

He hesitated before answering. "The Vly."

Fear dried my throat, turning my tongue to parchment.

"Perhaps we should turn around and go back," I suggested.

"Don't be foolish," Jacob replied, straightening his shoulders. "What is there to be afraid of?"

I wanted to shout that there was plenty to be afraid of, but pride stopped my tongue. This was my first hunting trip, and I wasn't eager to be branded a coward before I had a chance to shoot my first grouse.

"Very well," I said, affecting a nonchalance I did not feel. "Lead on."

Jacob bent down to break off a thin stalk of wheat, sticking it in the side of his mouth. I had seen him do this before when he was trying to work up his courage.

"Let's go, then," he said, striding forward confidently, but I noticed he cocked his rifle. "Come along, Dragen," he called. The dog obeyed reluctantly, slinking a few yards behind, still growling.

I tightened my grip on my own rifle. I had lovingly cleaned the barrel that morning with linseed oil and could feel it mixing with the sweat on my hands as I clambered after my cousin, lifting my knees high to clear the spiky stalks of winter wheat.

As we crossed the field, the sky darkened and a fierce wind swept over the meadow, rippling through the wheat. The stalks flattened as though a great hand were swatting them to the ground. The change in weather seemed to come out of nowhere—one minute the sky was clear and bright as a sparrow's eye, and in the next it was gray as the steel of our rifle barrels.

Jacob stopped in his tracks as Dragen's growls changed to whimpers.

"We should turn back," I said, the words bursting forth in spite of my desire to appear brave.

I saw my cousin's shoulders stiffen. And then I felt it.

I grew up in these hills. I was accustomed to sudden changes of weather, floods, and rock slides, as well as dangerous wild animals, from black bears and wild cats to coyotes. But this was different. The air itself was oppressive. I felt a sodden, sullen weight pressing upon my shoulders, pushing me toward the ground. A bleak, dense cloud threatened to envelop my consciousness; I was overwhelmed by a leaden feeling of hopelessness.

I had heard whispered stories about the Vly all my life, but it was not until I stood there with my cousin that I felt the full impact of that dark and gloomy place. It was as if all the will had been drained from my body, leaving behind a hollow, empty vessel. I could barely summon the strength to speak, let alone take a step forward. I had never believed a place itself could be truly evil until now. But young as I was, there was no doubt in my mind: the Vly exuded a palpable, supernatural malevolence.

I pulled at the sleeve of Jacob's linen shirt. "*Now*," I whispered through parched lips. "We should go *now*."

My cousin turned to face me. I took a step back, stunned by the change in his demeanor. His once-bright blue eyes were cloudy and tormented, the muscles of his face contracted as if in pain. His rifle hung useless at his side; with the other hand he clawed at the air, as if trying to grasp at phantom shapes floating before his eyes. Seeing him like that shocked me into action. Perhaps being younger, I was less vulnerable to the effects of that dreadful place. I summoned the willpower to shake free of the terrible darkness threatening to overwhelm me.

Gathering what presence of mind I could, I grasped Jacob by the wrist and dragged him from the field, back along the path. We retraced our steps, stumbling over exposed roots and rocks as we lurched back along the trail. The wind sliced through the trees, whipping at our feet as if trying to trip us; raindrops hurtled at our faces, stinging our exposed skin like tiny daggers. Still we pressed onward. I tightened my grip on Jacob's wrist, pulling him along behind me. Something told me if I let go of him I might never see my cousin again.

When we had gone a hundred yards or so, Jacob suddenly stopped short, jerking me backward.

"What is it?" I said, terror fluttering in my breast.

"Dragen!" Jacob looked around frantically, his face wild with panic. "Where is he?"

"Is he not behind us?" I asked, but my sinking heart knew the answer.

My cousin wrested his hand from my grip and stumbled back along the trail. I took off after him. Tackling him around the knees, I brought him down hard on the uneven ground, branches and twigs tearing at our clothing.

"Leave me! I must go back!" he cried. Throwing me off, he scrambled along on his hands and knees in the direction of the clearing. I fell hard against the trunk of an oak, the breath knocked from my body.

"No!" I gasped. "Jacob, no—don't go back!"

"I have to find Dragen!" he yelled. Sobbing, he stumbled back along the path. Sucking air into my burning lungs, I pulled myself to my feet and wobbled after him.

What we heard made us both stop short in our tracks. Long, low, and mournful, it was the unmistakable sound of a hound howling. It seemed to come from the edge of the open field, and it turned my legs to jelly. I looked at my cousin—he stood rigid and unmoving as the trees around us.

It had no sooner died out than it began again—a long, doleful wail ascending the scale until the surrounding hills seemed to ring with the sound. And then a second, even more terrifying noise— the frenzied yelping of a dog in mortal danger.

"Dragen!" Jacob rasped, his voice ragged. He lurched back along the path until he reached the clearing from whence we had come. I followed a few steps behind, pumping my legs to keep up with his long strides.

When we emerged from the woods we saw the dark form of a great hulking creature lurking at the far end of the open field. Standing in the shadows cast by surrounding trees, the animal had its head down—it seemed to be gnawing on something on the ground. Jacob stepped forward, and I followed behind, trembling. He raised his rifle and took aim. At that moment the creature raised its great head from the motionless form beneath it and turned its gaze upon us.

It was a gigantic hound—the biggest I had ever seen. It was nearly the size of a small horse, excessively lean and hungry looking. The beast took a step forward, out of the shadows. Its coat was gray as dusk, the gaunt eyes glinting yellow in the dim light cast by the feeble sun, hidden by the moody clouds that swept across the sky.

Jacob aimed his rifle and pulled the trigger. The shot echoed across the field, sending a shock up my spine. It was followed by a great flutter of wings, as birds from nearby trees took to the sky. The hound stood its ground for a moment, then, grasping its crumpled, lifeless prey in its fearsome jaws, bounded into the forest. Jacob started across the field in pursuit.

Summoning the last of my strength, I lunged at him. Wrapping my arms around his waist, I clung to him with all my might.

"N-o-o-o-o!" he bellowed, clawing at me in an attempt to loosen my hold. But terror tightened my grip. My arms felt made of iron, and I hugged him close, as though I wanted to squeeze the life from his body. I could feel my cousin's resolve weaken as his attempts to free himself grew feebler, until he collapsed onto the ground, weeping.

"Dragen!" he cried, digging his fingers into the dirt dampened by his tears. "My poor Dragen!"

"We must go," I hissed. "We must leave *now*!"

He turned his face to me. All the life had drained away from it. His vacant eyes gazed at me without really seeing, and his arms hung loosely at his sides. His body had no more life in it than a stuffed scarecrow impaled on a stake in the middle of a farm field.

"Come on," I said, taking his hand in mine. He submitted, docile as a child, and I pulled him back along the path as the wind whistled in our ears. The howling of the great hound resumed in the distance. The sound cut through our bodies like a knife thrust, and I felt my cousin stiffen as a sob grabbed at his throat.

"Dragen," he whimpered. "My poor, poor Dragen!"

Somehow we managed to stumble home, retracing our path to our little settlement of modest farmhouses. I saw Jacob enter his house before heading off toward my own. Pale and trembling, he had spoken hardly a word the entire way back, and I feared for his state of mind.

That night at dinner my mother noticed I was not myself.

"How did you fare on your hunting trip, Slade?" she asked, her sharp eyes fixed upon me as I stared at the untouched food in my bowl.

"Fine," I replied, stirring the stew listlessly with my spoon. My mother had made *waterzooi*, my favorite dish—a rich Flanders stew with carrots, leeks, potatoes, herbs, butter, and cream. But I had no appetite, which caused her to regard me suspiciously, for a twelve-year-old boy is always hungry.

"Did you shoot anything?" my brother, Maarten, inquired, swinging his legs back and forth under his chair. He was only seven and took after my mother, with hair as blond as summer wheat, and blue eyes the color of a cloudless day. I was darker, like my father, and carried an English first name, whereas Maarten had been named after my mother's father.

"We found no grouse," I replied, anxious to have the conversation at an end. I was haunted by poor Dragen's death, and confused by what my cousin had told me. I had no wish to share the information with my mother, who I feared had lied to me about my father's fate.

I excused myself soon afterward and went up to bed, on the pretext that I was unwell. I could feel my mother's eyes on me as I ascended the ladder to the loft bed I shared with my brother.

My sleep that night was restless and unquiet, haunted by the ungodly howls of the horrible creature. Its yellow eyes lingered in my mind's eye as I awoke the next morning, glad for the sunlight streaming through my bedroom window.

I knew there was one person I could turn to in such a situation.

My great-uncle, Frans van de Bogart, lived in a cramped, smoky farmhouse on the other side of Krumville. He still wore wooden shoes and could speak Dutch. It was said that no one knew more about local lore than Uncle Frans, and I had always felt a kinship with the old gentleman. After finishing my chores, I set out to visit him, hugging the farm fields along the side of the woods. The day was fair, with wispy clouds high in a deep blue sky, the sun warm upon my back as I hugged the low stone wall between properties. A chipmunk followed me for a while, chattering and flicking his tail boldly. I tossed the little fellow a bit of biscuit from my pack, which he grabbed up and scampered away with.

My uncle was seated in front of his cabin, mending a pair of old breeches. As I walked up the long dirt path to his door, a stick snapped beneath my feet, causing him to raise his aged head and peer in my direction.

"Who goes there?"

"It is I, Uncle—Slade Fletcher."

He frowned at me. "What brings you out here today? Have you no duties to perform for your mother?"

"I have finished my chores. I came to ask your advice."

"Did you indeed?" he remarked. "In my experience, advice may be freely given but is seldom heeded."

As he spoke, he continued to sew without interrupting the smooth rhythm of his work. His gnarled hand dipped in sure, swift movements as he sewed the patch on the material with tidy, even stitches. His dexterity was impressive, since he was completely blind.

"Well, boy," he said. "Don't just stand there—give your uncle a kiss!"

I climbed onto the rickety front porch, the boards creaking underfoot, and bent obediently to plant my face in his thick, oily whiskers. He smelled of saddle polish and tobacco, his beard stiff and prickly as the bristles of a broom.

"That's a good boy," he said with a satisfied sigh. "Come—what do you say we have some tea and *beschuit* in honor of your visit?"

"Thank you," I said eagerly. The long walk had caused my appetite to return, and I loved the crisp round Dutch breads, especially with honey or fresh-churned butter. I followed him into the dark interior of the cabin, the whitewashed walls streaked with soot from the single fireplace in the far corner of the main room. His heavy wooden shoes clattered across the floorboards as he poured water from an earthenware pitcher into the black iron kettle.

He hung the kettle over the hearth and threw another log on the fire, coaxing the flames higher with a leather bellows, then wiped his hands on his already stained trousers. Anyone meeting him for the first time would be astonished to hear that Uncle Frans was blind—he moved about more nimbly than many sighted men.

"What is your mother busying herself with these days?" he asked, settling his bulky frame into a sturdy oak-and-cane-backed "retiring chair." His family had brought it over from the Netherlands; the back was set at an angle so the sitter could recline comfortably.

"She's doing the spring cleaning," I said, sitting across from him on a low stool.

"She never could abide stillness," he remarked, stroking his beard and staring into the fire. It was hard to believe those clear blue eyes saw nothing, so keen was his expression. "I hope you are taking care of her, young Slade."

"Yes, sir, and the neighbors are always stopping by to see that she wants for nothing."

"That's as it should be. We folks out here need to look after each other." He grunted as he leaned over to toss on another log. "So, boy, what brings you over field and furrow to see your old uncle?" he said, wiping the ash from his hands. "What is it you wish to hide from your mother?"

I felt my cheeks burn from emotion as well as the blazing fire.

"I wish to hide nothing, sir—rather, I fear it is she who is dissembling."

"Is she, now?" he said, turning that pale gaze upon me. "About what, pray tell?"

I hesitated. As I sat before my uncle's cheerful crackling fire, the terrors of the previous day seemed the foolish fancy of an impressionable boy. But as I looked into those clear, kind blue eyes, the words came tumbling out. I omitted nothing—the sudden storm, the feeling of doom and despair that had seized my soul, and the tragic demise of poor Dragon in the jaws of the hideous hound.

When I had finished, my uncle sat back in his chair and regarded the fire—or rather, listened to it, as he could not see it. The logs popped and hissed, and the smell of green pine sap filled the room.

"There is an old verse I grew up hearing," he said, pouring a steaming cup of tea into a cracked earthenware mug.

*"The Vly, the Vly is dark inside,*
*Where strange and fearsome things may hide*
*Heed my warning, hear the cry—*
*Don't go nigh the Vly, the Vly."*

"But why?" I said. "What is in the Vly that is so terrible?"

He handed me the steaming mug. "Is it not rather I who should be asking you?"

I shivered in spite of the heat cast off by the blazing fire. My uncle laid a hand upon my shoulder.

"I believe I can tell you what you saw," he said softly.

"Wh-what?" I said, wanting and yet not wanting to know.

"The creature that devoured your cousin's dog—"

"What was it, Uncle?" I cried. "What on earth could be so fearsome and terrible?"

"It was Walpurga's Wind Hound."

"Who is Walpurga, and what is a—a Wind Hound?"

"Walpurga is the queen of the Wild Hunt."

"The Wild Hunt?"

"The last day of April is the spring equivalent of Midsummer's Eve—the very center of springtime. On that night the spirits of the dead return to the earth once more to engage in a mad dash on

horseback across the sky. It is a wild hunt of phantasms and spec-
ters, terrifying to behold. They are led by the goddess Walpurga
and her Wind Hound. That is why we celebrate Walpurgisnacht
with bonfires—to celebrate the coming of spring, but also to keep
away the spirits."

"What has this to do with my father?"

"Any mortal who chances upon the Wild Hunt may feel the
irresistible urge to join the hunt. Or, if they refuse, they may be
kidnapped and taken to the land of the dead. In either case they
may not be able to rejoin the living."

My uncle turned his sightless eyes to the fire. The flames licked
and danced in the grate, casting long, twisting shadows on the wall
behind, like the writhing forms of doomed souls.

"Perhaps I should not be repeating these tales," he said. "But I
fear you will return to the Vly, curious boy that you are. You have
too much of your father in you. I knew when my niece Catharina
married a Fletcher she was in for a hard time of it. But she loved
him, and I should like to think he loved her."

"He did—he does!" I cried, hot tears springing to my eyes.

"I believe you're right," said Uncle Frans. "But if he witnessed
the Wild Hunt, I shudder to think what has become of him."

"And the Wind Hound?" I asked in a voice barely above a whisper.

My uncle returned his gaze to the fire. "Walpurga's Wind
Hound is ravenous, and must be fed."

"It feeds—"

"On the living flesh of beasts—or men."

I nearly fainted from the thought that if the Hound had not gotten to poor Dragen first, Jacob or I could have been its victim.

"Surely these are merely superstitions!" I cried.

My uncle turned his sightless eyes toward me. "I would that they
were." A great sigh escaped his sturdy body. "I have never spoken of
this to you, but I was your age when I lost the use of my eyes."

I wanted to reply, but my mouth would not obey me. All I could
do was stare at him dumbly.

"It was just this time of year. I remember the bonfires blazing in the village that night—the one and only time I ventured into the Vly."

"Wh-what happened?" I said. My voice sounded very small and far away.

He shook his head. "I saw such things as mortal men should never see—nor would ever want to. Demons astride great black horses, hideous to behold, with glowing eyes—women, too, bare-breasted, their hair flowing out behind them. At the fore of the hunt was Walpurga herself, astride a great white mare with a flaming mane."

"And the Hound? Did you see Walpurga's Wind Hound?"

"Aye," he said. "It was the last thing on this earth I ever did see. When its yellow eyes met mine, I fell into a dead faint, and when I awoke, I was as you see me—completely blind. And now you must ask me no more," he said, rising suddenly from his chair. "I was lucky to escape Hugh Turner's fate. Had I not been struck blind, I think I should have gone mad."

"Just one more question, I beg you!" I pleaded.

"One more, and then we must talk of this no further."

"My father—was he—was his body recovered?"

Uncle Frans shook his head. "I should not tell you this, young Slade."

"Please—*please!*"

My uncle took a deep breath and let out a shuddering sigh.

"The coffin we buried in the churchyard that night was empty."

His words shot terror into my heart, like the blast of a rifle. But with the terror came hope—perhaps my father was still alive! My head swam, and I found it difficult to swallow. At last I recovered myself and sprang to my feet.

"Thank you, Uncle—and now I must go."

The sun was already low in the sky when I took my leave of Uncle Frans. As we stood on his tiny porch, he laid his strong, knotted hands upon my shoulders.

"Promise me one thing, young Slade," he implored, but even as he spoke the words I knew I would not. "Tell me you will return no more to the Vly."

I planted my feet firmly and inhaled the scent of pine smoke curling up from his chimney. "I cannot," said I.

"Then God help you," said he, and planted a kiss upon my forehead.

I turned to look back when I was halfway down the long drive to his house. He was still standing on the porch, gazing after me, as if he could see into eternity itself.

I had no wish to tread the woods alone with darkness descending, so I took the longer route leading through the village. Across the fields, I could see the great bonfire blazing in the town square, the sparks shooting like a thousand glowing eyes into the night sky. People had gathered to eat and drink and celebrate Walpurgisnacht Eve; shouts of laughter and singing floated across the fields.

Drawn by the dancing flames, I approached the circle of people around the fire. Suddenly I felt a hand grasp my shoulder. I spun around and found myself face to face with Hugh Turner. He wore an old-fashioned cloth cap at a rakish angle, his fair hair protruding from it, stiff as straw. His eyes were the eyes of a madman. He stared at me for a moment before intoning in a singsong voice:

> *"The Vly, the Vly is dark inside,*
> *Where strange and fearsome things may hide*
> *Heed my warning, hear the cry—*
> *Don't go nigh the Vly, the Vly."*

I tore his hand from my shoulder and stumbled down the road, away from the village. When I stopped at my cousin's house to see how he was faring, my aunt met me at the door to say he was in bed with a fever. I evaded her questions about what had transpired the previous day and set off for my own house. I kissed my mother good-night and went straight up to bed after dinner.

I lay in bed staring at the ceiling until my brother's breathing deepened and became more regular. Around me, the house slept; I alone lay awake in the darkness. There is something in the night, something sly and mysterious and inviting. Even as a child lying in bed, gazing out at the bright summer moon, I felt its beckoning. It spoke to a force within me that was not about life, but something darker. Perhaps it was the allure of death and oblivion, but it called to me nonetheless, heating my blood and sending my head spinning.

Now I lay gazing at that very same moon, grinning full and high in the sky, and I felt that it challenged me—no, dared me—to venture forth with only its cold white light as company. I threw off my covers, slid into my boots, and was out the door before my brother could turn over in his sleep. The sound of his thick breathing followed me as I crept to the kitchen, still and silent as the stars. The crockery, canisters, and bins of flour were alive with moonbeams cascading wantonly through the French lace curtains, throwing their reflected light into every corner of the room. I stopped, struck by the beauty of the moment, and by the knowledge that here, now, I was safe. Once I opened the door and ventured outside, I left the security of my family home behind.

I sucked in a lungful of air, put my trembling hand upon the door latch, and pushed. The door gave, and I stepped over the threshold and into the waiting night. I tiptoed across the small back yard and through the gate. The moonlight settled over the landscape like a cold white hand. Ahead of me the road lay, a ribbon of white stones and packed dirt awash in its pale light. I headed to the corral, whistling softly for my roan pony, Atticus.

I was answered by a gentle neighing and the clop of hooves trotting across the dusty paddock. Soon his head was on my shoulder, prodding gently as he sniffed for sugar lumps hidden in my jacket. I fished around in my pocket and found two, which I held out on my palm. His velvety muzzle tickled my outstretched hand as his lips closed over the sugar. He nickered with pleasure as he munched the cubes, nodding and tossing his head.

"Atticus," I murmured, "come along."

I had known Atticus from the day of his birth; it was my arm that pulled him, slimy, stunned, and sweating, from his mother's body when she was too weak to stand after hours of labor. It was I who washed and dried him and put his mouth to her teat, watching as he found the strength to suck it, pulling life into his spindly body. I was there when he was weaned, when he stretched and kicked up his legs with the other colts in the pasture, and I put the first saddle on him when he was two years old.

Mine was the only body he had borne upon his back, and I knew the feel of my legs around his ribs as well as I knew the touch of my own mother's hand. He had never thrown me, and I had never raised a hand to him. He knew neither whip nor lash, only the gentle pressure of my legs against his sides; the merest touch of my heels would send him into a full canter.

He sensed my excitement, as horses do, prancing and pawing the ground as I laid the saddle upon his back. When I sprang lightly into the saddle, he took off at a brisk trot, and soon we were cantering down the dirt road in the direction of the Vly. My fear had been replaced by determination to find out what had become of my father—even if I perished in the process.

The night was windless and calm, the pregnant moon overhead lighting my way. The creak of saddle leather blended with the even, rhythmic thud of Atticus's hooves upon the soft dirt as we ventured deeper into the forest. We stopped at a streambed so he could drink, and I heard the furtive rustling of nighttime creatures in the woods. The liquid *woot-woot-wootoo* of a barred owl high in the branches above us cut through the stillness of the night.

We continued, the terrain descending as a low-lying mist rose from the ground. As I approached the clearing where we had seen the great hound, I felt the same oppressive dread and nameless terror I had experienced before. This time I resisted, urging Atticus forward with a gentle press of my knees—but he balked and stood still, shivering, his ears pricked sharply forward. I had never known him to disobey a command before. I pressed harder, still with no response. I did something I had never done—I dug my heels deeply into his flanks. Startled, he leapt forward into the clearing.

A great gust of wind tore the hat from my head, and as I reached out to grab it, the sky itself seemed to open up. I was enveloped by an unearthly light, fierce and glowing, pouring from the heavens themselves. I was too astonished to be afraid, and as I gazed upward, a great roar shook the air. I heard the thundering of a thousand hooves, the battle cries of a legion of warriors, and the terrified screams of their unfortunate prey.

The sound, eerie as it was, scarcely prepared me for the sight that greeted my astounded eyes. Pouring from the cavernous rift in the sky, a spectral host on horseback galloped in mad pursuit of its fleeing quarry—a swarm of ghostly bison, deer, and elk. Accompanied by dogs of all sizes and descriptions, some of the hunters were misshapen gnomes with gnarled, demonic faces. Others were fierce-looking, well-formed men and women—some fully clothed, while others rode half-naked astride their charging steeds. Many of the women were bare-breasted, their wild hair flowing out behind them. These Amazons had the same fierce gaze as their male counterparts, clutching spears in their muscular bare arms. In front of the mass of riders was a tall, magnificent woman with long hair of burnished gold, at her side the same gaunt hound I had seen days earlier. I realized that it must be Walpurga herself, leading the chase.

I watched transfixed as they charged down from the heavens. My fear was replaced by a burning urge to join the multitude in their crazed dash across the sky. Atticus seemed to sense my eagerness, prancing impatiently beneath me. My gaze fell upon a rider mounted upon a tall chestnut mare, and I realized with a shock that it was my father! My heart fluttered and danced with joy in my chest—*my father was alive!* I urged Atticus forward to meet him, but my father's gaze met mine, and he shook his head, a great sadness in his eyes. I hesitated, confused—was I not to be with him, to speak with him once again?

I wrapped my legs around my horse's sides and squeezed. He sprang forward with a mighty leap, and we sailed, horse and rider, into the midst of the thundering herd of hunters. My ears rang with battle cries, my eyes were pierced with unearthly light, and my breast was flooded with such emotion it left me breathless. I seemed to experience every passion I had ever felt in my life, multiplied tenfold, a rush of feelings so intense it felt as if I must be going mad. Love, rage, jealousy, envy, terror, joy, and sorrow vied for mastery—but as these fell away, I felt the thrill of the hunt, the primal lust for blood. I heard the sound of my own voice shouting, as if very far away, joining the great commotion all around. I tightened my grip on the reins and urged my horse forward—until I caught up with my father. Riding next to him, I stretched out my hand. He hesitated, then reached his hand toward mine.

At that moment a great demon mounted on a black stallion came galloping toward us, a long spear held aloft in his misshapen hand. The stallion tossed his great head, frothing and straining at the bit. Just behind them I saw Walpurga's Wind Hound, teeth bared, charging toward us.

My father shrank back and tried to let go my hand, but I clutched his all the tighter. The demon rider closed in on us, his face a hideous mask of rage. His eyes were blazing red coals of fury, his skin green as tree moss. He raised his spear overhead, and my father pulled back from my grasp. Though my arm felt as if it was about to be wrenched from the socket, I would not let go, and held on to him with all my strength.

"No-o-o-o-o!" I cried, and closed my eyes.

Blackness descended upon me like a blanket.

When I awoke, the clearing was still and quiet except for the chirping of birds in the meadow. I lifted my head from the damp ground and opened my eyes.

I saw nothing but darkness, and realized I was now entirely blind.

"Atticus," I whispered. "Where are you?"

I heard the familiar soft whinny, and felt his muzzle nudge my shoulder. Another touch greeted me as well—that of a human hand.

"Hello, Slade."

Tears dampened my eyes as I grasped my father's hand in my own.

A good horse always knows the way home. My father insisted that I ride while he walked alongside Atticus. I relented, heaving my weary body onto the horse's broad back for the long walk back. On the return trip, my father recounted to me that fateful night he joined the hunt, drawn in just as I had been, enthralled by their powerful allure. He was astonished to hear he had been gone for a year; the time for him had passed as if it were a single day. We wondered if any explanation of the night's fantastical events would satisfy my mother. My father explained that he had tried vainly to warn me away from joining the Wild Hunt—but being a foolish and headstrong boy, I was beyond heeding the warnings of my elders.

I had succeeded in saving him, at the cost of my eyesight. Though it is a price I was willing to pay, I consider it my duty to warn others of the dark and dangerous things in this world. He who would venture into their midst should be forewarned.

*The Vly, the Vly is dark inside,*
*Where strange and fearsome things may hide*
*Heed my warning, hear the cry—*
*Don't go nigh the Vly, the Vly.*

# HEIRLOOM

## BY JOSEPH FINDER

T hey must think this is Nantucket," Walter said. "Is that a
Range Rover?"

"Oh, don't start," Ruth said in her scolding voice. "The
wife is lovely. I think it's wonderful they want to have us over. Give
them a chance."

"Give me a drink, I say. Though they're probably the white-wine
spritzer types. Hoity-toity."

"For heaven's sake, please, stop."

Walter grumbled something inaudible as he parked the truck
and turned off the engine and, heaving a long sigh, got out. Something crunched under his boots, and the air smelled fishy. They'd
recently put down crushed oyster shells over the dirt driveway. All
the rich summer folks seemed to do that. They probably thought
it made their places look more authentic, more Cape Cod, somehow. Like hydrangeas and split-rail fences and wind chimes and
fairy roses. They had no idea what a pain in the butt crushed shells
were, how you had to lay more down every year because of the ero-
sion, how the shells got caught in your lawn mower, how the weeds
always sprouted up through the bare spots and then you had to spray
Roundup, which could kill your dog. They never thought about how
it hurt your knees if you had to crouch down to work on your car.

Then again, people like that probably didn't know how to fix their own cars. They probably didn't even wash their own windshields.

Walter cast a shrewd eye on the sweet old house, probably one of the oldest on the Cape. An eighteenth-century Colonial with a steep gable roof and doghouse dormers and small-paned windows with shutters that actually worked. A big fat central chimney, painted white. The clapboard siding had been gussied up with a fresh coat of white paint, the shutters with black semigloss. The cedar roof shingles were weathered silver gray. Looked like the roof needed replacing, though.

"Will you wait for me?" Ruth said. Walter scowled but stopped and waited for his wife to catch up. She needed a hip replacement sooner rather than later. "Can you hold this, please?" She handed him the festively wrapped jam jar and clutched his right wrist for support.

"Welcome," a woman called. "Welcome!"

As soon as the screen door opened, a dog came hurtling out like a guided missile, heading right for Ruth, yapping, jumping up on her. A toy dog: a Jack Russell terrier with a small snow-white body, a tan face, and perky ears. Ruth gasped but then laughed with delight. "Why, look at you, poochie!"

The dog kept yapping shrilly. *"Anís!"* the young woman shouted. "Down! Down!" She ran across the lawn toward them and grabbed the dog by the collar, a band of Madras plaid. "Bad girl! Bad! *Anís*, no! Stop it! I am *so* sorry!"

"Nothing like a hearty welcome," Ruth said.

"I'm Morgan. It's so nice of you to come over." She was tall and blond and wore pink Capri pants, a lime-green alligator shirt, a pearl choker necklace. They all shook hands and exchanged the usual pleasantries.

"Hutch is out back tending the grill," Morgan said. "He won't set foot in the kitchen, but put the fire outside and all of a sudden he's *Mario Batali* or something."

"Anís is an unusual name for a dog," Ruth said.

"That licorice-flavored liqueur? We drank it constantly in Marbella, on our honeymoon. It's in that Hemingway novel, which one was it? *The Sun Also Rises*, I think. Anís del Toro—anisette of the bull? Hutch was an English major at Yale and never lets you forget it."

They entered the house, leaving the dog outside, and Walter handed Morgan the jam jar. She exclaimed over it as if she'd just won Mega Millions.

"Oh, it's nothing," Ruth said. "Wild blueberry preserves. Those wild blueberries grow like weeds on our property."

"I adore wild blueberries!" Morgan exclaimed.

Walter noticed they'd replaced the aluminum screen door with one made from mahogany. Bogus, he thought. Pretentious. At least they were taking care of the flooring. He'd always loved the old wide-board floor, creaky and uneven after years of settling, scarred by centuries of boots and shoes, the pumpkin pine having mellowed to an amber that polyurethane stain could never imitate.

"So you let your dog run loose outside, huh?" he said. "I guess you got one of them invisible fences put in."

"Oh, where you put that funny collar on them and it shocks them if they cross a certain line on the property or something like that? No, we'd never do that. But she's not going to run away. We feed her too well! She loves being off-leash, though. If only I could stop her from digging!"

"Oh, dear," Ruth said.

"We think she buries her bones and then digs them up later."

"What a shame," Ruth said. "Your lawn is so beautiful."

"Oh, but it's not. It looks good, but the grass is just *awful*. It's this terrible, coarse-bladed, wiry stuff that hurts when you walk barefoot on it. Like you're walking on a Brillo pad! Hutch wants to have it all dug up and replaced with, I don't know, whatever they use in golf courses. You know men and their lawns!"

"It's zoysia grass," Walter said coldly. "Drought-resistant. I put it in for the Murdochs ages ago because they didn't want to waste money on an irrigation system."

Morgan looked stricken. Her hand fluttered over her open mouth. "Oh my God, that's not what I meant at all. I mean, it's exactly what you want if you're not going to have an irrigation system. It's so much hardier. The thing is, we're going to have a swimming pool put in back there, and you know how all those trucks and tractors and things are going to chew up the lawn, so the whole yard's going to have to be reseeded anyway."

Walter gave her a quick, hard look; then his face seemed to relax. "Just don't use hydroseed. You'll be yanking out weeds for years. The soil's nice and rich, and I should know. I tilled in truckloads of Canadian sphagnum peat moss."

"Walter, remember how the Murdoch boy used to dig holes all over their lawn and you'd have to come back and reseed?"

He shrugged.

"Sure you do. It looked like they had a family of moles. He used to bury things, just like your dog. He called it his pirate treasure. Once he buried the Murdochs' television remote and he could never remember where he'd put it. And remember that box of cigars Tom bought you one Christmas and how it just disappeared one day and it turned out that poor Paulie had buried it in the yard, only he didn't remember where?"

Walter shrugged again. "Wouldn't have been any good if I found 'em anyway. The damp would have ruined 'em."

Ruth lowered her voice to a confiding whisper. "He was what we used to call feebleminded. Not quite right in the head. He looked like a strapping teenager but he had the mind of a five-year-old. Such a handsome young man…He always wore this funny red-and-black hat—you know those plaid hunter's caps? I call it an Elmer Fudd cap?"

Morgan nodded and smiled.

"Night and day, he was never without that hat. Winter and summer, no matter how hot it got. And of course he always had the earflaps down." A troubled expression crossed her face. "Walter was like a father to that boy. And then…" She fell silent and looked sad.

Walter said, "I'd be careful letting a dog that little run around outside at night."

Morgan looked at him quizzically.

"You know about the coyotes, don't you?"

She gasped. "Coyotes?"

He nodded. "Sure. At night you'll hear them howl and laugh. They roam around here in packs like wolves."

"They do no such thing," Ruth said. "Coyotes are loners."

"I guess you forgot what happened to the Costas' poodle," Walter said. "And he was even on one of them retractable leashes."

"Oh, that was such a terrible thing," Ruth said.

"Coyote came and grabbed it and ate it for dinner," Walter said.

Morgan turned abruptly and opened the mahogany screen door. "Anís! Anís, come! You get in here right this minute!"

The dog came scampering in.

"Now, I haven't seen the Pamet Puma, as they call it, but I've heard tell there's a big cat roaming around and feasting on small game and domestic animals. It ain't no legend, I hear. There've been sightings. When they can't find game, they get awful hungry..."

Morgan put a hand on Walter's shoulder. "Thank you so much for the warning. No one told us *anything* about that."

"Well, that's what neighbors are for," Walter said.

"What can I get you to drink? We have red wine and white wine—a wonderful Sancerre—and Hutch can make you martinis or just about any mixed drink you like."

"Just a glass of ice water for me," Ruth said.

"You probably don't have bourbon," Walter said. "I do like my Jim Beam."

"Are you kidding? Booker's is all Hutch drinks! Hutch! Come on inside and meet the Colemans."

A tall, gangly young man with tortoiseshell glasses entered from the other side of the low-ceilinged living room, the screen door clattering shut behind him. He was wearing a long black apron that said STAND BACK! I'M GRILLIN' on the front and he smelled of woodsmoke. He gave Walter an unnecessarily firm handshake. Hutch Whitworth, his name was. Hutch and Morgan, Walter thought. What kind of names were those?

"A Booker's for Mr. Coleman and a glass of water for Mrs. Coleman."

"Ruth, please."

"Ruth, do you prefer still or sparkling?" Morgan said.

"Oh, just tap water for me."

Walter took hold of his wife's elbow and muttered, "You don't want it from the tap."

"Of course!" Morgan said. "We have Evian or Fiji or...what's that neat bottle?"

"Voss?" said her husband. With a wry grin he added: "From the frigid aquifers of Norway." Under his apron he was wearing a light-blue gingham button-down shirt and shorts that actually looked pink.

"Tap is fine," Ruth said. "Really."

"Honey," Walter said. "You know about the well."

"The well?" Hutch said.

"Any kind of bottled water would be fine for her," Walter said. "Let's just leave it at that."

"Is something wrong with our well?" asked Hutch.

"They didn't tell you when you bought the house?"

"Tell us what?" Morgan said. "Is something wrong with the well water? Hutch, I thought we had it tested."

"We did. They said it was a little hard, maybe, but otherwise pure and clean as the driven snow."

"Charlie sold you the house, right?"

Hutch nodded. "Right...?"

"Charlie," Walter said with a low chuckle. "I love him like a brother, but you know, when you shake hands with him you count your fingers afterward."

"You mean he's...*dishonest*?" Morgan said, eyes wide.

"Charlie's the salt of the earth," Walter said. "Great guy. Great guy. But, well, you know...Like they say, a man's gotta do what a man's gotta do." He shrugged. "Who tested your well water? Kenny Fisher?"

"I think that was his name," Hutch said slowly.

"Sure," Walter said, nodding. "The only game in town. Kenny

and Charlie are old pals. Kenny's never gonna screw up one of Charlie's sales. Anyways, all that hooey about herbicides and pesticides and weed killers and stuff? There's no scientific proof it causes birth defects or bladder cancer or leukemia or what have you. That's all just scare talk. No proof."

"Walter," Ruth said, "I never heard anything about their well water. Where are you getting all this?"

"Sweetie, if you ever joined us for poker night you'd know a lot more about what's going on in this town than who's hitting the bottle too much." He winked at the young couple. "There's a reason they call us a quaint drinking town with a fishing problem."

Morgan's mouth was gaping open, and her husband's face was flushed.

"I always wondered," Walter said, "why the Murdoch kid was born, you know, feebleminded. They insisted it didn't run in the family, so you had to think, well, what if it *was* the water?"

"I think Estelle had a sister with developmental problems," said Ruth.

"Who can ever know with these things?" Walter said.

"You know, I'd love a tour," Ruth said hastily. "Can you believe we've lived next door for forty-three years and this is the first time we've ever been inside this house? Walter spent plenty of time over here, but not me."

"Sure," Morgan said, sounding subdued. "Let's get some drinks first. Hutch, I'll have a bourbon, too, come to think of it."

"Bourbon and water, coming up," Hutch said.

"Use the Evian," said his wife.

While Morgan showed Ruth around, the men stood next to the grill, highball glasses in their hands. It was one of those immense stainless steel numbers the size of a Volkswagen. The dog whined and pawed at the screen door from inside. "So the traffic noise don't bother you?" Walter said casually, watching Hutch flip bell peppers, orange and yellow and red. They had nice black stripes on them from the grill.

"You know, I don't even notice it anymore," Hutch said.

"No, you wouldn't. Not consciously." Walter took a long sip. In the lull, the whoosh of car tires on Route 6 seemed particularly loud. Then, as if on cue, came the blat of a motorcycle. "You probably saw that thing in the Sunday paper a few weeks back about how noise pollution can raise your blood pressure and give you anxiety and disrupt your sleep and what have you. Damages the fetus worst of all. Developmentally and all that. Scary stuff. But you folks probably aren't planning to have kids anytime soon, so it's no big whoop."

Walter could hear the young man swallow hard.

"We've been talking about hiring one of those acoustic consultants to design a noise barrier fence on the highway side," Hutch said.

"Why not," Walter said, nodding. "Worst that happens, you're out twenty, thirty thousand bucks. Call it an experiment, right? Though I always wondered if maybe they're selling you a bill of goods. It never works like they tell you."

"Actually, they're supposed to cut down noise as much as ten decibels."

"Build it high enough, maybe. Twelve-foot fence gonna look like the Berlin Wall, though."

Hutch shrugged. "We could sort of mask it with trees. Leyland cypresses, maybe."

"Huh," Walter said, unconvinced. "Sure. You might get lucky."

"How's that?"

"Your Leyland cypresses don't much like our winters."

"Ah." Hutch tried to turn a piece of zucchini, but it slipped through the cooking grate and landed in the coals with a hiss. The fire flared and crackled.

"Not helping you much, am I?"

Hutch chuckled. "You're supervising," he said. "Male bonding. Whatever."

Hutch's hair was thinning on top, Walter saw. The guy would probably be bald in a couple of years easy.

After a long pause, Walter said: "Well, I'm glad the house finally sold."

"This house?"

"You musta got a real nice deal on it."

"I—I thought it was on the market for only a couple of weeks."

"Going on six *years*, more like."

Hutch looked surprised. "That can't be true."

"Oh, Charlie. Man, I love him to death, but he musta relisted this house a dozen times over the years. Like they say, the last key in the bunch opens the lock. Guy could sell snow to an Eskimo."

"Wh—what was…? Well, they must have way overpriced it, then. We put in an offer half an hour after we saw this place." Hutch gestured widely with his hand, indicating not just the house but the sweep of open land. "You don't come across eighteenth-century Cape houses in this condition every day, you know, with this much land."

"Oh, it wasn't the price," Walter said.

"What—what do you mean, it wasn't the price?"

Walter noticed something and pointed. "What's that over there, a garden?" The sun was setting and the vast expanse of lawn was bathed in an ochre glow. The shadows had grown long. Walter's vision wasn't as sharp as it used to be, but he could make out a large rectangular plot fenced in by chicken wire and timber posts. It was situated right on the edge of the woods. That narrow strip of forest separated this house from Walter's farm.

Hutch looked and said, "My tomato garden. What about the house?"

"Just tomatoes in there, huh?"

"Heirloom. Twenty-seven different varieties."

"Any reason you put it way the heck over there? Seems like you'd get a hell of a lot more full sun if you moved it away from the trees."

"Well, you know, it's interesting: I noticed the grass over there was darker and greener and way taller than the grass next to it, even though it had just been mowed a few days before. I figured that for whatever reason the soil there was better. Just naturally richer."

Walter stared at the tomato garden for a long time. Suddenly his sun-creased old face had grown taut. He seemed to be deep in thought, and not happy thought.

"What is it?" said Hutch.

After a few seconds, Walter shook his head. "Huh? Nothing."

"Well, as I was saying, maybe it's the leaves from the trees—you know, they decay over the years and form a rich loam or compost or humus, I'm not even sure what you call it. But whatever it is, the dirt there is incredibly rich. I've never seen anything like it—the plants are immense and healthy and they're bearing loads of fruit, and they're *huge*. And the best I've ever tasted. You'll see what I mean— Morgan is making her tomato salad for dinner. We'll give you some to take home—we have way more than we can possibly eat."

The old man looked shaken. He cleared his throat. "Who dug your garden for you?"

"You really must think Morgan and I are just a couple of spoiled yuppies from the city," Hutch said, emboldened by the alcohol. "I did it myself, put the plants in myself, staked them myself. I like gardening. I actually find it relaxing."

"You come across anything?"

"Excuse me?"

"When you dug the garden, I mean."

"A lot of roots and some rocks is all." Hutch gave him a puzzled glance. "I suppose now you're going to tell me that's where the old cesspool was, huh?" He grinned wickedly as if to show he was onto the old man's tricks.

"Oh, no," Walter said softly. "Oh, no. Nothing like that. Nothing like that at all."

"Then what?"

Walter looked pensive. Like he couldn't decide how to answer. Finally he said, "I don't suppose you have any more of that fancy bourbon?"

\*    \*    \*

Dinner was punctuated by long, uneasy silences. The clinking of silverware, the sounds of chewing and smacking and swallowing seemed unusually loud. Ruth exclaimed over the cold cucumber soup and asked if that interesting flavor was fresh cilantro. The steaks were perfect, charred on the outside, tender and juicy on the inside, and Ruth asked Hutch how he grilled steaks as good as what you'd get at one of those expensive steakhouses in New York City. When Hutch revealed his secret—you coat the steaks in an emulsion of clarified butter and oil and kosher salt before putting them on a very hot fire, and turn them *only once*—he didn't sound very enthusiastic. He barely talked at all.

Ruth did her best to lighten the mood by telling funny stories about some of the more colorful characters who lived here year-round: the bossy postmistress who had a habit of "misplacing" your mail under a sorting table if she took a dislike to you; the elderly gentleman who had a llama farm and rode a motorcycle; the once-famous B-movie star who never left his house. Morgan smiled and laughed politely and made sure everyone's wineglass was replenished with the Pinot Noir from Oregon that had become their house red.

"Will you look at these tomatoes?" Ruth said after one particularly long stretch of silence. A wicker basket of cheerfully colored but strangely misshapen tomatoes sat in the middle of the antique French country farm table, an unusual centerpiece. "How extraordinary."

"This one's my favorite," Morgan said, selecting a bulbous deep-red one. "Don't you think it's obscene?"

"Oh!" Ruth said, giggling. The tomato's deep cleft looked almost lewd, like a buxom woman's cleavage. "What sort of tomato is that?"

"That's called a Mortgage Lifter," said Hutch in a brittle, almost annoyed tone. "Heirloom tomatoes have all sorts of funny names."

"Well, I think it looks just like the buttocks of a young boy," Walter said.

After several seconds of awkward silence, Ruth coughed.

Morgan got up to go to the kitchen, but on the way she turned around. "Oh, Hutch, you should ask Walter about the chipmunks."

"Chipmunks?" Ruth said.

"Yeah," Hutch said, perking up a bit. "I think the chipmunks are eating my tomatoes. It's like they wait for the tomatoes to get absolutely, perfectly ripe and then they take a bite—one single bite per tomato—like they're sampling each one. Then of course you have to throw them away, unless you want to catch rabies. It drives me nuts."

"Oh, sure," Walter said. "It's a cycle around here. They extend the hunting season so's people can shoot more coyotes because they're eating too many house pets. And of course coyotes eat chipmunks, so fewer coyotes, more chipmunks."

"Oh, but they're so cute!" Morgan said.

"They're cute until they eat your blueberries and raspberries and tomatoes, and then they're not so cute."

"So what do you do?" Morgan asked.

"Snap traps."

"Like—like rattraps?"

"Nah, mousetraps'll do you just fine. Put a little dab of peanut butter on there and you'll catch 'em easy."

"Well, I don't think I could do that," Hutch said. "I couldn't kill a chipmunk."

"Do those Havahart traps work on chipmunks?" asked Morgan, still standing at the kitchen door. "Catch and release them somewhere?"

"Oh, no," Walter said with a deep, rumbling laugh. "You gotta kill the little buggers. Snap their little necks." He saw their horrified expressions. "Hey, a man's gotta do what a man's gotta do."

"Oh!" Morgan said. "I almost forgot!" She excused herself and then returned from the kitchen with a platter. "Hutch's tomatoes," she announced.

"Come on, it's your great recipe," Hutch said modestly.

"Olive oil and a touch of balsamic vinegar and a sprinkle of sea salt is hardly a recipe, honey," Morgan said, dishing tomato salad onto salad plates. "Walter?"

"Looks tempting," Walter said. "But I'll pass."

Hutch glared at him. "Something wrong with the tomatoes?"

"Hutch!" Morgan said.

"Oh, these tomatoes are wonderful!" Ruth exclaimed, fork poised in midair. "I don't know what you did to them, but they're just *divine*! Walter, you have to try Morgan's tomato salad."

Walter smiled but shook his head.

"Walter started telling me something about the tomato garden earlier," Hutch said. "Right, Walter?"

The old man compressed his lips and appeared lost in thought.

"Did there used to be a toxic waste dump there, Walter?" Hutch smiled, but his voice was harsh and a bit too loud.

"Hutch," Morgan said again.

"I'm sorry," Walter said. "I really should have kept my mouth shut. There's no reason you need to know the history. What's past is past."

"Walter, what are you doing?" Ruth said.

"History?" Morgan said.

"Please. Forget I ever mentioned it."

"Walter, please," Ruth said, placing her hand on top of his. "Stop it right now."

Morgan and Hutch exchanged a quick glance, and then Hutch said, "No, I'd like to hear whatever it is that Walter doesn't think we need to know."

"Honey," Morgan said.

Ruth shook her head and exhaled noisily. "Oh, dear."

"I just don't think it's right that no one told them about the house," Walter said to her.

"Walter," Ruth said, "it's past my bedtime."

Morgan smiled and said lightly, "Well, now you *have* to tell us."

Walter looked at her, then at her husband, his face grim. "All right."

Ruth scowled.

"The Murdochs lived in this house for years," Walter said. "Tom and Estelle and their son, Paulie. Nice folks."

"You certainly spent a lot of time over here," Ruth said crisply, "when Tom wasn't around."

Walter rolled his eyes. "Ruth, we're not having this conversation again."

Ruth shifted in her chair, sat up straighter, her lips pursed.

"Now, how long ago did it happen, Ruth?"

Ruth shook her head almost imperceptibly. She seemed to be pouting over some old hurt, a wound that still hadn't healed.

"Eight years ago, I think it was," Walter said. "Hard to believe it's been that long."

The young couple watched him intently.

"Tom and Estelle had gone to Boston for the weekend, and they left Paulie at home alone. He must have been sixteen, seventeen, and even if he wasn't quite right in the head, he did fine on his own. When they came home, the house was empty. Nobody home. No Paulie."

Ruth was studying her half-eaten tomato salad.

When a few seconds had passed, Hutch said, "And?"

"It was like he just up and vanished. Not a trace. They called everyone they knew in town and they drove around, and—nothing. He was gone. It was the damnedest thing."

"What happened to him?" Morgan asked, sounding as if she didn't want to know the answer.

"They put up signs everywhere. There were search parties. The police didn't have any luck. Days went by, and then weeks and months."

"Was he kidnapped or something?" Morgan asked.

"I bet he ran away," Hutch said. "You wouldn't believe how many teenagers leave home and just, I don't know, live on the streets."

"They sold the house, must have been a year later. They said they couldn't live here. Too many memories of the kid. They moved down to Boca, but that didn't last long. Estelle had a heart attack and died maybe a month or two after they moved."

He went quiet, and Hutch mistakenly assumed the old man had finished his story. "I'm not really getting what this has to do with my tomatoes," he said.

Walter fixed him with a beady stare. "The family that bought the house—I don't even remember their names, they owned it so short a time—well, you know, the old cesspool wasn't up to code, so the town made them put in a septic tank. New state law. They hired Jimmy Rice to do the excavation, isn't that right?"

Ruth, still staring at her plate, nodded once.

"Jimmy was sitting in his backhoe loader digging the pit for the drain field, right about where the tomato garden is now, and when he emptied the bucket something caught his eye. Something bright red, like a piece of clothing, maybe."

"No," Morgan said, her voice tight.

"The damnedest thing. He got out of the cab and picked up this red plaid Elmer Fudd cap out of the dirt pile, and stuck to it was this white fragment of bone...I mean, Jimmy's son went to grade school with Paulie, so of course he recognized the hat right away."

"He dug up the...body?" Hutch whispered.

"Just that cap and a small piece of skull."

"What about the rest of the body?" Hutch asked. His wife looked pale and queasy, her hand over her mouth.

"Like I told you, I tilled in a lot of peat moss in that soil to make the grass grow better, and that stuff's real acid. Turns out acid soil really speeds up the decomposition of human remains. They didn't find the skeleton. They didn't find any bones except for a few slivers. The peat moss actually dissolves the bones after enough time goes by. And the thing is, the human body makes excellent fertilizer."

The color had drained from Morgan's face. She blinked hard. "Pardon me," she said. She rose unsteadily from the table, her elbow knocking a salad plate clattering to the floor, where it shattered. But she kept walking toward the kitchen.

Hutch's mouth hung open. He took off his tortoiseshell glasses and put a hand over his eyes. Ruth had folded her hands in her lap, eyes downcast, as if she were praying. Everything went terribly still, except for the faint whoosh of car tires from the highway and a distant retching noise that seemed to emanate from the kitchen or the bathroom.

"The family hired some fancy real estate lawyer in Hyannis who got them out of the sales contract. Some little loophole in the law about 'deceptive trade practices' or some such. And of course everyone started calling the Murdoch house the Murder House. Tom was arrested down in Boca a little while later. I guess the Cape and Islands district attorney's office found some witnesses that remembered him complaining about Paulie, back in the day. What an ordeal it was taking care of him. How he was at his wits' end. How it was straining their marriage and he didn't know what was gonna happen to that kid after they were gone and how he really hoped the kid died before they did."

Ruth said very softly, "You were one of the witnesses at the trial, Walter. Aren't you going to tell them about that?"

"I got subpoenaed, honey. I didn't exactly have a choice."

"But you were the one who first told the police about Tom. If you hadn't come forward, Tom wouldn't be in prison."

"He killed his own son, Ruth. He belongs in prison."

"I loved that boy, too. I wasn't as close to him as you were, certainly, but I did love him. But I never understood why you never said anything before then. Why'd you wait till Jimmy Rice found that poor boy's hat? What took you so long?"

"Until they found the hat and the piece of skull, everyone thought the boy ran away, Ruth. We all did."

"Still," Ruth said. "Who knows if Tom did it or not? Maybe he did, maybe he didn't. Maybe it was someone else. It just always bothered me how they could put a man in prison for saying nothing more than he was worried about what would happen to his son. They didn't have a single piece of evidence tying him to the murder, but the jury convicted him and the judge sentenced him to life without parole. That's not beyond a reasonable doubt, seems to me."

"Ruth," Walter said. "You were always sweet on Tom and you know it."

"And you—"

But she stopped short. Then she pushed back her chair and got up from the dinner table. "Please give your wife my thanks and also my deepest apologies," she said as she started limping toward the front door. "We're going home, Walter."

Even though the Colemans were next-door neighbors, the drive took a good three minutes, what with turning left on Route 6 and then making the complicated figure eight off the town center exit to circle back around to Hatch Road.

Ruth sat in silence almost until they pulled into their driveway. Then she spoke in a small, fierce voice. "Well, I hope you're proud of yourself."

"Ruth."

"I don't think we'll be invited over there again."

"They would have found out sooner or later, Ruth. People talk."

"They barely just moved in! And you didn't have to ruin that nice dinner. They worked so hard."

"They made me tell them."

"And you kept dropping hints so they'd ask. Why don't you admit it?"

He shook his head and tried very hard not to smile.

"Walter Coleman, this is all because they outbid you on the house, isn't it? I don't even know why you put in an offer anyway."

"It's not the house, it's the property. We could double the size of our farm."

"All these years the estate's been trying to unload the Murder House, and they finally find a buyer."

"They've had my offer on the table the whole time."

"Not a serious offer, Walter. Not a serious offer. You were bidding a fraction of what just the land's worth, not including the house."

"That's all we can afford."

"Well, you lost and they won. So just deal with it and stop torturing that nice young couple."

As they got out of the truck, Walter wasn't able to keep that wicked smile from spreading across his face.

Ten days later, a 1995 Caterpillar 416 backhoe lumbered up the long dirt road to the old Murdoch place and over the crushed-oyster section. It drove right across the lawn to the tomato garden around the back, leaving deep ruts in the zoysia grass, and then came to a stop, the engine running.

Behind the wheel, Walter was trying to recall some of the places where Paulie liked to bury his treasures.

His standing lowball offer had been accepted a few minutes after Hutch and Morgan had moved out. They'd engaged the services of a real estate attorney in Cambridge who got the sales contract voided on the basis of deceptive practices. The lawyer didn't have to try all that hard, either. Now, at a price less than half what the preppy couple had paid, the Murdoch property was finally Walter's.

He'd start at the tomato garden; why not.

Paulie Murdoch used to bury his little treasures all over the yard, seemingly without pattern. So the box could be anywhere, really.

It hadn't been a problem when Paulie ran off with Walter's box of cigars and buried them in the yard somewhere. How the boy loved his pirate treasure maps! But when he sneaked off with Walter's antique oak tool chest, the one that had belonged to his grandfather, the one where he kept the special photographs, something had to be done at once.

Not because the chest was an heirloom, though it was. No, it was those very special and very private photographs he kept inside, the pictures of forbidden things. Including the ones that documented the very special and very private games that Walter had convinced the teenage boy to play.

Yet the more insistently Walter had demanded the return of

the box, the more gleefully the feebleminded boy had laughed. All he'd say was that he'd hidden them somewhere so he could show Mommy and Daddy, who loved to look at pictures of their only son.

This was no threat. It was part of the game whose rules he'd made up and from which he could not be dissuaded.

What happened next—well, it was self-preservation, nothing more. A man had to do what a man had to do.

He pushed the left joystick forward to lower the front loader bucket to the ground; then he pulled the right joystick to curl it back. The sharp-toothed bucket chomped through the flimsy chicken-wire fence, buckling and crumpling it, furring strips snapping like matchsticks, and it scooped out the first load of dirt.

He'd find the damn box, no matter how long it took. He was a patient man. Now he had all the time in the world.

Then, suddenly, a strange impulse overcame him. He was not unacquainted with strange impulses. He engaged the parking brake, got out, and stepped through the hole he'd just torn in the garden fence, his boots sinking into the soft, rich soil. Then he knelt before one of the gangly staked plants and plucked a single perfect tomato.

It was blood-red and ripe and full, with a deep cleft. He held it to his nose and inhaled deeply of its musk. Then he sank his teeth into it. The juice squirted and dripped onto his jowls and spurted into his eye, but it was good.

*God*, was it good.

# THE BOCA BOX

## JAMES O. BORN

Okay, Manny, cut the shit. What's in the goddamn box?"
Detective Paul Tubman shifted so his gut rolled off the
Glock model 23 on his right hip. It was the extra layer of
fat that made him so self-conscious he wore a sport coat to cover his
pistol even in the stifling heat of South Florida.

The wiry man behind the counter was about twelve years older
than Tubman, probably just over fifty, with the lean, hard look
of a runner who'd spent a little too much time out in the sun.
"That an official inquiry, Detective, or interest from a prospective
customer?"

Tubman frowned and said, "Both."

Manny shook his head and said, "Sorry, I can't tell you. It's a
trade secret."

Tubman gave him a laugh and looked away to show his general
disgust at the squirrelly clinic operator. "This is bullshit and you
know it. Why'd you even have to move back to Boca Raton, where
every cop knows you?"

"My parents live here."

"Everyone's parents live here." Tubman shook his head as he
mopped the sweat off his forehead with his midmorning handkerchief. "It just makes my life a little more difficult. I have to explain

to my bosses why there's one of the most prolific fraud assholes of all time working in Boca Raton."

"I'm telling you, Detective, you got me all wrong. I've changed. I see a therapist and everything. This clinic is absolutely legit. We got nutritionists, exercise physiologists, and a plan designed to make anyone lose weight. The box is more of a gimmick. We tell people it's the last resort, but we really only had to use it one time."

"Only one of your clients failed to lose weight?" He couldn't put enough skepticism in his voice, so he threw in a good head shake and then turned so his wide shoulders would have at least a little intimidating effect on the short scam artist.

"I didn't say that. Most people who don't lose weight drop out long before we resort to the box." Manny looked Tubman up and down and even carefully pulled one side of his sport coat open to get a view of his belly. "You're still a young man and can handle some serious exercise. I think this program would be perfect for you. And if you didn't lose"—Manny looked down at the application Tubman had filled out before he realized who ran the clinic— "forty-five pounds by April, after following everything—the protein shakes, exercise, counseling—then you might realize that the box is plan B. But most people don't take plan A to its logical conclusion."

"So you're saying if I sign all of these releases, agree to follow your rules, sign the contract, and do everything and still don't lose every pound I want to, then I could find out what's in the box?"

Manny nodded his head. "Only if all else fails."

"You can see my concerns. Given your history and the number of people in Boca Raton who bought condos you didn't own, paid you to sell their time-shares, or bought into your investment schemes, I'd be crazy to just pay your initiation fee."

"In that case, Detective, unless you have other business here, you need to move on because I have a lot of clients waiting to sign up. Five hundred dollars to start is a tremendous deal. After that, you pay by the pound. No other program gives you that option."

Manny focused his dark eyes on the taller detective. "Three years in prison changes people."

Tubman said, "It changes druggies or killers, not common fraud artists like you." He didn't care if he hurt the man's feelings. Guys like that could hardly be offended. But he needed to do something drastic if he wanted to lose enough weight to satisfy Maria. She didn't think he had it in him to accomplish a goal like that, and she insinuated he was a lazy mama's boy and that was why she wouldn't marry him. He had to do something, and this was the clinic everyone was talking about.

The detective said, "And I lose forty-five pounds by April, even with the holidays coming up?"

Manny just nodded his head.

"And if I haven't done it by, say, March, we'll consider using your super-secret box over there?"

"You won't need it. The only questions are, when do you want to start and how do you want to pay?"

"I'd never trust you with my credit card info, so I'll be paying cash." Tubman couldn't take his eyes off the two-foot-by-one-foot box behind the counter as he slid his wallet out of his back pocket and slowly pulled out three twenties for a down payment. "I'll bring the rest by later this afternoon." He was excited by the possibility of changing the recent direction of his life.

Paul Tubman stared down at his salad with dressing on the side, using some of the tricks the counselor at the weight loss clinic had taught him. He took a drink of water before and after each bite, focusing on the sensation of food in his mouth, and tried not to think about all the stuff on the menu he would've preferred to order. To make matters worse, his friend, Carl Spirazza, perpetually lean and fit, gobbled down a plate of lasagna like it was an appetizer.

His friend looked at Paul and said, "I'm impressed, Tubby. I don't think I've ever seen you focus on a diet for this long."

Tubman ignored the unfortunate nickname he'd had since childhood. He attributed it more to his name than his size. He hadn't really started to expand horizontally until his midtwenties. "It's only been three weeks and I still got the holidays staring me in the face, but I've lost almost ten pounds, and even though I had reservations, the clinic certainly seems to be legit."

"They may be helping you lose weight, but their cost is way out of line."

"It's the first time I've been losing weight. I know Manny is a crook, but maybe he really did stumble into an honest-to-goodness business. It still kills me to see that box every time I walk through the door. You're a doctor, you don't have any idea what it could be?"

Carl shook his head. "Probably some kind of a gimmick, like an ancient saying written on a piece of paper. The way you describe the box, oblong, about two by one foot, it could hold anything. Or nothing. But there's no special device that could trim off weight you don't lose after four months of dieting. Unless it has something to do with liposuction."

"That's one of the things the clinic is very specific about. No cosmetic surgery. They leave open the idea that it could be a medical procedure, but who the hell knows what kind of procedure it is. They swear it's not a stomach staple or anything like that."

"You're doing good. You're ahead of schedule. Why even worry about it? The way things are going, you'll never have to worry about what's in that box."

Tubman shook his head. "If it were anyplace but Boca Raton. Why do I have to live and work in the fraud capital of the US?"

"Is it really that bad?"

"You have no idea. This place attracts con artists like Mormons attract wives. Thirty percent of the office space in the city is devoted to some type of illegal activity. It's been estimated that half the car accidents are staged. There's no reason for me to be optimistic about the clinic. I was blinded by a chance to impress Maria."

Carl frowned at the mention of Tubman's girlfriend. Most of his friends weren't happy about the relationship and thought the sexy Venezuelan took advantage of Tubman. Carl didn't say much about Maria. He just didn't want an asshole like Manny Katner taking advantage of him.

Tubman sighed and took a sip of water before shoving a piece of romaine lettuce with a spritz of vinegar on it into his mouth. "Maria hasn't even commented on it yet. The only thing she noticed was that I didn't eat much at dinner last Saturday night."

"Did she really tell you she wouldn't marry you until you lost weight?"

"She beat me to the punch. She said it before I even popped the question. It's really good motivation."

Carl shook his head and said, "Why do you put up with that shit? You're a great guy. People love you. I've got a couple of nurses in my practice that would go out with you in a heartbeat. You don't need to be bullied into doing something you don't want to do."

"You sound like my mom. Maria isn't bullying me. She's *encouraging me.*"

Now Carl lost all humor and looked at his friend. "Are you kidding me, Tubby? The only thing she encourages you to do is buy her gifts. I'm glad you're taking an interest in your health, but I think Maria is more likely to kill you than your weight problem."

"Then I'll die happy."

Paul Tubman purposely didn't wear a sport coat today. Instead, he wore a shirt and tie with his Glock on his right hip and his gold badge clipped on the belt next to it. It was the style most detectives in the coastal cities liked to wear. They weren't hiding the fact they were cops. They weren't undercover.

Palm Beach County had a clear divide between "the coast" and "western communities." The coast, at least in the minds of most the residents, was where everything happened and the cool people lived. The rest of the county was apparently created to service them. Tubman didn't feel that way. He was just happy to be able to shed the hot sport coat. It was also a chance to show off his frame with twenty-two less pounds only three weeks into the new year.

No one said anything at first, and he wondered if anyone really cared. Then his sergeant strolled down the aisle between the four desks used by the economic crime detectives and said, "Tubby, if you keep losing weight we're going to need a new nickname for you." The sergeant flashed one of her famous perfect smiles and gave him a wink. "I know you're going to that clinic run by Manny Katner on Dixie Highway. You think the whole place is legit?"

"Expensive, but legit. Look at the results. I'm halfway to my goal and I've got a couple more months to get to it."

"So what's the secret to the clinic?"

"It's a full-service clinic with a nutritionist, an exercise physiologist, and a counselor. The only secret is this box about the size of a small footlocker that has the words LAST RESORT written on the top. It's some kind of promotional gimmick but supposedly will work if all else fails."

The sergeant paused and looked at him. "What's in it?"

"I have no idea. I'd be lying if I told you I didn't try to figure it out every time I walked in and I didn't think about it ten times a day. But it doesn't look like I have to worry about it now, thank God. But curiosity is eating at me."

"You know what makes a good detective? Curiosity and patience. Luckily, you've always had both. Otherwise we got a couple of missing kids that would never have been found, whole bunch of Ponzi scammers who would still be ripping people off, and a string of unsolved robberies. Your curiosity is something I never want you to lose."

All the detectives noticed when the youngest sergeant in the history of the detective bureau entered her office. It not only meant the danger had passed, but she kept in shape like no one else. There were a slew of jokes about the pretty sergeant, but when it was time to get things done, everyone looked to her.

Tubman considered the rare praise from one of the tougher cops he'd known in his fourteen years with the Boca Raton Police Department. The agency had a difficult role in the community, which was dominated by demanding rich people but still populated by middle-class families. There were only a couple of bad spots in the whole city, and most of the cops were smart enough to know they had nothing to complain about—especially compared to some of the rough towns just a few miles up US 1. But the city had the unfortunate reputation among law enforcement for being the capital of economic crime. That was what kept Tubman's mind on little things like the box at the clinic.

Paul Tubman stretched his legs out onto the coffee table while they watched *America's Got Talent*. For the most part he tuned out the show, which, along with *American Idol*, often gave him a migraine. But he didn't care just so long as he had a chance to smell Maria's hair or admire her delicate wrists, which at the moment were obscured by the wide gold bracelets he had bought her for the anniversary of her arrival in the United States from Venezuela.

One of Boca's biggest jewelers gave him a fantastic deal on all the jewelry he bought. The jeweler loved Tubman after he had found the jeweler's missing daughter eight years ago. Tubman had gotten so involved in the canvass of the neighborhood, looking for the missing six-year-old, and his curiosity had driven him so hard, he'd forgotten to go off shift and had found the girl, lost and hiding in an abandoned store, after more than twenty hours on duty. The jeweler's wife had made him feel like Superman. Tubman had hung on to that feeling for as long as he could, and sometimes it was similar to how Maria made him feel special. It wasn't what she said or did. It was more how the other cops looked at him with her on his arm. The thirty-year-old former swimsuit model positively shone. She attracted attention wherever they went.

Now she turned her head on his shoulder and slid her arm onto his belly. As soon as she paused for a moment, then patted his stomach, the excitement grew in him. He'd been waiting for her to comment on his steady weight loss.

Maria sat up and looked him in the eyes. "You're really losing weight, aren't you, Paulie?"

"You like?"

"Yes, I like." He loved the way she made a "Y" sound like a "J." Her accent wasn't unusual here in South Florida. It was just unusual for a girl like this to be with a guy like him.

Tubman said, "You wanna see the new me in the bedroom?" He playfully wiggled his bushy brown eyebrows.

She gave him a crooked smile and said, "Not tonight. I want to see who moves on to the next round."

He leaned forward and kissed her forehead.

She said, "How much more are you gonna lose?"

He considered his answer. The chart at the weight loss clinic said he only had ten more pounds to go. All Tubman said was "Some."


Two weeks later, in early February, as Tubman banged through the front door of the weight loss clinic, Manny sat up straight behind the counter and said, "You're looking slim, Detective."

Tubman found it hard to be civil to a guy he'd arrested for everything from check fraud to stealing an old lady's social security.

Manny said, "The clinic director says you're almost to your goal and we can cut you loose soon. Very nice. Now do you believe we're not a scam?"

Tubman eased up to the counter and leaned on it so he could look Manny directly in the eyes. He did notice that his gut wasn't hanging down like a cow's udder anymore. "I'll testify you're not a scam if you tell me what's in the box."

Manny motioned him closer, and when their faces were only a few inches apart he said, "It's motivational."

Tubman stood up straight and said, "So it's empty."

"Not really, but no one uses it. It's too much effort."

"What do you mean?"

Manny shrugged his thin shoulders and said, "Come on, Detective, admit it, the program works. Give your inquisitive mind a break. You're never gonna need to know what's in that box."

He heard the voice and knew it was the sergeant before he even turned from the stand-up copy machine. She said, "Definitely can't call you Tubby anymore, can we?" To emphasize her comment, she slapped him square on the butt.

Tubman jumped and turned to see his pretty sergeant smiling at him. She'd always acted like one of the guys, and he didn't take offense at her action. Life was too short to be politically correct every minute of the day. He said, "I wouldn't mind it if no one ever called me Tubby again."

"Ever figure out what's in the box?"

"I talked to one of the assistant state attorneys about the possibility of probable cause for a search warrant to look in it. The clinic claims it's the ultimate cure. But the attorney said I had nothing. Also, there haven't been any complaints on the clinic since it opened. I guess the box is a gimmick, but it's awfully hard to just let it go."

"Let it go, Tub... Let it go, Paul. Enjoy your life. You shouldn't let outside influences affect you so strongly." She threw him a wink as she strolled away.

He knew the sergeant was right. She was smart, a good cop, and had good common sense. But he couldn't let go of the idea that there was something like that box in his town, and it drove him absolutely crazy. He'd always been by the book and didn't go for any shortcuts in law enforcement. He wasn't sure there was a shortcut for this one. He'd been worrying about it for months now. But it had gotten considerably worse the last few days. He realized it had something to do with his continued weight loss. Every pound that disappeared piqued his interest in the box that much more and put him closer to proposing to Maria. Technically, he was already at his goal. There was no reason for him to ever discover the contents of the box at the weight loss clinic.

Then he noticed something on the table next to the copy machine. A Snickers bar. Extra large. Detectives were always leaving candy around the office. It was a staple of police work. He couldn't help glancing around the D-bureau like he was about to commit a crime. He had the candy bar unwrapped and shoved down his gullet as fast as a kung fu master could throw a punch, but like an alcoholic, he felt himself sucked back into the wonderful world of food.

Two weeks. That was all it took to wreck four months of work. He hadn't put back the entire forty pounds, but by twenty-one, Maria was pissed. She'd ordered him to get back on the diet or go on a "No-Maria Diet."

Tubman decided he didn't get that much from her anyway, so he let his girlfriend put herself off-limits. Until she screamed, "*No más. I need someone fit and firm.*"

Tubman sipped a beer as he watched her collect a few things from around his apartment, then march out the door for the last time.

Now he was on a mission.

It was late March when he rolled back into the clinic, twenty-six pounds away from his goal. He couldn't admit to anyone at the clinic that he was tired of his attempt to put the weight back on and would be happy to quit stuffing his face with anything he found. But he was looking forward to slimming down again once he knew the contents of the box.

Manny's eyes bulged when he said, "What the hell happened to you? You miss a couple of appointments and blow up like a Macy's Thanksgiving Day float."

Tubman shrugged and said, "You know how it is, Manny, anything can happen on a diet. But now I only have a few weeks to get this excess weight off. There's got to be something we can do to get me to meet my goal."

"You bet there is. We're going to put you on a diet of nothing but protein shakes and work the living shit out of you at the gym."

Tubman held up one hand and shook his head. "No, Manny. I'm going to need the box."

"No, you're not. You proved you can lose weight."

Tubman picked up on the anxiety in Manny's voice.

Manny said, "You're just doing this 'cause you're crazy. You can't let it go."

"Then tell me what's in the box."

"I can't. I signed more nondisclosure agreements than you did." Manny's frustration was obvious and growing. "Look, Detective, I know you think I'm a douche bag."

"More of a scumbag."

"Whatever. I understand our dynamic, but I need to strongly recommend against the last resort."

"Why?"

"It's unnecessary. You've already proved your willpower."

"Then just tell me what's in the box." Tubman kept his tone calm and conversational, using his years of interviewing and interrogation to try to coax what he needed out of Manny.

"I can't tell you."

"Why not?"

"Just like you, I've got ethics. I signed on as manager of this clinic, and a lot of people depend on me now. More than I ever realized. If I break one promise or go back on one commitment, I'll start down the slippery slope. I'm like an addict. It's all or nothing. I like this life and I'm gonna follow the rules and not tell you what's in the box."

"The rules also say it's time for me to use the last resort." Tubman was resolute and wanted to get that across in his tone.

Manny said, "This isn't so much about what's in the box as it is what's in you. I think it's your own issues that have made you fixate on this stupid box. You're a head case."

"I'm a customer and a cop. I want to use it. I've earned it." Tubman wondered if Manny wasn't right. All that flashed through his brain was his urge to see what was in the box. It was blinding him to any sort of rational thought. Could a con man change?

Manny looked around the empty clinic, then said, "I'll set up an appointment." The resignation in his voice said it all.

Tubman said, "Bullshit. Let's do it right now."

"I gotta make some calls. The medical director is supposed to be present."

"Really? I thought you were in charge here. Come on, Manny, this sounds like a scam."

Manny shrugged and slid a sheet of paper across the counter. "Okay. Here's one last disclaimer."

Tubman barely read it. It said that the clinic was not liable, that he'd been advised of all the dangers and all the other bullshit that goes along with lawyers getting involved in something simple. He scribbled his name. Then looked up at Manny.

Finally the lean, older man said, "Go ahead. There's no one else around. I ain't gonna stop you."

Tubman took a deep breath as he slowly walked around the counter, savoring his victory. He stopped in front of the box and turned toward Manny. "What do I do?"

Manny tapped the top of the box, where instructions were clearly stenciled on. "Start by sticking your hands through the handles at the bottom of the box, then turn the knobs upward."

Tubman noticed the seam longways down the box's lid. He wondered why the box opened in such an odd manner as he twisted the knobs on each side. Turning the knobs with his hands through the straps at the bottom of the box was an awkward maneuver and forced him to lean down close to the box. He felt a series of clicks as some internal mechanism kicked in. As the excitement in him grew, he wondered if this was some ancient secret from the Far East. He loved solving puzzles, and this was one of his biggest challenges. He'd remember this drill for months.

Click, clack, the box was doing something. He could feel it as the knobs came to a stop. He glanced down at the instructions and saw that the last line said, TURN YOUR HEAD TO THE LEFT. Tubman complied.

Then he heard a noise like a heavy spring and out of the corner of his eyes caught the lid bursting open. Then the room swirled and spun as he went down on one knee and then flat onto his ass.

Manny rushed over as Tubman tried to recover his senses. Tubman leaned to one side and realized he was bleeding from his nose and lips, and the pain shot through his head and neck like electricity.

He stumbled back and slowly rose to his feet, staring at the wide-open box. It took him a moment to realize what he was seeing. It was just a simple, round leather pad on the end of a heavy spring dangling off to the side like a special-needs jack-in-the-box.

Tubman tried to speak, but he could only mumble. He recognized that his jaw was broken.

Manny said, "I'm sorry, but I promised the clinic owner I'd never reveal the secret. It was too valuable as a motivational tool. But the contract says it is available to clients. You see, Detective, I really do follow the rules now. But I wish you'd listened to me."

Manny helped Tubman to a chair as he continued. "It's no great technological advance, Detective. It just broke your jaw, and it's going to be wired shut for three weeks. I figure you'll lose about thirty pounds. It's a tough way to go, that's why it's always been the last resort."

Tubman glared up at Manny, but before he did anything rash, the detective remembered that he was the one who'd asked, "What's in the box?"

# MAD BLOOD

## BY S. W. HUBBARD

Two sensations awakened him: wet heat on his leg, sharp pressure on the back of his neck.

Trent opened his eyes to find Ducky wrapped around him. "Damn, Ducky—you wet the bed. *My* bed."

No apology. No whimpering. Just her breathing steady and hard in his ear, her little hands wrapped so tightly around his neck he could barely swallow. Then he heard noise from the kitchen: a shout, a crash, breaking glass.

His mother screamed.

Trent tried to pry Ducky off him. "C'mon, Ducks—I have to help her."

His sister tightened her grasp. The last time Trent had tried to get between their mother and Fredo, Fredo had tossed the boy across the room like yesterday's newspaper. Trent had hit the radiator hard and blacked out for a minute. When he came to, his mother, Ducky, and Fredo had all been standing over him.

"Told you he wasn't dead," Fredo had said, taking a drag on his tallboy.

The incident worried Trent. If he died, who would change the sheets when Ducky wet the bed? Who would get her shoes on the right feet? Who would open her SpaghettiOs? At six, she didn't know how to use a can opener.

In the kitchen, Fredo's voice rose from a low growl to a crescendo ending in "Lying fucking bitch!" Ducky flinched, burying her head in Trent's shoulder. The sharp ammonia smell of her piss filled his throat. The pounding of his heart made it hard to think. What was the likelihood his mother's phone was on her dresser, not in her pocket? What good would it do to yell "help" out the window at three in the morning in Flatbush?

A piercing shriek rocketed Trent out of bed, Ducky and all. He ran to the kitchen, his sister attached to him like an extra limb. On the threshold he stopped and covered Ducky's eyes. Their mother lay on the yellow linoleum floor, blood pouring from her neck like milk from a knocked-over half gallon. Drops of red speckled the front of the white refrigerator and the chrome legs of the table. Fredo had walked through the spreading tide, leaving clear footprints. One hand held the bloody end of a broken beer bottle; the other hand clutched his shaking cell phone to his ear.

Trent yanked his T-shirt over his head and pressed it against his mother's neck. Her eyes—apologetic, resigned—met his for a moment before flickering shut. Above him, he heard Fredo's voice.

"You gotta come, Nicky. I just poked her a little bit, but there's mad blood. Mad blood all over."

Trent and Ducky went to school the next day; it was the best way to escape the coppery-piney smell of blood and cleaning solution saturating the apartment. Fredo's brother, Nicky, and Nicky's wife, Carla, were taking charge. Last night, Nicky had shoved Fredo against the wall, calling him a stupid fuck face and a moron whack job, but when the paramedics arrived Nicky calmly explained how Trent's mother had tripped and fallen while holding a glass and accidentally cut her neck. His brother, Nicky told them, was too upset to talk about it. After the ambulance left, Carla, a woman who enjoyed giving a room a good cleaning, set to work wiping up the mess.

Now, in second period, Trent eased back in his seat and listened to Miss Snowden talk. Her voice rose and fell like the kind of music that doesn't have words. Sometimes she got so excited about what she was saying she would wave her hands above her head, then spin around and start drawing on the board. Trent noticed that the old teachers, like Mr. Weiss and Mrs. Bonaventure, hated Miss Snowden.

"So the arteries carry blood away from the heart, bringing nutrients and oxygen to the cells all over our bodies. And the veins carry the blood back to the heart, where it picks up more oxygen and the process begins again." Miss Snowden smiled out at the class. "I need an assistant. Teesha, come on up here and play the heart while I play the blood."

All the other teachers knew to leave Teesha alone. Held back three times, she towered over her fellow eighth graders. Her boobs were three times the size of Miss Snowden's. Teesha's eyes narrowed to slits when the teacher pulled her to the front of the room. Miss Snowden didn't care. She ran around the class passing out a stack of construction-paper oxygen molecules. Then she ran back to Teesha and begged for more. Then she ran around again. By the time the bell rang, everyone was laughing, even Teesha.

"Read chapter four, class," the teacher called to them as they left. "Tomorrow we'll continue our discussion of the circulatory system."

On the way to lunch, Trent fell into step with Teesha. Although she had a good thirty pounds on him, he wasn't afraid of her. "That Miss Snowden's something else, isn't she?"

"She nice, but she's dumb."

It didn't pay to directly contradict Teesha. "She knows a lot about science."

"But nothing about important stuff. Otherwise, why would she be workin' here?"

Teesha had a way of getting to the core of things. That was why Trent thought she might be useful. "I think maybe ACS might come to my house," he blurted.

"Hmm. Them caseworkers bad news. Your mother smokin' crack?"

"No. Fight with her boyfriend. She's in the hospital."

Teesha nodded. "Sometimes they put you in the system for that, sometimes not."

"I wouldn't mind foster care, as long as my sister and me could stay together."

"Huh! That ain't gonna happen. I've seen you with your sister—little girl with yellow hair, right? She don't look like you."

"Looks like her father. He OD'd a couple a years ago."

"They'll find a foster home for her right away, but nobody's gonna want you." Teesha elbowed him. "Everybody knows teenage boys are trouble. You probably go to a group home."

"Then Ducky would be alone."

Teesha looked down the long corridor toward the cafeteria. "Your sister's real pretty. Somebody might mess with her."

"Mess how?" Trent asked.

Teesha turned. Her dark, dark eyes held his without blinking.

Just what he figured.


That afternoon when they got home, the apartment looked totally different. Not only had Carla mopped up the blood, but she had also emptied all the ashtrays and thrown away all the beer bottles and Burger King wrappers. In Trent's room, the wet sheets were off the bed, replaced by a set with blue stripes that he'd never seen before. When he walked across the floor, his shoes didn't stick. Carla was still in the kitchen, banging around and singing to the radio. Trent and Ducky hesitated in the doorway.

"Don't this place look nice?" Carla asked. "Now try to keep it this way, wouldja?"

Trent didn't answer. Carla knew well enough it wasn't him and Ducky who spilled beer on the floor and flicked ashes on the sofa cushions.

"You kids wanna snack?" Carla peeled off her yellow rubber gloves and opened the refrigerator door. Ducky's eyes goggled. Milk and juice and eggs and cheese and a whole roasted chicken fought for space on the shelves. "Scrambled eggs," Ducky whispered, and Carla set about making them.

"Your mother's getting out of the hospital in a couple days," Carla said, her eyes never leaving the pale-yellow mound of eggs forming in the frying pan. "Now, it's important that she don't have any stress in her life right now, know what I'm sayin'? Some damn social worker person is coming over today to make sure this is a good home for kids. So don't you guys talk about what happened last night. It was just an accident, and everything's okay now, right?"

Carla banged the loaded plate on the table in front of Ducky.

"Trent and Demetria. Where'd your mother ever come up with names like that? Maybe from watching the afternoon TV, huh? Or maybe she saw those names in the movie magazines they got near the checkout at the supermarket. She ever read them while she's waiting in line?"

To Trent's knowledge, his mother had never been to a supermarket, only the bodega on the corner where there was never a line except for lottery tickets on a day when the prize went up over ten million.

"Well, Ducky's a better name for a little girl. That name Demetria is bigger than you are."

Ducky finished her eggs and was staring at a bowl Carla had set in the middle of the table. "What are those?" Ducky asked.

Carla cocked her head. "Whattaya mean? They're pears. Haven't you ever seen a pear before?"

Ducky shrugged. "In books."

After science class, Trent lingered in front of Miss Snowden's desk.

She smiled, her teeth as white and perfect as the strand of pearls around her neck. "Did you have a question?"

"I—I was wondering," Trent stammered. "How much blood is in your body?"

"Five-point-six liters—about six quarts." Miss Snowden answered without hesitation.

"How much can you lose before you die?"

"People have been known to lose almost all their blood, but if they get medical help right away and have a transfusion, they can survive. But without help..." Miss Snowden shook her head.

"Can all your blood pour out of one hole in your body?"

The bright enthusiasm in Miss Snowden's eyes dimmed. "Why do you ask?"

"No reason." Trent slung his backpack over his shoulder and turned toward the door.

"Trent."

He paused but did not turn.

"Did something happen? Did you see someone get hurt?"

Trent shook his head and kept walking.

In the middle of fifth period, Trent was summoned to the Guidance Office. The other kids in math class went "O-o-o-o" because a trip to Guidance meant that the dogs had found weed in your locker or the cameras had caught you fighting, but Trent knew neither of those things could be the reason for his call. The secretary sent him straight in to Ms. Jackson.

Ms. Jackson had long fingernails, a headful of braids, and round gold earrings. She was about as wide as a Jets defensive lineman, but not quite as tall. The last time Trent had been in her office it was because the cafeteria said he and Ducky couldn't have free lunch because their mother hadn't filled out a paper. Ms. Jackson had pounded a lot of buttons on her big black phone and said things like "Let me speak to your supervisor" and "That is not acceptable," and after about half an hour, he and Ducky were allowed to have lunch again.

Today Ms. Jackson smiled at Trent and told him to sit next to her on the little blue sofa with flowered pillows. This couldn't be good.

Ms. Jackson told Trent how, because of his mother's accident, the social worker from the hospital had called the school to check on him and Ducky. She said Miss Snowden had mentioned his questions. Ms. Jackson leaned forward and the beads in her braids made a little clicking sound. "It's very important that you answer my questions truthfully."

Trent focused his eyes on a spot above Ms. Jackson's left ear and began to talk. He and Ducky had been asleep when their mother got hurt. They did not see her fall. They did not see Fredo hit her.

Ms. Jackson did not ask, "Did Fredo call your mother lying fucking bitch?" She did not ask, "Did you see Fredo standing with a bloody broken bottle in his hand?" She did not ask, "Was your little sister so scared she peed on your leg?" She was quiet for a while and Trent thought she would soon let him leave.

Abruptly, Ms. Jackson spoke again. "Trent, what made you wake up that night?"

Trent didn't want to say about Ducky wetting the bed. He knew she shouldn't still be doing that at six. Maybe bed-wetting was something they put you in foster care for. He shrugged.

"Use your words."

He could hear her breathing, swallowing.

"Noise," Trent whispered.

"What kind of noise?" Her dark eyes seemed to look right inside him.

"Loud voices. A chair falling over. Glass breaking."

"So there was a fight." Ms. Jackson stood and reached for her black phone. "If you and your sister have been exposed to violence in the home, I'm obliged to report it."

"No!" Trent lunged for her arm. "Ducky can't go to foster care."

"The best way to prevent that is to get this violent man out of your family's life. Tell the police what happened and they'll arrest him."

"I'm no snitch," Trent said. "I can take care of my mother and sister."

"Trent, sometimes the strongest thing a man can do is ask for help." Ms. Jackson's face was so close to his he could count her eyelashes. "Tell the police and let them put this man in jail where he belongs."

"They don't put guys in jail for stuff like that." Trent knew there were men even worse than Fredo who had beat their raps and were walking around Flatbush.

Ms. Jackson rubbed her temples. "What he did was attempted murder. He'll be in jail long enough that you and your sister and your mom won't have to worry about him anymore. But the police can't do their work unless you tell them everything you heard and saw that night."

Trent looked past Ms. Jackson to the small window behind her. Outside was a brick wall. If it was Miss Snowden telling him to snitch he wouldn't pay attention. But Ms. Jackson didn't talk with a lot of big words. She didn't have information in her head about things that happened a thousand years ago. She just knew what was what.

"If you're brave, it will help your mother be brave." Ms. Jackson spoke softly.

This idea wormed into his head and stuck. Could his mother catch something from him, the way he caught colds from wiping Ducky's snotty nose? Was that all it took? His gaze fixed on the dim, dirty window. "So go ahead and call them."

After Fredo's arrest, Trent noticed that his mother seemed more like a TV mom. She got a new haircut that hid the scar on her neck and started waking up in time to make breakfast for them before school. She sang songs with Ducky and went to see Trent's exhibit in the science fair. Sometimes when her phone rang, she would glance at the screen, then switch her phone off. Soon Mr. Patel hired her to work the cash register at the Dollar Store. After that, she would bring treats home from the store: pink barrettes and a little plastic tea set for Ducky, baseball cards for Trent. The cards showed Matsui and Cabrera still playing for the Yankees, but Trent liked them anyway.

Around the end of May the carnival arrived in the parking lot of the Church of the Holy Savior: rides, games, funnel cakes and cotton candy. Trent couldn't be seen there with Ducky, so she went with their mother and he went with the guys from the neighborhood. As Trent and Justin and Phil made their way from the Viking

Ship to the Tilt-a-Whirl, Justin started laughing. "Yo, Trent—your mother throws like a girl."

Sure enough, his mother was trying to win a goldfish for Ducky by throwing Ping-Pong balls at an openmouthed plastic whale. She flung weakly from her wrist, and each ball bounced off the target. Trent went over and took the balls from her. As his friends cheered, he tossed the first two balls neatly into the whale's mouth. As he prepared to throw the third ball, he noticed Ducky studying him, biting her lower lip. He was Jeter: bases loaded, full count, bottom of the ninth. He wound up with his right arm and stepped forward on his left foot. The ball arced out of his hand, sailed through the air, and disappeared into the whale's mouth. Ducky's eyes lit up when the man behind the counter put a big orange-and-white fish in a plastic bag full of water and handed it to her.

Later, as the sun set and the parking lot was lit only by the neon of the rides, Trent saw his mother talking to another woman, who had her arm around his mother's shoulders. Sometimes his mother nodded, but her lips never moved. The goldfish swam around and around in the plastic bag his mother clutched in her hand.

As the woman turned and walked away, Trent saw that it was Carla.

In the middle of one night soon after the carnival, Ducky appeared beside Trent. He should have known *Pirates of the Caribbean* right before bed was a bad idea. It would be best to make her go to the bathroom before he let her into his bed, but he was too sleepy. He dozed despite the twine of her arms around his neck.

"He's back," Ducky breathed in his ear.

"Mmph. Pirates and skeletons aren't real, Ducky. Go to sleep."

"He's back. Listen."

Trent heard it. The rhythmic thump, thump, thump of his mother's bed bumping the wall. The urgent squeak of the springs. A grunt and a low moan. Ducky's hand tightened on Trent's arm. He pulled the covers over their heads.

In the morning, Trent entered the kitchen and sat across from his mother. Her head drooped over a mug of coffee as the milk formed a scum on the surface.. Fredo was chatty. "DA decided they didn't have a case against me." He leaned toward Trent as he spoke, the red and green and blue of his full-sleeve tattoo gleaming against the worn beige of the kitchen table. "Not enough evidence to go to trial, that's what my lawyer said. See, one person's story ain't enough to get a conviction. They need some *corroboration*." He tapped Trent's cereal bowl. "Know what that word means?"

Trent shook his head.

"Means someone else gotta *back you up*."

Trent's mother kept her eyes on her coffee.

"No one backed you up, boy. So here I am."

Ducky straggled into the kitchen, her wispy blond hair in tangles, her T-shirt inside out and backward with the tag right under her chin. She made a big detour around Fredo, hugging the wall as she edged toward her spot next to Trent.

She'd made it past the fridge when Fredo spoke. "C'mere, Ducky."

She stopped, her eyes darting from Fredo to their mother. Ducky wanted to know what to do. Their mother wasn't saying. Trent tried to pull his sister toward him with the power of his stare. She held his gaze for almost as long as it took for the B train to rumble by.

"Ducky."

That was all Fredo said. Just her name, not even loud. Ducky walked straight to him, never looking up.

Fredo pressed Ducky to his chest and rested his stubbled chin on top of her pale gold hair. His right index finger traced up and down her bony spine. "Missed my girls," he murmured, staring hard at Trent.

Bouncing Ducky on his knee, Fredo slid a bowl of Apple Jacks in front of her. She made no move to eat.

"What's the matter, little girl? You want some protein in your breakfast? Protein makes you strong." Fredo got up and crossed to the window. Behind him, the goldfish swished back and forth in its bowl. "Your brother knows all about that, right, Trent?"

Fredo grabbed the bowl and tipped it. The fish flopped into his palm. He popped the goldfish into his mouth and bit down. His big, dark head loomed over Ducky's shoulder.

He opened his mouth and spat the fish into Trent's cereal.

On one of the last days of the school year, Miss Snowden was on about scientific method.

"Class, the beautiful thing about science is that we're always making new discoveries. That's why an open mind is *essential* to scientific inquiry. Because even ideas that we were certain we were right about can sometimes turn out to be all wrong. Who can give me an example?"

Teesha gouged her name into the desktop with a broken pen; Jamal rested his head on his folded arms; Phil read a text on the phone in his lap.

"Jamal?"

Without raising his head, he answered, "Dudes used to think the world was flat."

Miss Snowden clapped her hands. "Yes! Good job! Who else?"

There were no more takers. Miss Snowden plowed ahead.

"Medicine is full of theories that were proved wrong. From the time of Hippocrates in ancient Greece, scientists believed that the human body was controlled by four humors: blood, green bile, black bile, and phlegm, and if there was too much of one element, a person would become sick." Miss Snowden got excited and started pacing around. "They believed a person could be cured by draining off some of the excess humor. So oftentimes doctors would make a cut in a sick person's arm or leg and drain out some of his blood. It was called bloodletting, and doctors believed this was a valid medical remedy for almost *two thousand years* before scientists tested the theory and proved it wrong."

How did Miss Snowden know all this stuff? Sometimes Trent wondered if she made it up. He raised his hand. "If the bloodletting wasn't curing people, how come doctors kept doing it for so long?"

"Excellent question!" Miss Snowden flung her hands over her

head. "Doctors had so few resources in those days—no antibiotics or fever reducers or pain relievers. But the patient believed that doing *something* was better than doing nothing. So because the patient believed the bloodletting would make him better, he sometimes did, in fact, get better. And the scientists who proved bloodletting wrong had to fight against the common perception that bloodletting worked. After all, it's just as easy to believe the blood carries humors as it is to believe it carries oxygen."

Trent looked at the veins crossing the back of his hands. Who knew what was really in there? Maybe the four humors were...evil...and fear...and craziness.

And rage.

A freakish heat wave gripped the city. Trent's mother spent her days selling no-brand suntan lotion and flip-flops at the Dollar Store. Fredo partied all night with his crew, then crashed all day at the apartment. Ducky got into the summer enrichment program run by the church ladies at Holy Savior. Trent shot hoops on the playground with the guys. In the middle of the day, when the asphalt got too hot, he sought out the air-conditioning and the computers in the Brooklyn Public Library on Linden Boulevard.

On the fourth day of the heat wave, Trent sat in his sweltering bedroom and waited. He listened as Fredo staggered in at dawn, and listened as his mother and Ducky left at nine. He listened as the morning routine of his neighbors gradually wound down to silence. At two-fifteen in the afternoon, the scorching streets of Flatbush were oddly deserted. Trent opened his bedroom door.

Even the dragon breath of the Fulton Street subway station smelled better than the air of the apartment. Puke, spilled beer, and closer to his mother's bedroom, Fredo's sweat and the burned plastic scent of his crack pipe. Through the open door, he saw Fredo sprawled naked on his back across the unmade bed. A half-empty bottle of vodka and a scattering of pills stood amid the clutter on the nightstand. He was coming down off a long high, and snored lightly through his open mouth.

"Fredo," Trent said.

He didn't stir.

Trent went into the kitchen. He took off his basketball shoes and left them by the door. He switched on the radio and turned up the volume. From under the sink, he got Carla's yellow rubber gloves and put them on. His hands trembled and he took a deep breath. In his mind he saw Ducky walking across that kitchen straight into Fredo's arms. He saw his mother sitting silent at the table. He heard Miss Snowden's voice.

From the top of the stove, he got the frying pan and took it to the bedroom. He listened to Fredo's snoring. He walked over to the mirror hung on the closet door. With one strong swing, he struck. The glass shattered into long shards.

Fredo's breathing never changed.

Trent chose the longest, sharpest piece of mirror and carried it to the bed. Standing naked in the bathroom, Trent had practiced finding his own femoral artery several nights in a row. Now he studied Fredo's legs. After all the prison weightlifting, Fredo had no fat on his thighs. His veins and arteries coursed clearly under his hairy olive skin.

Trent raised the glass shard over his head and plunged it into Fredo's thigh. The blood shot out like a pit bull released from its cage, angry and eager to be free.

Fredo awoke, more puzzled than pained. "Wha—? What the fuck?"

He rose from the bed and took a few steps. Blood pooled around him, thick and hot. It soaked the gray sheets and puddled on the uneven floor. Trent watched from the doorway. There was a lot of blood, but not all six quarts. Not yet.

The injured leg buckled. Fredo's eyes met Trent's. "Call for help!"

Trent took two steps backward as Fredo crawled toward him and the broken mirror. He threw the piece he had used into the pile of glass on the floor.

Understanding dawned in Fredo's glazed eyes. "You little bastard. You did this." He pressed his thigh with blood-slicked hands.

Fredo's healthy young heart pumped blood out of his body, emptying it with great efficiency. His eyelids flickered and Trent thought he might faint. The boy's fingers unclenched inside the hot rubber gloves.

But Fredo didn't faint. With a sudden burst of power, he flung himself at the bedside table. Too late, Trent saw what he'd overlooked: Fredo's cell phone. Fredo was weak enough now that Trent could have wrestled the phone away, but he couldn't afford to be found covered in Fredo's blood. The death had to look like an accident, like Fredo had crashed drunkenly into the mirror. For himself, Trent didn't care. He would happily have gone to Rikers or even Attica if it meant getting rid of Fredo. But he couldn't leave Ducky. She couldn't protect herself from whatever guy was bound to follow Fredo. As Fredo clawed for the phone from the front, Trent knocked the whole nightstand over from behind.

The phone fell to the floor. As Fredo scrambled toward it, Trent kicked it cleanly into the hall.

Now Trent was trapped by the spreading tide of blood. Once Fredo was dead, Trent could pick his way carefully out of the room. But he couldn't get between Fredo and the phone, not without Fredo grabbing at him with his bloody hands. He looked at the digital clock glowing green on the floor. 2:37. Fredo had been bleeding for four minutes. How much longer would it take?

Trent and Fredo heard the sound at the same moment: the click of a key turning in the front door lock.

Ducky's sneakers pounded down the hall. "Trent? Trent? The power's out at Holy Savior and we all had to leave. They sent me home with Elena, but her mom said to see if you were here."

Fredo dragged himself slowly toward the hall. Trent could see him open his mouth and draw breath.

The apartment door slammed shut as Ducky sailed past the

bedroom, heading for the kitchen. "Trent, where are you? Can I have a snack?"

Trent felt his throat swell with panic. Ducky couldn't see this. But how could he stop her?

Ducky had made it all the way to the living room and was doubling back.

"Trent? Tren—" She stopped outside the bedroom door. Her gaze rested first on the trickle of blood flowing steadily across the sloping floor. Curious, she squinted into the dim interior and saw Fredo prone, propped up on one elbow. Raising her head, she caught sight of her brother.

"Stay right there, Ducky." Trent tried to keep his voice calm, but it felt like Ducky was on the far side of Van Nostrand Avenue separated from him by six lanes of speeding buses and trucks.

"Phone," Fredo wheezed. "Ducky, get my phone."

Ducky glanced down. The phone lay a few inches from her pink sneaker. Then she looked back at Fredo.

"No!" Trent shouted. "Leave it, Ducky. Run into the living room. He can't follow you. He's too hurt."

But Ducky wasn't paying attention to her brother. Her eyes, pale and bottomless, stared unblinkingly at Fredo.

"Bring me the phone. Now."

Trent saw his sister bite her lower lip, the way she did when she was trying hard to color inside the lines. Slowly she crouched until her right hand closed over the phone.

Ducky rose. Stepping forward with her left foot, winding up with her right arm, she threw the phone overhand.

When all three heard the distant crash, Ducky gave a little nod. She faced her brother, ignoring what lay between them.

"I'm going back to Elena's, Trent. I'll tell her mom you weren't at home."

# DEAR MR. QUEEN

## BY JOSEPH GOODRICH

*March 2, 1977*

I gave Mrs. Zaborowski my story today, and she read it over the lunch hour. She thinks I ought to submit it somewhere. There are a few spelling mistakes and some other things I should fix, but then I'll send it to EQMM. Who knows what might happen?

*March 4, 1977*

Ellery Queen, Editor
Ellery Queen's Mystery Magazine
380 Lexington Avenue
New York, NY 10017

Dear Mr. Queen:

Enclosed you'll find "The Ubiquitous Fairchild," my latest mystery story. I hope you'll like it. I've enclosed a SASE for your response.

Many thanks,
Christopher Kenilworth
1203 Macmillan Street
Manderton, Minn 56031

P.S. I've just finished reading *The Wrightsville Murders*. I asked for it as a special present for my fourteenth birthday, which was last month. I had to write to a bookstore in Minneapolis to find it. It's brilliant. When will your next novel be published? I know your fans are waiting!

## April 25, 1977

It is now two o'clock in the morning. I'm listening to *Hobbs' House* on WCCO and drinking a cup of tea with milk. I shouldn't be up this late—tomorrow's a school day—but I can't get to sleep. Too full of thoughts.

Played "I Am a Rock" over and over again this evening. It keeps going through my mind. It seems so bitter, so calmly despairing. "I have my books and my poetry to protect me. I am alone." Will that be me someday, an encrusted, friendless old man? I hope not.

A rejection letter was waiting for me when I got home from play practice. (I'm essaying the role of Dr. Howard Fersig, an evil doctor, in *The Skeleton Walks*. It's a great part. Aunt Kathy's helping me memorize my lines. We open on May 13th.) I really thought "The Ubiquitous Fairchild" was a good story. I guess I'll try again. I know I can do it.

Uncle Wes's car just pulled in. He's back really late tonight.

I must try to sleep.

## April 26, 1977

A few thoughts, waiting for the bus. Should I join Mensa? Isaac Asimov is vice-president. Is my IQ in the top 2% of America's? I could send in the six dollars and see if I qualify, after taking the test they'll send me. All I need is a little self-confidence.

I've had an idea for a story. A murder story. Inspired by something that happened last night. There's the bus—more later.

## After Supper

I am being driven insane. By my classes. I've only got one I truly enjoy (English, with Mrs. Zaborowski). There are a few others that I can bear (I won't name them) and one that is downright *intolerable*: Drafting.

I just wasn't meant to hunch over a desk and draw geometric trifles on paper. I'm not a person who naturally can draw, use rulers and compasses. I am not fast at picking up mechanical techniques. I am fine in theory but dreadful in execution. It's torture. Mr. Calvin tries to help, but it's just no good. There's only one more month left in drafting, but guess what my next class is?

Woodworking.

They're trying to kill me.

## Later

Here's the background for that story idea.

Uncle Wes and Aunt Kathy have been living with us—me and my grandmother—for the last three months. Their house sold faster than expected, so they're staying here until construction on their new home is finished.

I like Aunt Kathy. She's soft and nervous and nearsighted and always interested in what I write.

Uncle Wes is a big man with a big gut and big gold teeth and a big square head covered with graying hair he combs over and over in the mirror before he goes out in the evening. He was in the Philippines during World War II and saw things he doesn't want to talk about. He scares me. Aunt Kathy's frightened of him, too. I can tell by the way she flinches whenever he calls for her. They fight sometimes—or, rather, he yells at her. He yells at her, then slams out of the house. She doesn't say a word. I find his behavior loathsome. I'm pretty sure that once, and maybe even more than once, he's hit her. And that is unforgivable. I swear that I will never be mean to any woman at any time under any circumstances. We must have standards.

Uncle Wes came home very late last night. He's a pal of the man who runs the A&W stand by the lake, and sometimes he brings back root beer and hamburgers, so I waited for him, just in case.

After a minute or two of silence, I went to the kitchen. No one was there.

I looked out the window. His Olds 88 was parked in the driveway, but Uncle Wes was nowhere to be seen.

I went down the stairs to the back porch, opened the screen door, and peered out.

Still no sign of him.

I was about to step back into the house when a flickering light appeared across the street. The flame of a cigarette lighter fluttered in the breezy darkness.

Uncle Wes was lighting Ava Templehoff's cigarette.

They were under the elm tree on the front lawn of the Templehoff house.

But, I asked myself, where was Ava's husband, Don?

That's when I had the idea for a new story. What if Uncle Wes and Ava Templehoff were having an affair? And what if Don wouldn't give Ava a divorce? And what if they had to kill Don so they could be together? How would they do it? It'd have to look natural. It'd have to look like an accident....

The Templehoffs' house is at the end of the block, right next to the splintery old bridge that crosses Whiskey Ditch. Uncle Wes and Ava could ply Don with drinks and then push him down the slope into the water. Or lead him down there, hit him on the head, and drown him. Or—

The scrabble of paws sounded on the bridge. Gretchen, the Templehoffs' blind eleven-year-old dachshund, waddled into view. Leash in hand, huffing and puffing, Don waddled along behind

Gretchen. Don is in lamentable physical condition. He smokes too much and eats too much. He wears a copper bracelet on each wrist, which he says helps his arthritis, but I doubt it. Whenever he comes over for some of Grandma's coffee cake and a chat, his joints hurt so much he can barely get up to leave.

...Or it could be a heart attack. They could get him mad and he'd drop dead. Then who'd ever know it was murder?

I can do something with this. I'll give it some serious thought in homeroom and see if I can't work out the details. It could be a real Jack Ritchie kind of story.

I even have a title for it: "No Hamburgers Tonight."

### Even Later

Uncle Wes arrived home at 2:29 a.m. Ava T. waited for him on her front porch. A pattern is forming. And I'm going to figure out just what that pattern is....

### April 27, 1977

Horrible day in school. That's all I'll say.

I will never forget the cruelty of others.

I'll never forgive it, either.

To make matters worse, there was an accident with the type-writer this evening. When I'd finished transcribing some notes for my story, I set the typewriter on the bed so I could sweep the eraser crumbs off my desk. I went out to the kitchen to get a cup of tea. When I came back, without thinking, I sat down on the edge of the bed—and that's when it happened. The typewriter slipped off the bed and hit the linoleum with a sickening metallic *chunk*. It's broken.

I loved that typewriter.

A bad end to a bad day.

\*　　\*　　\*

Uncle Wes arrived home at 1:36 a.m. He parked his car, walked across the street, and went into the Templehoffs' garage through the side door. My mind is working frenetically to weave circumstance into the stuff of fiction.

## April 28, 1977

A note on my methodology might be in order. When I hear the Olds 88 roll in, I go up to the attic and watch from the window at the head of the stairs—I can see the driveway, the street, and the Templehoffs' house quite easily from there.

Uncle Wes pulled into the driveway around 12:56 a.m. and went straight to the Templehoffs' garage.

I've figured out how they'll kill him. The character based on Don is crazy about his little blind dog. His wife accidentally lets the dog out, although it's far from any kind of accident, and the man drops dead from worry and overexertion. A perfect murder.

## April 29, 1977

Waiting for my allergy shot. Four-thirty in the afternoon. Today Mrs. Zaborowski read to us from *Notes to Myself,* by Hugh Prather. I'll look for a copy the next time we go to the B. Dalton's in Sioux Falls. It was beautiful and moving, and it really made me think.

I always seem to be looking for an idol, a hero. I revere Isaac Asimov, Alfred Hitchcock, Ray Bradbury, Robert Bloch, and Groucho Marx. I don't drift around without one, but I like a hero. I suppose I admire the person I want to be. I want to match their achievements and make a name for myself in the world.

Play practice from six to nine tonight. I intend to work on my story afterward if I'm not too tired. Mr. Christiansen told us we have to be off-book by Monday. I'm going to ask Kevin to help me with my lines during study hall.

Dilemma: I enjoy both writing and acting. What if I had to choose between the two disciplines? Which would it be? I think I would have to choose writing, though the rewards of the theatre are immediate and vastly pleasurable. There's something deeper about writing, I feel, something that calls to the deepest part of me.

It's just after midnight, so it's technically Saturday, April 30th. *The CBS Radio Mystery Theater* has just finished: "Good night, and pleasant dreams..." The reception from WBBM in Chicago was okay tonight. Not a lot of static, and I was able to hear the whole show. I hate it when sun spots, for instance, mess up the radio waves and I can't listen to E. G. Marshall and company. That's a show I'd like to write for. Himan Brown is a genius.

Uncle Wes isn't back yet. I'm worn out and I don't know how much longer I can last. I think I'll listen to Allan McFee's show on the CBC. I hope I can stay awake....

It's almost five o'clock in the morning as I take pen in hand. I'm exhausted, but I have to get this down before I crash into sleep—if I can sleep at all.

The facts. Concentrate on the facts. Write it all down.

About forty minutes ago, I awoke to the sound of a car door closing. I reached my perch in the attic window just in time to see Uncle Wes help Ava out of the Olds 88. Arm in arm they walked unsteadily across the lawn, stumbled at the curb, then staggered through the streetlamp's amber, leaf-dappled light to the darkness of the Templehoff lawn. After a minute or two, Ava left the shadow of the tree and Uncle Wes lurched back across the street to his car, got a bottle from the trunk, and followed her.

It looked like that was it for the night, so I went down the stairs, headed for bed. I was getting a glass of milk from the refrigerator when it happened.

Someone—a woman—screamed.

And a gun went off.

And went off again.

And again.

Then silence.

But not for long.

## May 3, 1977

The *Daily Globe* reports that the authorities view the events of the night of April 30th as a murder-suicide. An ailing Don Templehoff discovered that his wife, Ava, was involved in an illicit relationship with their friend and neighbor Wesley Lannen. Catching them in a compromising situation, he shot them both to death and then killed himself. Templehoff had a history of mental and physical problems dating back to his service in the Aleutians during the Second World War. He'd suffered a breakdown and been sent back to the States with an honorable discharge, a pension, and a Purple Heart.

The best part of the story wasn't printed in the paper, though. I've been keeping my ears open, and I've learned a few things. It's amazing what people will say in front of you if you pretend you're not interested.

Don met Ava at the Veterans' Hospital in Minneapolis in the summer of 1967. He was being treated for his joint problems. She was there visiting a former high school boyfriend—Wesley Lannen.

Ava quickly married Don, who'd come into a lot of money after the death of his mother. At her suggestion, Don sold his house in a suburb of Minneapolis and moved to Manderton...where Wesley was living with his wife, Kathy. The affair between Uncle Wes and Ava Templehoff began shortly after.

That was back in 1967. Which means their affair had been going on for ten *years*.

I will never understand people.

Don and Ava Templehoff were buried today. Uncle Wes will be buried tomorrow. But not in the same cemetery.

## *May 14, 1977*

Things have returned to normal—mostly. Other people, other events have drawn the public's attention away from Don and Ava and Uncle Wes.

One of those people who are drawing attention happens to be none other than Aunt Kathy. The change that's come over her since Uncle Wes's death is phenomenal. She reminds me of a prisoner who's been released after years in jail. Her natural warmth and exuberance, so long crushed by Uncle Wes's brutal behavior, are readily apparent. She has blossomed. Everyone in the house is happy for her. Me most of all.

My happiness is tinged with sorrow, however. Aunt Kathy is leaving. Not just the house, but the town itself. Uncle Wes's will left her a dairy farm in Wisconsin, and she's going to live there and run it. She should be very good at that, as she worked in an office before she got married. She's going to Rice Lake at the end of the month. I'll miss her greatly.

I don't miss Uncle Wes at all. I'm glad he's gone. Is it wrong of me to say that? Even if it is, it's the truth. And a writer must always tell the truth, if only in the secrecy of pages like these.

I've gone back to the idea I mentioned earlier. I'm still using it, but I've shifted some things around—names, details, etc.—in light of what's happened. I wouldn't want anyone to think I was exploiting the situation. I've come up with a twist I think is very clever, and I've written a couple of pages already. I hope to have a draft by the end of this week or the beginning of the next. I might have had one done by now, but the school play has taken up all of my evenings lately. It's been worth it, though. *The Skeleton Walks* opened last night at Memorial Auditorium. I'm happy to say it went very well. Lots of people were in attendance and there were many words of praise for me after the show. We have another performance tonight, and a matinee tomorrow.

Once again, the dilemma: writing or theatre? Who do I want to be? Harlan Ellison—or Peter Sellers? John Dickson Carr—or Alec Guinness? William Faulkner—or Tom Conti?

## May 17, 1977

I finished "No Hamburgers Tonight," and this morning I gave it to Aunt Kathy to type. She has a very nice Silent-Super Smith-Corona manual portable that I covet. It's the kind of typewriter I could sail to Europe with. Is it still possible to sail on ocean liners? I hope it is, because I crave adventure. I'm going to live in New York and Paris and London. And write stories and novels while I'm there.

## Later

Here I am, stuck in social studies. Per capita income and what causes inflation. Mr. Dahlquist is a good teacher, but I don't want to be here. I want to go to the public library and pick up the book that's on hold for me: *Tricks and Treats*, edited by Joe Gores and Bill Pronzini. Oh, will this class never end? Will this torment never cease? When will I be free to read and do whatever I want?

## 4:30 in the Afternoon

I'm sitting in the library, near hardcover fiction. I've just had the wind knocked out of my sails.

Aunt Kathy caught me as I was entering the library. I was surprised to see her, but before I could say anything, she took me roughly by the arm and dragged me down the stairs. She hurried me past the historical society's exhibits to the farthest part of the library basement. The scary part, with the barbed-wire samples and the iron lung and the American flag shot with bullet holes.

She took a crumpled mass of papers from her purse and thrust one of the pages at me. I recognized my handwriting. It was the manuscript of my story.

"How did you know that?" she said, pointing at the sheet of paper.

"Know what?"

She brought the page up to her eyes and read aloud: "'The police were more than willing to accept Ron Templeton's death as a suicide but for one thing: the gun was found in his right hand. Chief Sikorski was an old friend who knew that Ron was left-handed. Why would a left-handed man shoot himself with his right hand? The answer is—he wouldn't. It wasn't suicide at all. It was murder.'" She lowered the page and fixed her gaze on me. "How did you know that?"

"I don't know what you mean," I said.

She grabbed my arm again and pushed her face close to mine. "Yes, you do, and you damn well better tell me."

"Stop," I said. "You're hurting me."

"How did you know I put the gun in Don's left hand? *How?*"

"I made it up!" I said, jerking free of her grasp. "It's a story. I don't know anything."

Aunt Kathy looked at me for a long, long moment. "You didn't know," she said finally, so softly I could barely hear her. "You didn't know...."

No. I was just guessing. It's like I told her: I made it up. I didn't know a thing.

But I do now.

And so does Mrs. Zaborowski. Earlier today I gave her my other handwritten copy of the story because I couldn't wait for her to read it.

And now I'm really worried.

Because Mrs. Zaborowski is married to the chief of police.

And Chief Zaborowski was an old friend of Don Templehoff's.

## May 18, 1977

Aunt Kathy was arrested this morning and charged with the murders of Don Templehoff, Ava Templehoff, and Wesley Lannen. She quietly packed an overnight case and left without a fuss. As she went, she told me I could have her Silent-Super Smith-Corona manual portable typewriter. And then she was gone.

I feel horrible beyond my capacity to say.

I have learned a mighty lesson: words contain a ferocious power. We must be careful how we use them, for the consequences can mean life or death.

The human heart is a trunk filled with mysterious contents: lust, envy, hatred, fear. It is a trunk we open at our own risk.

All of this happened because of me. I looked into my own heart, and I am appalled.

I will never write another story.

## May 20, 1977

I had a talk today with Chief Zaborowski. He said they'd suspected Aunt Kathy from the start, and that my story played no real part in the investigation. He told me that murders usually aren't committed by strangers or enemies from the past who reappear after twenty years in prison or in any of the ways they occur in stories. Most often people are killed by people they know, people they love, people they thought loved them, and that's what happened here. He finished by saying the best thing for me to do is to get on with my life and not worry too much over recent events. I should feel no guilt. I did nothing wrong.

I want to believe him, but I still feel horrid. I don't know what to do. My life seems ruined, a blasted heath, a mess.

### May 23, 1977

I've finished a new version of "No Hamburgers Tonight." I'm not happy with it. In fact, I think it stinks. I'm just not sure. I'm not sure of anything anymore.

### Evening

I showed the revised story to Mrs. Zaborowski, and she read it over the lunch hour. She says it's "quite accomplished," and particularly admires the way I dealt with the boy's guilt over his role in the murder. She says I ought to submit it somewhere once I've fixed a couple of things.

Should I fix them and send it out? Do I have the heart to do it? What would Stanley Ellin do?

### May 25, 1977

Ellery Queen, Editor
Ellery Queen's Mystery Magazine
380 Lexington Avenue
New York, NY 10017

Dear Mr. Queen:

Enclosed you'll find "No Hamburgers Tonight," my latest mystery story.....

# THE DELIVERY

## BY R. T. LAWTON

Afew minutes shy of eleven on a sweltering Saturday night in July and heat was still rising up from the asphalt parking lot out front of the seven-story Gladstone Apartments, keeping temperature hot along the building like someone left the door open on a giant oven. Night air seemed to give off an aroma of deep-fried chicken grease, making the apartment's catwalk railings sticky to the touch. Most residents hung out on the open front walkways hoping to catch a breeze, anything to distract them from their own misery.

Some men lounged in work pants and damp T-shirts, rolling ice-cold cans of beer over their foreheads to cool their overheated brains. Young women in shorts and full tank tops stood loose on the catwalk, leaning hipshot against brick uprights while beads of perspiration turned their chests and faces slick and shiny. Older women in oversized dresses sat in cheap plastic chairs, all fanning themselves with magazines or stiff pieces of cardboard. Kids moved slow, sucking on ice chips swiped out of beer coolers when they thought adults weren't looking.

Everybody too hot to sleep and nowhere to go. Few had working air-conditioners humming in their windows. Those who did were the lucky ones, inside enjoying their comfort.

Down below on the main street, a pair of bright headlights bounced out of the southbound lane and pulled into the parking lot out front of the apartments. The small truck circled the lot like it was trying to make up its mind about something before finally slowing to a stop halfway between stairwells leading up at opposite ends of the building. All heads up on the catwalk immediately swiveled down toward the vehicle. Something new.

"Looks like a delivery van of some kind," speculated one of the old women on the fifth-floor walkway. "What you think they want here?"

"This a strange time of night to be making deliveries," replied her husband. "How would I know?"

"You gots better eyes than mine," urged the old woman, "and you know I can't read nothing that far away. Tell me what it says on the side of that truck?"

"I don't have my glasses on," muttered the old man, "and it's too hot to go get 'em."

"Let me have a look," offered a neighbor as he moved up to see over the railing. "I sees it plain, that's Crazy Carlo's truck. I seen him on television most nights, always shouting 'bout how good his sales are. You buy from him and he'll deliver anytime, night or day, makes no difference. Man's sure enough crazy, you ask me, making all kinds of deals, sell you anything you want, no money down. But you'd best pay up at the end, or his people come looking for you."

"What the hell's he gonna be delivering here?" asked the old man.

His wife kept fanning a self-made breeze in her direction with a piece of stiff cardboard. "We'll just have to wait and see, won't we?"

"Most honest people should be in their own beds asleep at this time of night," the old man continued, "or at least they be at their own home, not out running around."

"Don't mind him," the old woman said to the neighbor. "All this heat gets him cranky."

Down in the parking lot, a big Cuban in industrial-gray pants and shirt got out of the driver's side and walked around to the rear of the van. His short-sleeve shirt fit tight around his arm muscles, had a name tag said TONY above one pocket with a company logo above the other. His movements gave a slight roll to his shoulders as if he owned the streets and knew it. Raising his clipboard to eye level and consulting a sheet of paper on top of a stack of forms, he then glanced up at the seven-story building. Everything about him said he was here on serious business, so don't get in his way if'n you knew what was good for you.

"This the place, Edward," he growled, "so get on out here."

A short, stocky black man wearing blue bib coveralls and a white T-shirt got out of the passenger side and strolled to the rear of the vehicle. He, too, looked up at the building, but with a pained expression on his face as if he was counting the floors and it was going to be a problem. His closely shaved head gleamed in the overhead lights of the parking lot. Neither man seemed to be in a great hurry.

Holding the clipboard in one hand, the muscular Cuban used his other hand to unlock and flip down a heavy metal platform at the back of the truck. He pulled a lever. With a grinding noise, the platform slowly descended to street level. Big Tony and the short black guy stepped onto the platform. The Cuban pushed on a lever and the metal platform raised them up level to the truck floor. When the platform stopped, Edward unlocked a heavy padlock and raised the rear door on the truck. Both men disappeared inside.

Everybody on the walkways leaned forward to watch whatever came next.

In a couple of minutes, the two workers reappeared, using a two-wheeled dolly to maneuver a large wooden box out onto the metal platform and position it sideways. Pulling the rear door back down, the short black guy replaced the heavy padlock and stood up. At that point, the Cuban pushed a lever and they all descended to street level, where the crate was wheeled off the platform and onto the asphalt.

Consulting his clipboard again, Big Tony frowned. He looked up at the watching residents. "You folks got an elevator in this building?"

"It's broke," came the reply from somewhere up on the catwalk. "You'll have to use the stairs."

"Just my luck," muttered the short black guy.

Big Tony turned his head as he surveyed the approach to both stairwells, one on each end of the apartment building.

"Looks the same to me," he said. "Take your pick."

Edward shrugged.

"Like I care. Either way's a problem, going up or coming back down."

"Fine," said the Cuban.

They wheeled the large wooden box over to the open stairwell on their right. The big Cuban got on the upstairs side of the crate with the handles of the dolly clutched in his large hands, leaving the short black guy on the bottom to push uphill. The box bumped upward, one step, then another. By the time they got to the first-floor landing, both men had streams of sweat running off their heads and dripping from their elbows and fingers. At every floor, they paused a couple of minutes to catch their breath. Edward took advantage of these breaks to squeegee sweat off his bald head with the palm of his right hand, flicking the excess moisture over the railing before wiping his hand on his pants leg.

Watchers on the catwalks began slowly gravitating toward the stairwell where all the bumping noise was.

"Where you 'spect they going?"

"Don't ask me, I just know that thing ain't mine."

By the time the dolly's wheels cleared the last step and rolled up onto the fifth-floor landing, a crowd had gathered to ponder over the contents of the crate. Nothing was stenciled on the outside wood to give them a clue.

The Cuban wiped a red bandanna across his perspiring forehead before consulting his clipboard again. "Where's 507?"

One of the watchers jerked his thumb back over his shoulder. "Down there a few doors."

Big Tony eyeballed the crowd. "You folks gonna have to move back a bit, give us some room here."

A couple of watchers slowly drifted a few feet away. Nobody in a hurry to go anywhere.

"Lessen of course you want to help move this heavy crate your own selves," spoke up the short black guy.

"I already got a job," muttered one of the crowd as he retreated to just the other side of the door marked 507.

"Too hot to work on a night like this," muttered another as he flattened up against the wall to let them pass.

Four more doors down the catwalk, with the crate finally settled square in front of the correct apartment, Big Tony rapped his knuckles on the metal door and waited.

"Better knock louder," said the old woman. "She probably can't hear you over her noisy air-conditioner, especially if she's entertaining in there."

"It's all that entertaining company what gets her that big luxury air-conditioner she bought herself," came a female voice from the rear of the gathering, "whilst all we got is one of them broken-down ones what comes with the rent."

"Don't tell me about it!" exclaimed a heavyset woman up front fanning away with a limp piece of cardboard. "I seen all them mens she's got coming and going all hours of the night. She even got a man in there right now, cuz I seen him go in, but I ain't seen him come out yet. Stayed longer than most of her visitors. That's one busy woman if you ask me."

"If you had legs like hers, then you might have some men in your life, too," countered a young man with a sly grin on his face.

"Leastwise I don't have no dangerous gangsters showing up at my door," retorted the heavyset woman.

"Nor cops, either," added the old woman. "Every Friday afternoon I sees that same uniform policeman leaving her place with a brown paper lunch bag in his hand. What you think he's got in there? It's too damn late in the day for lunch."

"You can bet she's not making him sandwiches to put in that bag," joked the young man. His grin got larger.

"You mens," huffed the old lady. She elbowed her husband. "And you shut up if you know what's good for you."

"They's the ones talking about Mafia business and crooked cops," replied the old man. "Not me."

The big Cuban turned to glare at him.

"Now you done it," fussed the old woman. "Don't say I didn't warn you."

Before the Cuban had a chance to do anything, the apartment door opened behind his back.

"Oh, is that my delivery?" asked a high-pitched female voice. Loud music boomed from the stereo behind her.

Big Tony turned around.

In the doorway stood a slender young woman in a low-cut wispy top, tight silver lamé miniskirt, and black spike heels. Her thick black hair was cut short, her lips glowing fire-engine red; she wore large silver hoop earrings in her ears, with several bright-colored bracelets jingling on each wrist.

None of the men moved for a moment. "Lord almighty," one of them finally whispered.

"We're looking for a Miss Delilah," said the Cuban.

"That's me, sugar."

"Then this is yours. Where you want us to put it?"

"Just set it up here in the living room."

Edward wheeled the dolly over into the middle of the room and unstrapped the crate.

"You gotta sign for it," said the Cuban. He took a form off his clipboard and held it out.

She reached for it, but the paper slipped through her well-manicured fingers and dropped sideways to the floor. Bending forward at the waist, she picked up the document by one corner.

Immediately, all the men standing on the catwalk surged a little closer into the doorway. Those stuck at the rear put their hands on the backs and shoulders of those in front and stood on tiptoes so they could get a better look.

"Mens," grumped the old woman as she pulled her husband back from the crowd, "you only got one thing on your minds."

"Gimme the pry bar," said the Cuban standing by the crate, "and I'll open it up."

Edward patted his overalls. "Think I left it in the truck."

"Anybody here got a hammer?" inquired the Cuban.

"Let me through," came an authoritarian voice from the rear of the crowd. "I'm the maintenance man for these apartments. Yeah, I got one."

"As old as you are," quipped the young man with the sly grin, "you ain't gonna nail anything in here with that dinky hammer you got."

A few chuckles of laughter erupted.

His face flushed a bright red, the maintenance man pushed his way into the apartment.

"See how long it takes to get your plumbing fixed the next time it breaks down," he said to the young man as he elbowed his way past.

"Hell, I'm still waiting for you to fix my busted air-conditioner," came the retort.

"You'll wait your turn like everybody else. I'll get around to it one of these days."

"It's already been three weeks. Summer'll be over before you show up at my place. What's a tenant have to do to get some service in this rathole?"

"Maybe if you had better-looking legs," the heavyset woman shot at him with her own sly grin, getting some of her own back.

"Gimme the damn hammer so we can get this done," Big Tony directed the short black guy. "We don't got all night to waste here."

Claw hammer in hand, the big Cuban started prying one end off the crate.

"I can't see nothing from here," complained a younger woman in a tight-fitting halter top.

Sizing her up from his position in the doorway, the young man with the sly grin figured what his chances might be for later, took a short step inside, and then surreptitiously slid sideways along the living room wall, where he pulled the cord to open the front room drapes. A mass of faces suddenly blossomed on the other side of the window. He got a promising smile of thanks from the younger woman.

With an end panel of the crate removed, the short black guy reached in and started tugging on whatever was inside the wooden box. A black metal tube appeared at the top, with a black metal base at the bottom. Now the Cuban lent a hand and helped tug the object out of the container.

"What is it?" inquired the heavyset woman.

"Looks to me like one of them stair-steppy exercise machines," replied the younger woman.

"As much exercise as that woman gets at night, she don't need no machine to help her stay that skinny. She already got bird legs and snake hips. What more she want?"

"Can I try out my delivery?" asked Miss Delilah.

"We got to put it together first," said the Cuban.

"Send somebody out for food while we're working," requested the short black guy. "I ain't had nothing to eat since breakfast."

Tony dug in his pants pocket and came out with a twenty-dollar bill. He held it up for the crowd. "We'd like us a couple of burgers, some fries, and cold drinks."

Nobody moved.

"I'll throw in an extra ten for whoever goes and gets it."

A young boy weaseled his way through the mass and grabbed

hold of the money. "I know an all-night place across the street. Be back in a couple of minutes."

"And I want plenty of ketchup for my fries," added the short black guy.

The kid ducked through the mob and out the doorway. By the time he returned, the two deliverymen had just about finished putting the exercise machine together. He handed over a large white paper bag with a greasy bottom, waited for his promised ten-spot, then squeezed back out through the doorway. Tony opened the bag and started eating. Right behind him, the stocky black guy reached over to claim his share.

"Is my exercise machine ready now?" asked Miss Delilah.

"Yes, ma'am, it is," replied the Cuban between mouthfuls. "Go ahead and try it out."

There was a murmur of anticipation from the male population. A couple of older women in back snorted loud enough in disapproval to be heard up front.

Miss Delilah looked around at the gathering like she hadn't seen all these people until now.

"I can't try this out with everybody watching."

Big Tony gave a hard look at the crowd. He stepped forward, stretching out his arms in a shooing motion.

"Show's over, all you folks'll have to leave now. Let the lady be."

Those men inside the apartment slowly retreated to the doorway. The young man with the sly grin suddenly found himself all alone on the wrong side of the front picture window. When the Cuban glared in his direction, he hustled over to the door and threaded himself into the mass of bodies.

At a nod from the Cuban, Edward walked over to the front window and closed the drapes. Those watchers outside the window glanced at each other.

"Guess that's all there is."

"Getting past my bedtime anyway."

They began drifting off in different directions.

As Tony began shutting the front door, the maintenance man extended one foot to block the doorway.

"Hey, what about my hammer?"

"Come back later and pick it up from Miss Delilah." Then the Cuban kicked the offending foot out of the way and slammed the metal door.

With warring emotions between being treated so poorly by the deliverymen, yet now having an excuse to visit Miss Delilah later at night and all alone, the maintenance man couldn't make up his mind whether to be angry or elated. Finally he stomped off to take care of other duties.

A couple of hours later when the maintenance man was up on the sixth floor outside apartment 608, he heard a door open up one floor below him. Then it was quiet for several minutes. He poked his head over the rail and leaned cautiously out far enough to observe some of the fifth-floor catwalk. Mostly all he could see was those two deliverymen from their knees down, but he managed to catch parts of their quiet discussion.

"All the lookie-lous gone?"

"Yeah, everybody must've gone off to bed."

"Past my bedtime, too. Let's get this crate out of here. We still got a lot of work to do with this."

There was some grunting and heavy breathing and then the lower part of the wooden box loaded on the dolly came into view. With a left turn, the dolly and its cargo headed for the open stairwell. When the two deliverymen got to the end of the catwalk and started down the stairs, the maintenance man pulled back a little so as not to be seen himself. Seeing how carefully the muscular Cuban and the stocky black guy maneuvered that wooden box and dolly going down the open stairwell, it appeared the crate was as heavy going down as it had been coming up. Of course the two workers could just be tired by now, he thought. After all, it was long past midnight.

Waiting until both deliverymen had the crate up on the raised metal platform and were putting it into the back of the truck, the maintenance man went down the stairwell at the opposite end of the building to stay out of their view. Down on the fifth-floor cat-walk, he was about to knock on the door of 507, when he noticed his hammer was already outside the apartment, lying in front of the closed door. No lights shone around the curtained picture window. He put his ear to the metal door. No music from the stereo, no sound at all.

Damn, he'd have to find another excuse on another night to come see Miss Delilah.

As the maintenance man walked toward the same open stair-way that the deliverymen had gone down, the sole of his left shoe slipped on a wet patch. He glanced down. On the walkway cement shone a small smear of thick liquid.

Red paint? No, more likely it was ketchup. Them damn deliv-erymen must've dropped some of that extra ketchup the short black guy had ordered for his fries. The stuff had landed on the catwalk. Lucky the dolly wheels hadn't run through it, else it'd be tracked everywhere. There was another smear about five feet further along. And another closer to the open stairwell. Also seemed like there were smears on some of the steps all the way down to the asphalt.

Hell, he might as well take care of this mess before the owners saw it and raised a fuss. Bad enough that tenants complained about all them broken air-conditioners. Be worse yet if one of them com-plainers slipped on this red stuff and claimed a lawsuit for injuries whether they was hurt or not. Crazy people in this neighborhood would do anything to make a little money. Best go get a mop.

# MOKUME GANE

## BY TOM ROB SMITH

Taro Oshiro entered Aokigahara, the forests at the north-west foot of Mount Fuji. If regarded with a dispassion-ate eye, these forests were a place of outstanding natural beauty. The trees and boughs were unusually close together, knot-ted around boulders; there were no easy paths, which caused some to feel a sense of claustrophobia; vines like rope cords could ensnare your feet, but there was exceptional serenity. The forests were not popular with ramblers. Few creatures lived among these trees: a fact science had so far failed to explain. There was no rustling of leaves, no birdsong—a silent sea of white cedars and pines. Perhaps partly because of its stillness, perhaps because it was located in the shadow of a sacred volcano, perhaps for reasons unknown, Aokiga-hara had become the most notorious suicide spot in Japan.

Taro Oshiro had only been walking for a few minutes, but he was now entirely enclosed by the forests and cut off from the world. Upon entering the cover of these trees, many spoke of discomfort and fear, the unsettled presence of the tormented souls who'd taken their own lives—some would venture only a few hundred meters before running out, believing there was darkness seeped in the soil and emanating from the tree trunks. In contrast, Taro Oshiro, a man nearing his fortieth birthday, felt entirely at ease. He came here often, walked for many hours through these strange forests, not out of appreciation for their beauty but because he owed the forests everything. He walked here out of gratitude.

Born poor, in a depth of poverty that offers few escape routes even to the most ambitious, Taro Oshiro had been unable to flourish in school, holding in contempt his fellow students for the smallness of their dreams, desiring good grades, or praise from a teacher. His mind was restless; he disliked hierarchies and was suspicious of authority; one thing was clear—entirely unemployable, he must become his own boss, control his own destiny, for he was no good at taking orders. However, even the humblest of fledgling enterprises requires a small amount of start-up capital, and his parents had none, nor would they sell anything to invest in him. They didn't believe in him. He was turned down by relatives, friends, professional moneylenders who listened to his plans, found him arrogant and awkward, and took pleasure in declining his requests. No other moment in his life shaped his character more sharply. He learned a bitter lesson. He owed this world nothing.

A setback, he told himself; he'd devise a solution, and that would make his eventual and inevitable success all the sweeter because he'd done it alone. He paced his village for days and days; his toes bled, his feet blistered, he didn't sleep, until, finally, exhausted, he slumped in the sun, his mind still trying to find a solution even as his body implored him for just a moment of sleep. In the haze of his exhaustion, the sun warm on his skin, he heard the chitchat of two women from the village taking an idle stroll. This was the lifestyle of the rich with nothing else to do except gossip. Unaware they were being overheard, they loudly and indignantly discussed a popular novel called *Tower of Waves* by Seichō Matsumoto. Taro Oshiro had no interest in fiction; he didn't understand how people could concern themselves with matters that weren't real—there was enough in life to be busy with; nevertheless, he remained still, unobserved, listening to their discussion about a story which ends with two lovers killing themselves in Aokigahara. Such melodrama was of no concern to him until he heard how this story had caused a great number of readers to copy the fictional characters. Like a hunting animal's, his ears pricked up—inspiration struck.

The next day Taro Oshiro packed a bag and set off for Mount Fuji, entering Aokigahara and vowing not to leave until he'd found what he was looking for—his future. Unlike any forests he'd walked in before, he found Aokigahara difficult to navigate; the compass he'd brought with him didn't work; the needle would spin listlessly. The dense foliage forced him to climb trees in order to check his position, glancing at Mount Fuji before climbing back down and realizing he'd been completely wrong, he'd been going north when he'd been sure—absolutely sure—he'd been traveling south.

On the fourteenth day he saw her, a shadow in the trees, slumped against the trunk as if the tree were pregnant with this young woman. She was no older than twenty, alone; no lover hung by her side. Out of obligation, rather than common sense, Taro checked her pulse, an unnecessary act since her skin showed signs of decomposition. He scolded himself; he was not here to check her pulse—he was here to check her purse. He looked around to see if she'd brought a bag, a purse to pay for the bus fare to reach the forests, and sure enough, he found a small bag and her purse; he took the modest amount of money and anything that he might be able to sell. Unfortunately, she was a young woman and, judging by her clothes, not rich. His gains were modest.

It was the body of a dead businessman, found two months later, still wearing an expensive gold watch, and with a wallet full of cash, that gave Taro the capital he required. For two months, he'd lived in those forests, like a wild animal—his patience had been rewarded. After cleaning himself at an onsen, he caught a bus to Tokyo, where he would enact his plans, turning a gold watch into a business empire. Carefully, he stole regular glimpses at this fine gold watch, made in Switzerland. He was careful not to allow the other passengers to see, terrified that they might call the police, he would be shamed, and his plans would collapse before they'd begun. Privately he took the philosophical approach that life continues regardless, and he was merely part of the process. The dead decompose. Life goes on, it feeds on the dead. He was not going to feel guilty; the man had killed himself, giving up even though strapped to his wrist was more wealth than Taro Oshiro had known in his entire lifetime. At least he was turning their wasteful deaths to some productive end. But he was well aware that no one else would see his actions that way and that the origins of his business must always remain a secret between him and Aokigahara.

The discovery of the gold watch was over twenty years ago, and Taro Oshiro was now a wealthy man; his various businesses employed over five thousand staff; he'd weathered financial storms; his disdain for banks and moneylenders meant that he never over-borrowed. His personal wealth was such that he did not need to work again: he could live out the rest of his days in lavish luxury. Needless to say, his restless mind had no interest in retirement; he was not driven merely by material gain but by a hunger for success and perfection. Though it would have made sense never to return to the forests, since they were the scene of a crime, the dark seed from which he'd grown his career, he could not turn his back on the forests that had helped him when no other person had wanted to hear his name. Whenever there was a problem that required a great deal of consideration, a merger, a whistleblower, a takeover, he would drive to Aokigahara and walk among its trees. He felt a connection here and a greater attachment to these trees than he did to his own parents. This was his home. The child Taro Oshiro might have been born in a village. But the great and respected businessman had been born here, in these forests.

The problem that occupied him today, as it had done for some years now, was the irresolvable fact that Taro Oshiro was unloved. He wasn't a sentimental man; he felt no need for a companion and would've been content to live alone, except that remaining a bachelor could not be considered the act of a successful man. He could not accept the way in which people would dismiss his great achievements by saying "But has he found love?" To remedy this situation, he must find a wife. Wealth meant that he could easily have formed a dishonest relationship based on material gain, but once again, he could not tolerate the idea that people would whisper behind his back that his wife was merely with him for the money. If he was to marry, the woman must love him, love absolutely, there must be no possibility that it could be considered anything other than a success. However, there was a problem. He'd discovered that women did not love him. He was a handsome man, exercised regularly, there was no physical reason why a woman might not find him attractive, but any woman who spent long enough in his company began to withdraw from him; they pulled away, as if sensing that something was not quite right with him, something askew and invisible to the eye. They recoiled, not immediately but inevitably. The kind of woman he required by his side, the kind of woman whose adoration was beyond question, always declined his advances.

As he walked through the forests he opened his heart, sometimes spoke aloud, resting a hand on the trunk of a tree, hoping the answer would come to him here—perhaps Aokigahara would give him one more thing, just one more. He'd already bought the wedding rings after reading an article on the ancient metalcraft of mokume gane, in which two metals are melted together, forming a ripple pattern not dissimilar to the grain found in wood—curves and swirls composed from the random movement of precious metals. The rings symbolized everything he was looking for—two people becoming inextricable upon marriage, a perfect union. In an effort to concentrate his mind, Taro Oshiro carried these rings with him at all times, crafted from the most expensive blending of platinum and white gold, inside a box decorated with the same craftsmanship. Strangely, he loved the box more than the rings, since the lid looked as if it had been sliced from the trunk of a magical metal tree.

Up ahead, among the trunks of the trees he knew so well, he saw another shape also familiar to him, a human shadow—he'd seen so many bodies in these woods he felt no curiosity, only mild disdain for this senseless act, and he was about to turn away when the shadow moved. This person was not yet dead.

Moving with some speed, he walked toward the figure, moving quietly, not wishing to necessarily interrupt, closer and closer until he saw a beautiful young woman not much older than twenty, tying a noose. He'd never seen such beauty and sadness. The woman's skin was perfect and pale. She was tying the noose with great inefficiency, bursting into tears every few seconds, her hands trembling. On the ground there was a pile of crumpled letters—love letters, he guessed. Yes, she looked as if she was suffering from a broken heart, not that he had any experience in such matters. From his position, hidden among the trees, he watched the young woman as she neared the end of her preparations. He felt the edge of the box in his pocket and imagined saving this woman, how grateful she would be; she was young, with no perspective on the world; he'd help her recover from this broken heart and she would love him unconditionally. She would be blind to whatever element of his character made other women turn away. The forests had rewarded their devoted child once again.

Taro Oshiro stepped forward, declaring:
  "Please reconsider."

The woman was so startled she let go of the rope, lost her footing on the trunk of the tree, and fell to the ground. Taro Oshiro ran forward, scooping her up in his arms. Her eyes were fragile glass. Instead of speaking, she burst into tears, resting her head on his shoulder. It took her several minutes to calm down, and finally, looking at him, she said:

"I am too foolish."

He thought it an odd remark—too foolish for what? Not for death, which would accept fools and the wise alike—but her humility made him feel comfortable enough to stroke her hair.

Her name was Aya Tanaka; she was a university graduate who'd fallen in love with her professor, a wise and brilliant man who'd seen their love affair as no more than a fling—he'd discarded her, as he'd discarded many others. She'd never loved anyone else. She believed that her death would cause a scandal and the professor would never be able to break anyone else's heart. Taro Oshiro threw his jacket over her shoulders and she rested against his chest, coiled up in his arms; in truth, he felt sorry for the professor, about to have his career ruined, and was pleased, if nothing else came of this incident, that his career would survive. However, her story proved she was principled, idealistic—hopelessly naïve—a woman whose love for him would not be scorned; no one could doubt her integrity. Now there was a simple test. He was waiting for the moment when she would start to recoil, when she would pull away, but it never came, despite their talking for many hours; on the contrary, she became more tactile, she would stare into his eyes, she would call him the kindest man she'd ever met.

"I never thought I'd experience kindness again."

She was perfect. She was blind. She was smitten, and she would associate the thought of leaving him with death—she would be forever loyal. She didn't even know he was rich. By the end of their conversation he was ready to give her the ring and make her his wife. Fearing that she might be scared by such speed, he made a supreme effort to control his urge to propose. Instead, he said:

"Are you strong enough to walk?"

"Yes."

"Then let's leave this place, leave it forever; you must have dinner with me, you must stay with me in my home in Tokyo until you remember how wonderful life can be."

She smiled:

"I remember already."

She touched his arm.

As he walked through the forests, with Aya Tanaka leaning on his arm, the trees brushed against him and the vines caught his feet; he found walking difficult and tripped several times, something that never happened when he walked alone. He paused, looking around at the strange shapes of the trees, and slowly his tremendous feeling of happiness began to ebb away. Happiness was replaced with another feeling, one he was more familiar with—suspicion.

It was odd that this young woman hadn't asked anything about him; she hadn't asked if he was married, she hadn't asked why he was in the forests; Aokigahara was too notorious for a pleasure stroll, no ramblers came here, yet she had made no attempt to gather his story. She was self-centered, that was true—even so, it was odd. She smiled at him—she smiled a lot for a woman who'd just tried to end her life:

"What's wrong?"

She was quick to notice his change in temperament; not so blind after all.

"Nothing," he lied, and began to walk again. This was wrong. What were the chances that he'd arrive at such an opportune time? In fact, had he even seen the woman try to kill herself? All he'd witnessed was the crude paraphernalia of suicide, and there had been very little of that; normally a suicide victim took an overdose of sleeping pills to make sure, very few came into the forests with merely a rope and not even a bag to conceal the rope. What was more, she'd readily accepted his affection, considering her heart had just been broken.

Taro Oshiro's heart began to darken like storm clouds at sea, obliterating the horizon, with lightning flashes of rage. He was being tricked. Why hadn't he checked those love letters on the ground? They could've been faked, written by her, but now they were left behind, vital evidence he could have used to see if this professor was even real. How could he have been so quick to believe? Pretty Aya Tanaka had done her research—he was a famous businessman, after all, an eligible bachelor; maybe she'd noticed that he took long walks in these forests. Several people knew about the rings he'd purchased—hadn't his assistant shown him the article on mokume gane? Yes, she had, she'd arranged the appointment with the jeweler. Now that he thought about the matter, at least ten, perhaps twenty people knew he'd made the rings; it could easily be deduced that he was looking for a wife; a plan had been hatched; this woman in the forest was part of a trap, she'd followed him, running ahead and setting up her position; it would've been a simple task, and here she was, hanging off his arm as if they were already married.

No, it was far worse, this girl knew the secret of the gold watch— the secret of his origins. Perhaps her mother had been on the bus; she'd seen the watch and had recognized his photograph in a recent business magazine. He'd been a young fool for taking the watch out so many times and admiring it so carelessly. With such information this woman would have an unbreakable grip over him. She'd be able to shame him at any moment. He stopped walking, short of breath:

"Sometimes I get lost in these woods. Let me climb this tree and check that we're going in the right direction."

Aya Tanaka ran forward, hugging him tight:

"Please be careful. I don't know what would happen to me if you fell."

He felt sick at this grotesque piece of playacting.

*You'd be fine,* he thought, *just fine; you'd take my wallet and my watch and make off with your modest gains, except that would be disappointing since you have a bigger target in sight, marriage; you want to take everything I have. You want it all.*

He climbed the tree, looking at Mount Fuji. They'd been heading in the correct direction. They'd be out of the forests in less than thirty minutes. He climbed down. And smiled; she wasn't the only person who could act:

"These forests are quite extraordinary. We're heading the wrong way."

"Are you sure?"

There was the proof he needed! The conclusive proof! She knew her way around these woods, unlikely for someone who was supposed to be befuddled by a broken heart. But he would not let her go. He took her by the arm.

"Trust me."

And he changed direction, turning back into the woods.

# ANGELINA

## BY MARY ANNE KELLY

You never saw Angelina unless she was watering her lawn. She would come out early, do the front and then the back. She never missed unless it was raining, so she had the best lawn in the neighborhood, where the lawns are stamp-small but neat and lush.

It's dead quiet over here in South Ozone Park except for the intermittent scream of planes in and out of Kennedy airport. But after you've been here a couple of years you don't hear them anymore. My Molly wakes up when she hears the cat coming home next door and that means I'm up. We go around the block, left, in case that loose male dog is hanging around the boulevard. We pass Angelina as she's lugging her hose down her driveway. I think when she sees us turning the corner she knows it's time to do the yard. Then we come home, the *News* is on the stoop, and we have our breakfast.

I was concerned when I hadn't seen her for a couple of days. I knew she had a daughter, so I wasn't too worried. But then Angelina's lawn started to parch and I really thought something might have happened so I went up past the statue of Saint Anthony and I rang the bell. Angelina's got the air-conditioner cranking from June to September and the brick house has that fortress feel to it.

It took her long enough. I was just about to walk away when she opened the door a crack. "Hey," I said, "I didn't see you for a while. How you doin?"

She looked at me with uninterested eyes.

"You okay?" I said. "I mean, if you want me to carry the hose out for you, I can."

Angelina shrugged. "Na," she said. She made a mouth like when you get a piece of bad calamari. Her housedress was as usual black. I remembered her husband was dead three years, a mere flash in a Sicilian pan. And she looked like she hadn't been sleeping.

"You want me to call your daughter?"

Suddenly there was life under those heavy lids. "No!" she said. Behind her the television droned.

I thought of my son, still in bed. "I gotta go. Listen, you want my number? Just in case you need someone to call in an emergency?"

For a second I thought I saw a spark of interest. But "No." She tipped her head in polite dismissal. "So long." She shut the door.

I had my crossword-puzzle ballpoint in my pocket and left my number on a coupon and stuck it in her mailbox anyhow.

Then I didn't see her for a while. I'd never had more to do with her than a careful nod; now there I was thinking about her every day. It was one of those real hot summers. One evening it was so hot we overloaded the electric, and the air-conditioner broke down before supper. All the windows were thrown open and a squirrel came right up on a branch bold as you please and looked at us. "Close the window, Anthony," I worried, "or he'll come in and we'll never get him out." But Molly jumped up barking and that took care of him. "Westies are ratters at heart," my husband informed us, his voice tight with respect. He was in a good mood because he'd just finished paying the bills. He suddenly recalled when he was a kid and Angelina's husband used to string the clothesline over a vat of boiling water on the barbecue and smear the line with peanut butter. Then he'd shoot the squirrel and it would drop into the boiling water. Anthony stopped eating. I must have turned pale. "Whatsa matter?" Tony laughed. "You don't eat meat? Whaddya think, it comes like that all nice and ready in a package?"

I stood up and scraped the rest of my rigatonis into the trash.

"And," he remembered with a jolt of sudden interest, "he had the best grapevine in the neighborhood. He gave Nonno his shoot." He chewed a wad of mozzarella and washed it down with our homemade. "Come to think of it, the vine we have in our yard came from Nonno so it must have come from that one. A man like that"—he shook his head sympathetically—"would be sorely missed."

I stood at the window looking out at the backyard. The vine above the picnic table was heavy with grapes and bees.

The next day I went up and rang the bell again and this time she answered right away. "Whatsa matter now?" she said.

"Look, Angelina, you want me to water your lawn?"

"No. Good-bye."

"Listen." I put my hand on the door. "I don't mean to be pushy or anything. Don't misunderstand me, I just—What is that, anyway? That aroma? What is that?" I peeked in past the yellow velvet living room enshrined in fitted vinyl. The kitchen was pink and gray, like fifties poodle skirts.

"I gotta sauce onna stove." She pursed her lips and flapped her two arms folded on her stomach. "Braciole."

"Wow."

"Anh. You gotta nose. So what?" The door shuts, caboom, in my face.

Nice. No good deed goes unpunished, I'm thinking. Huh. Well, that's the end of that. Her daughter must be coming for her to be cooking. Whenever she comes she's loaded down with shopping bags of broccoli rabe and like that. At least I know the old girl won't starve. And I go home.

Ten days pass. Now Angelina's got no more front lawn. It's brown and it's all over. My mother-in-law tells my husband her neighbor told her that Angelina's daughter got a firm offer on the house from a Pakistani family and she's pushing Angelina to move to a "maturity" condo in Jersey. Personally, I've never cared much for the daughter. She wears those slithery leisure suits and drives a Mary Kay executive convertible. I know because she parks this on my corner, worried that the drug dealers who live next door to her mother will steal it. I hate to tell her, but they probably wouldn't be caught dead.

And where is Angelina going to find Locatelli cheese in the wilds of New Jersey? Where is she going to find veal like at Suino d'Oro? Over here she can take the Q10 up to Liberty Avenue and she's got everything right there. Or she can take her shopping cart and walk. It's not that far. There's a kind of intimacy strangers share when they see each other every day. Now I'm not one of these do-gooders my husband accuses me of being. It's just I get a feeling Angelina's maybe fading away because she has nothing left to live for. It makes me think of that dog we avoid. He's old and he's mean and he lives over in the airport parking lots, existing on scraps of who knows what from the Domino's Pizza garbage disposal. Once in a while he comes around the boulevard and my softhearted neighbor, who is Dutch, puts out rice in a plastic bag folded over like a dish. He hangs around a day or two, suspicious and hungry, then slinks back across the parkway. Every time I see him he looks baggier. I avoid him because my Molly isn't fixed and that's all I need. Sometimes, late at night, teenagers from Lefferts Boulevard throw stones at him and I can hear him barking back, outraged but weary.

Sunday night Molly gets a full walk before bed. Monday morning is recycle day and all the cans are out, plus, you get a lot of really old stuff thrown away and you wouldn't believe some of the great things people throw away: old books and perfectly good iron frying pans! I noticed Angelina's recycle garbage was just a lot of empty tomato soup cans. But hey, none of this concerns me. My husband wants me to mind my own business and I do. I hurry Molly past the drug dealers' house, whose recycle bins are loaded with broken Bombay Gin and Johnnie Walker Black bottles.

A smeary, rotten stench is oozing from their garbage bags and I yank Molly—who yearns for just that sort of thing—briskly away.

Monday rolls around and who do I see on the street meandering behind the garbage truck but this dog. I mean, doesn't anybody do anything around here about stray dogs? They must, I figure, but everyone knows what happens if you call. They come and get it and the next thing you know they put it to sleep. I'm standing on my porch and I'm thinking what is he? Shepherd? Rottweiler? And a side order of Husky, the tail, despite everything, still more up than down. That has to tell you something. A big old guy, big feet, big head, big balls hanging down. Everything loose like he was once good and stocky. What this guy needs is someone who loves to cook.

So I already know what you're thinking but I'm way ahead of you. Anthony is watching a SpongeBob video and eating his favorite: buttery Eggos. Tony is sound asleep on the couch and the truck is tucked in on Rockaway Boulevard so he's not going anywhere. I lock the door. It cost me all the doggy biscuits I keep in my pocket for Molly to lure him around the block. I spot a jump rope on fat Anita's front lawn and I slip it around the damn dog's neck. Now I'm dirty and already I'm annoyed. And maybe I'm dead if he decides to go for me. But I've been attending Anu Butani's yoga class on Thursdays and I'm starting to get it so I ease myself into well intention.

I go and I ring Angelina's bell. No answer. But meanwhile I know she's home because she's got an opera on, Puccini, which is good because we want her in that kind of mood. The only trouble is Angelina won't answer. And next door, the venetian blinds upstairs crack a little bit open and I can almost feel myself being observed. I'm not giving up yet, though. I take the pig's ear I was saving for Molly's big-job reward. I rub it all over Angelina's front doorstep, then push it halfway in the ledge of her mail slot. I look in that old dog's big brown anticipating eyes. "You're going to have to take it from here," I tell him, and I pull the jump rope off his head.

I walk away and the stupid dog comes gangling after me. "Look," I say, walking him back to the stoop, "you come with me, I'm going to chase you away and you'll wind up back by the garbage container. Stay here, play your cards right, and you can be eating cavatelli every Tuesday. Make a decision."

I walk away holding my breath. He doesn't come after me but now I'm afraid to turn around and see if he's staying there. I just keep going, then I go home and take my Molly around the other block, by Lefferts Boulevard. There's only so much you can do.

Well, a couple of weeks go by. I'm still walking Molly around by Lefferts Boulevard by Don Peppe's restaurant and the supermarket there. She loved it while it was new and fresh, but after a while she's not interested, she just won't go. She wants to go back her old way. If you've ever known a West Highland terrier you know they can be very stubborn. So this day I take her back our regular old way. The smell of garlic mingles with olive oil and thick tomatoes from the yard—and basilico. Basil grows like a weed from the gray cement under the brick from every house around here. What a smell! It's got to be Angelina frying sausages and what do I see? Angelina's backyard chain-link fence is locked with one of those school locker combination locks and who's in there? Angelina's back door slams and I hear, "*Bruno! Bruno, venga a chi!*" There's that big old dog lying down on an apricot chenille rug on the dirt. He does not move but his tail thumps encouragingly, swatting the dust. Good thing there's no grass to ruin. I pat myself on the back and walk home slow. Bruno, eh? *Bene.*

Then one day, Sunday, the phone rings and to my surprise it's Angelina. She's all upset. The drug dealers who bought the house next to hers are having a party. Everyone in this neighborhood knows they're drug dealers. They've got so much money they don't know what to do with it. Two guys. One of them is really handsome, in a dark and dangerous, drug-dealer sort of way. I personally thought he looked kind of nice. Running slowly to his four-by-four with darkened windows in a happy, thrifty gait.

They have a fiberglass boat on the driveway, wrought iron bars on the windows and doors. Right away when they moved in, it was instant landscape and all exotics; bonsais, eucalyptus, and palm trees even outside. They have no idea what winter is like here. The cement people from Howard Beach arrived in a beautiful truck and did the whole driveway and the courtyard in pink cement. The word on the street is the pink comes from the blood of the drug dealer's tardy clients. Only that's too good to be true, my husband says. On feast days, they have so many lights up it looks like carnevale. Sometimes, when you hear shots at night, you know right away where they're coming from.

So Angelina is very upset on the phone because these people are having a party since yesterday and the dog can't take that mambo jambo music no more. Also, a van pulled up and eleven blond Polish girls were ushered in from a van. Or maybe Russian. They could have been Russian! She called the cops but they won't do nothing till eleven at night and she's going potza. Bruno barks the whole time. If they don't a stop soon, she's a gonna get out her husband Jasper's pistoli he had since Mussolini and she's a gonna shoot a the bastards one a by one in the head!

*"Calma, Signora."* I soothe her as best I can over the phone, and peek out through my blinds upstairs from my bedroom. There's a whole posse of snazzy cars with bras on their front fenders and smoked windows you can't see through parked by that house. One of the cars bumps up and down on humungous tires to rectum-vibrating hip-hop.

What am I supposed to do? I listen to her go on and on. She's "a gonna move to Florida!" She's "a gonna take a the dog and never talk a nobody again!"

I feel bad because there's something in her voice that tells me maybe she believes it herself. My husband's busy helping Lefferts Louie and Richie the jeweler put the new air-conditioner in the wall. "Who is that?" Tony jerks his head and wants to know, in a bad mood.

"Angelina," I mouth silently.

"Oh," he grunts, "the ball-breaker."

I've got my cutlets ready for frying and the water's starting to roll for the pasta. I figure as long as you let somebody vent, you mostly don't have to do anything at all.

"So, Tony," Louie jokes, "how long do you think till you get the hell out of this neighborhood?"

"Seven years, I figure," Tony tells him, shifting the air-conditioner up and off of his shoulder.

Seven years. Frozen, I sit down with the phone on Anthony's little trucks on the floor.

So it's two days after that, it's raining and I'm upstairs in my closet with the cardboard box from the new air-conditioner, playing emotional tug-of-war with clothes I haven't worn in over a year. The doorbell rings and it's two detectives, the one short, the other tall. Now we have gold badges, close shaves, and the unforgettable smell of Old Spice. They're investigating a drug deal that's about to go down around the corner.

"About time," I mutter.

"Are you aware there is drug traffic from that location?" the tall one says suspiciously.

"Yeah. Everybody knows," I say right back. Who the hell is he? "It's not like they're living the low profile."

"Let me put it to you this way," the short cop says. "We'd like to use your upstairs back window in the next couple of days."

"Come on in," I say, and they do. Wait till I tell Angelina this, I think.

"What are the chances of getting a reward?" I ask the short one while we're going up the stairs.

"Let me put it to you this way," he says, "none."

As soon as they leave, I put a leash on Molly and nonchalantly we walk over there. It's five o'clock and butter yellow. We're just turning the corner when I see Angelina's daughter's car parked in front of my Dutch neighbor Elly's house. That takes care of that, I think, and Molly and I head slowly home. Molly is no fast walker, it's more like you're accompanying a serious student of dirt. So I'm still out on the corner when I see Angelina drive by in her daughter's car. I'm happy to see she's done something to her hair. She's driving with the top down and there's Bruno on the front seat, tongue jauntily flapping like a long necktie. I didn't even know Angelina could drive. Angelina looks right at me and gives a sort of a start of a wave but she's busy driving. I watch her drive all the way down Lefferts, past Don Peppe's and onto the Belt.

For a while I linger outside. It's still hot but the air doesn't hurt like all day. Tony and Anthony are over at Holy Child playing CYO basketball so I have some time to kill before I start supper. There's this new little cappuccino place on Lefferts and I go there for a ristretto. It's kind of a rickety place and they let me bring Molly if I sit outside and she stays under the table. On the inside there's this big mural on the wall of the hills of Abruzzi and I sit there looking in at it. A big loneliness fills up my heart as I sip my coffee and feed biscotti crumbs to my Molly. Who would have thought I'd have seven more years to live out in South Ozone Park? I read on the menu that the mural is not of the Italian hills but the Colombian rain forest. I don't know what's come over me. Then I get up and go home.

The kids from down the block come running up when they see me. They're wild with excitement. "Did you hear what happened?"

"What?"

"All the cops were around the corner!"

I thought of my upstairs window and how now no undercover cops would be sitting there spying and my heart sank. "Did they arrest them already?"

"Nope. She got away!"

"Who? She?"

"Angelina! She got the hell away!"

"What are you talking about?"

"Yeah! She got away with a lotta the money." Abel bounces up and down. "She took it from the safe house!"

"No, dopey"—Frankie smacks him—"she *was* the safe house!"

"I don't understand," I wail.

"She got clean away on the bus," fat Anita says.

"They're gonna catch her up by Union Turnpike," Melissa—eyes like saucers—informs us. "I heard them yellin' when they got in the car."

I say, "How about the two guys next door who are dealing the drugs?"

"They no drug dealers, man," Abel says like I'm stupid, "they two gay guys."

I look down the boulevard. There's no traffic on the Belt. She could be in south Jersey by now. She probably is. All of a sudden the sun falls onto the roof of Don Peppe's restaurant and at the same time Mikey lets his racing pigeons fly off. They circle over our heads and then out over Kennedy airport. It's a beautiful sight.

I wonder if Bruno is going to like Florida.

Let me put it to you this way, if it was just Angelina, maybe I'd tell. But Angelina and Bruno? Hey. *Bona fortuna.*

# THE REMAINING UNKNOWNS

## BY TONY BROADBENT

T hey say your whole life passes before you at the moment of death.

They're wrong; their timing's way off, not even close.

Not if you count life in seconds. Not when a single second can seem to stretch for an eternity and a millisecond carry the weight of a lifetime, several lifetimes, sometimes, and the very next instant buy a subway ticket to heaven or hell for anyone within blast range. *Fiat lux. Fiat nox. Fiat nex.*

Latin? From a kid from Brooklyn?

Believe me, there are times it surprises even me, but you'd be amazed what you can pick up sitting cross-legged in a library; be it guarded by snow-covered lions way across the East River or one that arrives in a stack of moving boxes filled with nothing but dread sorrow.

Patience. Fortitude. Lessons carved in stone or wisdoms clawed from mountains of rubble. If life teaches you anything it's that you take what insight you can, when you can, from wherever you can find it. Then you hold on to it by every means possible. In the end there's nothing else. You go out with what you came in with. Beyond that first cry and last sigh, there's really nothing else.

Dust to dust. Ashes to ashes.
Smithereens to smithereens.
*Illegitimum non carborundum.*

I suppose I'd daydreamed of another life; not too clearly that I
remember or anything very much in particular; simply a thousand
and one other things for me to do than follow family tradition and
don the uniform of a New York cop.

Fat chance.

My older brother had upped and escaped the inevitable and
done so with rare distinction, all but barring my path out with the
measure of his success and the towering nature of his achievements.
Inimitable? You better believe it. On my best day I couldn't even
come close to reaching such unfathomable heights. At least that's
what I thought, no matter what Teddy did to try to ease the gap,
ease the burn. A little difference of eight years between us; it might
as well have been eighty; he was always the golden boy, I only ever
had feet of clay.

He was the hero; I was the hothead. And so it goes.

Teddy was nothing if not all-conquering. A scholarship to Holy
Cross, topped by what must've seemed a preordained *Sanctae Crucis*
Award, and from there on to Dartmouth and an MBA garlanded
with the laurel leaves of a Tuck Scholar. The inevitable siren calls
from the big Wall Street investment banks and huge early success
in the worlds of high technology and the Internet even before most
people knew what in hell any of it really amounted to and all the
world soon in every way his very own oyster. In rapid succession: an
impossibly beautiful wife; a four-story Park Slope town house that
everyone said was "to die for" even if it was only in the better part
of Brooklyn; an unending passion for vintage Rolex sports watches
and purple silk ties, dozens of each; a place out on the Vineyard
for the summer; a private jet to call on whenever he needed to hop
down to the Islands for some much-needed R&R and some time

on his sailboat. And then September 11th. And all our worlds come crashing down.

And I am born again.

"You on air, Bobby?"

The voice sounds a thousand miles away, even with the amplifiers inside my blast helmet, but I give a thumbs-up, get a quick slap on my shoulder from my partner, Brad. I've got air coming through my respirator. I'm good to go.

All nearby buildings have now been evacuated, all nearby roads blocked off, all vehicular and foot traffic diverted, inner and outer perimeters marked by lines of yellow police tape. The outer perimeter pushed back more than double the usual distance and reinforced with aluminum barriers and faded blue NYPD sawhorses; any damn thing that can be dragged into service. The inner perimeter now a rectangle of fluttering plastic tape not one but two hundred feet from the target vehicle, doubly secured by squad cars and fire trucks parked nose to tail, three deep in some places. And I begin another Long Walk.

It's the job of the NYPD Bomb Squad to attend any suspicious package or potentially lethal device found anywhere in the city's five boroughs. For any number of reasons, the Squad never consists of more than thirty or so officers. Any more than that, on "the Job," would have way too many cooks in an already overheated kitchen and to keep things focused we work in teams of two.

Two heads being better than one, it was up to Brad and me, crouched down behind our NYPD emergency vehicle, to interpret the pale-gray tones of the X-ray as seen on a laptop computer screen. Our very lives, mine certainly, depended on how carefully we read it. What we saw was an image of a complexity and level of sophistication previously only reported in terrorist bomb incidents abroad and, up to that moment, not seen anywhere on the US mainland. The X-ray images also showed additional dark spots and instances of flaring, which could indicate the presence of shielded radiological material.

The heart of the improvised explosive device appeared to be a lead-lined box—eighteen inches or so, by six, by nine—attached to a mess of wires and metal tubes, some of which would be functional, some not. All of it meant to blind us to the exact nature of the bomb and the full extent of what without any sense of irony we refer to as our "unknowns." And with the distinct possibility "the package" could be "hot," the ripples of concern spread further and further out, as Brad enlarged, enhanced, then wirelessly transmitted the X-ray images to ever higher and higher command posts and to other more experienced bomb techs for further analysis and advice. Yet even after everyone and his scrambled-egg-wearing brother has weighed in on how best to render the package safe and a reversal of standard protocol has given us early success, it still comes down to me taking the Long Walk armed with only a set of hand tools; knives, clippers, hooks, forceps, scalpels, crimpers, tape; your everyday toolbox.

I've never been sure whether my father died of a heart attack or a broken heart. He'd more than proved himself the toughest of old birds. No one made detective supervisor without having been to hell and back and then some, but Teddy going like that, out of a clear blue sky, without warning, only for it to be relived over and over and over again on television and in every newspaper and magazine, and the shock of it forever ongoing, there were dimensions to it he just couldn't grasp or didn't want to. It wasn't the world he'd given his life to protect, it was something other; it was as if he'd died of what someone in one of Teddy's books had once called Future Shock. And with Teddy having always been the apple of her eye, I'm sure Mom would've gone the same way, but breast cancer had already savaged and taken her. And looking back on it, a small mercy perhaps in the bigger scheme of things, but at least Teddy had been there by her bedside when she'd left us, we all were.

A bomb requires very few working parts: a power source, a switch, an initiator, explosives, and a container. The low- or high-explosive incendiary device; a mix of solid, liquid, jelly, or powder; made from over-the-counter firecrackers, propane, gasoline, and ammonium nitrate–based fertilizer; or from illegally sourced commercial and military-grade nitroglycerine, dynamite, TNT, or plastic explosives. When such a bomb explodes it can create blinding light, searing heat, toxic gas, and blast waves moving at up to 26,000 feet per second. An invisible, utterly incomprehensible force that nothing on earth can outrun and that compresses and hits with such speed and violence it's not until a second wave follows, a few milliseconds later, that any bystanders can even hear the deafening eruption. And by then the pitiless, shapeshifting, shrapnel-filled horror is already upon them and has utterly devoured them.

My father had always held himself a good Catholic, in that he'd strived all his life to adhere to all Ten Commandments, as well as the thousand and one rules in the *NYPD Patrol Guide*. The fact that he pretty much succeeded in following most all of them, in spirit, if not always the exact letter of the law, said a lot for him. Not that anyone ever called him out on anything; there was never any hint of wrongdoing. It's just that New York policing is tough business and New York City mired in politics, at every level, in every department. And ends sometimes justify means. So, Christmas and Easter and weddings and funerals aside, he'd venture into the confessional only after whatever high-profile case he'd been working on had been officially closed, as then both his desk and his conscience were perfectly clear. It was much tidier that way, for New York, and for him. He was ever a pragmatist. I think that's why he stopped going to Mass after 9/11; God had struck out the two apples of his eye in an almost wrathful vengeance, after which there was little left worth praying for or even living for anymore, at least not in his book.

It sobers me to know that the amount of highly enriched uranium needed to build a bomb that'd bring New York or any major US city to its knees need weigh no more than seventy-five pounds, would fit inside a suitcase, and could all too easily be transported by any size car or SUV. Our worst imaginings delivered in the kind of vehicle we see on our city streets every single day and that we're utterly blind to and can't positively ID without inside information. So I always ask myself: Is this a "dirty bomb" designed to release a radioactive cloud that would render parts of Manhattan uninhabitable for generations to come? Or does it contain some biological agent or toxin that would spread death and disease on the wind?

If the NYPD Bomb Squad is called out, all of New York City's own prevention measures and all of the nation's many security resources; everything from border checks to cargo monitoring at port of entry; all the countless airline security checks; as well as the entire intelligence-gathering apparatus of every department of Homeland Security; every single one has failed. One single fact alone enough to stop me dead in my tracks: nine million shipping containers enter US ports every year and only five percent of them are inspected before they get loaded onto trucks and trains and vans that head everywhere in the contiguous Forty-Eight.

The Bomb Squad is the last line of defense, the very last of the first responders. It's only after a terrorist bomb has exploded and extracted its bloody toll that the ambulance and triage teams, the doctors and nurses, aid workers and morgue attendants, all arrive; enough officially planned-for bodies to man all the border crossings to all nine circles of hell.

I'd been gone for almost three years when my father died unexpectedly. I was with the Marine Corps, in Iraq; locked, loaded; desperately trying to seize the day; though in my heart of hearts I seem to remember I'd originally enlisted to go hunt for Al Qaeda in Afghanistan. I was granted emergency leave. I don't know if any strings got pulled by NYPD brass, but I guess someone somewhere thought it would've been unseemly for so respected a senior police officer not to have his only remaining family member at his funeral, especially as that same someone on high also decreed that the memorial service would take place at St. Patrick's Cathedral.

Over the years I'd come to realize that the death of any New York City police officer, in the line of duty, is always a big deal, the ripples spreading far and wide. The sea of NYPD officers, five rows deep in some places, marking the route the casket will take; every officer in best dress blue. Police officers on motorcycles, reds and blues flashing, leading the procession; the deep throb of their engines merging with the pipes and drums of the NYPD Emerald Society, ever resplendent, in dark-blue tunics and kilts, Kelly-green sashes and plumes.

The coffin, hidden beneath a carpet of flowers, saluted by mass ranks of white-gloved hands; the massed pipes keening "An Inspector's Funeral" as the escorts remove it from the hearse. The casket hoisted onto the shoulders of six former colleagues and slow-marched into the church. The American flag; of green stripes, not red; tucked in tight around the coffin to ensure the deceased is correctly identified as a fallen NYPD officer all the way to the gates of St. Peter.

Eulogies from the pulpit by New York's police commissioner and mayor; final prayers for the dead and departed's safe passage into the afterlife offered by the officiating priest; the casket shepherded back into the street to the haunting sounds of "Taps." *Fidelis Ad Mortem*. And I sit quietly through it all; the pomp, the circumstance, the ceremony; my eyes never for one moment leaving the flag-draped coffin. For I, too, am "Faithful Unto Death."

Are the concentric circles of remembrance, the differing layers of enclosure, the only real key to the substance of one's life, one's death? The one true indicator of goals achieved; battles fought; honors and prizes won? One's importance recognized, recorded, and marked by the exact number and order of veils required to sanctify what was once the all-too-human core? As when a deep moat, heavy portcullis, guarded gate, narrow passage, and stout doorway are all barriers to be negotiated before you gain entry into that sacred inner sanctum in which resides the beloved or despised king, queen, president, dictator... or father. Are the secret, hidden pathways to our hearts and minds really so very different?

Today's package has already been recorded in multiple NYPD logbooks as a VBIED; a vehicle-borne improvised explosive device. The tricked-out black Chevy Suburban; the same model sport-utility vehicle used by most state and federal agencies; displaying "official" registration plates an exact match of those on a Suburban used by the governor's security detail up in Albany. CCTV has captured what looks to be a Caucasian male, in suit, tie, sunglasses, exiting the suspect vehicle; hair neat, no beard; same blank face adopted by security agents the world over. But that little conundrum is as nothing to the problems the Chevy presents us with since a very diligent traffic patrol officer first tagged it.

We began, as always, from a suitably safe distance, using the Remotec F6A. First order of business for our little caterpillar-tracked robot: to use its steel claw to shatter one of the SUV's black-tinted side windows so we can get a camera inside. Video shows third-row rear seats removed and, in the expanded cargo area, four large metal drums, three propane tanks, a gun locker filled with bags of fertilizer, and half a dozen large plastic tubs duct-taped together. It's all very neat and tidy, very expertly done, and very scary. What's equally disturbing is that the rest of the interior is a goddamn mess of fried-chicken boxes, paper wrappers, plastic utensils, and coffee cups and lids. There's also a briefcase, several sealed file folders, a backpack, a thermos, and a short length of metal pipe capped at both ends. Any and all of which could conceal a bomb. Best case, it could all turn out to be harmless. Worst case, everything from the handle on the briefcase to the plastic knives and forks could have been molded from Semtex or C4. We plan for the worst. Multiple booby traps.

It's as if the truck has been driven by two different people, polar opposites, one of whom must've Googled the long and varied history of bomb making, read *The Anarchist Cookbook*, or watched how-to videos on YouTube. And if anything was meant to tell us we were being taunted and played with, it was that. I think I took most exception to the cup with the I LOVE NY on it; big red heart of the Big Apple, smack in the middle; a cruel mockery of the bomber's intent.

Six years active duty with the Marines; first tour, in Iraq, with 2nd Battalion, 25th Marines; a transfer to Combat Logistics, my EOD training at Camp Lejeune, before being assigned to 2nd MLG, 2nd Explosive Ordnance Disposal Company. Two more tours; made sergeant; a couple of medals; a return stateside; an honorable discharge; two years Reserve, no recall. There was little surprise, me wanting to join the NYPD, more than a little at me wanting to stay in EOD, as a technical officer with the Bomb Squad. Family history prevailed, though, and I was accepted and soon set about relearning the craft, as civilian bomb disposal procedures are way different from those in the military.

Homeland presents a unique terrain. Safety of the public is paramount. On home ground it's a given everything is automated, shielded, and at a distance. There are no snipers; no one in the crowd waiting to command-detonate a hidden bomb; at least not yet. So IEDs are only dealt with by hand as a very last resort. That's why every three years every bomb tech in the land undergoes rigorous retraining at a special FBI bomb school, in Atlanta; followed by time at the Hazardous Devices School in Huntsville, Alabama.

That way every bomb tech is kept up to speed on terrorist bomb-making techniques and bombings from around the world. The one "known" that keeps us all so utterly focused: that it's just a matter of time before some terrorist group or other is able to put together a sophisticated bomb big enough to take out an entire metro. And maybe so, but I'll be damned if it's going to be New York City. One thing's for sure; it ain't happening on my watch.

After a deal of deliberation it was decided our first task was to take out all the garbage. Clear the playing field; see what was left; and only then attack the mysterious lead-lined box. An officially sanctioned reversal of standard ops that meant us first hitting all the possible secondary devices with the pan disrupter—a weapons-grade high-strength stainless steel cannon mounted atop the Remotec, so called because it can deal with most threats. We never fail to bless all the many techs who invented, then modified it, in all the many theaters of war, as the P-D fires specialized ammunition or a high-velocity jet of water powerful enough to punch out, disrupt, sometimes even completely dismantle an explosive device before it can trigger. It was definitely our best bet. And so "Robby the Robot" went to work again, with me very happy to be at the joystick end of the business.

Fools rushing in? No. At this stage, it's all still well within the perimeters of "knowns." Given the improvised bomb smorgasbord spread out before us, there could be any number of mechanical or electrical triggers, even chemical sensors. A simple pull-wire; a ticking Timex wristwatch; a mix of clock timers, digital timers, cell phones, or automobile remote-entry devices, as favored in Iraq and Afghanistan. So we immediately deploy a multiband radio frequency jammer, as much to negate the OnStar RemoteLink mobile app we know is an available option on the Suburban, as to block all signals from all surrounding cell towers and antennas. We don't want anyone to be able to start the vehicle, control the door locks, or trigger a bomb remotely, be it from down the block or a thousand miles away.

As one of the very few unmarried NYPD bomb techs, I get a lot of ribbing from the other guys in the squad. It's just them urging me to follow in their footsteps and let some woman make an honest cop of me. As, if I do say myself, I do seem to attract more than my fair share of pretty women. Women far too good for me, I'm then told. I'm always surprised, though, when a woman knowingly dates a police officer; I know firefighters are supposedly top of the ladder; but, hey, who am I to complain if one of them decides to hook up with me? I tell them, statistically speaking, it's far safer being a NYPD bomb tech than a regular NYPD patrol officer, as some of the people at large on New York streets can prove far deadlier than any bomb. Even so, when we've all met up at some function or private party, I've always been impressed by the wives of the other bomb techs; how they shut out any and all talk of danger; how they know it, but don't think it; which I think is its own very special kind of bravery. My mom always said that about the spouses of all serving NYPD officers. As a Marine, I came to think the same about all the husbands, wives, children; the fathers, mothers, brothers, sisters of all those who serve in the military. *They also serve who only stand and wait.* There are times I think waiting for a loved one to come home, safe and sound, is the toughest duty of all.

We do it by the numbers. Send in the Remotec; gain entry to the target vehicle; and, one by one, disarm all objects flagged as secondary devices. Locate, identify; aim. "Fire-in-the-hold!" Retreat a ways, reassess; reengage. Until every potential IED has been rendered safe, save for the lead-lined box wired to God-knows-what. We have no idea how many layers there still are to "the package" or how multiple or varied are its hidden depths. We've assessed the explosive profile as best we can; taken every kind of precaution;

expended all known "knowns." It's the remaining "unknowns" that continue to gnaw at the soul.

My father died in an automobile accident, responding to a call for extra backup from a rookie cop going to the aid of his partner. It was happenstance my dad was in that neighborhood, on his way uptown to some official function. So he radioed in, set the mag-mount flashing atop the car's roof, and did what he'd always done, went off in pursuit of bad guys. It was later determined that a man and his two little boys had just exited a crosswalk when the younger boy dashed back into the roadway to retrieve a toy he'd dropped. The older boy turned to pull his little brother to safety, the father turned to gather them both back up, and suddenly there they were the three of them, dead ahead. I wonder whether my dad saw them or us—himself, Teddy, and me—as we'd once been; the three of us; him, his little hero, and me, the hothead. Only, his one-and-only Teddy was gone forever and I wonder if it broke his heart anew. Whatever it was he saw or felt, he hit the brakes too hard, swerved too violently, the car skidded, a piece of metal in the road blew out a front tire, the Crown Vic bounced against a parked car, rolled, and slid first on its side, then on its roof, for some hundred yards or more before a delivery truck slammed into it. The Vic spun round and smashed into a light pole. The impact broke my father's neck. He was dead before the paramedics got to him. He was posthumously cleared of any and all charges of reckless driving or of endanger-ment; the accident officially recorded in the books as being the result of him having suffered a massive heart attack. And so it goes.

All that's left now is for a hooded man inside a bulky green bomb suit weighing ninety pounds, fingers bare beneath cuffs of Kev-lar armor, fingerless spandex and leather gloves already edged with sweat, to start walking downrange from "the package," and all without the company of a friendly robot on an electronic leash. "Where are you, R2-D2, when I need you?" I whisper, as the words of a stern-faced FBI instructor come to mind: "Start remote. Stay remote. Be remote."

If only. Only, not today; today's little problem calls for the personal touch; a closer, hands-on inspection, in the vague hope of producing more "knowns." A process that will have me kneeling down and saying numerous Hail Marys while I attempt to locate, then cut, the correct wire or wires, sever the right circuit or circuits, and oh so carefully remove the blasting cap or caps, and defuse the bomb or bombs that still remain "unknowns."

Thoughts of one's own mortality not unnaturally turning to what makes life so sweet; what about all those pretty women who at different times have chosen to walk into this NYPD bomb tech's life? Haven't they filled me with joy; given life purpose? Well, yes, but maybe not in the way you might think. And, sadly, there's no getting around the truth of it, because after only a couple of months or so of us getting to know one another, it's always me that seems to come up short in any relationship.

It's not that any of my girlfriends has ever come right out and told me I can't or won't make a proper commitment, but in one way or another they all tell me there comes a moment, as if out of the clear blue sky, when I look horribly, terribly afraid. Me, the man of action trained to take bombs apart with his bare hands. They all seem to stumble for the right words, but in one way or another they tell me the look on my face literally terrifies them and then starts to haunt them. Even the memory of it fills them with dread. And in the end it's the growing chill inside that kills it dead. Cold always kills. The opposite of love isn't hate, it's fear, and so all the pretty women become ever more frightened. And when people get frightened, and don't know why, they get angrier and angrier and they lash out. Things fall apart. The heart cannot hold.

It confused the hell out of me the first few times it happened, but deep down I suppose I always knew there was no real mystery to it. It's the look my brother's wife, Jackie, had on her face, the day she saw the TV images of the terrorists flying those commercial airliners into each of the Twin Towers, over and over and over again, and the buildings bursting into flames and slowly collapsing, over and over and over again, and her Teddy gone forever, having simply gone off to work that morning. The horror deep-etched into her face from looking over the edge, into the abyss, seeing the tortured mass of steel, concrete, and glass still burning white hot; still spewing dust clouds that plastered tears to cheeks and threatened to choke the life out of every living New Yorker. The look of horror thousands upon thousands of people woke up to every single day for weeks and months and years afterward. Yet, over time, even the deepest pain fades to distant memory; both a curse and a blessing; and people forget and they move on. There are those, though, that can't ever let go; they just learn to mask it. And with me, it seems, there are times when the mask slips and the full horror of that September day is relived anew. *Mea culpa. Mea culpa. Mea maxima culpa.*

I take in the truck's interior. The backpack, briefcase, cardboard files, the bits of plastic rubbish; only ever intended to confuse and cause a bomb tech's heart to flutter; have all been blown to pieces by the P-D, but not all; the pipe bomb remains intact and I see for the first time it's spot-welded to one of the wheel arches. The landscape of threat has been radically altered but is no less deadly. I look at what remains of the primary device and see that the lead-lined box has been split open at one end; enough to reveal the rat's nest of wires inside. I close down that part of my imagination that fears for my own mortality; look without focusing to see if anything else presents itself as unusual; and try to see inside the mind of the bomb maker. My only task, at that precise moment in time, to identify something, anything, that might clue me into some "known." The different bomb-making techniques used in Northern Ireland, Iraq, Afghanistan; in Israel, Spain, Russia; and almost every other country around the globe; are all known. Bombs that have exploded and brought bloody terror to London, Madrid, Belfast, Baghdad, Tel Aviv, Moscow, Mumbai, and Kabul have all left unique signatures and every scrap of knowledge has been gathered and recorded; all of them now "knowns." I wonder which of those "knowns" now await me here.

Some years later I bumped into Jackie, on Fifth Avenue, outside a grand hotel, steps from St. Patrick's. She was with her new perfect husband and their two perfect little boys; the perfect husband, to my eye, no match for Teddy, but by the look of him, a definite contender. Even I couldn't damn her for that; everyone does what he or she needs to do to survive. She saw me see her trying to avoid seeing me. Then she looked at me, deliberately, and stared for what seemed an eternity. She ushered her new perfect family further up Fifth, in the direction of the park, and turned and walked toward me. Still impossibly beautiful; tall, slim, willowy; camel coat, shoes, handbag; so chic, so elegant; her expensive silk scarf a perfect complement to her shoulder-length blond hair; as flawless as ever I'd seen her; the uptown girl of every man's fantasy.

She looked me up and down; took in my shoes, clothes, and wristwatch. She shook her head, the curtains of her hair moving in perfect time, and told me in no uncertain terms it was a heinous crime for me to spend my whole life trying to be like my brother. I shot back; said I was very much my own man, thank you; and that I'd fought long and hard, every single fucking day, for years, in the Marines, in pursuit of the very people who'd carried out the attacks on 9/11. For some reason I even felt the need to tell her I'd joined the NYPD Bomb Squad, the moment I got back from Iraq, to continue with the fight. The bitch didn't even miss a beat. "You still won't be better than Teddy, you facing death, on purpose, Bobby, every single time you go try to dismantle some stupid asshole bomb," she said. "Teddy's gone forever, Bobby. He's never coming back. Get over it. Go get a life, why don't you, before it's too damn late?"

She fucking blew me away. And as I watched her walk out of my life, again, I just stood there blinking, like a stunned survivor of a bomb blast, my mouth opening and closing, gasping for air, still not believing what'd just happened.

It's true. I worshipped Teddy. I hated him. I envied him. I loved him.

I needed him. I wanted to be like him. And, like him, I'll never know when it happens, not even as it happens, the blast will move much too fast for me even to register, let alone respond to. And it will happen, one day; I know it will; it's simply a question of when.

But I ask you—is it a crime to walk in a dead man's shoes?

As I walk the Long Walk, nothing but the scratchy noise of the respirator in my ears, the world reduced to what I can see through my visor, it's not for me to ponder why someone has built this bomb whose only purpose is to spread terror. I have no time to curse or hate. It's not for me to condemn anyone. Whether "the package" represents present danger from enemies foreign or domestic; from without or from within; my only task is to defuse and/or demolish any and all rogue explosive ordnance brought into my city, my homeland; that and nothing more. The rest I leave to the politicians and to fate. You go mad otherwise.

I know I can face the very worst the world's worst terrorists can conjure up and even contemplate the beginning and the end fused into a single moment again as happened that fateful September day. And I can do so without giving way to fear. Love may conquer all, but not all fears. Love opens you up to fear in ways unimaginable before that love ever took hold of your heart. I can walk into the mouth of hell every single day, but I will not take a woman or child I love in there with me. Nor will I ever put a woman in a position where she believes her only path to continued happiness is by my side. For me that's a nonstarter. So I've chosen to live alone and alone I will stay. It's my battle to win or lose, then, even though I admit it's not at all a path I ever imagined I'd seek out for myself.

And so my entire life; the best of times, the worst of times; all the people and events that have formed and framed my life within its sudden-seeming all-too-brief span; comes down to a lead-lined box, not much bigger than the one my last pair of Nikes came in, split open at one end to reveal a digital timer with its face smashed. And beneath the tangle of wires, which after some gentle twisting, pulling, and prodding I see are attached to nothing but themselves; I come at last to an exposed blasting cap connected to four different-colored electrical wires; three if I count the yellow one I've just cut; two, once I've cut the green. Two wires, then, red and black; one the color of life, the other of death; and the eternal clock still ticking down; digital or analog; sand falling through an hourglass; it's no matter at all to me now, as all time is relative. And I feel the wire hot in my blood; taste the stale air in my face mask; and catch the salt tears starting to sting my eyes. Are we our memories? Is that all we are? Ever were? Will ever be?

*What lies behind us and what lies before us are small matters compared to what lies within us.* Ralph Waldo Emerson wrote that. I know. I must've read that old quote a thousand times on the tiny brass plaque on the bookcase that stood next to my father's armchair. Even though there was no way, back then, I could fully understand the true wisdom contained in those words, they always hit home. And never more so than when I was a teenager desperately trying to find my own way out. The words still hit home. When all else is dead and gone, it's what lies within that truly counts. How else can you ever know why you are, who you are? Why you do what you do? Why even though what you do may appear as a crime to others, those same events, when seen from where you stand, point to the only possible path open to you? And you must always be true to yourself. Right?

One day, after one of my visits to the New York Public Library, on Fifth, I visited with my dad, at his office, at One Police Plaza, in the hope I could get a ride home; he wasn't in, but on his desk, another brass plaque, more Emerson: *He has not learned the lesson of life who does not every day surmount a fear.*

Truly, is there really any other way to live?

Yet no one asked my brother, Teddy, if he could take the worst; nor was it asked of anyone else who died in the Twin Towers, or of any of their surviving family members; or of anyone else in New York. Death was visited, on all, from above; without warning, without pity, and without remorse; by unforgiving strangers from strangely unforgiving lands. It's no way for anyone to die.

After that first dreadful year, following 9/11, Jackie went out of her way not to see my father or me. We'd always been worlds apart, anyway, but her putting distance between us—and events in New York—was, I'm sure, the only way she thought she could take back control of her life. So she relocated to another city, on another coast; found herself a new husband; and had the children she never had with Teddy. The falling Towers broke her into a million pieces, too, and the dense clouds of grief smothered and killed whatever love she'd once had for Teddy. Everything became dead ground.

That's why, once she'd sold the house in Brooklyn, she got rid of everything of Teddy's that would in any way remind her of him. That's why she let me have anything of his I wanted; any and all of his personal things; and I took everything, literally. All his books; his CDs and DVDs; all of which arrived at my Brooklyn apartment in stacks and stacks of neatly lettered moving boxes. Everything of his for me to read and/or listen to; at last for me to know the secret heart of him; so he could live again, inside me. I even inherited his collection of vintage Rolex wristwatches; his purple silk ties; his suits, his shirts, his sweaters, most of which fit me, for a time, anyway, until I bulked up a bit. His shoes still fit. Like his suits, they were the kind of shoes I could never have afforded. English.

French. Belgian. Handmade. I know there were women who had given me a look, then a date, only because of those shoes, those clothes. I never minded that. In fact, I wore it well.

What I do still mind, though, every single second of every single day, is a big brother gone forever, blown all over the island of Manhattan. Knowing that the emptiness that followed can never be filled; no bedrock ever solid enough to build a future upon; only shifting sands, no matter how deep you dig down. So, yes, it's true, I did rush to fill the hole inside me; my own personal Ground Zero. All I could do was try to fill up the huge gaping hole with the best of him and the worst of him. His was a different generation; different hopes, different dreams; different music; different rock stars, film stars, sports heroes, but they all became my heroes, too, just as he had always been.

There are times when I can do nothing but rip off my blast helmet and push down the protective collar and go throw up before I can even start to remove the rest of the bomb suit. Afterward, I always seem to catch myself, for an instant, reflected in a vehicle's wing mirror or blacked-out window and I just stare and stare and have to really think hard whose face it is. Is it Teddy? Or is it me? And when death comes, as it does to us all, will it honestly really matter?

I saw for myself that Teddy never let anyone or anything stand in his way. In everything he ever did, every goal he ever set himself, he was single-minded, fearless; he just went for it, hell for leather, damn the torpedoes. He was like that in high school. I know, because I went to Bishop Ford, too, and they were still telling stories about him when I was there. He was the one to emulate, the one to follow. I'm sure he was just the same at Holy Cross and Dartmouth, and then on Wall Street. I didn't need my father to tell me that staying focused was how Teddy always succeeded, but he did, at every single, sad, sorry opportunity.

And me? I was always the big disappointment. I was hotheaded

Bobby, hot-tempered Bobby; always-getting-into-hot-water Bobby; no hell's kitchen ever too hot for our damn Bobby.

And maybe that's the one thing that ever truly separated us.

We were fire and ice. Eternal opposites.

Though I do admit I seem to have grown so very, very, very much colder since the Twin Towers fell.

For the inescapable truth is I chose the road I traveled by; it was not the road that Teddy took, but it might just as well have been.

They say your whole life passes before you at the moment of death.

They're wrong, even if by no more than a few milliseconds; for I am already dead before I cut the bloodred wire. Blown to smithereens by the blast triggered by what lay hidden deep inside; my fate forever sealed by the lie beneath the lie; the falsehood now fully revealed; the father, the son, the brother, if never quite the twin; my death mask, but a momentary reflection of what lies inside the ever outwardly expanding heart.

# DOUBLE JEOPARDY

## BY STEVE BERRY

He stood before the machine, studying the chrome switch marked ON/OFF, mustering the courage to end his son's life.

The boy lay on the bed, the once-adorable face obscured by thick white bandages, just a nose and tiny mouth visible, blue lips clutching an oxygen feed. Only the respirator, standing before him, allowed the child's six-year-old lungs to accept each breath.

The brain was gone.

That was what the doctor had said yesterday. She'd tried to be gentle, knowing the situation, but how do you gently tell a man that his only child had no chance? At least Kristen had died instantly, spared the agony of having her body kept alive when no semblance of life remained. Only three days had passed since their new Navigator, driven by Kristen, careened off Highway 16 into an oak tree. The air bag deployed but did little to stop the engine from slamming through the passenger compartment, killing her and horribly maiming Marty. The boy's thin body was burned and battered, nearly every bone broken, yet somehow he'd survived long enough to make it to the hospital so doctors could connect him to the machines.

For seventy-two hours he'd stood beside Marty's bed, delaying

Kristen's funeral as he anguished. His options had been made clear earlier by a hospital counselor.

What an interesting service.

Someone to help when the plug needed to be pulled.

The wiry older man had offered little advice, simply agreeing with the obvious. The need for such a service was clear—risk containment—since it was bad for business to have grieving families filing lawsuits claiming that overanxious doctors and cost-conscious administrators had rushed them to judgment. The counselor was the patient's advocate, supposedly speaking only for Marty, urging caution but never discouraging the inevitable.

And that was the problem.

Everything had become painfully obvious.

Marty had, for all intents and purposes, been dead for three days. There'd not been a sign of life, except what the machine forced upon his damaged organs. A finger placed within his tiny palm brought no response. Where before his son had clutched the offering and held on while they crossed the street or found their car in a parking lot, here there was nothing.

He stared down at Marty.

God, he'd miss him.

He was a blessing in every sense, something neither he nor Kristen had expected. She was nearing forty and he was approaching fifty, and they'd tried for decades to have children, without success. The doctors had offered little hope—age and nature were working against them—but they kept trying and, finally, Marty was born. They loved each other, got along wonderfully, even worked together every day. He practiced law and she made sure the office ran smoothly. Clients called her most times instead of him. Everyone loved her. It was hard not to. Friends wondered how they could be together so much.

He'd not even had time to grieve for Kristen yet.

Marty had delayed that.

It seemed he'd bury them together, side by side, in a plot under more oaks near the ocean. The thought wrenched his stomach and he felt his knees weaken.

No time for that.

Marty needed him.

The doctor said that once he switched off the machine the end would come fast, so everyone had retreated to give him privacy. Kristen's parents stood out in the hall, respectful of his task. His own parents had long been dead. Marty and Kristen were all the family he had. Crying had never come easy for him, and he could not recall the last time a tear had formed in his eyes. Now, suddenly, rivulets started to flow.

Last Christmas they'd taken Marty to see *The Nutcracker*. Marty had worn a precious new suit bought specially for the occasion and had been enthralled by the spectacle. For days afterward he'd imitated the dancers and hummed the tunes. He was proud that his son appreciated art. Such a bright little boy.

But now...

In a few minutes his son would be dead and a part of him would die, too, just as a different part of him had been extinguished three days ago when he'd been required to identify his wife's mangled body. After, he'd tried to flush the blood and disfigurement from his thoughts, remembering her as the beautiful woman she'd always been.

The same was now true for Marty.

He wanted to think of him as a blond-haired, violet-eyed little boy with all the energy and enthusiasm life, opportunity, and privilege bestowed. Maybe he would have one day become a lawyer, taking over the practice. Then again, perhaps he would have chosen another career, something that made him happy. Either was fine. He'd given him life, and all he ever wanted was for him to succeed. Now he would give him death.

He stroked the child's head.

"The best boy in the whole world," he whispered.

That was what he'd always told him, since Marty was an infant, held in his arms at three in the morning. Or when they'd played together in the backyard—hide-and-seek was Marty's favorite. Or when the boy had brought home from preschool a picture painted just for Dad. It was never anything recognizable, mostly smears of paint, but to a father they were masterpieces.

He recalled the last time he spoke to his son. Three mornings ago as he headed out the door for work. Marty was finishing off a bowl of Apple Jacks at the kitchen table. Kristen was dressing and would soon follow him to the office, after dropping Marty at school. He'd kissed the child on his forehead and told him they'd do something fun that evening. Maybe ride bikes around the neighborhood. Marty had only recently mastered a two-wheeler with training wheels. He recalled the smile and the words he'd said.

*"The best boy—"*

*"—in the whole world," Marty finished.*

He'd started doing that lately. Accustomed to the phrase. Always smiling back at him when he completed the sentence. It was something between them, special for a father and son.

His gaze stayed locked on his son.

"The best boy in the whole world," he mouthed again.

He wondered what he'd done to deserve the misery life seemed to have imposed. Four days ago things were good. He was having the best year ever. Money was plentiful, the bills low, they were planning a trip to Disney World in the fall. Every day for the past month, while fighting sleep at night, Marty had scanned the resort's brochure in his bed.

He turned back to the machine and knew what he had to do. Just a flick of a switch. He tried to imagine what the feeling would be like as he watched Marty die, and the terror of that vision kept his hand frozen at his side. He thought of Kristen and wondered how all this had happened. The police had offered little in the way of explanation. The day was clear, the roadbed dry, their car in good repair. Something must have distracted her, the authorities concluded, and she'd momentarily lost control, enough that the vehicle left the asphalt and found a tree. She knew the road, had driven it hundreds of times. On that day—just a simple errand to the grocery store, on the way home from picking Marty up at school, for some sour cream so she could make stroganoff for dinner. He loved her version. Pink from red wine and always served over rice since he didn't particularly care for pasta.

The thought of food turned his stomach.

He'd not eaten in two days.

He sucked a breath and steadied himself.

His son did not deserve to die, and he did not deserve for his son to be taken. But circumstances had assumed control. Kristen was gone and Marty was about to be. Was it that they had challenged nature? Become pregnant when they shouldn't? Was nature striking back? It sure seemed that way. For this case, this trial, he would not walk away with the dispassionate objectivity of a lawyer doing his job. This time the verdict was against *him*.

And he would pay the price.

He reached for the switch.

A spark of static electricity popped as his fingers touched the metal. The shock caused him to yank his hand back, as if the machine were telling him no, not now, not yet.

But he knew better.

Act before his courage vanished.

He touched the switch again.

No spark this time.

He closed his eyes, bit his lower lip, and with tears streaming down both cheeks he flicked the toggle down.

Ten seconds passed.

Twenty seconds.

Marty's chest heaved. A groan seeped from the boy's mouth and for an instant he wanted to reengage the respirator, but the doctor had warned him that the body would labor until it realized there was no brain. Ignore the pleas, he was told, and let nature take its course.

Damn nature.

Another moan and his heart pounded.

The chest collapsed. Shivers racked the child's limbs.

The sight clawed at his heart.

Then, nothing.

Color drained from the skin and a sickening silence signaled Marty was gone.

He bent down and lightly kissed the child's bandage.

"The best boy..."

But he couldn't finish.

He turned and stared at the door leading to the hall. Framed in the rectangular window were the tearful faces of Kristen's mother and father as they watched their grandson die.

The box lay on the table beside the bed. Silver, wrapped with red ribbon and a bow, which he'd brought with him earlier. He slowly tugged on the ribbon, unwrapped the bow, and opened the lid. Wrestling one last burst of courage from his fear, he reached inside and gripped the gun. A semiautomatic, bought years ago for late nights at the office. It had never left the drawer in his desk until today.

He turned back toward the bed, never let his eyes leave the boy, and raised the barrel to his head.

The door of the room swung open and someone screamed *No*.

But his finger was already pulling the trigger.

And his last thought was a hope.

That God was indeed merciful.

# THE SECRET LIFE OF BOOKS

## BY ANGELA GERST

Oh no, I'm not working....I do my tapestry
and play cards....
—COLETTE, IN A LETTER TO A FRIEND

Colette set aside the Parker pen she'd bought twelve years and a lifetime ago when she could still walk and even dance a few slow steps. Before she reconstructed her story, every event that preceded the murder must be replayed in her mind, starting with that first cold rain.

Paris rain sent signals. Sometimes it sounded like the radio hissing in code, or scratching fingers, or furtive pebbles thrown against a window. That day it had whispered like a ghost with a secret. Ignoring the pain, she'd dragged herself across the divan and opened the glass doors to the balustrade. From the gardens rose a mixed essence of iron and hyacinth, flor-metallica, the kernel of spring. She could almost taste it. Something stirred along her knotted spine, something light and quick.

Far below, umbrellas were popping open all over the Palais Royal. There was the countess Liane unfurling her chartreuse lampshade, fringed no less. Two steps behind, Liane's dull young husband scuttled after her Pekingese. Hah, the purse, the prince, and the pooch. But Colette's dry little smile faded when she spotted Jules Roland zagging toward the arcade. A parcel teetered on his palm. Oh, Lord, he's bringing me lunch. "Quick, Pauline! Roland is coming!"

Her housekeeper appeared in the doorway, thick gray hair slipping from its pins, one cheek slightly puffed, as if a toothache had blossomed. In her hand was the ice pack Colette had insisted she use to keep the swelling down.

The doorbell rang.

"Fast, isn't he, for an overblown chef?" Colette's laugh was brightly malicious. "Tell him I'm away, on the high seas with Maurice."

"But, Madame, you agreed to see him. He telephoned yesterday from the Petit Corsair."

"*Always* his restaurant. I may be forgetful, but there's a sameness about his talk. He condemns his rivals. He denounces the black market. Two notes, both flat." She reached for her tapestry. "And his madeleines! I'd rather dunk shoes in my coffee. Accept his gift if it looks good, then show him the back of your hand."

"Eat my supper, sing my song." Pauline pressed the ice pack to her cheek. "The concierge adores him."

"Because he feeds her, too."

The bell rang more sharply this time.

"Madame!"

"All right, bring him in, the fat old bore." Her laughter erupted again, coarse as a crow's. Colette had always admired those intelligent birds. "And I'm sure he says the same about me."

"No one could call you a bore, Madame."


"Ortolans! In April! You are too kind."

"No, no. It is you who are kind." Still in his damp coat, Roland arranged five grilled songbirds on the tray Pauline had set out.

"Cover them. I won't lunch for an hour yet." Roland could have his fifteen minutes, but she was damned if she would eat with him. He reeked of mothballs. And that moustache! It made him look like a pimp. She caught his irritated glance. A peevish pimp, with razor scrapes on his neck.

Soundlessly he placed a dome over the birds, his pulpy fingers leaving smears on the silver. Colette tried to imagine those hands caressing her, and from the depths of her soul she, who had savored all that the body offers, shuddered.

"The only ortolans in Paris," Roland was saying. "Yesterday I bought twenty off a hunter at an outrageous price." But I bring the best to you, said the silky smile. "I spend Sundays in the country—Barimonde."

Was that appalling grin an allusion to the well-known fact that she hailed from Saint-Sauveur, a stone's throw from Barimonde? Were they, God help her, compatriots? From her raft, as she called the divan, she pulled the table closer and picked up her wine. A speck of politeness forced her to offer Roland a glass, too.

He settled into a chair and unbuttoned the coat she had no intention of proposing he remove. "I beg pardon for disturbing you, but I have a favor to ask." Implicit were the words: And I have been sending you truffles and foie gras and raspberries all through the war and these two years after.

Yes, she thought, Pauline is right. I have indeed eaten Roland's supper. "If I can help you, I will."

"Oh, Madame, you'll be the making of me!" His hands clutched each other—red kitchen scars, larval whiteness. "Raymond Oliver will twist in the wind."

"If you expect me to injure the greatest chef—"

"I express myself badly. Certainly Oliver is a genius. But the Palais Royal can support two chefs of genius."

"What do you want from me, Monsieur Roland?"

"Come to my wedding on Saturday."

Astonishment froze her tongue. Who would marry that moustache? Whoever the woman, Colette knew she herself would be the prize, flaunted like spoils of war. Her name would be yoked to Roland and his restaurant, and Colette well understood the power of her name. The princes of Monaco worshipped her brilliance. Sartre sat at her feet. The press would erupt. Crowds would rush to dine at Petit Corsair. Raymond Oliver would never forgive her.

A stark image cut through her thoughts: her wheelchair. "I leave my apartment only for literary occasions. Ask something else."

There was no disappointment in Roland's face. The pimp had anticipated her refusal. "Then may I name my new dessert after you? And, as I am a photographer, may I take a picture of you?"

"Photography, too? Bravo!"

He coughed delicately. "Perhaps eating it?"

His sly eagerness offended her more than his enterprise. Still, one session and it would be over. No public appearance. No wheelchair. And afterward, no more gifts. She would insist on Cartier-Bresson. An amateur's snapshot must not distort the careful image she presented to the world: wisdom shining from ancient eyes that said, Even wisdom isn't the end of me.

"Your dessert must have marzipan and meringue," she improvised. "And cherries."

"Certainly." His spongy fingers smoothed that despicable moustache. "One more thing—my bride. May I bring her to meet you? She would be gratified that a woman of such grandeur is my friend."

The only answer to this was a rude noise. Colette chose silence.

"Gisele is young," Roland went on in a gluey voice.

"How young?"

"She'll be eighteen in October."

"Seventeen, then."

"But she's a real woman, tall, intelligent. She has read all your books."

"All?"

He frowned as if so many questions threatened him.

"How do you know this clever young woman?"

"Her parents are suppliers of mine. The war was hard on them, both sons lost, barns destroyed. Recently I loaned them enough to keep their farms going—no interest until they're back on their feet. They agree I have much to offer their little Gisele."

"And little Gisele? How does she feel about marrying her grandfather?"

"Madame! I am only forty-seven! And it's all the same to Gisele, she said so herself."

"Well, then. By all means, bring me your bride."

A satisfied Roland buttoned his coat. As soon as the door hit his heels, Colette lifted the dome and, with a few passes of her knife and fork and her remaining teeth, crunched down the ortolans. Not superb, but quite good, really. And for once Roland hadn't bored her. After coffee, she settled back with her papers and pen. Tapestry could wait until tomorrow or, if she captured her story, the day after.

Monday ended as it began, on her raft in the rain, her blue lamp burning a hole in the dark. Tuesday washed into Wednesday. The sun came out. All week Colette's fingers roamed restlessly between her needle and her pen. On Friday Maurice's telegram arrived at breakfast, which Pauline served with a scarf tied around her swollen face.

"He'll be home in seven weeks." Colette passed her the telegram, but Pauline was in too much pain to read it. "And if you don't get to the dentist I'll pull that tooth myself." She clacked the sugar tongs at Pauline.

"Maybe tomorrow."

"Idiot! Today the abscess bursts and tomorrow you're dead of blood poisoning." Colette snatched up the telephone and arranged for Dr. Delibert to see Pauline at eleven.

"But your lunch—"

"Ask Madame Boyer to bring me some little thing. She can take care of dinner, too. By the time Delibert gets through with you, you'll need a month in the country."

"Oh, please stop!"

"Just teasing, my dear. Delibert is an artist."

*   *   *

Madame Boyer poked her frizzy orange head around the door. "I've brought you an omelet and a few early radishes." Although the concierge insisted she couldn't linger, she accepted a glass of wine.

Colette ate quickly, running bread around her plate to capture whatever her fork had missed. "Wonderful! You're a subtler cook than most professionals—Roland, for example." Her praise was meant to inspire. She didn't want another omelet for supper.

"Roland is an assassin."

"True, his coulibiac smacks of murder." Colette recalled Roland's attempt, as soggy as a wet sock. "But when he cooks simply—baked foie gras, grilled ortolans—the goodness comes through. Roland knows what's good, give him that. When he finds it he twitches like a divining rod. That child bride had better—"

Madame Boyer stood up. "I can't stay."

"Finish your wine. Nobody expects you to be on duty every minute."

"Nobody expects anything of me." She dropped back into the chair, her eyes too bright for that little bit of wine she'd dipped her beak in.

"A man?"

Boyer nodded.

"Not…"

"Roland. Yes. We were to be married when I'd saved enough to invest in his restaurant. He's expanding. I was to take charge of his staff." She began to moan. "And now he's thrown me over for a—a *pissant*!"

"Pull yourself together! You're not the first woman tossed aside by a man. Have you given him money?"

The orange head jerked up. "Are you mad?"

"It's purely an affair of the heart?"

This triggered an explosion of sobs, so unbecoming in a woman Boyer's age, at least forty, and a widow to boot. Colette herself had never shed a public tear. Not when Willy left. Not when he sold her rights to the Claudines. For a sou. Not when her mother died. She topped up Boyer's glass. There was no wine for omelets or broken dreams. This soft Vouvray would have to do. "Tell me about it," she said, indulging her avidity, her fever to know, which still raged after seventy-four years of probing the universe. Perhaps Boyer had something new to add to the annals of inconstant love.

It took half an hour, but in the end, out came the same old story: Who gives most is drained and abandoned. Colette stifled her yawn. The ardent concierge would survive, even thrive; she was already planning her own bistro on the cheaper side of the Palais.

By Sunday afternoon Pauline had recovered enough to serve coffee and those incomparable napoleons when the countess dropped by with her Pekingese. At sixty-five, her years eased by couture, spas, balms, Liane was the youngest and richest of Colette's friends from her music hall days.

"Where's Henri?" Colette inquired.

"Communing with his horse. Day and night he rides in the Bois. Alone. My spine can't take it anymore." Boredom filled every powdered line in Liane's face. Only the jewels on her fingers winked with life.

"Spend more time on your back," Colette advised. "In the old days how you loved the jab of a man's spur."

"Pain, joy. Who can tell them apart? Right, Topaz?" The countess leaned toward the dog at her feet and stroked his throat until his liquid eyes drooped.

If age sat lightly on Liane, Colette's years were impossible to hide. Passive resistance was all she could muster: scarves, lipstick, the warmth of her intelligent eyes. Not that time had diminished her essence. Her grip was strong, her hair as lively as bedsprings. And, as she had informed Marcel Proust fifty years ago, her soul was stuffed with red beans and bacon rind.

"Now, *this* is joy." Liane dug into the golden crust. "Roland is a genius."

"Wrong." Colette loved to contradict countesses. "Raymond Oliver made the napoleons." As any gastronome could tell. But Liane's forte was jewelry. In food as in men she had no taste at all.

"Those two. Always sending me treats." Pastry cream clung to Liane's lips. "Though I prefer Roland's. He's better looking than Oliver."

"With that moustache? Ugh. He got married yesterday, poor girl."

"Married? The rascal never said a word!" Liane waved a hand, airy as a silk scarf, and her sleeve fell back, exposing a gold bracelet six inches wide and studded with rubies.

Colette couldn't tear her eyes away. "What a glorious cuff! It has a sado-maso quality I adore. Let me try it on."

Liane's arm stayed just out of Colette's reach. "It brings bad luck. It belonged to a Gypsy, who sold it to a princess, who sold it to me. Only the owner can wear it."

"That magnificent clasp! A fish?"

"Mermaid, and put down your hand. Even a touch brings grief. Speaking of which"—Liane covered her arm—"how long will your dear husband be away?"

"Too long." Colette explained that Maurice was promoting her books in the world's richest land, "now that Europe has again reduced itself to ashes."

"My darling Colette"—Liane helped herself to more coffee—"nobody reads in America."

"Oh, but there are so many of them, even nobody is ten thousand."

Nights, Colette worked on her story, writing and rewriting, never closing on the end. Like her long-ago cats, she slept in snatches. Every morning from her window she watched the day break, earlier and earlier as the equinox drew near. She could set her clock by who was moving below: the dairyman at five-thirty, followed twenty minutes later by Madame Boyer with her market basket. At an unfashionable seven, Liane's Henri left for the Bois in his riding clothes. At eight, around the time the concierge staggered home under the weight of those endless cabbages, Colette had her first cup of coffee and a slice of bread. Page by page, the days passed. Outside, the gardens grew tender and hazy, with shoots of penstemon rising like dark green exclamation points at the ends of pastel sentences.

Three weeks after his ortolan visit, Roland introduced the bride to the monument. "My wife is a compatriot of yours, Madame."

Gisele was taller than her husband and self-conscious in her blue and white Sunday best. A rash on her chin marred her prettiness, but cornflower eyes lay shyly in her oval face, and when she said, "Proud to meet you, I'm sure," her rolling *r*s were pure Burgundy.

Colette used her tenderest voice. "What village, my dear?"

"Barimonde." In Gisele's mouth, the word sounded as final as death.

"Ah, yes. Me, I left Saint-Sauveur half a century ago. For this!" Colette swept an arm toward the glass doors. "Tell me, Gisele, does Paris please you?"

Shrug.

"The gardens?"

"Very small."

"You like animals?" Not many farm girls did.

Shrug.

"But you've read my *Barks and Purrs*?"

"It was required at school."

At her nape, held there by tiny combs, Gisele wore a twisted braid thick enough to uncoil to her heels, exactly like Colette's when she first came to Paris, a barely fledged country bride on the arm of potbellied, middle-aged Willy.

It was the braid that decided her. She would win over this raw young compatriot, who couldn't possibly love her husband. Perhaps she could smooth the girl's way, help her discover that love wasn't everything, or even necessary. Although at twenty, hadn't she been deeply in love with Willy? Love was important starting out. Love launched one. Well, she would do what she could.

"Never mind tea," she said to Pauline, who had rattled in with a tray. "We want chocolates and champagne. Use the etched glasses."

Vintage Clicquot and sweets lightened Roland at least. He devoured nougatines and proposed endless toasts: to his magnificent friend, to his obedient bride, to his new dessert, to his restaurant. By the time he reached *la France!* his cheeks had pinked up. A jolly pimp today.

They discussed Cerises Colette, the fabled dessert, and Colette laid down conditions—a new dress for herself, a travel allowance for Cartier-Bresson—and while they settled the details, Gisele munched handfuls of hazelnut brittle and guzzled champagne. Later Colette played piano, music hall tunes easy on her fingers. To her surprise, the country bride played, too, a few pieces by Schumann.

When long shadows filled the gardens and the fountain lights flickered on, Pauline brought the coats.

"Will you visit me again?" Colette asked.

Roland beamed. "With pleasure."

"Not you. Your wife, when you're busy in your restaurant. She'll be lonely then."

"I'm supposed to help in the kitchen," Gisele said.

Colette turned a hard eye on Roland, who was sliding Gisele's coat over her shoulders. "Monsieur Roland! Your wife is not a galley slave. Her music needs work. And books! This is Paris. She must keep up. I myself will be happy to read with her of an afternoon."

Gisele frowned. "I don't want—"

Roland squeezed her elbow so tightly she gasped. The scars on his hand burned red at the bone. "My wife will be pleased to visit whenever you call."

Twice that week Colette and Gisele met over coffee and chocolates. Gisele stuffed herself but refused to play the piano again because "it makes me sad."

When Colette talked about Willy or her famous friends, Gisele listened with unfeigned interest, but if books were brought out, or even the newspaper, she stared at the windows. "I have never enjoyed reading," she said blithely to the only woman ever elected to the Academy Goncourt.

"You must read more. Reading leads to reading. There's a novel you'd enjoy—*The Irish Harp* by Germaine Beaumont. It's a grand Gothic romance of the sort I would write if only I could. On the second shelf."

Gisele slouched over and studied the rows of lettered spines. There was a wary look in her peasant's eye, but also a desire to please. "If I must read," she sighed, "I prefer this." She took down a copy of *The Innocent Libertine*. "At least you wrote it."

"In spite of the title, my novel may bore you," Colette warned. "Now let's have a nice game of piquet."


Why am I wasting my time with this illiterate girl? Colette asked herself at the end of the week. There were Goncourt Prize submissions to plow through, roses to stitch. Her new story was languishing. She wondered if her unconscious mind was preparing a coda to *Gigi*—the after-the-happily-ever-after—Gisele her model.

She dismissed the notion. It was hardly unconscious if she could describe it. More likely, she was playing at mother, since her own daughter rarely came to call. Or pretending the indifferent Gisele was the ghost of her own young self.

Next visit, perhaps sensing Colette's withdrawal, Gisele confided her longing to escape the apartment over the restaurant. "I'm dying. He won't let me out, except to visit you."

Truly, Gisele's complexion had worsened, pale as winter endive. She was standing with her back to the balustrade, cocooned in a sweater. "He thinks he owns me."

"My first husband owned me, in a way," Colette confessed. "I was so young and in love I didn't mind. Until I grew up and discovered the difference between being owned and being possessed."

"There is no difference. And I hate it." Gisele's face turned cold and blank. Colette had once seen a farmer with that face, cramming corn down the throat of a goose.

From her raft, she formed a sudden impression that a spider had crept onto Gisele's wrist. "What is that?" She grabbed Gisele's arm and pushed up her sleeve. Blue-black contusions stained the white skin. "He beats you?"

"When he's angry he pinches my arms and neck."

Two things were clear to Colette, who understood danger: Pinches lead to slaps, and this country girl was pining. She sent Gisele home with a pocketful of chocolates, then telephoned Roland.

"Your wife has hurt herself." She cut off his surprised effusions. "Poor little thing insisted she fell, but there are bruises in the oddest places; do you follow me, Monsieur Roland?"

He did.

"Lack of fresh air makes her dizzy. You must let her out for long walks in the Bois every day." When he hesitated, she added, "Is it next Wednesday that Cartier-Bresson is supposed to photograph the cherries and me?"

Roland needed no more than this quiet reminder of her power to give, and more to the point, to take away.

That night when sleep wouldn't come Colette revisited her childhood in the fields and forests of Saint-Sauveur, where she and her brothers had wandered from dawn until dusk, in every season. How necessary it was for her mother's savage children to roam. Even now, flooded by pain she never acknowledged, Colette could smell the almond husks, taste the ice and dust of Lancet's brook, feel the garter snake, electric in her hand.

By her third day of freedom, Gisele's complexion was verging on roses. "The Bois is full of lakes," she chirped to Colette. "The Count de Rossat showed me."

"You know Henri?" From her window this morning, Colette

had watched Gisele cross the gardens at the same time as Liane's husband. A coincidence, she'd thought.

"He and the countess often have supper at the Petit Corsair. The countess is very kind, always asking for me." Gisele plopped down across from Colette. "Is Henri really a count?"

"As a matter of fact, he is. He's got the title, she's got the money. The perfect marriage. They're wild about each other, so Liane says." Colette smirked, but Gisele didn't notice.

"Piquet?" Gisele tore open a new pack of cards and set to work.

"You shuffle like a sharper," Colette said, watching cards and fingers fly. "I mean that as a compliment."

"I've begun *The Innocent Libertine*."

"Is that so?" Colette lifted an eyebrow.

Gisele blushed.

A single piercing shriek interrupted Wednesday's first cup of coffee. From outside? Colette couldn't tell, and Pauline had gone to the apothecary. Somewhere below, a door slammed, followed by a brief silence, then more shrieks. Curiosity finally drove Colette to hobble on her canes to the balustrade, where she watched a kitchen boy from Petit Corsair gallop across the gardens and disappear into her building. Excited voices followed, and seconds later Pauline burst into the room, accompanied by a breathless Madame Boyer.

"Oh, God, oh, God." A feathered go-to-market hat fluttered against the concierge's orange curls. "I found him! Me! Why me?"

"Found who?"

"Cherries all over everywhere!"

"Will someone kindly tell me what's going on?"

"Roland is dead!"

"Have you called the police?"

Curls and feathers nodded.

"Where—"

"Lying in the alcove," Pauline said. "Stabbed through the heart."

"With his own fruit knife." Madame Boyer groaned. "I recognized the handle." Her eyes darted from Colette to Pauline. "The kitchen boy told me everything started at two this morning when Pauline rang up the Petit Cor—"

"I did no such thing!"

"Well, he thought it was you. Both boys sleep near the pantry, but nothing wakes the little one." A tear dribbled down Boyer's nose. Her story came in garbled bits that Colette reassembled in her orderly mind:

The woman who called herself Pauline had an urgent message about the photo session. Roland must arrive at seven, not nine. He must bring two Cerises Colette and ingredients for a third.

"Ah, the cherries," Colette said.

"The foyer is littered with them!" Madame Boyer rushed on. "And Roland was supposed to come alone because Madame hates a crowd in the kitchen."

"That's absurd." Colette threw out her hands. "I love a crowd."

"I'm only repeating what Pauline—"

"Are you deaf? It wasn't me called the kitchen boy."

"If people are going to keep butting—"

"Go on. We won't say another word."

"Yes, well, the woman who called herself Pauline said she knew it was short notice and extra work, but there'd be a publicity bonus. Madame herself wanted to make the dessert. She intended to whip the meringue, and Cartier-Bresson would photograph this historic event."

"Whip meringue? With my arms?" The blue lamp swayed over Colette's head, and she pushed it aside. "That my name should be dragged into this."

"What about me!" Anger overcame the fear in Pauline's eyes. "How could those idiots believe such monstrous lies?"

"Because the monstrous is so often true. Look at Europe." Colette folded a pillow under her neck. "Or me."

From far off came the whine of police sirens.

"They'll be here any second. Hurry and finish your story."

"I'm talking as fast as I can!" With rough fingers, Madame Boyer tweaked her feathers. "So Roland gets out of bed in the middle of the night and labors until dawn. Anything to promote himself." She tossed her head like an angry rooster. "Just before seven he loads his trolley and walks out to his doom. When I found him I rang his establishment, even before I called the police. Not that his bumpkin bride was at home. Out galavanting like the tart that she is."

A faint knock interrupted her denunciation of Gisele, and the kitchen boy sidled into the room. "P-pardon," he stammered. "The p-police want Madame Boyer."

As he followed the concierge out, Colette noticed bruises like spiders on the back of his neck.

Cartier-Bresson came and went, sorry to lose his session with Colette but thrilled to photograph a crime scene. At ten o'clock, Inspector Ducasse mounted the stairs. A thin man with small eyes, he displayed not a shred of deference in the presence of monuments. There was something disagreeable, even English, about him, Colette thought— maybe the baggy tweeds or the thick-soled, too-serviceable shoes.

While Colette gave her account of Roland, Ducasse frowned at her canes as if he inferred secret stilettos from the curved handles. She used one to hook her workbasket. "Fishing from my raft, Inspector."

He didn't crack a smile.

She found a skein of madder rose and held it to the light. "I often sit by my window. Not much activity this morning. The dairyman. Our concierge off to market. At no time did I see Jules Roland. He must have pushed his trolley beneath the arcade."

She didn't mention that Gisele had left for her walk later than usual. And that Henri hadn't gone for his ride. Let the sour inspector find things out for himself.

Without warning, Ducasse whipped a small cloth out of his pocket. Inside the folds lay a carved ivory comb. "Do you recognize this?"

Colette shook her head. "Should I?"

"It was under Roland's body. Doesn't your protégée wear trinkets like this?"

"Gisele? You'll have to ask *her* what she puts in her hair."

Next, Ducasse struck at Pauline. "You were friendly with Monsieur Jules Roland before his marriage?"

"Certainly. When he came to see Madame I guarded the silver."

Don't be insolent, Colette tried to warn with her eyes.

"You never met privately with him? On your day off? In the evening?"

"Never."

"Was two in the morning your usual time to call him?"

"You're barking up the wrong tree, Inspector. I have never in my life telephoned Jules Roland."

"The kitchen boy swears it was you."

"Slander is a crime in France!"

"So is murder."

With the ferrule of her cane Colette tapped Ducasse's knee. "The boy is mistaken. Pauline was with me. We played cards from midnight until dawn. I'm an insomniac and sometimes she humors me." Colette's Burgundian accent was suddenly as thick as clotted cream. "My Pauline didn't budge from this room."

"Coming from you, I must accept that, Madame. Who besides your immediate household knew about the photography session?"

"The entire Palais Royal, I imagine."

"I imagine so, too." Ducasse sighed.

After he left, Pauline touched Colette's sleeve. "Thank you."

"Not at all, my dear."


Over the next days, Colette watched Ducasse and his men invade the Palais Royal, where each building had its concierge and its theories. Shop owners, residents, street urchins—all passed through the inquisitors' wringer. Pauline hobnobbed everywhere and carried every tale back to Colette.

Other suspects besides Pauline had serviceable alibis:

Raymond Oliver had spent Wednesday in bed with influenza.

Madame Boyer had been haggling over onions in front of all the world.

The kitchen boys, both dotted with Roland's pinch marks, vouched for each other.

Only Gisele's hours roaming the Bois couldn't be verified. On Sunday morning, the police took her away, for questioning, they said. They warned the count not to leave Paris, and that afternoon over coffee Liane fretted out loud to Colette:

"Henri was at his mother's country estate from Tuesday night through Wednesday afternoon. Wasn't he, Topaz?" Liane had left her dog in the arcade and kept stumbling over his absence, now and then leaning down to stroke an empty place near her foot. "But the young widow, now, that one has gained a few francs. Her parents have, too. Did you know Roland held a mortgage on their farms? One hundred hectares of pure gold—truffle oaks, a trout stream, the vineyard."

"Everyone knows he made them an interest-free loan," Colette said. "He loved to lower his eyes and mention his generosity."

"Generosity, my foot! I'm sure he kept a sharp eye on their land. Ready to pounce at the least provocation."

"My dear countess, are you suggesting Roland would have destroyed the parents in order to punish the child?" She watched Liane closely. "For example, are Gisele and Henri having a fling?"

"Heavens, no. Not that I would mind. When Henri and I tied the knot we put flings in the contract." Liane's laugh came from deep in her chest, and Colette knew her old colleague was telling the truth, about her indifference, at least.

"Gisele probably moons over my handsome Henri." Liane widened her eyes, which nevertheless failed to sparkle. "He tells me they often meet after his ride and sit chastely by the lake. He reads to her, one of your books, I believe. That's the beginning and end of their fling. If Gisele murdered her husband, I can assure you my Henri wasn't involved. He's much too lazy for murder."

"Gisele is certainly capable of murder," Colette said. "But we Burgundians kill strictly from passion. We never premeditate."

"Well, there are plenty of other suspects." Liane inclined her supple body toward the raft. "They say your Pauline was madly in love with Roland."

True to herself, Colette hid the anger Liane had squeezed from her tired heart. "Oh, Roland chased after her for a few weeks before the war. But Pauline is a woman of taste. She found him even less appetizing than his tripe lyonnaise."

On cue, Pauline came in from reconnoitering the neighborhood. "Countess," she said. "What's wrong with Topaz? He refuses to set one paw inside the lobby."

"I know. I think he's afraid." Liane tapped her nose, and Colette noticed the Gypsy bracelet outlined under her sleeve, rubies puckering the silk. "My poor little puppy must smell Roland's blood."

"But the floor has been scrubbed with carbolic."

"When it comes to scent, dogs have perfect pitch. Think of truffles."

Truffles, Colette mused after Liane had gone. The oak tree's dirty and delicious little secret. "Pauline, I have an idea." She pushed the telephone toward her housekeeper. "Invite the inspector to come here. Now, if he can."

Ducasse was too busy. "If you have new information," he said over the telephone, "it is your duty to tell me at once."

Colette imagined his office—the cast-iron stove, the battered desk, a smell of cheese. Was Gisele somewhere nearby, tired and frightened in her Sunday dress? "Nothing new," she hedged, "but our minds sort facts differently. Gisele didn't murder her husband."

"In affairs of the pen I defer to you, Madame. At the Sûreté, we rely on logic. The peasant loves the prince. The chef blocked her way."

"You read too many romantic novels, Inspector. A jeroboam of prewar Chambertin says there's nothing but friendship between Gisele and Henri."

"I'm a teetotaler, but supposing you're right, that leaves greed. Different face, same coin. Roland loaned his in-laws a million francs, collectable at will. He was about to ruin them. We found his letter demanding the money or the farms."

"This letter—he hadn't mailed it?"

"No. It was on his desk, in plain sight."

Colette sifted probabilities. "Gisele couldn't have seen it, or she would have warned her family."

"No married woman could have missed it. Face it, Madame, your protégée decided to take care of Roland herself. If his threat to her parents doesn't convince you"—Ducasse paused for drama—"my men found something else. The coin flips back to love."

"You may as well tell me, Inspector, so I can refute you."

"Refute this—behind Gisele's chiffonier was a note asking her to come to the Bois at dawn; in other words, a few hours before Roland was stabbed. Signed 'your dear friend' in farcically crude handwriting. The transparent disguise of the exalted Count de Rossat, who was certainly advising Gisele step by step."

Robespierre must have left progeny, Colette thought, listening to the fury in Ducasse's voice.

"Anonymous notes? Dashing about at dawn?" She affected a chuckle. "What a lot of work for a man who had nothing to gain from Roland's death."

"I repeat, the answer is love. With Roland dead, Gisele and Henri would be free to marry. The count has no doubt begun to tire of his elderly wife."

"Nonsense. My husband is sixteen years my junior, and we're the best of friends. I'm a realist, Inspector. Marriage has nothing to do with love."

Had she, three times married, really uttered those words? Had seventy-four years so eroded her heart? "Men like Henri need a purse. And Liane's purse is colossal."

"Roland's estate goes to Gisele."

"The estate of a chef?" Colette clucked her tongue. "Another thing. Why would a murderess leave a trail of bread crumbs—letters, combs, a knife from her own kitchen?"

"I said the girl was in love, I didn't say she was clever, for all that she carries your novels around in her pocket. Though I must admit, she fooled *you*, Madame."

Fooled? Every instinct told her Gisele hadn't murdered Roland, and yet there was something hidden about the girl, something buried far deeper than truffles. Colette considered how carefully Gisele had selected *The Innocent Libertine* instead of the Gothic romance, a choice meant to flatter, so she'd assumed at the time. And the secret note Gisele had apparently left for anyone to find. Why, in spite of the note, had Gisele gone for her walk later rather than earlier?

The libertine and the note.

Yes.

A connection slipped into place.

"You're right, Inspector, Gisele has fooled me. Bring her here, and I'll give you irrefutable proof of her innocence."

The day turned chilly, but her fur blanket put an animal warmth into her legs. Ducasse had agreed to bring Henri as well as Gisele. These days wherever Henri went, Liane followed, so in a few minutes there would be four at her table.

She ticked off her arsenal: Tapestry? Handy. Workbasket? Out of reach on a shelf. Lipstick, a touch of kohl. She was ready.

Like a country hearth, the blue lamp invited her visitors to bask inside a circle of light. Pauline offered chocolates, tea, and madeleines, but only Henri, careful of his worsted, was eating. Freshly hennaed and slimmer than ever, Liane sat next to him.

Colette embroidered her tapestry, needle weaving a story she might afterward tell with her pen. Stitch after stitch fleshed out a rose. "Gisele," she said, "on Wednesday, why did you leave so late for the Bois?"

"I was watching for Henri."

"Do you walk together every morning?"

"Sometimes we meet after his ride."

"Are you in love with him?"

"Oh, really." Two words out of Henri's lockjawed mouth, and already Ducasse looked annoyed. As did Liane.

"Of course not." Gisele's voice was casual, indifferent to Henri. In her simple white blouse and gray skirt, she looked like a postulant with a prayer book in her pocket.

"Did you kill your husband?"

"No." That was all. No trembling chin. No fluster. Formidable child. When this was over Colette intended to invite Gisele to play bridge with Maurice and Cocteau.

"Did you know your husband meant to seize your family's farms?"

"No."

Ducasse jumped in. "The letter was on his desk. You must have seen it."

Colette silenced him with a look. "Tell me about the anonymous note," she said to Gisele, possibly the calmest person in the room.

"It came Tuesday night. Someone knocked, and when I opened the door I saw an envelope on the floor with my name on it."

"*Your* name?"

"Yes." Some emotion, irritation perhaps, at last crept into Gisele's voice.

"You're sure—"

The chair creaked under Ducasse's impatience. "It was her name. I saw it myself." He turned to Giselle. "Madame Roland, why did you ignore the count's note?"

"Really, Inspector." Henri's face slackened into petulance. "I did not send that note."

Colette cast her line in a different direction. "Gisele, did you bring my novel?"

From deep inside a gore-seam pocket, Gisele pulled out the little book.

"Open to page forty-seven."

With painstaking fingers, Gisele leafed through the pages. "Here." She offered the book to Colette.

"Just read from the top, my dear."

"My eyes." Gisele rubbed her lids. "Blurry today."

"Would you like more light?"

"I am waiting." Ducasse's voice came from far away.

Colette's heart beat in her throat. "You will wait forever. Won't he, Gisele?"

The country bride shook her head, an ivory comb slipping from her braid.

"Read," Colette said.

"Chapter…" A capillary pink suffused Gisele's neck. "Chapter…"

"There are no chapters in my book."

Gisele pressed a hand to her cheek.

"You can't read, can you, my dear?"

"No! I can't!" Her face twisted with rage, Gisele stabbed a long finger at Colette's name on the cover. "Names I recognize. Numbers. The kitchen boy helps me with menus and things. I saved the note for him to read to me later." Still no tears, but Gisele's face was on fire. "'Reading leads to reading,'" she said, mocking Colette's easy aphorism. "For me *nothing* leads to reading. At school they thought my eyes were bad. My friends helped me. That's how I got Henri to read this to me." She pitched *The Innocent Libertine* across the room. "Satisfied? Now that you've shown the world how stupid I am?"

"My dear child, I've shown the world how innocent you are."

No one spoke.

While Colette waited for the truth to sink in, she drifted on her raft, past Henri, fingering his tie, past Ducasse and Liane, both sipping tea. On the mantel glass paperweights glowed, chrome yellow, cobalt, all the colors of tropical fish.

She circled back to Liane. "Countess, would you be so kind? Fetch my crewelwork needle?" She pointed at her workbasket across the room.

"Is this what you mean?" Liane held out a fat needle, its eye cocked like a wink.

"The very one. Bring it here, will you?"

Something must have shown in Colette's face, because Liane hesitated before coming close.

"Thank you." Like a mongoose, Colette grabbed Liane's wrist and pushed back the sleeve, exposing the Gypsy bracelet.

"Don't touch it!" Liane screamed. "It'll bring you bad luck."

But the bad luck was all Liane's, her arm trapped in Colette's steel grip. A few jabs with the needle released the mermaid catch and, like a hinged shell, the bracelet fell open.

Bruises, fading from purple to sulfur, girded Liane's hidden skin.

"Your own little fling?" Colette asked. "Did Roland forget himself and hurt you where others could see?"

"She's covered with bruises," Henri murmured. "For Liane, pain equals joy, something I can't give her."

"They battered each other." Colette pictured the scrapes on Roland's hands and neck. Scarred by Liane's fingernails? The tips of knives?

"He was blackmailing me," Liane whispered. "He took pictures with a hidden camera and threatened to publish them."

Colette, once married to a baron, understood Liane's predicament. If Roland exposed her to the world, Henri's mother, descended from kings, would be unable to endure the infamy. She would push Henri into divorce. And divorce would cost Liane her title.

Worse, half her assets—for Liane, true infamy. She had to shut Roland's mouth, search his apartment, implicate Gisele.

If only Topaz could speak. Dogs don't shy away from blood, they're carnivores. But a tender pooch might shy away from the scene of a murder he had witnessed.

Shouts, Liane's sobs, mingled with Colette's thoughts. Let the inspector sort out the pieces. She'd done enough. She snapped off her lamp, and silent as a ghost, Pauline appeared with the coats.

When they were gone, Colette turned to watch the sky through her window. It was the sky of Paris, the color of cats, and slowly darkening. Already the moon hung over the gardens, but there was an hour still, she thought, of good light. She picked up her pen.

# THE VERY PRIVATE DETECTRESS

## BY CATHERINE MAMBRETTI

I n his later years, my dear friend Allan Pinkerton confessed he shared my opinion that, in the ordinary course of business, a private detective eye encounters few persons of interest. In most cases our clients grossly overestimate both their adversaries and themselves. All claim to be "reluctant to consult you" and hint that the only reason they've made their way to your door is that they're too ethical to stoop to handling the matter personally. "The characters I wrote about," Pinkerton said, "had to be spiced up for publication. However, there was one case about which I never wrote, a case which involved an extraordinary person, who, as it turned out, grossly overestimated me."

The woman arrived at the Chicago office one November morning in 1856 without an appointment. Pinkerton's secretary, Harry, took her coat and showed her into a secluded waiting room. At five minutes to noon, Pinkerton escorted a typical client out of his private office, then said to Harry, "Lunch with the accountant. Be back before my next appointment at one-thirty." When he grabbed his bowler off the bentwood hat stand, he noticed the woman's coat on the rack and turned to Harry with a question-mark eyebrow.

Harry put a finger to his lips and stepped up to the closed wait-ing room door. He slid aside the copper disk that hid the peep-hole, so Pinkerton could take a look at her. "Not the usual society peacock who needs proof her husband's cheating on her," Harry whispered.

Pinkerton agreed. The woman was a wallflower, if he had ever seen one. She wore a black bonnet, behind whose veil her face was nothing but a blur. He wasn't even sure there really was a body inside the voluminous hoopskirted dress. Its balloonlike sleeves might have been filled with air instead of flesh and bone. The bon-net's wide bow and the stiff, mannish white collar of her charcoal-gray dress completely hid her neck, which could have been long and scrawny or short and thick—or she might have had no neck at all.

The only thing about her body of which he was certain was "There's a backbone inside that corset." She sat up as stiff, in his words, "as if she had a broom handle up her arse," reading a book she had selected from the agency's small library.

"What's she reading?"

"A translation of Machiavelli," Harry said.

On the table beside the horsehair armchair was an unusually wide leather reticule of the kind that terrified Pinkerton, who was well known to suffer from an unreasonable fear of ladies' reticules. His worst nightmare was that his wife might one day ask him to reach into her reticule while it sat across the room from her: "Allan, fetch my hanky for me, won't you, dear? It's just over there in my reticule."

"Did she say what she wants?" Pinkerton whispered to Harry.

"No, she just said she'd prefer to tell that to Mr. Pinkerton. I said your schedule for the day was filled, and she said she could wait."

"After I leave," Pinkerton whispered, "tell her I won't be able to see her until late, four o'clock at the earliest, and if that isn't accept-able she can make an appointment."

When Harry passed on this information, the lady declined to leave. Instead she sat there all day, while a series of gentlemen told Pinkerton they were more sinned against than sinning, like a long line of vindictive supplicants at the devil's own confessional.

"My name is Mrs. Kate Warne. I'm a widow."

Even up close, Pinkerton told me, he found her so ordinary-looking as to be literally indescribable. Except for her eyes. They were blue and cold as the heart of an iceberg, eyes that even her black veil could not obscure.

"How may I help you, Mrs. Warne?" he said, as usual trying very hard not to sound bored.

"I've come in response to your advertisement for detectives. I'm willing to submit to a thorough background check."

To say he was surprised doesn't describe what he felt. "I must admit, I never thought of hiring a female detective. For that matter, Mrs. Warne, I've never imagined a woman would want to become such a thing." It was just after four o'clock on a gray autumn afternoon. In the streets of Chicago, lamplighters would soon begin their work. The window behind Pinkerton was the room's only light source. He considered asking Harry to bring some lamps into the room, then thought better of it. The interview would soon be over.

"You astonish me, sir," she said. The dying sun briefly penetrated her veil. He caught the slightest twitch of an eyelid. As if she feared her face might reveal something about her, she looked down at her gloved hands and the wide leather reticule in her lap. "What I mean is, I assumed all detective agencies must employ lady detectives, or I would never have inquired about the position. It never occurred to me that I would be proposing an innovation." She raised her eyes to him, but now their cold intelligence was muted, as if she had drawn another, thicker veil across her face. Her face was a complete blank, a veiled blank.

"Have you ever heard of a female detective?" he asked.

"No, but I assumed a detective agency would never advertise

specifically for ladies. Public knowledge that you employ lady detectives would undoubtedly diminish their...stealth. I suppose that's the word. Better not to alert a criminal to the possibility that the woman with whom he's conspiring is actually his nemesis." For an instant Pinkerton thought he must be looking at a daguerreotype, so expressionless was her face. It was uncanny, he told me. He had never known a woman who could hide her feelings so well.

He didn't like to ask a lady to leave, so instead he examined the desktop, as if he were searching for a document there and needed to get on with his work.

She said nothing.

Finally, he said, "Surely it goes without saying, the last sort of employment a widow should seek is employment as a private detective. A lady's companion or a nanny might be more suitable, and certainly more in demand."

"Mr. Pinkerton, I don't have the temperament to coddle either old women or children. Besides, I have no credentials—at least written ones—for such ladylike forms of employment. I believe I'd make a fine detective. I can be stealthy. I'm very plain. No one ever gives me a second look."

The room was dark now, but he took his watch from his vest pocket and pretended to check the time. "Mrs. Warne, the hour grows late. I've business to attend to." He rose and walked to the door, which for propriety's sake stood open. "It would be ungentlemanly of me to turn you out of my office," he said, certain it was clear that was exactly what he was doing.

"Now that I understand you have no lady detectives in your employ," she said, "perhaps you'd be so kind as to entertain a proposal that I be the first. I've been alone for some time. My husband left me very little to survive on. I'm at a crossroads in my life and must seek employment. If you won't listen to me, then I'll take my proposal to your chief competitor."

He thought she must know it wasn't much of a threat, but she had piqued his curiosity. He wondered how far the woman would carry the conversation. He poked his head out of the door. "Harry, bring lamps in here, will you?"

"As I said, I'm more than willing to have you inquire into my background," she said as he returned to his desk. "In fact, I beg you to do so."

Harry entered with a lighted lamp in each hand.

Pinkerton thanked him; then to Mrs. Warne he said, "I don't like to work here after dark, not with all these papers. Even the walls are covered in paper. The building's nothing but thin lathing and a bit of plaster. God forbid a fire should break out in the neighborhood."

"I won't keep you long," she said. "I've no intention of telling you my whole life's story. Quite the contrary."

"Then please don't tell me, either, why you want to be a Pinkerton detective. I don't care what your reasons are. I doubt they're good ones. Just tell me why you think you can do a man's job."

"I'm not suggesting I can do a man's job," she said. "I'm suggesting there are jobs of detection no man can do."

"Such as?" said Pinkerton.

"Have you read Mrs. Browning?" she asked. "Then 'Let me count the ways.'"

Pinkerton didn't recognize the quotation, but he was lawyerlike and said nothing.

"First, there are some secrets no man could ever worm out of another person and certain places where a man can never go," she said.

"Such as?" he persisted.

"Secrets no woman will tell a man, not even her lover, and especially not her husband." She looked around the office, as if before then she had paid no particular notice to her surroundings. Her gaze came to rest on the lever-lock safe behind Pinkerton's desk. "There are secrets every man would love to confide in someone, especially a woman, things he needs to get off his chest but couldn't confess to another man, not even to a priest." She looked Pinkerton in the eyes. "You know that's true."

He snorted skeptically but did know it was true.

"Second," she said, "there are many places where a man can't go."

"And a woman can?"

"Can a man enter a lady's bedroom while her husband's at home? Can a strange man enter an infant's nursery even if its mother keeps watch?"

Pinkerton's mustachioed lip curled noncommittally.

"Can a man enter a girls' dormitory or a brothel's inner sanctum or a nunnery or a seamstress's fitting room or—"

"Enough. I concede your point. However, I'm far from convinced that you, Mrs. Warne, are the sort of lady every woman will invite into her boudoir and in whom every man will confide. You said it yourself, or I wouldn't tell a lady this, but you are plain."

"Exactly why people confide in me," she said. "It's as if they think I'm not really there."

"Can you dissemble? In my experience few women are capable of cold, calculated investigative subterfuge of the kind a detective must engage in daily. Besides, women lack the physical skills I require in a detective."

"What skills?" she said.

"Every Pinkerton must carry a firearm and know how to use it," he said.

She put her gray-leather-gloved hand into the reticule on her lap and pulled a Derringer out by its barrel. "Be careful." She offered him the gun.

He took it. By its weight he could tell it was loaded. He placed it on the green blotter in front of him, its barrel pointed away from them. "My operatives carry revolvers and can shoot a man between the eyes at twenty paces—if he's stupid enough not to turn and run."

"I'm an excellent shot with all manner of firearms," she said.

"May I ask how you learned?"

"Perhaps Chicago girls don't learn to hunt by the time they're twelve, but in other parts of the world, it's common," she said.

"And what part of the world are you from, may I ask?" Like the rest of her, her accent was nondescript.

"I won't say." She retrieved the Derringer and slipped it back into the reticule. "I also have a small flick knife concealed upon my person."

Pinkerton smoothed his moustache with the thumb and index finger of one hand, as I often saw him do to hide a smile. "I might consider hiring you as an office clerk," he said. "Can you write and do arithmetic?"

"I have perfect penmanship, am an expert computer, including the calculus, a precise bookkeeper—but I'm not interested in clerical work, thank you," she said. She didn't rise to leave, however.

Pinkerton was flummoxed. He simply couldn't fathom why any woman, let alone an unprepossessing widow in need of funds, would be willing to risk her reputation and possibly her life as a detective. "I'm not saying I'm considering your proposal, but if I were to employ you in any capacity, let alone as a detective, I'd first need proof, not only of your marksmanship, but also of your absolute integrity."

"I expected you to say that. I've told you I'm willing to submit to an exhaustive background check," she said. "I'm also ready to demonstrate my marksmanship."

"All right." He left the office and closed the door behind him. "Harry, give me a copy of the thanks-but-no-thanks employment application," he whispered.

Harry smiled, opened a drawer, and pulled out a lengthy printed form.

"Thank you," she said when he handed it to her. She skimmed it. "I'm sorry. I can't fill this out."

"But you just said you'd provide 'exhaustive' information about yourself."

"No, I said I'd submit myself to an exhaustive investigation."

It occurred to Pinkerton that the woman might be slightly mad.

"Mrs. Warne," he said, "when did your husband die? Are you all alone in the world? Any relatives or friends in Chicago?"

"If you're asking me for references, I have a banker, but I'd prefer not to give you his name."

"I wasn't, actually," he said. "I was wondering if you were lonely and had come here out of a misguided notion the Pinkertons might provide some companionship."

She smiled as if he'd made a joke. "Not at all. I came here to have my background checked by the nation's best investigators and then to be employed as a detective."

Suddenly Pinkerton thought it might be a good idea for someone to investigate this woman, because there was something decidedly peculiar about her. The Chicago police ought to be tipped off. "All right, then. Will you at least supply your address?"

"Why should I?" she said. "Surely your detectives can track it down."

"Why should they have to?"

"Because in no better way can I demonstrate my skill in eluding followers and performing other necessary deception than by making your investigation of me as difficult as possible. Surely that's a better reference for detective work than any banker's word."

He snorted. This was the strangest bird he'd ever met. "Excuse me." He left the office and closed the door behind him again.

"Harry, send a man outside to follow the lady home," he whispered.

Harry nodded.

Pinkerton held the door open for Mrs. Warne. "Very well," he said. "I'm game. You can expect a letter from me within two days in which I'll detail your personal history. Good evening."

The streetlamps were lit when she exited under the sign of the Eye That Never Sleeps. Because she wore dark clothes and kept away from the lamps, the Pinkerton who followed her lost sight of her several times. The passages between buildings along the street were dark, but once he caught sight of a man lurking in an alley and wondered if he'd have to save the lady from attack. Eventually she took him on a tour of Michigan Avenue shops, the last of which was a corsetiere. The shop's display window was heavily draped. The solid oak entrance bore a sign that said men were not permitted on the premises. He knew there might be an exit in the rear, but he couldn't afford to leave his lookout in front.

As it turned out, Pinkerton had only himself to blame for sending a lone operative to follow a woman on a shopping spree.

The widow had eluded Tim Webster, one of his best operatives. After that it took Pinkerton's men two days to inquire at banks for an account holder named Mrs. Kate or Katherine Warne. When they located her bank, they bribed a teller for her address. The teller also said she had opened the account only the day before she had shown up at the agency. Pinkerton contacted the police about the strange widow.

Then, a day later than promised, he wrote to her at the LaSalle Boarding House for Ladies on Dearborn Street:

> I congratulate you on evading my man. We found your address through your bank, the First State Street Bank. In doing so, we confirmed what you said about having a bank account in good standing, but we also learned you opened the account only the day before you visited my office. If you still wish to pursue employment with my agency, please return to the office at four o'clock on Friday to complete the interview. Be prepared to supply basic information about yourself, including your husband's full name, your maiden name, and your date and place of birth.

Harry greeted Mrs. Warne with a polite smile, then disappeared into Pinkerton's office. When he emerged, he asked her again to take a seat in the waiting room. Fifteen minutes later, he escorted her into Pinkerton's office, which was filled with stale cigar smoke. Before Pinkerton rose to greet her, he deposited a half-smoked cigar in a floor-standing glass and bronze holder.

Again Pinkerton had the feeling he was watching a wallflower fade into the wallpaper. She wore the same gray dress she had worn before and held the same bonnet and the same reticule in her gray-gloved hands. Without the bonnet, for the first time he could see her virtually colorless hair. "Do you mind if I smoke?"

It was a test, and she seemed to know it. "Of course not. I occasionally smoke a lady's cheroot myself. I don't suppose you have any?"

"I do," he said, and opened a mahogany case so she could choose one. From her reticule she pulled an ivory holder, into which she inserted the cheroot, and she held it to her lips as he lit it for her. She exhaled and said, "Would you care to learn how I eluded your man?"

"Yes."

"The corsetiere's shop has an exit from the fitting room into an alley very near the omnibus route," she said.

"Clever enough to prove you're capable of evasion," he said, "but I still need your bona fides. Will you tell me your husband's name?"

"More than 'Mr. Warne' I cannot say."

Pinkerton didn't even try to hide his displeasure. "No woman as honest as you claim to be should object to telling me her husband's name. How do I know you really are a widow rather than a female confidence trickster?"

"Do I look like a confidence trickster? Is that what you're saying?" She removed the glove from her left hand and showed him her ring finger, with a pale indentation where a wedding band appeared once to have been.

"Where's the ring?" he asked.

"I lost it."

"I can't hire you with so little information," he said. "I couldn't vouch for you to a client otherwise."

"Why not? If any client asked, all you'd need to say is that your men did a thorough search of my background and found nothing objectionable."

"What makes you think my men did anything but inquire at a few banks?" In fact, George Bangs had spent a long time discreetly investigating the boardinghouse. He'd learned enough about the proprietress, one Mrs. Wanda Jean Cole, to know she couldn't be bribed to permit a private detective to rifle through a lodger's dresser drawers. He'd also asked about the deportment of the women who lodged with Mrs. Cole and learned that none were of the sort who might sneak a gentleman friend into their rooms. There were six lodgers in all: a retired schoolteacher, the spinster sister of a Lutheran minister, an elderly German woman in her dotage, a wheelchair-bound invalid and her companion, and Mrs. Kate Warne, a widow who had taken the room only two days before she first visited the agency.

"My operatives are engaged in important matters. Why should I expend valuable resources to investigate you?" He thought he caught a bit of disappointment in her eyes, but she was a hard book to read. He couldn't imagine what she was up to. "I can think of no legitimate reason not to supply a little information to any prospective employer."

"With all respect, sir," she said, "the great Allan Pinkerton isn't just any prospective employer. A good detective, let alone a great one, ought to be able to investigate a prospective employee's background easily. I don't feel it should be my responsibility to do your job for you."

Pinkerton's face grew more florid than usual. "I wouldn't accept a statement like that from a man."

"I'm a very private person, if not yet a private detective," she said. He thought he spotted a hint of fear in her eyes. "I value my constitutional right to be secure in my person."

"I'm not asking you to tell me anything that isn't in the public records. If it's public, then it isn't private. All I really need is a birth certificate or marriage license. Or just tell me where you were during the last census."

"I can't give you that information," she said. "However, I realized there was a chance you wouldn't be satisfied with what you found out about me. Since I must find employment by the end of the month, even if it isn't as a lady detective, I came prepared to make a bargain."

*So that's it,* Pinkerton thought. *She really is a confidence trickster, and a brazen one at that.*

"I keep all the records of my life in a small strongbox," she said.

"And if we find the strongbox, you'll turn over its contents to me?" His voice would have dissolved anyone else's backbone, but Mrs. Warne still sat up ramrod straight.

"Yes." She seemed to hold her breath while he considered the ramifications of accepting her offer. What she called a "bargain" sounded to him more like a wager. Pinkerton was working on a complicated investigation in the Deep South for the Adams Express Company. A clever, respectable-looking woman like Mrs. Warne might, indeed, be of some assistance in the more delicate aspects of the case. The risk was that if he failed to find the strongbox he'd be obliged to hire her even if she had larceny on her mind. He wasn't above hiring a detective with a shady past, regardless of what he might have told her about requiring proof of integrity, but only if the man was honest about it and wanted to change his ways. But this wasn't a matter of a shady past. It was a matter of no past at all.

"Describe this strongbox," he said.

"It's roughly the length and width of that envelope on your desk," she said. "It's polished brass, one inch deep, and has a small keyhole. No markings anywhere on it. If you find it in a week, you must promise not to pick the lock or open it by force, but instead deliver it to my hands intact." She removed the half-smoked cheroot from its holder and stubbed it out. "When you hand it to me intact, I'll give you the contents and you'll hire me."

"And if we don't find it?" he said.

"You'll hire me without further ado."

"You're asking me to find a needle in a haystack," he said.

"Isn't that what you do for a living?"

"Let's shake on it," Pinkerton said. He didn't often offer to shake a woman's hand. She had a good, firm handshake.

The moment she left the office, he told Harry to have Webster tail her. "And tell him not to lose her this time."

Then he called three other operatives into his office: Bangs, Joe Howard, and Tom MacDonald. He explained the challenge. George Bangs would team up with Webster, and they would take the night watch over the woman. While Webster followed her away from the agency, Bangs would head straight to the LaSalle Boarding House for Ladies, and when Webster and the woman eventually got there, Bangs would fill him in on the plan. Howard and MacDonald would take the day watch.

One operative from both pairs would follow her whenever she left the boardinghouse, while the other would sit tight and watch the house, and if the opportunity arose would look for a way to get into her room and search for the strongbox.

"What do we do if she leaves the boardinghouse and spends the night somewhere else?" Bangs said.

"I have a feeling this isn't the kind of woman who sleeps anywhere but in her own bed," Pinkerton said. "At least, she pretends to be, but if she spends the night with a man, I want to know right away, because I'll call off the investigation."

The next morning, Pinkerton met with Bangs and Webster after they had been relieved by Howard and MacDonald. "Did she leave on your watch? Where did she go?" he asked.

"No," said Webster. "Went straight home from here and didn't leave again while we were there."

"Could she have left through a back door without being seen?"

"The only other door's on the side of the house, the basement door," said Bangs. "We could see both."

"Let's face it," said Pinkerton, "she came here prepared. She'd already concealed the strongbox when she made me the offer. The most likely place is somewhere in the boardinghouse. We already know that neither the proprietress nor the other residents are likely to let us in. So work something out with Howard and MacDonald. We need to find a way to get inside and search the place."

He sent them off, then poked his head out at Harry. "Any appointments scheduled for this morning? Good, I don't want to be disturbed." After that he sat behind his desk, smoking one cigar after another, blowing smoke rings, and staring at the wall into which the wallflower widow had seemed to fade.

A small strongbox filled with papers could be concealed in many places, but since it contained the secrets of an intelligent woman and since she had described it as being of a type that could easily be broken into—or she wouldn't have had to warn him against opening it—then it was most likely concealed in a very secure place.

He poked his head out at Harry once more. "Send somebody to the First State Street Bank again and find out if Mrs. Warne has a safe-deposit box there. Send the operative in here the minute he gets back."

He closed the door, sat back down, lit another cigar, and blew more smoke rings. The next most logical, secure place for a flimsy strongbox would be a locker or the lost and found at a train station.

He walked to the door and poked his head out at Harry. "Send somebody to all the train stations. Slip a quarter to the guys at the lost and found and see if any of them have a small brass strongbox with a keyhole. Size about nine by five by one inch deep. Slip a couple of quarters to the stationmaster to get a look inside the public lockers. Send the operative in to see me as soon as he gets back."

He closed the door, sat back down, and blew more smoke rings. If the strongbox was in none of those places, he'd have his detectives make a list of all the places she visited while they followed her, including the corsetiere's shop. He would send his handsomest detective to call on all the shopgirls. Just after noon, he sent the operative nicknamed Ladies' Lad Leo to chat up the shopgirls on Michigan Avenue.

\*　　\*　　\*

Six days later, the strongbox still had not been found.

By the time Kate Warne entered his life, Allan Pinkerton had given up legwork. His potbelly made it hard to enter a building surreptitiously in broad daylight, let alone squeeze through windows at midnight. But he wanted to be the one to search the boardinghouse. That meant the only way in was to jigger the lock on the basement door.

When they were sure Kate Warne wasn't there, Howard and MacDonald drove a wagon carrying a huge piano crate to the alley beside the boardinghouse. They unloaded the crate at the mouth of the alley with as little commotion as possible, so curious neighbors wouldn't be drawn to the spot. Howard stood watch, and Mac-Donald cried "Yeehaw!" to the horse pulling the wagon and drove it up onto the boardwalk across the street, terrifying passersby and distracting everyone while a potbellied burglar behind the piano crate picked the lock on the basement door.

Pinkerton was convinced that Kate Warne was every bit as private a person as she claimed to be, so that meant she wouldn't trust her secrets to a flimsy strongbox hidden anywhere in a boardinghouse full of strangers except her own room.

With an Eye That Never Sleeps cocked toward the kitchen door, he crept up the back stairs to her third-floor room. The lock was so easy to pick he wondered why she had even bothered to lock it. In case a cleaning woman tried to enter, he locked the door behind him with a skeleton key, then surveyed the room.

An oval mirror hung at head height beside the door. A rag rug covered the floor. One double-hung window with a lace curtain faced the house next door. The only picture on the walls was a watercolor of a weathered old lean-to, signed w. j. cole, '54. It concealed no wall safe, nor had he expected it to, but he was habitually thorough in his searches.

A bed with a brass headboard was pushed against one wall. Between it and the window stood a deal chest of drawers, over which hung another mirror. On the other side of the bed was a small table covered with a doily, on which stood an oil lamp. Against the wall opposite the window stood a large, mirrored chifforobe with nothing in it but a dressing gown and an empty hatbox. The chifforobe was too heavy for him to move away from the wall, so that meant Kate Warne couldn't have moved it, either. The deal chest held only a few undergarments, which it especially embarrassed him to finger through, because from the mirror above it his own Eyes That Never Sleep watched over him. He edged the chest of drawers away from the wall and looked behind it. Nothing. The drawer in the table held a Bible and a small pewter-handled mirror. There was nothing under the mattress, but under the bed pillow was a small brass case with a mirror. He hadn't imagined a plain woman could be so vain.

In the end, the only possible place of concealment was under the floorboards covered by the rag rug. But when he'd rolled up the rug and moved it out of the way, he saw that the thick, dark varnish on the boards was unmarred and better preserved than the rest of the floor. The floorboards didn't conceal a hidey-hole.

The strongbox simply was not there.

Then it hit him. He felt a complete fool. He'd been bested by a mere woman. Why hadn't he thought of it before? She must carry the strongbox in that damn reticule from which she had fetched the Derringer and the cheroot holder, and which no doubt contained many other strange accoutrements of womanhood. It made him wonder if all women knew that all men fear the contents of a woman's reticule.

"I've found the strongbox," Pinkerton wrote her. "If possible, please come to the agency tomorrow morning at nine o'clock, which is before my first client is scheduled to arrive. Be prepared to reveal the contents of the strongbox. If your credentials are adequate, then I'll hire you as a private detective."

At precisely nine, Harry ushered the black-veiled Mrs. Warne into Pinkerton's office. Pinkerton rose to greet her, unable to suppress a smug grin, until he saw she didn't have the reticule with her.

There was nothing in her gloved hands. *She never intended to let me read the papers in the strongbox*, he thought. *She can't admit defeat.*

"Please be seated," he said grimly.

"I'm disappointed in myself," she said. "Obviously, I'm not as clever as I thought."

Pinkerton fell back in his chair. "It seems to me that not only did you overestimate yourself, but you underestimated me. Finding missing things is one of my specialties. In one area, though, I myself am clearly inadequate, namely, the ability to comprehend the female mind. I actually thought you'd keep your word."

"I'm sorry," she said, her voice quavering. "I never thought you'd find it."

Pinkerton lit a cigar. "I'd offer you a cheroot, but I see you're without your reticule and have no holder. Would you like one anyway?"

She looked down at the gloved hands lying limp in her lap. "My reticule? I didn't realize I don't have it. I didn't even miss it when I bought the omnibus ticket. I carry coins in the palm of my glove."

"But surely you left your reticule at home on purpose," he said.

"Why would I do that?"

"Without your reticule, I can't prove I won the bet. You carry the strongbox in it."

She froze. For a full minute not even an eyelid twitched. Then, slowly, she drew the veil up and back over the bonnet.

He saw a very different face. A wry lip was curled in amusement. Her ice-blue eyes were filled with triumph.

She rose. "Follow me." She opened the office door on her own. Pinkerton watched her hoopskirt sway past Harry's desk before he understood what she had commanded him to do.

She opened the waiting room door and swept in, seeming not to care about the alderman who hid his face behind a newspaper.

Pinkerton and Harry were in close pursuit. "Oh, Mr...." Pinkerton said, before he caught himself. "I apologize. Harry, take the gentleman into my office."

Kate pointed a gloved finger at the table beside the chair where she had last sat when she visited the agency. On it was a shallow brass strongbox.

"You've failed to live up to your side of the bargain, sir," she said. "Now you must hire me."

Pinkerton closed the door. "I'd be a fool not to hire so clever a woman," he said. "Besides, I pride myself on being a good judge of character, and I judge yours to be excellent. I suppose I can live without knowing anything of your background."

"It may surprise you, but I don't want you to live without knowing anything of my background." She reached inside her stiff white collar and extracted a thin gold chain, from which dangled a tiny key. She took off her gloves to unhook the chain, slid the key off, unlocked the box, and opened the lid. "Here." She offered Pinkerton the contents.

The box held only an envelope. "You won the wager," he said. "You don't have to reveal the contents to me. I'm a man of my word."

"I know you are," she said. "Take it." Kate sat down in one armchair, Pinkerton in another.

The envelope he held was fine laid-linen paper. It had once been sealed with red wax, which was stamped with the initial *W*, but it had been carefully slit open with a paper knife and was now empty. He turned the envelope over. All that was written there was *Mrs. Kate Warne.*

"You mean to tell me that your only documentation is an empty envelope with your name written on it?"

"Yes."

"Absolutely nothing else?" he said.

"Nothing. I don't even know who wrote that name. It isn't my handwriting."

"And your husband's full name? Why is that a secret?"

"Because I don't know it," she said. "Frankly, I'm not sure I am or ever was a Mr. Warne's wife. I'm not sure I am the Mrs.

Kate Warne whose name is written there. I assume I am, but only because I have that envelope addressed to Mrs. Kate Warne."

He studied her calm face. "I don't understand. You seem to say you dropped from the sky one day, fully grown and with literally nothing to your name but an envelope."

"You make me sound Olympian. I wish I were," she said with a sad smile. "But what actually happened was less dramatic. One day I found myself seated on a bench in a train station with a reticule in my lap, which contained a Derringer, a coin purse with a little money, and that empty envelope." She tapped her left arm. "And I had a flick knife strapped to my forearm."

Pinkerton tongued his cigar from one side of his mouth to the other a couple of times. "I've heard of amnesiacs, but never actually met one."

"Amnesia," she said. "That's what I concluded, too. Although even now I don't know when I learned the term."

"Did you have a bump on your head?"

"No."

"If you can't remember anything, how do you know you learned to fire a weapon as a child?"

"I don't know," she said. "I just do. The same way I know what amnesia is, and calculus, without remembering a single lesson, and bookkeeping. I also have a feeling I was born somewhere in New York State and that I'm around thirty years old."

"Many ladies carry a Derringer, but why, do you imagine, do you carry a flick knife?"

"Maybe I'm part of the Underground Railroad," she said. "You're an abolitionist. I had hoped it might be a sign you'd recognize."

"Why in tarnation did you decide to apply for a job as a detective?"

"It isn't easy to explain," she said. "But neither is it a long story. Pretty short, actually. It begins in the train station two days before we met. After I had been sitting there awhile, a porter walked up to me and asked if he could help me find the right track. I didn't know the answer, so instead I asked directions to the ladies' waiting room.

"It had a full-length mirror on the wall. I looked in it and didn't recognize my face. It was just a very plain face. No one I knew. Even now I don't recognize my face in mirrors, no matter how often I look. I even keep a mirror under my pillow to look at first thing every morning.

"Anyway, I knew something was terribly wrong with me. I couldn't live in a ladies' waiting room. I needed a safe place to go. So I went back out into the station and asked the porter for directions to the first safe place that came to mind, the nearest bank.

"But when I reached the bank I realized I needed an address in order to establish an account, so I bought a newspaper to find a decent boardinghouse. On the same page as the ad for the LaSalle Boarding House for Ladies was yours for detectives. It struck me that if anyone would be interested in a lady who carried a Derringer and a flick knife, it would be you, and if I could interest you in hiring me, you'd conduct a thorough check of my background.

"I never imagined Allan Pinkerton wouldn't be able to figure out who I am."

# THE BIRDHOUSE

## BY STEPHEN ROSS

He strangles her.

There is nothing I can do.

The man is in a white shirt and brown pants. He is big. He has short red hair and a face that smiles. The woman is a nurse. She is young, thin, with blond hair tied up.

He strangles her on the lawn on a beautifully sunny afternoon. She is dead.

I see this through the window. The panes of glass are old and wavy. It's the only window in my room, and it's open by an inch.

The man is standing over the nurse's body. He is looking at her. I don't think he had planned to kill her. He seems to be thinking: What to do next?

Outside my window is a small garden. It's flanked by a hedge. It must be a private place. He must have thought he was alone when he put his hands to her neck.

There had been an argument, a heated exchange. The nurse had pointed her finger at the man and had made threats. He had struck out, taking her throat into his grip. It had happened fast. He killed her quickly, in silence, and with efficiency.

The man walks away.

I can't see where he has gone.

I am left sitting to stare at the lifeless body of the nurse on the lawn.

What can I do? Should I watch the soft breeze gently move the leaves of the hedge? Should I listen to the sound of the robin, or whatever it is, I can hear singing in the tree?

Should I admire the birdhouse?

At the rear of the garden stands a little white birdhouse. It stands about seven or eight feet from the ground at the top of a pole. It is a grand miniature house with a red roof. It has a little balcony for birds to promenade upon, and a little hole for them to step through, to go inside to hide from the storm.

I couldn't hear clearly what the man and the nurse had been arguing about. They had spoken in whispers. Hers had been a sharper voice, with an accusatory tone. I had heard her say: "I know." I had heard her say it more than once.

The man has come back.

He has brought something with him. It's dirty white in color. It's some kind of bag and he is lifting the girl's feet. He is dragging the bag up around her legs. I think it's a laundry sack. He is putting her into it.

Within seconds, the man has hidden the nurse's body in the sack. He ties the rope at its opening and seals her in.

He looks at my window.

He stares.

I can't read his mind, but I know what he is thinking. I see the change in his expression. He is concerned.

He walks up to my window.

Outside, the garden is drenched in afternoon sunlight. With the contrast in light, I imagine that the view through the window into my room is not immediately obvious.

He presses his face to the glass, and he looks directly at me.

I can do nothing.

He looks about my room.

There is nothing I can do.

He returns to the nurse.

He lifts up the laundry sack and hauls it over his shoulder. He walks away, out of my view.

I hear my breath. It's racing. My vision has begun to blur. I must relax. My heart must be pounding. I can't feel it, but it must be turning over like a motorcycle engine.

I stare at the birdhouse.

I focus on it.

It is a pleasant little house. A craftsman has spent many hours fashioning its shape and design. If I were a bird, I would be very pleased by it. I would seek refuge there.

I stare at that birdhouse until it's all that exists.

The door to my room opens, and I'm brought back. The door is behind me. I can't see who has opened it.

I hear soft footsteps. It's the sound of one pair of shoes on the wooden floor.

It's the man.

He stands at the foot of my bed. He looks at me. I'm sitting up, propped up by pillows, looking back.

The man is older than he appeared through the window. Now that he's closer, I can see lines and wrinkles on his face. His red hair is flecked with gray. He is easily taller than six feet. He is big. He is fat. He is still smiling. His smile is infectious. I would almost like to smile back.

He studies me.

I dare not close my eyes.

He picks up the clipboard that is hung on the end of my bed. He reads it. As he reads it, he begins to nod to himself.

"Is someone there?" a voice asks.

The voice shocks me. It's loud after the quiet of the afternoon.

The voice is from Fulton, the man in the bed next to mine. The big man glances over at him. His smile becomes a grin.

Fulton's head is wrapped in bandages. I've heard that his sight will return, but for the present, he is blind.

"There is someone there, isn't there?" Fulton demands. "I heard footsteps. If you're trying to play a game, you can fuck off. I'm in no mood."

Fulton is a Scotsman. That's about all I know about him.

The big man with the short red hair places my clipboard back on the hook on the end of my bed. He quietly walks out of the room.

I am not a bowl of fruit. I am not a vase standing on a table with a selection of flowers sticking out of me. I am not an ornament. I am not a decoration. I am not a damn objet d'art.

The three doctors stand at the foot of my bed. They have the same looks on their faces as they did yesterday.

They talk about me as though I am not there. They know I can hear them. They know I can see them. They talk about me as though I am little more than a chest of drawers and incapable of perception or understanding.

I don't know why they bother. I have been in this room for five days now, and each day in the afternoon, they visit, and they stand at the end of my bed with the same faces.

Hopeless.

They don't say that out loud, but I hear it in their pauses. They think I am hopeless.

Nothing is hopeless. I refuse to ever accept that. I can't feel or move an inch of my body except my eyes—I can move them, and open and close them. I will not surrender to this. It is not hopeless.

What did that Churchill fellow say? *We shall never surrender.*

That's me. Me and Churchill.

I wish they would put me near a radio, or by a gramophone.

Nine days, and I'm bored.

Fulton talks a lot. He sings songs with dirty lyrics. He tells obscene jokes—the vilest, most disgusting of jokes—and he swears a lot. And all in that Scottish accent of his. Glasgow, I believe. His accent could cut a glass bottle in half.

Fulton knows I'm there. He's never seen me, but he's been told I'm in the bed next to his. My name is Joseph. At home I get Joe. Fulton calls me Fucking Yankee.

Fulton talks a lot. He talks a lot about his family.

I can't talk back.

I can't do anything.

Nurse Anne is my guardian angel. She talks to me and understands that I can't answer. She talks to me as though I'm part of the conversation.

Nurse Anne visits several times a day. She feeds me, and she cleans me. She is intimate with me. She deals with me in a way no other human being ever has had to since I was a baby.

I'm completely immobile, but my body still functions like that of a normal man. I would happily climb aboard another aircraft for another mission with a near-certain threat of death rather than do what she does. If I ever get out of this mess, I will tell her how very grateful I am.

What I really wish I could tell her is what I saw in the garden. I saw a man in a white shirt and brown pants murder a nurse.

A murder seems so out of place during a war.

I am no innocent. I have killed. I have fired upon countless aircraft, and many have erupted in flames and spiraled to the ground. Enemy aircraft are not piloted by ill wishes and bad intentions. I have killed men. But I have not murdered a single one of them.

Those men were willing to die, as was I. Whoever takes to the air and engages is prepared to meet the end of his life. It was just my bad luck to live.

We took flak over France. I was flying escort to a bombing raid in a Mustang. The B-17s had dumped their payloads over Koblenz, and we were homeward bound, and then we got it. It was like the Fourth of July. The big bombers were getting hammered. One got it bad, and I flew through a shard shower of red-hot metal. It gutted my fuel tank and took out most of my flight controls.

By the time I saw England, I had no fuel and no play left at all in the tail. I crash-landed in a farmer's field. Crippled. Hopeless.

A nurse does not ask to die. She is there to comfort and heal us madmen. Who was that fat man with the short red hair? Why did he murder that poor girl?

I can see my father sitting there in his armchair, smoking his pipe, listening to news of the war on his radio and clawing at his newspaper as he reads of casualties and deaths. I can see my little sister lying on her stomach on the floor, reading a book and asking questions, or talking to herself. I can see my mother, in the kitchen, worrying.

I wonder if they have heard. I wonder how long it has taken for news of my accident to travel from Britain, across the Atlantic, and to my home in Hartford.

When I was younger, I couldn't wait until I got out of there. Now I simply can't wait until I get back. But what will be waiting for me?

I am not a man anymore.

I don't know what I am.

Maybe I'm just a bowl of fruit after all?

He is a cook!

Nurse Anne has found a wheelchair for me. She has taken to wheeling me about. After three weeks in that room, I was beginning to lose my senses.

Nurse Anne has parked me in the games room. I, the bowl of fruit, can watch people move and play, and talk and laugh.

The hospital isn't really a hospital. It's a grand house that has been commandeered by the military for the duration. It's the country house of Lord Somebody-or-other. The good lord isn't here. He has moved out and taken his family, his servants, and probably his good silver. He'll be back at the end, I would say. If we win.

The games room is probably what had been the good lord's drawing room. A table has been set up for table tennis. Men sit about, playing cards, reading, engaging in casual banter. The atmosphere is convivial. There is a gramophone. Someone likes Al Bowlly. I hear him a lot.

We are all airmen here, all with our wings clipped, all resting from the storm. It is mostly British pilots, with a couple of Poles, a couple of New Zealanders, and a couple of fellow flyboys from back home. No one I know.

The fat man with the short red hair is a cook. He works in the kitchen. He is still smiling. He has smiles for everybody.

He moves about, dressed in a white apron, with a pot of coffee and a plate of small, thin sandwiches, probably cucumber. The Brits like those.

He chats with everybody.

Everyone likes the fat man. People respond warmly to him. A Brit with a ridiculous moustache and voice remarks that he does a good job on the grub.

The fat man doesn't smile at me. He doesn't even bother to look at me. I am of no interest. I am no threat. He has read my clipboard. Hopeless. Can't move. Can't talk. Just eats and sleeps.

I overhear the cook's name. Derek.

I stare at him.

The words are on my tongue, ready and waiting. But I can't even open my mouth. Nurse Anne has to wedge a small piece of wood between my teeth to keep my mouth ajar so as I can breathe comfortably.

I wonder why Derek the cook hasn't poisoned my food yet. Am I really that hopeless?


It's a clear night, and the moon is up. The little garden outside my room is illuminated. It looks like a fairy tale through my window, with the little white birdhouse with the red roof glowing in the lunar light.

Nurse Anne and another enter my room. They remove the pillows propping me up and lay me down.

Nurse Anne wishes me a good sleep.

I stare at the ceiling. It's lit up by the glow of the garden.

I can't sleep. I'm thinking about that nurse. Why did she have to die? What did that fat cook do with her body? It has been four weeks now. That poor girl.

The sun is in my eyes. Nurse Anne is not aware of this. She probably thinks she has done me a favor, wheeling me outside.

She has wheeled me into the garden outside my room. The garden is quite small, just a little patch of lawn, and it is indeed very private. No other windows face onto it other than my own, and for the first time, I see my window from the other side.

I can't see into my room—the sun is too bright. All I see is a distorted reflection of Nurse Anne, the birdhouse, and me. I know now why no one has taken me anywhere near a mirror. Even allowing for the deformation in the wavy glass, I can see I am scarred.

Nurse Anne sits in a garden chair beside me. She seems upset. She is not herself today. God forbid she should be worrying about me.

I believe I have become her special case. She has given over a great deal of her time to looking after me. She bathes me, she feeds me. She talks to me and tells me of all her dreams. In return, I keep no secrets from her.

I close my eyes.

The sun illuminates my eyelids, and I see a sort of vivid red color.

I do have a secret. There is a secret trapped inside my head that cannot get out. My only fear in my life now is that it will stay there until the day I die.

Nurse Anne moves me. She has realized the sun was in my eyes.

I wish I could put my hand on hers. Something is troubling her deeply. She is trying to hide the fact.

"I had a friend," Anne says. She is looking at the ground. "Her name was Judy. She disappeared a few weeks ago. She was a nurse here at the hospital. We both trained together in Croydon."

There are tears in Anne's eyes.

I try to move my hand, to place it on hers. I try with all my will and with all my strength.

My hand remains motionless.

"We all thought Judy had left," Anne says. "We thought she had gone back home to Swansea."

Anne looks at me. I have never noticed how beautiful her eyes are until this moment. Pale blue. Caught in the English sunlight.

"They found Judy's body in the river."

Anne looks away.

"There's a river, it's about four miles from here. They don't know if it was an accident, or how she came to be in it."

Anne puts her hand on mine. "We must value our lives, Joseph. Life can be so short."

She says no more about her friend.


I wake to the sound of an explosion. I hear aircraft. Many aircraft. I hear volleys of ground fire. I thought I had dreamed of the air-raid siren.

It's night. I'm on my back, laid down for sleep. I can't lift my head. I see a pale orange flickering on the ceiling of my room.

The hospital is near an airfield. It's two miles away. It can only be that. There must have been an attack.

I hear the roar of aircraft scream over the house. Two or three of them. Spitfires. Give them hell, boys.

A doctor drags me off my bed and into my wheelchair. Another doctor gets the mad Scotsman out of his bed. Fulton's bandages have been off for three days, but he still can't see clearly. He is led by the hand.

Everyone is taken downstairs into the servants' area and the kitchen. We are all lined up along the hallways. Nurses and doctors are running and yelling. There are shouts about a dogfight. It's above the house.

The RAF has engaged a group of Luftwaffe bomber escorts. A wing of the hospital has been strafed by aircraft fire. Theirs or ours? No one knows. There have been deaths.

Oh, how I long to be in the air, to be up there at the controls and fighting. I have no doubt every man sitting on the floor, or in his wheelchair, about me, feels exactly the same way.

You don't know life until you live on the edge of it, where your every action in the raw heat of the moment determines your fate; where a crazy idea, a sudden instinct, or just sheer dumb luck sees that you live and don't die.

"Wait until I get back up there," Fulton grunts. "I'll fuck them bastards up and no mistake."

I see Anne. She's at the other end of the hall. She's bandaging a doctor. He's kneeling on the floor. It appears he has been hurt. It looks like blood on his face.

The cook is handing out cups of coffee and keeping everyone's spirits up. Jovial is the fat man. Always cheerful is the fat man with the short red hair.

Eventually, he settles near me. He sits next to the Scotsman. He lights a cigarette. He shares it with my foulmouthed friend. They chat quietly while we listen to the fighting above the house.

I learn that Fulton is a gunner stationed at Duxford. His bomber was attacked over the channel by a Messerschmitt and he took shrapnel in the face. He was lucky to have survived. Damn lucky.

My Scottish neighbor talks about Cambridgeshire, where Duxford airfield is. He likes it there, but the airfield is soon to be transferred over to the USAAF.

"Fucking Yanks," he says. He grins at me and then passes the cigarette back to the cook.

It occurs to me that the Scotsman is talking a lot, and that the sympathetic ear of the cook is doing a lot of listening.

The cook asks a question about the Scotsman's barracks. The Scotsman answers. It's a vague question, nothing significant.

It's all surface conversation, idle talk while waiting for the fighting to finish. But underneath it, the cook is drawing out a reasonable understanding of the layout and floor plan of Duxford air base.

My God, is the cook a spy?

I close my eyes.

Of course he fucking is.

George is looking older. He's twenty-four, like me, and he looks forty-five. He looks old enough to be my uncle. George is my good friend. I've known him since high school.

He doesn't know what to say.

He looks at me and then away. He talks about the weather. He talks about the weather in New York and drums his fingers on the armrest of his chair.

George is a drummer. He's stocky and looks as if he should be in pro football. Back in Manhattan, he plays in a swing band. Here in Europe, he's a navigator. I bet he hasn't seen a drum set for over a year.

George adjusts his collar. He dressed up for the visit. He's not casual. His hair is combed. He really doesn't know what to say.

It is subtle.

The cook makes his rounds with tea and cake in the games room. He is a happy, friendly face and always ready for some conversation. He is a fat, jolly man. He is your friend, and for a moment, he can make you forget about your pain.

This is not a battlefield, this is the drawing room of Lord So-and-so, and we're all friends here. We're all fellow combatants. We're all on the same side. Our guards are down.

A young English boy—barely eighteen, shot down on his first mission and lost a leg—tells the cook about a tricky flight path he encountered.

An Australian talks about his aircraft. He's proud of it.

Someone mentions that Hatfield airfield over in Hertfordshire has been patched up and reopened since it was bombed three months ago.

It goes on.

The cook doesn't ask for any of this. He doesn't solicit a word. But he is there, attentive, and ready to mop it all up, to wring it all out in his bucket.

The penalty for spying is a bullet in the head. That's why Derek the cook killed Judy the nurse. He is a spy. She found out about him. She had said, "I know." This was what *she knew*.

I will get that fat son of a bitch.


I am screaming inside.

I have spent every moment for more than a week trying to move. I have tried to move every part of my body. My legs, my arms, my toes, my fingers.

I have tried by sheer force of will to induce my throat to make a sound, any sound, so as to be led back into speaking words.

My brain is in chaos.

I can't move. I can't speak.

I will not surrender to this. I will not give in. I have no idea if I will ever walk or talk again, but I *will not* surrender. This secret must come out. It has to come out. It cannot stay buried inside my head for eternity.

Nurse Anne looks at me.

She probably wonders why I am crying.

I close my eyes.

The only part of my body I can move is my eyes. The only part of me I can feel is my eyes.

I open them.

Nurse Anne has gone. I'm in the garden and staring at the birdhouse. The sun is directly overhead, and the birdhouse looks radiant.

I'm no more than a few feet from where that poor girl was murdered. This garden was the last thing she saw. It was the last place she knew.

There is a wire on the pole.

My eyes are blurred from my tears, but I can see a wire. There is a wire attached to the wooden pole holding up the birdhouse.

The wire runs up the pole out of the ground. It goes up into the birdhouse. It's painted white, like the white of the pole.

It is certainly a wire. There are two tiny clips holding it in place.

Blink and you would miss it. Stare at the damn birdhouse as long and as often as I have, and you will eventually see it.

A question comes to my mind: Why have I never seen a bird in the birdhouse? Not in it, not on it, not near it?

There are plenty of birds here. I hear them in the trees all the time. Is the birdhouse some kind of radio transmitter, or an antenna?

Is this how the cook transmits his information? Is this why the nurse and the cook were in the garden?

Of course it fucking is.

Nurse Anne returns. She has a handkerchief. She wipes the tears from my eyes and face.

George has brought news from home. My mom and dad send their love. My mom is praying for me every day. My sister is sending me a book, maybe someone can read it to me.

After that, George doesn't know what else to say. He drums his fingers on the arm of his chair.

He looks at me more today. This time, he is more relaxed.

I wish I could drum back. Maybe get up a rhythm along with him. I used to be able to pick out a reasonable tune on a piano.

I get a sudden, crazy idea.

I blink.

I blink in a rhythm.

George stares at me as if I am nuts.

I keep blinking.

He keeps staring.

Finally, he gets it.

"SOS?" George says. "You're blinking SOS?"

I blink the Morse code for YES.

He nods. He understands.

Eyes closed short for dots. Eyes closed long for dashes.

I ask him how he is.

"I'm fine," he says. "Thanks for asking." He looks incredulous. He laughs with amazement.

I wish I could cheer and leap from my bed. I wish I could hug and kiss the great oaf.

Wait until he hears what I have to say next!

# THE HONOUR OF DUNDEE

## BY CHARLES TODD

*Southwest England, 1920*

Alice Miller came home from the churchyard after her husband's services and walked directly into what he always called his study, the small room where he kept his memories and his books.

The box was on a shelf in the captain's chest along the far wall—quickly found and quickly carried away. She held it before her as if it contained something virulent, something that she might breathe in or touch if she were not very careful.

It wasn't enough to set it at the bottom of the garden. She walked through the small orchard to a copse of trees beyond it, close by the lane that went to Manor Farm. She had no shovel, not even a spoon to dig a hole. The ground was wet enough in this marshy country to serve her purpose. Scuffing in the thick layer of leaves, she made a shallow pit and put the box in it.

She had asked Harry to get rid of it as he lay dying, but he'd shaken his head and said it would stay in the chest as long as he drew breath. She would have taken it away as soon as she heard his death rattle, but there was the doctor, one of his nurses, and a neighbor come to comfort her. She hadn't been alone since.

Dusting off her hands, as if to rid herself of contamination, she turned her back on the box and strode away, her eyes on the distant roofline of her cottage.

It was more than a week later that the children from the tenant farm discovered the box, the covering of leaves blown away and one corner standing higher than the other three.

Running to it, digging it out of the rotting leaves and muddy earth, they studied it for a moment, trying to decide what might be inside.

Toby tried the hasp. "It doesn't open," he said.

Lionel, leaning over his shoulder, said, "I'll find a rock and bash it."

"No." Tim, the eldest, shook his head. "We don't know what's inside. It could break."

"Pa has something in his workbox that will spring it," Lionel offered.

"Let's take it home," Toby agreed. They brushed off the worst of the debris clinging to the box and set out for the farm.

But no amount of prying would force the hasp, and at length, bored with their find, they dropped it in the sitting room and went out to finish feeding the chickens.

Mrs. Tasker discovered it as she brought in more wood for the fire. Her first thought was to toss it in with the kindling, dirty as it was, and then she decided against it, because the brass hinges and hasp wouldn't burn properly. On her way back to the kitchen she dropped it in the dustbin.

There it lay until her husband hauled the dustbins off to the tip.

An ex-soldier, scavenging for anything he might sell, discovered it on Saturday evening, and carried it away with him, trying to open it as he walked. But the hasp wouldn't give and a good shake indicated it was empty. He gave up. Cleaned and then given a shine with scavenged brown shoe polish, the box was more presentable. He took it to the pub and offered it to the barkeep in return for a pint.

Grumbling, the barkeep accepted the barter, and set the box on a shelf behind the bar. There it lingered for more than a week, until he noticed it one evening and shook it to see if it rattled, as in coins.

It didn't, and he set it on the bar, intending to hand it back to the ex-soldier when next he showed his face, demanding payment for the ale he'd drunk, telling him that he didn't care to be played for a fool.

Captain Jarvis saw it there, took it over to his table along with his whiskey and sandwich, and studied it for a time before trying the hasp. When it didn't open, he sat back, gave the matter some thought while he finished eating, and then went back to the bar.

"Where did you get this?" he asked the man, who was busy serving a young couple.

"It's yours for the price of the ale it cost me," the barkeep replied sourly.

Without hesitation, Jarvis reached into his pocket and handed over several coins. He had taken the box and walked out the door before the barkeep realized that he could probably have asked a pound or more for the damned thing, and he swore under his breath.

Captain Jarvis went to the hotel down the street and put in a call to Scotland Yard, asking for Inspector Rutledge.

When Rutledge finally came to the telephone, the captain said, "Jarvis here. Did the Yard ever find that box missing from the Dundee Rifles Officers' Mess?"

"No. It appears to have vanished. Why, what have you heard?"

"I think I have it. Sandalwood. There's even still a scent about it. And the hasp, of course. Shall I bring it to London with me?"

"I'll come to you. Where are you?"

Jarvis looked out the door of the telephone closet. A dozen or so people were coming into the hotel, laughing together as they walked toward the dining room. "I'm just outside Sedgemoor. A village called Worthington. I hadn't planned on staying the night here, but I'll wait for you at the hotel."

He walked back to Reception, still holding the box in one hand. Several people glanced his way as he passed, but he thought it might be because he was a stranger.

A room was to be had, and he went out to fetch his valise before going up.

It was the next morning when Rutledge arrived, driving down the High until he spotted the Monmouth Hotel. The Poldern Hills were a low purple smudge in the hazy sunlight, and a ring around the sun promised rain.

He was given Jarvis's room number and took the stairs two at a time on his way to number 26. If this box did belong to the Dundee Officers' Mess, it would be the first fresh clue in nearly two decades in connection with a theft that had ended in two murders.

Rutledge tapped at the door, his mind still on the box. When Jarvis didn't answer, he glanced into the bath down the passage, then retraced his steps and went into the hotel dining room. But Jarvis wasn't there, either. Returning to Reception, he asked if the captain had left.

He had not, and Rutledge took the room's second key from the clerk at the desk, and went back to number 26. The door was not locked after all, and when he stepped inside, he could see that the shades were still down and the lamp had burned itself out. Putting up the shades, he saw that Jarvis was still in his bed. But the sheet covering him was black with blood.

The captain had been stabbed in his sleep, for there was no sign of a struggle. And although Rutledge searched the room thoroughly, he could not find the box.

His first duty was to send for a doctor and alert the local constable. He did neither. Hamish, the voice in his head, a legacy of war and shell shock, disapproved, grumbling about taking matters into his own hands.

Shutting the door behind him and locking it, he went back down the stairs. Jarvis had somehow found the box in the vicinity of Worthington, for he'd called from this hotel. The question, then, was where had he been before he put through that telephone call?

He wasn't ready to question the hotel staff and alert them to the murder.

Instead, he went outside and found Jarvis's motorcar, and searched it for the box. Nothing. Looking up and down the High Street, he calculated his choices. It was just after one o'clock when Jarvis had telephoned London. If he were passing through and in a hurry to be on his way, why would he have stopped? For a sandwich, perhaps? The pub nearest the hotel was the Water Wheel. Rutledge went there, but drew a blank. Walking on, he saw another pub, a little larger than the first: the Duke of Monmouth, named for the Protestant bastard of Charles II who had instigated a short-lived rebellion against the accession to the throne of the King's brother, the Catholic James II. His likeness adorned the sign, a young and still innocent face.

Rutledge stepped inside to find the barkeep sweeping the floor.

"We're closed," the man said, barely turning to look at Rutledge.

"Yes, of course," Rutledge answered pleasantly. "I seem to have misplaced a friend. He was to meet me here today. But he wasn't at the hotel, and I wondered if I had the days wrong." He went on to describe Jarvis.

"You must've," he was told. "He was here yesterday. Came in for a drink and a sandwich."

"I'm sorry to hear that," Rutledge said. "He was bringing me a book. He didn't leave it, by any chance?"

The man shook his head.

"It could have been in a box."

"The only box was one he had off me. Bought it for the price owed me."

"Did he indeed? Why am I not surprised? He collects boxes. It was yours, you said?"

"Not mine. An ex-soldier down on his luck sold it to me for a drink. A week or more ago, I should think."

"What did it look like?"

"A box," the barkeep said, irritated by the questions. "Wood, with brass hinges and hasp. It was heavy enough to have something inside, but when I rattled it, I didn't hear anything move. If I'd known he collected such things, I'd have raised my price."

"Where is that ex-soldier now?"

"I haven't seen him since, and I'm not likely to. For all I know, he pinched the bloody box from somewhere."

"Can you describe him?"

"Middling height, brown hair, walked with a limp. Here, I thought you come in about your friend."

"So I did. Perhaps he went looking for your soldier."

"Why would he do that? I didn't tell him how I'd come by the box."

Rutledge thanked him and left.

Outside, a misting rain was beginning to fall, wetting down the dust of the road.

As he walked back to the hotel, he considered the ex-soldier. Unlikely to want the box back, if he'd sold it for a drink, and unlikely to have the money to redeem it anyway. Unless he'd discovered its worth. But how had he come by it in the first place? It was ordinary enough not to be a tempting item to steal. The church poor box would be a better choice.

Hamish said, "And no one has reported it lost."

True enough. The box had sat unnoticed for a week at the pub. Then Jarvis had spotted it and bought it, carrying it to the hotel with him to put in his call to London. Afterward he must have requested a room. With the box still in his hand? Or had he left it in the motorcar?

Not the motorcar. It could have been taken from there without killing Jarvis.

Rutledge went to the hotel and asked the clerk in Reception if he had been on duty yesterday when Jarvis had asked for a room.

"I was," the man said, warily, as if preparing himself for a question he felt uncomfortable answering.

"Did he have anything with him when he came to the desk to speak to you?"

"His hat." The clerk squinted in thought. "A box or packet or something."

"Was there anyone else here when he asked for a room?"

The clerk laughed. "Half the county, or so it seemed. There was a private luncheon for Squire's birthday."

"When the party was over, did anyone ask you about the man registering just then?"

"Mr. Albert Harrison thought the new guest was someone he'd met in France during the war. But the name he was after was Dunne, Lieutenant Dunne. Not Jarvis. He seemed disappointed."

"Did Mr. Harrison return later in the evening?"

"I was off duty after five o'clock. I couldn't say."

Rutledge asked him how to find Harrison, and went back out into the rain to start his motorcar. Harrison lived in a house just west of town, and Rutledge found it with ease from the clerk's description of the low stone wall in front. He stopped, went to the door, and asked for Harrison.

The maid who had answered his knock asked him to wait, then escorted him to a small sitting room down a passage, where a thin man with red hair rose from his chair and frowned.

"Do I know you?"

Rutledge waited until the door had closed behind the maid. "My name isn't Dunne," he replied. "I used that to gain entry. Rutledge, Scotland Yard. I've come about Captain Jarvis."

"I don't know anyone called Jarvis."

"You asked about him at the hotel yesterday after the birthday luncheon. You thought he might have been someone named Dunne."

"I did no such thing."

"Someone returned later in the evening, stabbed Jarvis to death, and took only one thing from his room. An old box with brass hinges and hasp."

"I'm afraid I don't know what you're talking about. Why should I want an old box? As you can see, I'm comfortably set here. I can buy whatever strikes my fancy."

"I'm not sure it has anything to do with money. And he wasn't intending to sell, he was holding the box for me."

"You say I asked someone about this Jarvis. Who was it?"

"The clerk at the hotel."

Harrison stood up and went to the door. "We'll see about this. Take me to this clerk."

They drove the distance in silence. Rutledge had the feeling that Harrison was very angry, and he was prepared for anything. Except for one thing—when they reached the hotel, they were informed that the clerk had taken the rest of the day off.

"He felt ill, he said, and asked if I could take over," the young woman behind the desk informed them.

Harrison said something under his breath. Rutledge ignored him. "Where can I find this man?"

"I'm not allowed to give out personal information about the—"

"Rutledge, Scotland Yard." He took out his identity card and showed it to her.

"What's Mr. Phelps done, then?" she asked, a worried frown on her face.

"His direction," Rutledge snapped.

"I'm coming with you," Harrison said when the clerk had finally complied.

He found the cottage without difficulty. It was down Pudding Lane, the second house from the corner. Rutledge knocked sharply, but no one came. He tried the latch, and the door swung inward. He called the man's name once more, then walked into the front room of the cottage. There were signs of hasty departure in the bedroom, clothes strewn everywhere and the wardrobe standing open.

He turned to Harrison. "I'm not sure what this means. But I'd advise you not to leave the village. I'll want to speak to you later."

Harrison said, "My good name has been impugned. I'm going with you."

There was no time to argue. Around back, Rutledge saw that a bicycle had been ridden through a muddy patch, the imprint of the tires already filling with rainwater.

"There's a chance we'll catch him. Let's go!"

They ran around to Rutledge's motorcar, and drove back to

the High Street. The question was, which direction had the man taken?

Harrison said, "He won't have gone toward London. To the hills, then."

Rutledge agreed, and turned west out of Worthington. He soon found the rough, uneven track that Harrison pointed out.

"There's a hamlet tucked under the ridge," he said. "Several people from our village once lived there. It's desolate now." They soon came upon the scattering of cottages, most of them in various stages of decay. Harrison added, "These people lived by the moor. Whatever came to hand, including cutting withies and rushes for thatching. The men died together at Gallipoli, and their families came into Worthington in search of other work. Sad case, really. They were watermen, set in their ways, unwilling to change, any of them."

"Wait here, in case he tries to leave," Rutledge said, and began going from door to door down the muddy street.

It was in the last cottage that he found the clerk, Phelps. A bicycle was propped against the far side, almost out of sight, and the door stood ajar.

Someone had got there before Rutledge. The clerk was lying on the rotting floor in a pool of blood, a knife in his chest. And the box was nowhere to be found.

He splashed through the puddles, hurrying back to the motorcar. Harrison called, "Did you find him?"

"I did. He's dead."

"Good God," Harrison said. "What's so damned important about this box?"

"It belonged to the Dundee Rifles Officers' Mess. Someone broke in one night in 1903 and took it, leaving behind two dead—a sergeant major and a corporal. Everyone was questioned, but the inquiry got nowhere. Captain Jarvis knew about the box because his father had been an officer in the Rifles. That's why he believed he recognized it when he saw it in a pub here in Worthington."

"It was here in Worthington? How did the pub come to have it?"

Rutledge told him about the ex-soldier. "On the whole, I believe the barkeep. He was glad to be rid of it when Jarvis offered to buy it, and then regretted that he hadn't asked more for the thing."

"Where's the ex-soldier now?"

"I wish I knew."

Harrison said, "There might be a way of finding that out. The rector of St. Mary's sometimes feeds men looking for work. It isn't as bad now as it was just after the war. He might remember your man. How long had the box been at the pub?"

"A matter of a week or ten days, according to what I was told."

He turned the motorcar and drove back to Worthington. The church of St. Mary's was at the far end of the village, and the rectory stood beside it, an early-Victorian building with scalloped trim on the eaves and the dormers.

Mr. Swift was an elderly man with snow-white hair and bright-green eyes. He recognized Harrison at once, and welcomed both men, leading them back to his study, where a small fire struggled against the dampness of the day.

Rutledge explained the reason for calling, and the rector listened intently, frowning over the deaths of Phelps and Jarvis.

"But what's there about this box that someone is still killing people over it?" he asked, dismay in his voice.

"If we knew that, we'd be a long way toward finding our man," Rutledge said. "In the officers' mess where a regiment is quartered, in this case in Scotland, there are the battle honours, the regimental silver—sometimes quite an impressive display of it—and the regiment's flags from various engagements, among other important objects. One of these was the box, and the police were told that it was the Honour of the Regiment."

"Hardly reason to kill for possession of it," Harrison put in. "Besides, it's a Scottish matter, I should think. Why is the Yard involved?"

"Because the Scottish police traced the thief to England before losing him."

"I remember the story now," the rector said slowly. "Just after the Boer War—I had been living in Carlisle then. The Dundee Rifles were appalled that the box was lost to them. Later, one of their officers wrote a book about the regiment during the fighting on the Somme. It was nearly wiped out, and he blamed it on the loss of the box."

"Legend has it that the regiment will thrive as long as the box survives. If it's lost, the regiment will be lost as well. John Graham of Claverhouse, First Viscount Dundee, was one of the first martyrs of the Jacobite Wars," Rutledge went on. "He was killed at Killiecrankie in Scotland in 1689, fighting to keep James the Second on the throne after he'd been replaced by William of Orange and James's daughter Mary. As he lay dying, one of his officers cut a lock of his hair and placed it in a wooden box. It was said that he caught the man's arm, told him to build an army and carry the box before it into battle. As long as he did, the army would be victorious. And the regiment has been very superstitious about that box ever since it was formed."

"'Bonnie Dundee,'" Harrison said. "Yes, of course. I learned the song as a boy."

"But why wish the Rifles ill?" Mr. Swift asked. "If it *was* a thief, why take the box and leave the silver? It doesn't make sense."

"The speculation at the time was that the thief was interrupted by the sergeant major before he collected the silver. Another theory was that he held a grudge against the Rifles."

"Good God," Harrison said. "But that must mean the thief is here in Worthington."

"Precisely. We must find that ex-soldier, and learn how he came to have the box."

"He couldn't have known its value," Harrison replied. "Not if he sold it for the price of an ale."

But in spite of all his efforts, Mr. Swift couldn't recall which of the many soldiers coming to his door was the one they sought. "They're all so alike, thin and hungry. They eat and move on."

"A dead end," Harrison said as they walked out of the rectory.

"Not quite," Rutledge said. "I can't imagine that the hotel clerk knew the value of the box. Someone else saw Jarvis with it, and questioned Phelps. He'd have gone to him as soon as he'd lied to me about you—I expect, in the hope of being paid handsomely for keeping his head and sending me off on the wrong track. And he was killed for his trouble. Who are the oldest residents of the village? I've often found they're a well of information."

"The rector—"

"He hasn't lived here for twenty years or more."

"Mrs. Hobson, then. She lives on the other side of the post office."

The rain was letting up as they drove there. Mrs. Hobson, surprised to find the likes of Mr. Harrison on her doorstep, was flustered. She asked them to step into her front room, and sat on the edge of her chair after they had refused her offer of tea.

Rutledge noted that she looked to be in her eighties, but her back was as straight as a rod, and she was dressed carefully, her white hair done up in a smooth bun on top of her head.

"We've come," he began, "to make use of your memory. I'm told by Mr. Harrison that your mind is very clear about the past."

"Oh, well now, I wouldn't go that far," she said, nervously smoothing her apron over her thin knees. "I do have my off days."

"You've lived here in Worthington all your life, I understand. Do you remember anyone who went off to be a soldier in a Scottish regiment?"

"Oh, dear," she said, drawn unexpectedly into the past. "That does seem like such a long time ago. We were so young, Willie and I. He swore he'd die if he couldn't marry me, but I'd already given my heart to Mr. Mills and there was nothing I could say. He went off and tried to sign up with the Buffs, but they turned him down. Coming back through London, he met some soldiers of the Dundee Foot, as it was called then. And he went off to India with them. The next thing I heard he was a sergeant. Then something happened out there, and he was disgraced. Drummed out of the regiment. When he came home he claimed he'd been invalided out. But his wife told me later that it was wrongfully done. That he was innocent."

"And was he, do you think?"

"He was a broken man. I think he loved the army more than anything. More than me, because he forgot me soon enough and married another girl," she added with a wry smile. "He died not long after that, leaving a widow and a son. Harry took it hard, went wild after the funeral, always in trouble somewhere. Then he left Worthington for a bit, and when he came home, he was a different man. Calm and settled, ready to marry his sweetheart. As if all the wildness was over."

"When did he come back to Worthington?" Rutledge asked.

"It was just after the Boer War, as I remember."

The Dundee Rifles, as they'd become, had fought bravely in the Boer War as well as along the Northwest Frontier in India, adding to their reputation.

Rutledge glanced at Harrison. "Where can I find this Harry?"

She shook her head. "He's in the churchyard, sad to say. He died two weeks ago."

"Children?" Harrison asked.

"A boy and a girl. Sally is married and lives in Glastonbury. The boy's been in Borstal, sad to say. Sowing his wild oats, like his pa before him, only his pa never had any trouble with the police."

But he might well have murdered two men in Dundee, Scotland, Rutledge said to himself. "Where's the boy now?"

"Teddy didn't come home for his father's funeral. He said he was in Manchester, and never got word until he went back to London. But I think he wanted to stay away from people who knew him. Embarrassed, like."

Or was wanted by the police in Manchester. Aloud, Rutledge said, "Give me his name, if you will."

She looked distinctly uneasy. "I didn't intend, talking to you, to get the boy into trouble."

"We can't be sure he is," Rutledge told her. "Until we speak to him."

"Teddy Miller. His mother, Alice, lives by that copse of trees just at the end of the High Street." She hesitated. "You won't tell Alice, will you, that I betrayed her boy? She looks in on me from time to time. I've grown fond of her company."

Rutledge thanked her for her help, and as they returned to the motorcar, he said to Harrison, "It appears your name is cleared."

"In for a penny, in for a pound," Harrison replied, stooping to turn the crank. "I miss the war sometimes, and the feeling that I'm alive because I'm about to die."

"If he's killed two men, like his father before him, he'll put up a fight."

Harrison didn't answer. He got in the motorcar and settled himself next to Rutledge.

They found the house without any trouble, and went together to the door. It was opened by a middle-aged woman, one side of her face dark with bruising. "Yes?" she said, wariness in her eyes as she held the door half-closed so that they couldn't see beyond her into the passage.

"Mrs. Miller?" Rutledge said pleasantly. "I've come to speak to you about your late husband. Mr. Harrison, here, tells me that he died only recently."

"Yes, two weeks and three days ago," she answered, her eyes clouding with grief. "It was a hard blow."

"How did he die?"

"Of a cancer," she said. "In his lungs. What is it you wanted with him? I've paid all his debts I knew of. There's not much money left."

"Could we come in? It will only take a moment."

"I'm—I'm in the middle of preparing dinner," she said, her voice rising. "Could you come again another day?"

"I'm afraid not. I have to return to London shortly." He put a hand on the door, and she cried out.

"Stay here," he said to Harrison, and set out at a run around the side of the house toward the rear. He was just in time to see a young man of perhaps twenty dashing out the kitchen door, heading for the orchard and the copse of trees beyond. Rutledge went after him, and they were halfway through the copse before he brought the fleeing suspect down. Getting to his feet, he hauled Teddy Miller up again, and said, "I'm arresting you for the murder of one Captain Jarvis and a hotel clerk named Phelps."

"I didn't do anything," Teddy Miller said, still breathing hard. "You don't know anything about me."

"I know you slapped your mother for getting rid of your father's old box. Where is it now?"

"Wouldn't you like to know," Teddy sneered, trying to shake off Rutledge's grip on his shoulder. "Maybe I burned it."

"Not likely," Rutledge said. "Or you wouldn't have killed two men to retrieve it." He marched Miller around the house to where his mother stood in the doorway, her face streaked with tears.

"I didn't tell them anything, Teddy," she called to her son, her voice edged with fear. "Truly I didn't."

"He won't be around to harm you, Mrs. Miller," Rutledge said, pushing Miller toward the motorcar. "He's in police custody now."

Harrison joined him, holding the door as Rutledge, his mind on Hamish, pushed Teddy Miller into the rear seat.

"Will she be all right?" Harrison asked, looking over his shoulder at the stricken woman. "I'm not sure how much she understood about this business. But she did say to me, 'It's brought nothing but evil, that box.'"

"She could be arrested. Time will tell. But for what it's worth, I don't think her husband ever told her where the box came from. And she was too frightened to betray her son."

They drove directly to the constable's office, and it was a good hour before Constable Hull quite grasped what had been happening while he was quietly making his morning rounds. He went to see the bodies, and then insisted on interviewing Mrs. Miller.

She recognized the two knives used in the killings—they had come from her own kitchen—and began to cry.

They set about searching the house, but there was no sign of the box. When Hull had left to question Teddy Miller again, Rutledge went out to scour the orchard and small wood. It had begun to rain in earnest, and he was forced to return for an umbrella. He found Mrs. Miller in the kitchen, and when she looked up at his face, he knew he had been searching in the right place.

Half an hour later, he'd found the box, this time buried a little deeper. For that Mrs. Miller could indeed have been charged. He couldn't decide whether she had tried to shield her son or whether she was determined to be rid of the box that had cost her family so dearly.

"I tried to open it once," she said as he brought it in and used a cloth to wipe away the water and the earth that clung to it. "But the hasp doesn't work."

"No. It's a puzzle box," he said, and fumbled for the hidden key. Suddenly the front moved, and then swung out. Mrs. Miller came to stare over his shoulder at the contents. Inside was a faded, brittle square of silk, and on it lay a lock of hair curled into a half-moon.

Hamish said something, but he was drowned out by Mrs. Miller.

"That's all?" she was exclaiming, shock in her voice. "He killed for someone's hair?"

He wasn't sure whether she was speaking of her husband or her son. "It's a talisman," he explained. "A lucky charm to those who served in the regiment this belonged to."

"I hated the box," she retorted. "I saw my husband's face whenever he looked at it. And I shivered."

"Why do you believe it's malevolent?" Rutledge asked, restoring the hair and the silk to the box and closing it.

"Harry told me once that it held his father's heart. I didn't know whether to believe him or not. If I'd had my wits about me, I'd have told Teddy that it was buried with his father. But I was too frightened, when he thought it was gone forever. He wanted to pass it down to *his* son. Well, he won't never have one now, will he? And the box will go back where it came from. All nice and tidy, that, only I'm left with no husband and no son on account of it. Will they give me a reward for its return, do you think? It's only fair, considering."

# HEDGE

## BY JONATHAN STONE

I'm writing these words in complete darkness.

I can't see this pen or paper in front of me.

I'm forming these words carefully in straight lines across the paper—assuming this handwriting will be clear enough to read—whoever ends up reading it—if anyone ends up reading it.

I'm writing this purely by feel. Like everything I do in here. The darkness is so black, so absolute, my eyes are useless. Still in working order presumably, but with no current function. I've never seen what surrounds me here, and if I am brought out of here the way I was brought in, I never will.

I can only feel for, and imagine, what it looks like around me. I'm reduced, literally, to my imagination. Sometimes I catch myself wondering if there's anything really there, at my ink-black periphery. But of course, I know there is. I know too well the solidity, the thickness, that is there.

I gave up kicking. I kicked furiously for a little while, then began to worry about conserving my energy.

I gave up screaming. The screaming made me feel better—a release—but only for a moment. It's such a tight, close space, my eardrums rang from my own screaming. Soon enough I knew it was pointless. It was only wearing me out.

I can only speculate about where I am. My initial kicking yielded only a sense of the solidity of my container. And the solidity of what surrounds me, beyond my container. The solid, discouraging thunk and thud of thickness, of substance. Of don't-kid-yourself-you-ain't-goin'-nowhere.

It's about three feet high, give or take, too low to stand up in, so I periodically clench my legs, pump them, shift them, have done that since I got here. I keep count, track the repetitions in my head, to make sure I'm doing it long enough to qualify as exercise, to keep my blood flowing.

Not surprisingly, you quickly lose all sense of time. You have no way to gauge it. They took my watch, of course, its dim dial a beacon of order and organization. Who would have thought I'd miss its seconds, minutes, and hours so acutely?

It's dank. Which is why I assume I'm belowground. How far belowground? Three feet, fifteen feet, a hundred? In an old mine shaft? An abandoned well? An industrial fill site? An old cave? I have no idea. Or is the dankness just my own mustiness at this point, my own anxious sweat, a coating of worry?

It's silent. The noise of life totally gone. I hear only my own sounds—the beat of my breathing, my shifting—which I am acutely conscious of one minute, then forget about the next, and am again conscious of the minute after that. Part of the antipodal rhythm in here: hyper-self-awareness, and then, a moment later, no sense of a self at all.

The air pipe is about eight inches wide. It lets them drop me food without my ever setting eyes on any of them. Without their risking my seeing them, identifying them.

Potatoes. Fresh fruit. A can of beans. A carton of juice. There's a little porcelain bowl in the corner. My hands stumbled onto it when I first felt around me, and its function was immediately obvious. The stench I have to bear. Overwhelming at first—you gag as it marinates at such close range, but then, as the days wore on, it was hardly noticeable. Smell, like sight, is a sense that can be suspended by circumstance, apparently. And when (on the second day? the third day?) they lowered a clean bowl balanced in a simple rope sling, I understood well enough. I took the clean bowl off the sling and carefully—very carefully—put the filled one in it.

It feels like a coffin. But it's *not* a coffin, I remind myself. It's somewhat taller, a little wider. If it felt *too* much like a coffin, if it felt too much like you were buried alive, you might go crazy. It needs to feel just enough like it is *not* a coffin. They know this, I'm sure. They know how to keep you—they need to keep you—just this side of sanity. Crazy, you have no value to anyone—and that's not the condition they want you in.

No noise, no sound, except the slight scratching of this pen skating across the paper, the click of my punctuation landing on the page, correctly, I hope, in the otherwise utter, exaggerated silence around me.

This thick stack of paper, these dozen pens, mysteriously here for me, greeting my searching hands on my arrival.

Trying to keep straight lines, keep enough space between them, not bunch them too close. I'm carefully rotating the pens, switching to a new one every few pages, to maximize the chances that my words are actually making it onto the page.

I'm writing this as fast as I can, because I don't know how much time I have.

Maybe only another minute. Maybe another week. Maybe a month. Maybe eternity. (I'm trying not to think about that last too closely, trying to push the thought away, but it's hard to push anything beyond these thick dank walls.) And although there is the chance they want me to write only to see what I know—and then they'll bury it along with me—there's also the chance they want me to write it for some actual, future use, where my story, my version of events, is genuinely valued.

Because the paper and pens are presumably here for a reason. Merely to keep me sane? Or to drive me crazy? Or for some purpose opaquely between those two?

––––

IF YOU WERE awake, alert to the world around you, if you were honest with yourself, you saw it coming. We all did.

The only surprise, really, was that it hadn't happened before.

You could certainly hear it, couldn't you, in the commentary of your coworkers, delivered in a jaded tone of inevitability. You could read about it in the sober news articles, see it quantified in the accompanying charts, couldn't miss it in the strident, alarm-bell editorials.

You could hear the phrases—the verbal shorthand—passed slickly, knowingly back and forth like hors d'oeuvres at a cocktail party.

Bandied around by the cable commentators, by your frail and alarmist eighty-five-year-old neighbor, by the couple behind you in the theater just before the film starts.

*Growing income disparity. Richer and poorer. Two Americas—separating fast.*

*Disappearing middle class. We're becoming South America.*

(You were at those dinner parties, weren't you, where you discussed or at least acknowledged the two Americas, in the form of outrageous CEO pay and equally absurd minimum wage, and the dangerously growing chasm between rich and poor, the protesters camped in city parks across the country—and yet blithely and eagerly and with no sense of irony in the next moment you exchanged recommendations on landscape crews or designer clothing sales or highlights of your last golf round. No inherent accusation. I saw you at those parties. You saw me.)

If you were alert, you saw it coming—a by-product of the slow-motion collapse of our financial system—its immense granite and marble pieces in their thunderous fall to earth sending out a vast rising cloud of unemployment and a billowing dust of anomie, desperation, and foreclosure, on homes, futures, lives—combined with a government that, it turned out, couldn't protect its citizenry in the aftermath of a bad Gulf storm, or win little wars of its own devising against third-rate countries with crackpot dictators—a government paralyzed by partisanship and infighting like a parlor full of quarrelsome aunts—so how could it ever be effective against the guerrilla nature and craft of what was coming....

So it became in a way inevitable, and finally, it was here: our latest import. Like fresh flowers from Peru and Uruguay. Like our silent diligent busboys and landscapers and masons from Mexico and Guatemala and Honduras. Like our coffee from Colombia and Brazil. Simply the latest South American product.

Kidnapping.

Not like snatching the Lindbergh baby, though, with catchphrases and newspaper headlines and newsstand sales. Not disenfranchised white-trash moms or laid-off dads using a stolen kid as a pawn. Not taking a kid from a mall parking lot. Not kidnapping for emotional leverage in a disastrous marriage or as a political statement, but much more pure and direct than that.

Kidnapping for money. Simple commerce. The business of kidnapping. A business we'd never had. A vast new enterprise galloping onto the American economic landscape, with a cottage industry of security firms, private police, alarm systems, tracking devices, springing up around it.

Yes, at some level, inevitable. An utterly logical extension of social forces and events—illegal immigration, income disparity, economic meltdown, and our battered but still mythic virtues of private enterprise and free-market capitalism.

A broad social problem that fractured like a fragile jigsaw puzzle into individual problems, each piece its own island of woe. A social problem, arriving where you never really believe broad social problems will arrive—at your own doorstep.

———

SPEAKING OF DOORSTEPS: follow me now across this particular one…that of a fancy building where the hum of Fifth Avenue goes suddenly silent behind me as I enter the building's vaults and coolness. Where I announce myself and my destination, which solicits a raised eyebrow of appraisal and then a quick nod of approval from the uniformed doorman. Where the whispering whoosh of soft oiled mechanics is all I hear ascending in the dark cherrywood elevator—with a plush bench with embroidered cushion along one side for a weary matron or pampered child. My entry into the apartment is closely supervised by the uniformed maid, leading me along a corridor of original neoclassical, Impressionist, and New York Brutalist canvases, and antique maps dating to the Renaissance, letting out in a mahogany den anchored by an immense Louis XIV desk—huge leather chairs facing it, and a fireplace behind it where perfect blond logs smoke and crackle.

It could be the apartment of a corporate law firm's senior partner, or the New York residence of a multinational's CEO, or the Manhattan retreat of a Midwestern industrialist or a Silicon Valley venture capitalist. It is in fact the home of my brother.

He could be any of those. It doesn't much matter, for the purposes of this record. In fact, his social group crosses the borders of all those occupations. They whack the little white ball around together expertly, second nature, while they throw deals each other's way.

We occupy different universes, which intersect, only glancingly, on Thanksgiving and Christmas. His adorable young daughters have never flown commercially. His goateed chef, Armando, travels everywhere with them. I've observed a steady process of increasing insulation—big tracts of land, private schooling, home delivery of groceries and goods—anything to cut off interaction with the world at large.

But the more our lives have diverged, the more our bonds of love must be proved to each other, and provide proof to ourselves—*See, it's not about worldly circumstance, it's about something deeper*—to reaffirm the pride in our connection.

He just bought an island off Nova Scotia. He's also got one in the Caribbean. His friends are buying them, too—it's the thing to do. The island of their existence was at first merely metaphorical. Now they're isolating themselves physically as well. Islands used to be an impractical fantasy—inaccessible, wildly impossible to build on and maintain. But personal jet travel—and the absurdly outsized returns in a previously humming world economy—have revived the allure of island life.

"Coming along," he says of his Nova Scotia property. "Guesthouse and dock are done. Main house has a ways to go. I'll have you up soon." I'll get my few days, shoehorned in between his high-powered, like-walleted guests—his friends.

We rarely talk business. He's an investor, a capitalist. I'm an investigative journalist. (I'm a freelancer, and the small circle of online publications I work for now each want their own coverage of, their own angle on, the kidnapping story—a story too pervasive, too personal to *not* be covering—and like all my assignments, it will help pay my modest but rising rent.) He is establishment, the power structure, there to maintain it and enhance it; I'm there to question it, challenge it, rattle it, shake it up. We are like brothers lining up on opposite sides of the scrimmage line, brothers divided by a civil war—but have rarely said anything to acknowledge it. In truth, we both enjoy it, I think—bracketing the world, encompassing the world, from its opposite sides.

But now our lives are at risk of intersecting beyond the holidays. Because if certain criminal parties learn that an investigative journalist on their trail is the only brother of a wealthy financier, grabbing me both silences me and promises a payday—maybe too tempting a combination to resist. So I owe my brother this visit, to say what I'm working on (I wouldn't let him deter me, and he wouldn't bother to try), and to warn him how it makes us both a target.

And once pleasantries are aside, and I explain the nature of my latest assignment and my concerns, I double-check—only in passing, making the assumption—that he is already carrying some kind of kidnapping insurance.

He pauses a long beat, looking at me. Examining me. "I have no kidnapping insurance."

The risk professional? The consummate arbitrageur of risk and return? My puzzled expression asks: *Why not?*

He smiles grimly—his shifted lips a parallelogram of irony—and mutters gruffly: "Too expensive. Can't afford it."

*Meaning what?*

"Me, my wife, my kids, we're uninsurable," he says. He looks out, explains in simple terms to the neophyte. "To take the risk of covering me, anticipating what kidnappers would ask, an insurance company would want...well..." and here, I can tell, he is careful to avoid the specifics, "... it would come to a sum that you, that I, that anyone, would find incomprehensible. So it's just not worth it." He smiles at the irony. "We've got too much money to be insurable."

I'm silent. I've never imagined such a problem.

He explains a little more. How it's actually worse than that. More complicated. The insurance companies can't tell what he's worth. "So they can't assign a value or formula to me. And they won't work without their formulas.

"But here's the thing. My business life has been built on risk. Assessing it, quantifying it, minimizing it. Being proactive and anticipatory about it. Acting on risk. This is just another case of risk. That's how I'm looking at it."

*Proactive and anticipatory. Acting on risk.* Calculating life down to the financial, to its plus and minus columns. That's how he's gotten where he is.

He turns serious, dutiful. "I've started interviewing guards," he says. "Seen some impressive candidates. It's not a terrible arrangement, for them or me. These guys will be your fourth for golf or tennis. They'll drive your ski-boat. Even make a decent meal or two on the chef's night off. Ex-military, most of them. Physically fit, mentally sharp. Of course, you've got to watch your women-folk." He smiles wolfishly.

So he *is* protecting himself and his family, at least. But we both still know that he is sitting across from his greatest liability. A condition that long precedes my accepting the kidnapping assignment. For the wealthy, poor relations are always a burden. Their ruined evenings and sleepless nights. For everyone like my brother, it will always be someone like me—someone entrenched in the messy daily world he tries to absent himself from—who will define and demonstrate where familial responsibility begins and ends.

———

AND NOW, OF course, it has come to pass. And if the kidnappers know what they are doing, they have begun with my wife, given her an impossible sum for us to cobble together, but one that *he* can handle—not without a wince or two—so that it is she who must approach him. With her anxiety, with her tears, with my two- and four-year-old daughters in tow, she'll presumably make a far more effective salesman on his threshold than some cold South American voice on the phone.

I see my wife there in that same lonely leather seat opposite his massive Louis XIV desk, or standing by his plane amid the wind and engine noise on an agreed-upon tarmac, making the case to him, wondering why she even should have to, resenting his somber nod, knowing he has already decided what to do, or what not to. Already, perhaps, without her knowledge, through his network of contacts, engineering my release.

———

AND NOW LET me pull you into the dark with me again. A far different quality of dark than the one that surrounds me now.

Wait with me…pulse pounding…in the dark of a storage closet of an insurance company that happens to sit two floors above the trading floor of a brokerage firm—a brokerage firm where my research, my interviews, my tips, my instincts, have all led me.

A dark alive with anticipation, with a sense of mission and purpose.

A dark that *I* controlled, that *I* had chosen and arranged. By flowing in with dozens of glum wordless workers, who assumed I was simply reassigned from another building, as a number of the other workers actually seemed to be, so all my carefully practiced excuses were never needed—in fact, I never had to say a word. This silent, invisible army of the underclass, the army of night, in which a new soldier with his ID and brown uniform isn't even noticed, much less questioned. (ID and brown uniform copied from photos on the Internet site of the maintenance company that had the building's cleaning contract.) I earned only a wan welcoming smile or two from squat matronly Filipinos and Malaysians with no English.

Pushing my cart of supplies around the halls of the insurance company—restocking bathrooms, dumping office trash cans, replenishing my cart from the various supply closets, learning the floor's layout as I go. Toward the end of the shift, slipping silently into the storage closet I scouted earlier, arranging the packs of paper towels and rags and smocks just so, to settle into the black silence….

Post-9/11 New York fire laws require that during office hours, stairwells between floors (and between companies) in high-rise buildings must be open and accessible.

So that when the brokerage firm's trading day is in full swing the next morning, a new mailroom attendant (in the required uniform of pressed black slacks and white button-down shirt) is working the day shift, already out on his morning rounds….

\* \* \*

Hushed carpeted lobby, expensively coiffed receptionists, paneled walnut and mahogany walls, a serene corporate preserve high above the street, far above the fray, operating as if unshaken, untouched, by the utter turmoil of the markets it serves, as if all is well, nothing is changed, like a man in top hat and tails strolling through the rubble of a bombing—and moments later, my dowdy mail cart and I are bursting through the regal matching mahogany doors as if through swinging saloon gates, onto the trading floor—vast cacophonous sheer space filled with computer monitors and white-shirted loose-tied bodies—leaning forward, slouching back, striding confidently, rocking nervously, a dense Bosch tableau of headsets and torsos and screens. A futuristic locked-away warehouse of men and their blinking machines, and you couldn't ascertain which were beholden to which, which the masters, which the servants.

And as I stroll, head bowed—docile and dull—down the central corridor of this cacophony—traders murmuring, shouting, declamation, tintinnabulation—I have the sense of all commerce passing through these electronic portals, all the pounds and bushels and barrels and crates of oranges, coffee, lemons, rubber, salt, rapeseed oil, bioengineered corn and soybeans—all digitally routed through, paying homage and tithe to, this electronic crucible. The economy is in collapse, but this gear of it spins ceaselessly on an unstoppable flywheel—the continually floating, continuously adjusting assignment of value to products, of money to goods, of dollars to donuts.

I pass the desks at the end—quieter here, something more measured and mundane traded here—and push my mail cart—by instinct, by intuition—through a further, interior-most set of double doors, to another trading area—same monitors, same white-shirted young traders—but the room is much smaller, a narthex off the nave, and when I enter, a few traders turn, and look at me, and frown suspiciously.

I step closer to the monitors—an aborigine drawn to the blink and gleam.

On the monitors there are first and last names, with a five- or six-digit number next to each name....

I become light-headed, breathing deeply to steady myself. Comprehending fully, bluntly, irrevocably, what I am seeing. The blinking numbers, the tiny digits, as fragile and as clear as a life. A life, assigned a value. I watch, dumbstruck.

Listen to the smooth explanatory pitch I was subjected to over the next few days, as various silver-tongued spokesmen tried to justify, to dissuade me from my article, to *educate* me. "It's clean. Antiseptic. A marketplace solution. Matching buyers and sellers. It's a redistribution of wealth. We broker it. We're middlemen. The South Americans know they'll get their money—they don't want to be in the business of killing, they prefer the business of not killing. We assist them in assigning a value—in determining that fine trading point between what they can get and what they can't, what the maximum reasonable payout is, above which they likely won't get a thing. And on the other side of the ledger, the victims' families, they know we're the experts. They know we have the experience in what the kidnappers will take, what they'll accept. So they turn here. They know we'll stake them, work out a payment plan they can afford.

"And as middlemen, as providers of the stable marketplace and the necessary and reliable software and experience and expertise, we take our cut. And for that cut, there's almost no killing....

"It's contained. Systematic. Gives the kidnappers an organized clearinghouse. Keeps them calm. Keeps people alive."

Bring kidnapping to America, and we will Americanize it. Streamline it, polish it up, PowerPoint it.

Pork bellies, soybeans, coffee, lives, freedom.

Trading freedom.

Freedom—America's signal promise—converted now to supply and demand.

What's a life worth? On the one hand, of course, that can't be determined. We're not in a position to judge. It's the exclusive, murky province of philosophers and of God.

On the other hand, we determine the worth of lives all the time. Every salary review. Every war reparations board. Every carat of every engagement ring. Three thousand perish, and we appoint a special master to examine and assess each claim, to distribute based on future income potential, current earnings, current responsibilities, current and future suffering. A life's worth can't be determined, and yet we do it every day.

And I was therefore sure, looking at those monitors, that somewhere, in data, on disc, there was a system. A score. Like a credit rating, which every financially functional American adult has assigned to them, so why not something similar? Your *worth* rating. What will it take, what will it cost, to get one/you/him/her back? A shorthand, a set of metrics, within which the traders negotiate, they parry, they get to yes.

And it occurred to me that such a rating wasn't measuring something so vague as "a life's worth." It was measuring something far more specific. Something unaccustomed to measurement.

It was measuring love.

How much did a spouse love a spouse? How much did a family love a child? How much exactly? Because that's what determined the price. The price to get them back. And those prices in aggregate in turn helped determine a proprietary algorithm, and the question was how you stacked up, rated, on the algorithm. Did your family want you back more than the mean? Or less than the mean? Did you want your child back more? Or less?

One's freedom—all it required was enough love.

Those monitors: an enormous blinking Love-O-Meter.

Love, quantified.

Love, American style.

WHEN I CURL into sleep in this blackness—for a few minutes or a few hours, I can't really tell—I pull up my knees, pull my collar up over my face, to make some recognition, at least, some gesture of order, of a differentiated state, to aid my descent into slumber. And I have another tradition that carries over from curling into sleep in my own bed in my own home. I think of my daughters. I minutely construct their faces, their big swimming wide curious eyes, their smooth soft cheeks. I picture them folding into sleep themselves—blissful, unconscious, as natural as breathing, and their example leads me, instructs me, inspires me.

My brother's two daughters are only a few years older than my own. They are surrounded by adults—day nanny, night nanny, ubiquitous chef Armando, maids and handymen and gardeners. The girls have gotten the sense that they're on more than equal footing with the adults. That they are, in some way, in charge. They have picked it up, presumably; felt it in the air. The predictable result? An insolence, an arrogance, a bossy willfulness. First-class brats—literally.

Yet he dotes on his girls, my brother does, lights up when they float silently into the study or kitchen in the morning, often not yet dressed, in their silk catalog pajamas. He watches them fascinated, admiring. And I understand. They move in a rarefied realm, a magical sphere, and when you are with them, you move within it a little yourself. That's how it is for dads and daughters. A helpless addiction to their aura. No different from my own.

His daughters are lightweight. Trusting of adults. Easily transportable. Perfect kidnap candidates. But they weren't taken. Instead, it was me.

———

As I THOUGHT about the numbers on those screens—later looking closely at the photos of them I snapped with my unobtrusive little palm camera—I could see that each blinking number, each "price," included a fraction. Which confirmed that the traders were earning a percentage. *We take our cut,* as I'd been told. But it wasn't a simple fraction. It didn't take a genius to see it was a *fraction* of a fraction. Which presumably meant that some other party was taking a cut, too—an unchanging, consistent cut, given the math. My brother's words in passing returned to me: *They won't work without their formulas.*

Insurance companies, I thought. After nearly choking themselves in a feast of their own toxic CDOs and credit default swaps and other exotica, going back to their roots. Their core competency. Insuring lives. Because everyone was upping their life insurance, buying more, lining up for it. To say nothing of kidnapping insurance, which had always existed for executives on South American business trips, but now there's suddenly a broad new need for a host of new kidnap financial products. And are the insurance companies just the dumb-luck beneficiaries of this chaotic new world, or do they have a hand—a substantial, steady hand—in creating it? The percentage of a percentage revealed on those screens in that dark, quiet, interior trading room would seem to be giving me my answer.

And to maintain the value of the policies? To keep customers paying their premiums? To motivate a steady stream of new buyers? It was obvious to me that the marketplace would require the occasional killing. The killing must go on to some degree, to hold insurance rates steady; to stabilize income and guarantee return.

The insurance companies: using death and chaos as a hedge.

Death and chaos. Always a smart hedge.

You can generally count on them.

The insurance company where I crouched waiting in the dark—it wasn't just fire doors and stairwells that connected it to the trading floor of the brokerage below it. It was an idea—the same cynical, practical, highly profitable idea. I had passed between the two companies as easily, as permeably, as fluidly, as the cynical idea itself.

———

OF COURSE, THERE need not be the traditional envelopes of cash anymore. The transactions could all be paperless—wire transfers, bank account to bank account, made and confirmed on the Internet from a laptop anywhere. With neutral, third-party "holding" accounts for the cash in transit, while the deals, the drop-offs, the physical transfer and reclamation details, are finalized. That's how it *would* work. If the marketplace I discovered did not need to keep itself secret.

So to camouflage the existence of such an organized marketplace, there are still the smudged, crumpled envelopes of cash. To make the kidnapping continue to look primitive, dangerous, uncontrollable, criminal.

I'm pulling one of those envelopes out of my pocket now.

A white stationery envelope like any other.

A discarded envelope. Its contents already removed. Precisely the kind of envelope that *could* have held cash. But it was not stretched or creased or crumpled that way. It looked fairly pristine, as if it had held, if anything, only a note, and it seemed somewhat out of place, of course, there beneath me on the dirty car floor behind the front seats, where I had just been shoved forcefully, facedown, out of sight.

An envelope I scooped up and stuffed into my pocket in the brief few seconds before—hovering above me, working silently—they tied and adjusted my blindfold, bound my hands with duct tape, and delivered the little pinch in my arm that would put me out.

An envelope I scooped up because I recognized in an instant—from childhood, from my past, in a millisecond ignition from my unconscious—my brother's handwriting on it. Which I still might *not* have recognized, but for what was written in it. In his distinctive arrogantly looping lettering, precisely the words I had seen written before, on cards with gifts, on previous envelopes, so many times over the years: my own name and address. But here, the address underlined repeatedly, for emphasis—and next to it, some further instruction I had no time to decipher.

I have the envelope out now. I am turning it in my hands in the dark. I have been taking it out of my pocket, turning it around in my hands, putting it back, since I got here. I can't see it, of course. I can't check or confirm here in the dark what my instincts told me in an instant, can't get another look at that handwriting. But I have had nothing but time to think through, to imagine, what would be written on the note inside it.

On the back of the envelope, I can feel an embossed return address. I have run my fingernail along its ridges slowly, incessantly in the dark, trying to carefully count the letters in the embossed name, to see, to feel, whether they correspond to my brother's. Trying the same thing with the next line, the street name and number.

*This is my brother. This is where he lives. Go ahead. Take him. I offer him up to show you that you can't threaten me. That you don't frighten me. To show you that I am bigger than the emotions that you rely on, better than the game you play. I am in control—not you. As proof, I give you my only brother. To show you that my money, my holdings, my assets, will always come first, and that I will make any sacrifice neces- sary to protect them. A sacrifice all but biblical. My own brother. To show you by example that I will pay for no one. Are you contemplating grabbing any of my family? I am showing you the outcome before you even try.*

Proactive. Anticipatory. A contrarian play.

True to his profession, a hedge. A hedge against calamity.

There are multiple possible versions, of course. I mull them obses- sively here in the dark. Maybe something like this: *Someone I know, someone I'm close to, is about to blow the story wide open. Expose the insurance companies, the collusion, the vibrant market behind closed doors. But I know how you can gain six, eight months. Six, eight months more profit. Kidnap him. Take him. You won't hear from him, you'll buy yourselves, the industry, months more profitabil- ity. Millions more in policies and assets. Yes, he's my brother. Which shows you where my loyalties lie, doesn't it? And what would I like in exchange? To avoid the same fate. Make sure we're left alone—me, my wife, my girls.*

Or maybe it *was* cash. The simplest deal of all, the deal tailored best to the blunt mentality on the other side. *Some money in the envelope now. More to come, when you prove you have him.* My brother paying his modest tithe to the system—paying what *he* is comfortable with, what *he* decides, setting the terms himself. And if those who took me decide to then try for more, they will soon see he doesn't play games. A deal is a deal. He won't go higher by one dime. I am the proof. *I said take him, and I meant take him.*

Yet how could I really think it's my brother? Is there really any evidence beyond my brief glance at that envelope (I'm fingering the embossed return address again now, counting the letters, matching them to his own name, to *our* family name)—amid, after all, their hustling and jostling me, pushing me down, sandwiching me between the rows of seats, the car jerking and squealing into motion. . . . With any chance to examine the envelope again, to verify, having disappeared into the darkness with me. . . .

Yes. A far more compelling piece of evidence, really. In front of me, in front of you, all along.

The pads and pens.

They would have been put here only if someone knew this box would host a writer. That this box would shortly contain someone who felt he had something to say, a story to tell. There's even more reason for these pens and paper if someone knows roughly *what* I'm going to write, and wants me to write it to see what I know.

But I can't help thinking there's more to it. A larger, sardonic purpose of my brother's own.

To demonstrate to the writer how useless it is to write it down. To mock him by giving him all the materials, all the time, yet while he works he knows that it will very likely be buried with him. How impotent, how futile his commitment is. How childish, how unrealistic, his view of his own importance, his own hushed, determined bid for immortality.

Go ahead, jot away. Scribble into the darkness. Because the metaphor is the reality: it *is* scribbling into the darkness. As unseen by you as it is likely to remain unseen by anyone else. It is mere artifact before it is even out of the box.

The world moves not by words, not by ideas, but by money. Mammon trumps all. My being inside the box, or outside the box, is merely a matter of cash.

Write to your heart's content, he is saying to me. Rip the lid off an industry, expose fraud, right wrongs, summon justice. The world goes on without you. The world tramples you underfoot, figuratively and literally. You are a voice deep beneath the ground. A voice unheard.

It is a mockery, a lesson, a puzzle, a deal—all rolled efficiently into one. The operational efficiency he always strives for, my brother. The stack of empty paper, the pile of unused pens. It bears his signature. It's what *he* has written to me. Clear in message, clear in tone. Without resorting to words at all.

———

I HAVE BEEN here long enough, pondered the possibility, toyed amateurishly with the physics. How long will I have if the air supply is cut, if the eight-inch pipe is stuffed up with a rag or crumpled T-shirt? That's how they would do it—not to have to see the victim, or think about him or her. How long would I have? A half hour? Fifteen minutes? Ten? Five? In which case, will I go bleary?

Illogical? My mind and writing hand sloping toward the nonsensical? I'm no scientist, but certainly it would be a process...the oxygen slowly decreasing, competence vanishing, the brain giving in before the body. My mind—my trusty, true, sole, final companion—giving out just before the rest of me, sacrificing itself as if selflessly, in some ultimate, elaborate hallucination, some final incandescence, before the permanent dark. The $CO_2$ gathering, hanging in the blackness, starting to explore the seams and crevices and crannies of my box as if with curiosity, as if in reconnaissance, until it coils in on itself, until there is no more for it to explore....

———

Voices.

Voices above me.

A murmur—I can't hear specific words. But it isn't the silent delivery of the daily food drop. It's multiple voices, movement up there.

My brother's voice? I think. The negotiator, making the deal?

Trying to be a faithful scribe here. Keeping pen to page.

Heart pounding with anticipation...

Hands shaking...

Head spinning...

Short of breath...

All the signs of my own excitement...

Voices...

Suddenly muffled.

Fainter now...

Do I still hear them?...

Did I ever?...

———

I AM WRITING these words in the light.

Stunned to be blinking in the brightness.

Stunned by what I see.

A huge warehouse of thick concrete containers...dozens of them...

Each with an air pipe extending from one end...

Each container twenty, thirty feet from the next...thick enough, far enough apart to fool us each into thinking we're alone...

The air pipes extending up, like chimneys, to fool us into thinking we are buried deep...

Extending up to a high catwalk, from which the food is obviously dropped...

Thick concrete containers in orderly rows. A graveyard of the living.

Organized. Institutional. I should have imagined such efficiencies of scale—a trading floor, after all; corporations, after all. Why could I not imagine that my unseen tenders were tending all of us, like a herd of animals in a barn? Keeping us fattened up to fetch our price at auction.

I should have imagined something like this....

Victims wouldn't normally be allowed to see this, I'm sure. I'm sure you're released as you were brought in—blindfolded.

So why the exception for me?

My brother. He must have paid. I must have been wrong about him. He has saved me.

Then where is he?

Where are my captors who have finally let me go?

Where is anyone?

The concrete containers are all still sealed. But I am somehow outside mine....

Moving alone through this light-flooded warehouse...

Imagination my only companion...

The warehouse is so vivid.... The light is so strange....

Pen still up. Like a sword for battle. Writing, writing it all...

And at last I can see these words and letters as I write....

I can see them, even in this utter darkness....

A warehouse of containers...

So am I released from mine?...

I must be.

I am.

I am released.

Pen down.

# THE LUNAR SOCIETY

## BY KATHERINE NEVILLE

Society, however, cannot exist among those who are at all times ready to hurt and injure one another... Beneficence, therefore, is less essential to the existence of society than justice... Justice is the main pillar that upholds the whole edifice. If it is removed, the great, the immense fabric of human society... must in a moment crumble into atoms.

—ADAM SMITH, 1759

*Lichfield, England: Winter 1798*

Tonight was the night of the full moon.

The night of justice, at last, thought Dr. Erasmus Darwin.

Tonight's meeting at Birmingham would be their first meeting in many "moons"—indeed, in scores of them, several years in fact. And today, as Darwin thought wryly, was most appropriately a "Moonday," a term that his confrères of the Lunar Society—their unofficial gaggle of scientists and inventors, or "Lunaticks"—had humorously dubbed themselves and their choice of meeting nights over these past forty years. For despite membership that often rotated, whether due to death or wars, travel or exile, those who could meet had traditionally met each month on the Monday nearest the full moon, in order to ensure safe return on horseback to their homes. At least, that was the reason that Darwin's eccentric band of "loonies" had always given outsiders.

The doctor limped across his library to peer through the frosty Italianate windows, waiting for his carriage to be brought round. Since he had shattered his knee many years ago in an accident, his horse riding days were over: Physician, heal thyself, he mused. For tonight it seemed far too late for recriminations. Over anything.

In the nearly forty years of the Lunar Society's scientific explorations, they'd become internationally famous, jointly and separately, reaping awards and honors, as well as vast fortunes from their manufacturing, scientific discoveries, and inventions: whether it was their harnessing electricity with their early cohort, Dr. Franklin; or Joseph Priestley's isolating oxygen; or naturalist and physician William Small's creating new metals; or Wedgwood and Bentley's inventing new forms of ceramics; or Watt and Boulton's supplying steam engines and copper coinage; or their collective engagement in building canals and launching balloons—Darwin himself being the first Englishman to fly in one. Not to mention the risks they'd taken to their reputations and even to their lives, in supporting liberal movements like the American and French Revolutions.

But tonight's private meeting in Birmingham, as Darwin recognized better than anyone, might prove their greatest risk of all.

He suddenly felt a chill not caused by the weather. Though the temperature alone might be enough to discourage any sane man from venturing abroad on a night like this. For hadn't today been marked in the almanac as the coldest in fifty years? Only this morning, Darwin's milkmaid had protested to her master that she could not milk the cows, for her fingers were blue, and the hot froth of milk had turned to slush the moment it hit the pail.

No, Darwin knew quite well that this chill of his wasn't for fear of the rough journey that lay ahead, nor was it caused by the bitter climate—at least, not weather-wise. It was the political climate that numbed him to the bone, the changing climate throughout England, which threatened him and his closest cohorts, and had grown ever and ever worse, these past three years.

Indeed, tonight's gathering had been presented overtly as a simple "dinner invitation." For by law, the members of the Lunar Society could actually be imprisoned for "holding a meeting": ever since Prime Minister Pitt had passed his Seditious Meetings and Treasonable Practices Acts. The former required that all intellectual societies, such as their own, must be licensed by the State in order to exist. And the latter banned members from merely discussing either religion or politics.

In addition, there had been the riots of "Church and King"— roving mobs of faceless men who'd ranged throughout the countryside, burning homes and meetinghouses, targeting Freethinkers, Quakers, Unitarians, any dissenters not belonging to the official Anglican Church. The Lunar Society itself was hardly left unaffected:

Matthew Boulton and his partner, James Watt, had set live cannon outside their Soho steam engine manufactory to protect the Works against marauders, who were bent upon demolishing free enterprise; chemist Joseph Priestley saw his home devastated by the mob, his valuable scientific instruments looted and smashed, and he'd fled to exile in America, in fear for his life; ceramics industrialist Josiah Wedgwood was found dead under suspicious circumstances, in a room locked from within. And now, Joseph Johnson—the publisher of Erasmus Darwin's own vast, erudite, and widely acclaimed botanical studies—had just been jailed for selling seditious works!

They'd all felt the noose tightening round the throats of liberal thinkers like themselves. Experimental science such as theirs, which had blossomed in the Age of Reason, was lately deemed treasonable behavior; their own skills were turned against them as a weapon, a crude bludgeon to pound them into conformity. The members of the Lunar Society—isolated and reviled by royals and the masses alike—watched in horror as England herself, slowly yet willingly, sank into the mire of her own ignorance....

Darwin shook such thoughts away as he saw, just outside his imposing Georgian manor, that his horses had been harnessed and the carriage brought round, the coachman seated on the box. It was time for the journey to Birmingham that he had postponed for so long. This journey that, in truth, he had both desired and dreaded these past three years. It could not be put off any longer.

Turning from the windows, the doctor caught a brief glimpse of his reflection inside the mullioned glass: that beefy yet trustworthy face that men admired and numerous women had, quite improbably, fallen in love with; his massive arms, thick neck, and bull-like torso, which gave the impression of substance.

For the first time Darwin felt the full weight of his sixty-six years of trials and travails. He hoped the tide might be turning at last. For tonight, Darwin and his eminent colleagues were together about to step off a steep and daunting precipice, an act after which there could be no change of heart, no turning back.

But wasn't that what justice was all about? thought Darwin. For, as wise men had known since Solomon's day, there was no justice, for anyone, in slicing the baby in half!

Limping to his desk, Darwin opened the black leather satchel sitting there—it was another of his own inventions, a "medical bag," as he'd dubbed it—which contained the tools of his trade. Then, from the box beside it, he carefully lifted the artifact from its wrappings: it was a ceramic medallion that fit neatly into the palm of his meaty hand. Though the doctor's hands might appear to some to be as awkward as grappling hooks, his dexterity was such that, using only his thumb and forefinger, he'd trained himself to tie a surgical knot within the confines of an eggshell! It was a skill and precision that had always been his hallmark, and which, he thought, might well come in handy in the mission that lay ahead.

The medallion itself was no secret: indeed, its image was legendary. Created about ten years ago, by a cofounder of the Lunar Society, the great ceramist Josiah Wedgwood, it was a beautifully crafted cameo, carved of black-on-yellow jasper. It portrayed the figure of a dark man, who knelt upon one knee and looked beseechingly skyward. His hands, manacled with irons, were clasped in prayer: a slave. Above this figure letters were printed in the shape of a rainbow. They read:

*Am I Not a Man and a Brother?*

Ten years ago, when Wedgwood and his fellow Lunar members had first learned from Darwin that local Birmingham manufacturers made a successful trade in forging such manacles and leg chains for British plantation owners in the West Indies, they'd been horrified and infuriated. Wedgwood had retaliated by creating this medallion, in honor of the recently formed "Society for the Suppression of the Slave Trade."

And to further the destruction of a business which Lunar members found abhorrent—the sale of and trade in human beings—they made sure that the cameo was copied and disseminated everywhere. This heartrending image and its motto—whether worn by men or women, on a pin, a button, a hair ornament, a bracelet, a snuffbox—both the image and its motto had spread swiftly from England to the Continent to the Americas. But the popular, ubiquitous black-and-golden cameos were missing one critical element:

The artifact that Erasmus Darwin now held in his palm was in fact the prototype, the original casting, a gift ten years ago from Josiah Wedgwood to Darwin, his closest friend. As such, it was the only cameo in existence that contained the secret lacking in all the others, a secret known only to three people—and one of those was now dead.

Now, with infinite care, Darwin wrapped the fragile object in a soft, supple layer of sheep's wool and placed it in his satchel, topping the whole, against possible prying eyes, with vials of opium, and the herbs of his standard medicaments. Then he shut the bag and took up his walking stick, and he went into the entryway. His manservant, awaiting him there, bundled the doctor in thick robes for the journey, then assisted his master to labor down the steps in the bitter cold, and to squeeze his bulk into the waiting carriage.

But within the dark confines of the carriage, Erasmus Darwin could not help thinking about two worrying things that had nagged at him all along:

First, that if tonight's mission took off, like that hydrogen balloon he'd sailed from Derby so many years ago—as he, perhaps recklessly, prayed that it would—then the rest of their journey might equally prove more fraught with danger than if it had failed upon the launching field. And second, that by unveiling this long-kept mystery that was hidden within the medallion, they might open a Pandora's box too difficult ever to shut again.

Darwin would soon know the answer to both these worries: for that third person, the cameo's original genius—both of its inspiration and its creation—had agreed to join their illegal gathering of "Lunaticks." At Birmingham, tonight.

## Birmingham, England: The Full Moon

For the first time in three years, the members of the Lunar Society were together again. The conversation around the table, thus far, had been light and filled with pleasantries, against prying eyes and ears.

They had lost so many, but the five were here at the long table: in addition to Erasmus Darwin was his fellow founder and their host this evening, the senior member at age seventy, Matthew Boulton, who'd begun as a successful buckle maker and had gone on to create copper coins for the realm, and to fund the engine manufactory of the man seated here beside him, James Watt, now age sixty-two. Then Darwin himself, the famous botanist and man of medicine; and at his other side the chemist James Keir, followed by "young" Samuel Galton, age forty-five, the wealthy son (paradoxically) of a Quaker gunmaker. Sam, a latecomer to Lunar membership, had experimented in optics and color following the works of Isaac Newton. Not present were inventor Richard Lovell Edgeworth, retired to his farm in Ireland, and Joseph Priestley, who still languished abroad in self-imposed exile in America.

The sideboard, which had been laden earlier in the evening with fat capons, ham and fish, Cheddar and Stilton, puddings and baked apples, had now been cleared off by the "newlyweds," as Darwin still liked to think of the two young folk, who'd just arrived tonight from their home in Shrewsbury: the beautiful and bountiful Susannah "Sukey" Wedgwood, who, a bit more than two years ago, had married her favorite childhood playmate: none other than Darwin's young son, Robert. A marriage that Erasmus Darwin cherished, and that would have filled Sukey's father, Josiah, with joy, had he lived to see it.

As Robert was setting around the stone beakers of ale, flasks of whiskey, and platters of sweetmeats, Sukey now joined the group, sitting among these men of science as if she were one of them—as she'd often done, even as early as the age of seven or eight, by her father's invitation.

Sukey Wedgwood was a treasure. Everyone knew the famous paintings of the Wedgwood clan, done when Sukey was young, and executed by "Lunar" artists like George Stubbs and Joseph Wright, who'd happily attended their meetings, participated in their experiments, even lived among them.

And Sukey was special in other ways: while all the Lunaticks believed that girls should benefit by a scientific education, and had trained their daughters accordingly, none had done more than Josiah Wedgwood, with Sukey, his favorite daughter. The boys might run the manufactory, but Sukey had Josiah's spirit and spark, his scientific curiosity, and even his headstrong stubbornness; her father had favored her beyond all his passel of other children. Now Sukey was a fully blossomed young woman, radiant in her youth and in her recent marriage—which, as everyone knew, had brought to her new husband, Robert, a dowry of more than twenty-five thousand pounds from her father, Josiah's, estate—a vast fortune to bestow upon such a mere slip of a girl.

And tonight, she'd come hither from Shrewsbury, to bring another bequest.

In anticipation of this, their host, Matthew Boulton, made certain that the servants were kept away, and that all the dining room doors were shut and locked. Standing beside his son's lovely wife, Erasmus Darwin placed his medical satchel upon the table, and withdrew and unwrapped the medallion, placing it in Sukey's waiting hands. Her husband, Robert, had already prepared the burner apparatus, and its blue flame, so familiar to all the scientists around this table, shimmered amidst the yellow candlelight.

Sukey stood beside the flame, her face illuminated from below, looking upon the cameo in fascination, just as she'd looked in all those portraits of her as a child watching scientific experiments, gazing into an orrery or watching a bird in a glass cage.

"Gentlemen," Sukey said, regarding the face of each man around the table, these men who had been her mentors and father figures. "You are gathered here tonight to engage upon an enterprise that may prove to be a dangerous risk, and a risk for something that perhaps may be founded upon nothing more than the fantasy of a dead man and upon its explanation, tonight, by myself, whom you've only known as a girl. This medallion represents my father, Josiah Wedgwood's, last will, which he wrote in secret ten years ago and entrusted me to interpret as best I could, for nothing was written down except what has been writ here, within this bit of colored jasper." Sukey paused and added, "God help us, each and all, to determine, once we have seen it, what will be the right path."

The men stood and gathered closely about Sukey; they all waited as she held the medallion lightly over the flame, with the uncarved side down. Slowly, within the yellow-and-black field of the raised carving itself, a shape began to emerge around the figure of the Negro slave: a large, luminous triangle that glowed in the dim light.

Then Sukey turned the medallion over to reveal its other side. And Erasmus Darwin gasped: "Good Lord, so he'd planned it all along...."


## *Philadelphia, Pennsylvania: Spring, Third Quarter Moon*

Joseph Priestley dismounted from his lathered horse and took the sweaty reins in his hand to lead his beast to the wooden trough to drink. His clothes were caked with mud. What a night it had been.

The noted chemist and former Unitarian minister had ridden all day from his isolated place in the countryside; he'd departed from home, with just some cash and the clothes on his back, the very moment this morning that he had received the written message.

But now he was dismayed by what he saw here around him: he'd not been in Philadelphia in nearly five years—not since he'd first arrived on these shores, an exile with the stench of his burnt house back in England still clinging to his clothes. His reception was poor, for at the moment of his arrival, the American Congress itself, in pandemonium, was clearing out of the city whilst the yellow fever raged all around them. That epidemic, it was said, had by now claimed the lives of more than four thousand Philadelphia souls. Even tonight, here beneath the bright blue moonlight, the streets appeared to him deserted and desolate.

Now, for the first time, the peril of Priestley's immediate situation struck home to him. How would he even find a place to shelter himself, much less his horse, here in the Negro quarter of the city? But here was precisely where he'd been directed to go. He patted his horse on the flank and peered up the street anxiously.

Just then, in the cold moonlight, he saw a lone figure striding along the quai; the chap raised his arm aloft in a gesture of greeting. Priestley waved back and was about to call out, but the man gestured for silence. Priestley took his horse's reins and went to meet the other.

"Hallo, Reverend Priestley, we've been expecting you," the chap said, *sotto voce*. "We mustn't be seen here, there's a curfew, you know. I'll explain when we reach our destination." And with that, he took Priestley by the arm and the horse's reins in his other hand, and led them away from the river, through the maze of ramshackle streets.

Priestley glanced over at the fellow as they went: he was a tall, slender chap of about thirty, clean-shaven, wearing a well-cut vest and breeches, his straight black hair tied back in a queue—exceedingly handsome. And somehow familiar, Priestley thought. Could this be the mastermind he was to make contact with, or merely an emissary?

They reached a stable, where a small black boy came out and took the horse's reins. "Horatio here's rather young, but an excellent stabler," the man assured Priestley. "He will curry your horse and clean his hooves and make sure he's fed. And we'll do the same for you!" he laughed.

Then he led Priestley up the steps of a darkened building and rapped at a door, which was opened by a young mulatto woman. Mellow light flooded out, they entered the room, and the door was shut and bolted behind them. There a fire flickered in the hearth, a kettle swung from the soup arm above the flames; the overwhelmingly delicious aroma of victuals reminded Priestley of just how long it had been since he'd eaten. The man had already filled a large plate for his guest, and he dismissed the young woman.

As Priestley expressed his deep gratitude and broke bread into his plate of soup, the younger man studied him.

"You do not recall having met me, Reverend Priestley," he said at last.

"You are familiar to me," the scientist assured him. "Though at this moment, I can't think when or where."

"It was five years ago, here in Philadelphia, that we met," said the other.

Priestley thought again how remarkably good-looking this young man was, more so here in the firelight, his cheeks flushed with health, his intelligent brow, the chiseled profile like a noble Roman cameo....

"We were both then in the company of Thomas Jefferson," said the other.

And then Priestley knew.

"You're the cook," he said, in complete amazement. But here, in different clothes, in a position without subservience—dear Lord, the chap looked as white as anyone else! The younger man was nodding in wry amusement. Though, of course, thought Priestley, he couldn't have felt all that amused. After all, the man now sitting before Priestley, when last they'd met, had been Thomas Jefferson's slave!

"James Hemings, at your service," said the fellow. "I'm free now: two years ago, my cooking finally bought me my freedom. I've just been back to Paris, where I'd first learned my trade when my former master had been Secretary to France. For five years we lived there, up until the Revolution; my sister Sally and I were among the household staff. I procured everything for Mr. Jefferson, from horses to houses. We were briefly in England, and that was where I met professor William Small, a founder of your Society."

As flabbergasted as Priestley was at these revelations, now the connections were falling into place. Scotsman William Small, a physician and natural historian, had for some years been professor at the Virginia College of William and Mary, and mentor while there to the young Thomas Jefferson, whom Priestley himself, even now, mentored through their correspondence. After William Small's return from America to England, he had also become one of the founding members of the Lunar Society: like Priestley and the rest, Small had never been reconciled to anything about the slave trade.

But something still puzzled Priestley.

"The message I've received," he explained to Hemings, "the one bringing me hither tonight, had directed me to make all haste here, to '*Come to the aid of a Man and a Brother.*' That is a motto you must know, referring as it does to an African slave. Yet, Mr. Hemings, you tell me that you, grace to God almighty, are now a free man."

"Reverend Priestley," said James Hemings, "was there a symbol written on the letter you received? Perhaps a triangle?" When Priestley nodded, mystified, James added, "You have heard, perhaps, of 'the Triangular Trade'?"

It was a term that Priestley knew as well as anyone might, who was opposed to the slave trade: the highly lucrative business of interdependent financial traffic, called "triangular" because on the first leg, guns, shackles, and muzzles were exported from Europe into West Africa, where they were deployed to capture whole villages of innocent people; the ships there would refill their empty holds with cargos of captured humans—"black gold"—who were bound on the "middle passage" for perpetual enslavement in the West Indies and Americas; and the vessels then returned, on the final leg, laden with luxuries like coffee, chocolate, sugar, rum, and cotton for gluttonous European consumption. It was a business so lucrative, as Priestley well knew, that it had run its three-hundred-year cycle virtually unchallenged, creating fortunes for some of the noblest families in Europe—and with no end in sight.

"Reverend," said James Hemings, "I may be free, and living in a free state like Pennsylvania, but all of my relations in Virginia, even my sister, are still enslaved by a man you know well. As I said, I've just returned from France, where, as you are aware, four years ago the French revolutionary government abolished slavery. While there, I realized that the war with England and the current crises in France make it impossible to know what will happen there next. The safest place for a free black man may well be England; I do not know. Reverend Priestley, mine are a people who have spent hundreds of years awaiting a miracle. We cannot wait to learn what the French or the British may plan to do."

Priestley, a humanitarian who did admire Thomas Jefferson, but who loved freedom more, felt at this moment that he might weep from the weight of his emotions.

"I now understand why the Society sent me here with such urgency," he told James Hemings. "I am to meet with you, to plan a concerted effort, hands across the seas, to create a multinational abolitionist movement!"

"Actually, Reverend Priestley," Hemings said, "you are here tonight, just as the message said, to come to the aid of a man and a brother." Hemings paused and added, "Now I would like to introduce you to the man you have been beckoned here to meet."

At this cue, a tall, dark man in elegant clothing entered the room. He was a person of substance, as Priestley could tell by his demeanor. He seated himself before the hearth, between Hemings and Priestley, and turned to address the latter.

"I am called Horace Wright," the newcomer said. "I am a trained master chef with twenty years of experience, and have recently, this past year, learned even more chef's technique from our young friend here, who is a master of French cookery." He smiled toward James Hemings. "However, I have learned that I cannot ply my trade openly—not even here in Philadelphia, where we of African descent are deemed free."

"Why can you not?" asked Priestley.

"Because, sir, several years ago, President George Washington signed into law the Fugitive Slave Act, empowering whomever desired to do so to seize enslaved peoples who had escaped bondage, and, with the reward of large bounties, to return them to anyone who claimed to be their 'rightful masters.'"

"From whom had you yourself escaped?" asked Priestley, already sensing what that answer might be.

It was James Hemings who supplied it: "Horace escaped from President Washington and his family," he said. "He was their chef. His name was not Horace then: they called him Hercules."

### Shrewsbury, England: Summer, New Moon

Sukey Wedgwood Darwin stood upon the terrace of their country house, one arm about the shoulder of her husband, Robert Darwin. His arm was wrapped around her waist. Robert looked down upon her lovingly.

"Susannah," Robert said, "your father, Josiah, did not die of natural causes. What caused him, do you think, to take his own life?"

"Father was dying of a cancer in the jawbone," Sukey said. "Your father gave him enough laudanum to relieve the pain—and perhaps a bit more. Father took it, and locked the door. But Father only left us as he did, because he knew that we would set in motion the mission he himself had fought and prayed for all his life. As indeed we've done."

"Only thanks to you, and to your well-celebrated infernal grit," Robert commented blithely. "Those old men of the Lunar Society may have dreamed of, or even wished for, a better world. But you're the one, my darling, who actually set those wheels in motion."

Sukey shrugged. "I only gave them the key to their dreams and wishes," she objected. "The rest they are accomplishing themselves, with very little help from me!"

"Admit it to me," said Robert, "that you and my father, the 'doctor,' actually 'doctored' that medallion!"

"That triangle—my father's message about the 'Triangular Trade'—was already present on the medallion," said Sukey. "Could I help it that all those names mysteriously appeared on the reverse? How could I have known that those names were the names of famous slave owners, whose slaves were already mounting, on their own, an important resistance to the slave trade? Could I help it that the Lunar Society rushed to the aid of these men, or that Messieurs

Watt and Boulton had already minted copper coins that could pave their paths to freedom? My dear, far be it from me to interfere with a plot that may free hundreds of families that are still in bondage! Indeed, this entire scenario may have been the work of the angels!"

Robert bent and kissed his wife on the lips. "You are the angel," he said.

The two were silent for several moments.

Then Sukey said, "Robert, when we have children, let us be sure that each and every one of them understands what we, and our parents, have lived for. Let us vow to one another that, no matter what the future brings, and at all costs, our children will destroy this vile abomination of slavery, that they will know and respect what the Lunar Society once stood for—as manifested in its secret code."

"And what exactly is that?" asked Robert Darwin. "For I'm afraid that my father never shared any secret code with me."

"It's simple," said Sukey. "We believe in reaching for the moon."

## End

Postscript: Another of the "favorite" slaves owned by George Washington's family, Oney Judge, managed to escape to freedom, and later, so did six relations of James and Sally Hemings, once owned by Thomas Jefferson. Sukey and Robert Darwin's son Charles became a lifelong, bitter opponent of slavery, and was inspired by his grandfather Erasmus's example to pursue scientific research that supported the common origin of all humans: *The Origin of Species.*

# HIGH STAKES

## BY R. L. STINE

I noticed the man as soon as Denny and I stepped into the bar. His eyes were so unnaturally blue, like polished sea glass, they didn't belong in that leathery, tanned face. He had a head of thick, white hair brushed straight back, his cheeks creased beneath a two-day bristle of beard, a blue bandanna loose around his throat, probably covering a tortoise-skin neck.

He appeared to be alone in a red vinyl booth against the back wall, one hand wrapped around the stem of a martini glass, the other rolling a short cigar between his lips.

I saw all this in a few seconds. I'm good with detail. I have a quick eye and a good lockup memory. For a while, I thought I wanted to be a journalist, before I decided to write novels, before I decided to be a wife.

Some people think having a father with a fortune of money makes life easier. But for me, it made it all so much more confusing and difficult because it opened up so many possibilities, I found it impossible to choose.

So I chose Denny. And now, I had no business studying the man in the back booth because I had to devote myself to celebrating our honeymoon, true love and all. I really was acting head-over-heels and the whole cliché. And not just because Dad was so against Denny and so opposed to my rushing to get married.

He was right. I'm only twenty-three, and I'd only known Denny for a month, after all. But Dad didn't understand. I knew he was posing as a father figure, doing what he thought he was supposed to do, his duty to warn me away from the man who could only be after our money.

But I've always thought of my father as an offshore adviser. He was two wives past my mother and most of the time barely remembered that I—Ashli Bennett—existed, except as a name on a bunch of trust accounts (which don't start paying off till I'm twenty-five).

Denny wasn't after my money. He just wants us to be happy. He's so adorable and *eager*. He hardly ever lets *go* of me, and I love that. As much as I love the dimples on his cheeks, so boyish, and his dark eyes, and his expression, so appreciative and humorous at the same time, as if he's enjoying the world's best joke.

Oh, God. Listen to me. Am I a living romance novel? Is *that* what I've become? No *wonder* Dad was appalled and refused to be a witness at our city hall wedding.

But so what? Here we were, our arms tangled around each other, leaning together on tall stools at the bar, a wall of dark bottles gleaming in pink light in front of us, and the soft shusssh of the ocean through the open windows. The air felt salty and cool against my burning cheeks, and Denny's light kiss at the back of my neck sent me shivering back to romance-novel world.

Cameron Cay was my dream honeymoon spot. I didn't have the nerve to tell Denny the island was named after my father, Cameron Bennett. Yes, Dad was chairman of the partnership that owned it. Mom and I came here every winter of my childhood—until Dad took his profits and dissolved the partnership—and suddenly our winter destination became a resort in Anguilla.

Not bad, either. But Cameron Cay lingered in my fantasies. If you want to psychoanalyze me, you'll probably drag up something interesting in my wanting to honeymoon with Denny in a place my father once owned. But so what?

The bartender was a slutty-looking young woman with white-blond bangs, dark raccoon-eye makeup, and balloony red lips like everyone in the movies. She wore white short shorts and a sleeveless tee that showed off her blue tattoo of a grinning monkey head. I wanted to ask her why she chose a monkey. But she only looked at Denny (as if my head wasn't leaning on his shoulder).

He ordered two glasses of Prosecco, and I said, "Come on, Denny, it's our honeymoon," and told her to bring a bottle of Cristal. He was pouty after that. He doesn't like it when I make him look cheap. So I kissed him a lot and ran my hand slowly up and down his thigh, and he got over it pretty quickly.

We carried the bottle and glasses to a table. Except for an older couple staring out at the water in silence by the window and the blue-eyed man in the back booth, the bar was empty. Lovely steel-drum music played from a speaker somewhere above us. The breeze off the ocean made me shut my eyes. I wanted to remember this, remember all of this.

We clinked glasses. "To us," I said.

"To us *forever*," Denny added.

The champagne was perfect. Denny squeezed my hand. He leaned across the small round table, brought his face close to mine. "Maybe we should take the later snorkel boat, Ashli. That way we could spend the morning...in bed."

I tilted the slender flute and took another long sip. "I like the way you think, Mr. Sparano."

"Hey, thanks, *Mrs.* Sparano."

We clinked glasses again, kissed, and drank. I felt as bubbly as the champagne. I'm not embarrassed to say it. We ordered popcorn shrimp and fried calamari, finished the bottle of Cristal, and ordered another one.

It was late and my head was fizzy, a little hard to focus, when I realized the blue-eyed man had joined our table. The cigar was gone but the martini glass remained in his hand. He raised it across the table to Denny and me. An opal ring gleamed on his pinkie finger. "I just want to offer my congratulations," he said, a smile creasing his weathered face. "Your honeymoon, right?"

We clinked glasses.

His glassy blue eyes were trained on me. I'm used to men staring. I'm not exactly a loser in the looks department. But his hard gaze made me glance away. The sea air had suddenly grown colder. I shivered.

He slicked down his white hair. I turned back. I liked the way his eyes crinkled at the sides. And I liked the deep crevices down the sides of his face. Made me think of a movie cowboy. He smelled of cigar smoke and a strong spicy aftershave.

He and Denny were chatting about something. The ocean was too loud in my ears. I couldn't make out the words. Was it the champagne? I was swimming sitting up. I gripped Denny's wrist. My life buoy.

"Clay Davies," the man said. "Everyone calls me Davies." It took me a short while to realize he was telling us his name.

"Where you from?" I asked. I poured the last of the second bottle into my flute.

He shrugged. "Here and there." He gave me a lopsided smile, almost an apology.

"What do you do, Clay?" Denny asked. I squinted at him. My new hubby was definitely more clear-eyed than me.

"I'm a gambler" was the reply. He watched us for our reactions. But we both just nodded.

"You came here for the casino?" Denny asked.

He shook his head. "No. No casinos for me. I gamble for high stakes. No cards or dice or horses. High stakes."

I struggled to clear my head. "You mean—?"

He emptied his martini glass and set it down on the table. He twirled the opal ring slowly with his other hand. "I bet on people," he said. He licked the last of his drink off his lips. The smile had disappeared. The crazy blue eyes moved from Denny to me.

"High stakes?" Denny giggled. Maybe he was as drunk as me after all.

"Do you like to gamble?" Davies asked Denny.

Denny tilted his head. Like when a dog thinks hard about something. One of his cute habits. "Sometimes."

Davies reached into his white beachcomber pants, then slapped a twenty-dollar bill on the table. He glanced around. "This place is dead." He climbed to his feet. "Come to my room. I'll show you what I do."

I made a face at Denny. I shook my head. I didn't want to go to this man's room. I wanted to go to *our* room. Had Davies forgotten we were honeymooners?

Davies took my arm and helped me up from the chair. His hand felt like dry sandpaper against my skin. "I think you'll find it interesting. Really. Only take a minute."

Denny was on his feet. He tugged me aside. "Let's just see what he wants to show us."

"No, honey, I really—"

He put a finger on my lips. "Our honeymoon, right? We want to come back with some good stories. This will be a story. I know it."

I started to giggle. The champagne, I guess. I held a hand over my mouth, trying to stop. I planted a sloppy kiss on Denny's neck. He gave me a conspiratorial wink.

He held on to me as we followed Davies out of the bar to the elevator. The steel-drum music followed us, and I could still hear the steady rush of the ocean. I realized it must be late. The lobby lights had been dimmed. A white-uniformed woman bent over a vacuum cleaner.

Davies walked with a slight hitch, as if one leg was longer than the other. He hummed to himself as we walked. The back of his neck was crisscrossed like lizard skin. I couldn't stop staring at it.

As the elevator doors slid open, a young couple in matching blue

sweat suits staggered out, holding hands. I guessed they were heading for a late-night walk on the beach. We rode up in silence. I
didn't feel like giggling anymore. Something about this adventure
had sobered me. I knew I should try to be alert.

Still humming, Davies opened the door to a suite on the fourth
floor. The front room was all white wicker, a sea-blue carpet, and
seashell designs on the wallpaper. French doors were open to a balcony that overlooked the beach. My eyes swept past the couch, a
few chairs, a glass dining room table.

"Come in, come in." Davies scurried about, turning on lamps.

"We... can't stay," I said, my eyes on Denny.

Davies motioned to a closed door on the right. "That's my
friend's room. He's on the mainland tonight." His blue eyes flashed.
"So, while the cat's away..." He rubbed his hands together.

*Weird,* I thought. *While the cat's away? What does* that *mean?*

Denny had a blank smile on his face. I couldn't read his thoughts
at all.

A gust of wind made the curtains leap at the open doors. I
grabbed Denny's arm. I saw a tiny lizard scamper across the dining
room table. "Let's go," I whispered. Denny waved me away.

"This way," Davies said with a short bow and a sweep of his
hand toward the door on the left. He pushed the door open. I felt
a wave of frozen air. He had the air-conditioning on full blast. He
clicked on a ceiling light as we followed him in.

I blinked. I saw a king-sized bed piled high with pillows. The
same shell pattern on the bedspread as on the wallpaper. A wicker
dresser against one wall.

"Whoa." A low cry escaped my throat when I saw the coffin. It
sat on the other side of the bed. The dark wood gleamed under the
ceiling light.

Denny burst out laughing. "Davies, do you sleep in that thing?
Are you a *vampire*?"

All three of us laughed. Davies laughed longer than we did. He
pressed his hands over the front of his Hawaiian shirt, as if holding

himself in. "I hope not," he said finally. He strode toward the coffin. "Isn't it the most beautiful wood? Have you ever seen mahogany like this?"

He waved us closer and reached to tilt up the lid. The inside was silky and red. I thought of my satin sheets back home.

"It's actually crushed velvet," Davies said. He ran a hand along the side. "So soft. Want to feel it?"

"What is it doing here?" I asked. The shrillness of my voice surprised me.

"You sell coffins? You're an undertaker?" Denny made another joke, but this one fell flat.

Davies's grin didn't fade. "I told you. I'm a gambler. I thought maybe you might also be a gambling man, Danny."

"It's Denny." He took a few steps toward the coffin. "I don't get it. What kind of game—?"

Davies had his eyes on me. He saw me back up toward the bedroom door, but I didn't care. "It's quite simple, really," he told Denny. "I make a bet with people. A high-stakes bet." He rubbed the bristly white stubble on one cheek.

I could see he was spelling it out slowly, building suspense. Toying with us. "What exactly is the bet?" I couldn't keep the impatience from my voice.

He gazed hard at Denny. "I bet that you can't spend a night in the coffin. That's all. That's all there is to it." He tapped the edge of the box.

I knew he wasn't telling us something. Hey, I grew up in New York City. I'm a Barnard girl. No way I'm going to be taken in by a cheap carnival trick. "You mean—?"

"Most people are too claustrophobic," he said. "They panic. They don't last the night. Or the fear overwhelms them, the fear of being dead, of spending eternity in one of these."

Denny walked up and slid his hand along the smooth wood. "I still don't understand. Do people run out of air? Is that it? They have to get out or suffocate?"

Davies shook his head. "No. Look. Vents. I put air vents on both ends."

"You pump in poison gas or something?" I asked. I don't know *where* that thought came from. "You put something through those vents and the person has to jump out?"

"No. Nothing like that," Davies insisted. "You come in at seven or so. You lie down. I close the lid. I lock it. You have a nice sleep. No torture. No tricks. At seven the next morning, if you're still inside, I pay you a million dollars."

I rushed forward and tugged Denny's sleeve. "That's insane. Let's go. Good night, Mr. Davies."

To my surprise, Denny shrugged me away. "A million dollars?" he asked Davies. "Is that the bet?"

Davies nodded.

"That's wild," Denny said, eyes on the casket bottom. "Too easy. I mean, I'm not claustrophobic at all. I could sleep in there for a week. You'd totally lose your money, Davies."

Davies adjusted the bandanna around his neck. "Sometimes I lose. But sometimes I win. Want to try it? We can both go to the mainland tomorrow and get bank checks. Mrs. Sparano, tell you what—you can hold the two checks."

"Denny, please—" I wanted away from there. But the color on Denny's cheeks told me he was excited. He was even breathing hard.

He pulled me back into the front room, and we argued about it. My point of view was there had to be a catch. Denny's point of view was, even if Davies was crazy, it was easy money. No way Denny could lose.

I pleaded and whined. "I don't want to do this. Even if you want a honeymoon story to come home with. He's a creepy man, and the whole idea is creepy. Keeping a coffin in his hotel suite?"

"Sure, it's weird, Ashli. But that's how the man makes his living." Lame.

But then Denny had the clincher. "This money can be *my*

contribution to the marriage, Ashli. A million dollars. Not *your* money. My wedding gift to you. My contribution. Money I earned for us."

My head still wasn't clear. But I could see how important this was to Denny.

I turned and saw Davies watching us from the other room. "Well?" he called. "Do you want to wager with me?"

"Oh, what the hell," I said. "It's our honeymoon. Let's make it *two* million dollars. Can you do *two* million, Mr. Davies?"

In the sober light of morning, it still seemed like a crazy idea. But Denny's excitement hadn't worn off, and it was catching. I actually felt giddy, totally light-headed, as we took the taxi boat to the mainland to pick up the bank check. And we joked about how making a profit of two million dollars on our honeymoon would *definitely* make a good story to tell our friends—and even our grandchildren.

"What's the worst thing that could happen?" Denny asked over our lunch of shrimp and crab salads and a nicely chilled Chablis, served in the shade of our beach cabana.

"Davies could be a penniless fraud and not have his half of the bet?"

Denny shook his head. "I checked him out online, Ashli. He's loaded. He owns diamond mines in South Africa. I'm serious."

It took a few seconds for that to soak in. I stared out at the ocean and watched a white, skyscraper-tall cruise ship inch by, out where the water met the sky.

"The only downside," said Denny, "is it'll mean I'll be separated from you for so long."

That tender line won him a delightful afternoon of lovemaking. We took a short break for one phone call. I called the bank and asked about Davies's bank check. At first, they refused to violate his privacy, but I finally managed to wangle them into saying that the check was good.

Okay. So, by the time seven rolled around and we made our way up to Davies's suite, we were both happily exhausted, even a little dazed, and Denny assured me he'd have no trouble at all sleeping through the night.

Davies met us at the door. He was dressed entirely in white, a crew-necked white sweater, very fleecy and luxurious-looking, over white cargo pants. He had shaved, exposing his crinkled and creased tanned face. He shook hands solemnly with both of us. Very businesslike now. No offers of a drink or chitchat about the weather.

We compared bank checks. Davies folded the checks together, then handed them to me. "I know you'll keep them safe till tomorrow morning."

"No worries." I tucked them into my bag.

Davies squeezed Denny's arm as we walked into the bedroom. "Nervous?"

"Not at all."

"You shouldn't be. It's easy. An easy two million. Unless you panic."

"I won't panic," Denny told him.

The coffin lid stood open. I gazed into the red interior and suddenly felt queasy. I guess from thinking about Denny lying like a corpse all night. Not sure if I could do it. I need a lot of room to roam around in. Always have.

A lingering kiss, and then Denny hoisted a leg over the side of the coffin and lowered himself to the red velvet. "See you in the morning, Ashli."

"Sweet dreams." The words sounded stupid, like I was making some kind of joke. But Denny smiled and stretched out on his back.

Davies carefully closed the lid. He clicked the silver latch and locked it. "You okay in there?"

"I'm enjoying it immensely." Denny's muffled voice from the air vents on both ends. "Ashli, go ahead and deposit his check. We've already won."

Davies uttered a humorless chuckle. He led me to the door. "I admire his confidence. Really."

I didn't know how to reply to that. So I just said, "See you tomorrow morning," and strode quickly down the hall to the elevator.

The sun was red but still high in the sky. I took a walk along the ocean, letting the spray cool my face. The water churned with high waves, and whitecaps frothed onto the shore. I took off my sandals and let the cold water wash over my feet.

I felt more tense than I'd expected, all knotted up and unable to think of anything else but that crazy-eyed Davies and Denny flat on his back in that narrow box. Two tall white cranes stared at me from a flat rock ledge. The air grew cooler as the sun lowered itself over the water.

I returned to the room for an hour or so and tried to take a nap. But I couldn't get comfortable. I realized I was hungry. We hadn't had dinner. I walked down to the coffee shop, slid into a sea-green booth, and ordered a grilled cheese and a glass of Pinot Noir.

I was sipping the wine, still waiting for my sandwich, when a young man burst through the restaurant door, his eyes taking a fast survey of the nearly empty room. He had scraggly blond hair over a pink-cheeked face. He was short and pudgy and had a red-and-white-striped polo shirt half-tucked, half-untucked over baggy white tennis shorts.

His eyes stopped on me. He nodded, his lips moving, and hurried over to my booth. "Mrs. Sparano?"

I set down the wineglass. "Yes?"

"Is your husband with you?" He had a hoarse, almost comical voice. His cheeks had darkened to red.

I gestured across the table. "Obviously not. Actually, he's lying in a coffin right now."

I expected him to show some surprise at that. But his face showed only alarm. "That's what I was afraid of," he said. He slid into the seat across from me. "Mrs. Sparano, my name is Kyle Jeffrey. Did your husband make a wager with Clay Davies? Did Davies make him lie down in a coffin?"

I nodded. "Yes. Is something wrong?"

I saw beads of sweat form a line on his forehead beneath the blond hair. "Well, yes. I'm so sorry to interrupt your dinner. But I'd say we have a situation here."

My hand bumped the wineglass, nearly toppling it. "A situation?"

"You see, I'm Davies's caretaker."

I swallowed. "Caretaker? Meaning he's... sick?"

"Yes. He's uh... unbalanced. I mean, mentally. He's been a patient at our hospital. But we're transferring him. We decided to give him a short holiday here. He insisted on bringing his coffin with him."

Kyle shook his head. "Unfortunately, I left him alone. I had to go to the mainland yesterday. I left him alone for one night and—"

I felt my throat tighten. "He's really *nuts*?"

He pressed clammy fingers on the back of my hand. "He isn't dangerous. But he likes to play these crazy games with people. And sometimes..."

The waitress arrived with my sandwich on a large pink plate. I shook my head and waved her away. "Is my husband in danger? Would Davies harm him?" My hand shook as I pulled the two checks from my bag and waved them in front of him. "We made a bet. He gave me his bank check and—"

Kyle took the checks from my hand and tucked them into his shirt pocket without looking at them. "Let me hold on to these. I'm so sorry. We'd better find your husband. I'm sure he's okay, but—"

"Find him? What do you mean *find* him?"

But Kyle was already on his way out of the coffee shop. I climbed to my feet and hurried after him. I heard the waitress call out, but I didn't turn around.

"I don't understand." I had to run to catch up to him. "What do you mean *find* him?"

As we reached the lobby, I saw the front doors swing open, and Clay Davies strolled in. His white sweater was pulled down over his rumpled white pants. The sweater had a long dark streak on the front, some kind of stain. His face was red, hair damp, matted to his forehead.

Kyle moved to block his path. "Clay? Where've you been?"

The older man blinked, startled to see us. "Out," he said. He made a vague gesture toward the doors.

I stormed up to him. "Is my husband okay?"

He studied me for a long moment, as if he'd never seen me before. The blue eyes, so jewel-bright before, suddenly appeared cloudy. "Is he okay?" He repeated my question, as if he didn't understand it.

Kyle took Davies's arm, not too gently. "Upstairs, Clay. Come on. Let's discuss this upstairs."

It seemed to take forever for the elevator to appear. I pressed the button three or four more times. "Is Denny okay? Just tell me that," I pleaded.

The door finally slid open. A herd of chattering people stepped out. I followed Davies and Kyle into the car. We rode in silence to four. Kyle kept shaking his head unhappily, moving his lips as if talking to himself.

Down the long hall to their suite. Clay dropped the room key card. He fumbled for it on the carpet. Then it took three tries to click in and open the door.

The front room was dark. I didn't wait for them to turn on a light. I went running to the bedroom at the back. "Denny? Are you all right? Denny? Can you hear me?"

I flung the door open and lurched into the brightly lit bedroom. "Denny? Denny?"

Then I tried to utter a scream, but my breath cut off. I stared hard at the far side of the bed.

The coffin was gone.

"Where *is* it?" I gasped. I spun around. Davies had stepped up behind me. I gripped the front of his sweater. "Where is it? *Where?*"

He twisted his face in an expression of disdain, as if the answer was obvious.

"I buried it," he said.

I could feel myself go into a kind of shock. I knew from the beginning Davies had a trick up his sleeve. But the idea of Denny lying helpless, buried underground in that locked coffin, was too much to bear.

Luckily, Kyle took over. Maybe the caretaker had had to rescue victims of Davies's insanity before. He quickly arranged for a resort bus, a driver, and two workers to accompany us with shovels. The bus rattled and shook as the driver followed the rutted one-lane road toward the tiny cemetery on the harbor end of the cay.

Kyle sat up front, leaning over the driver, urging him to make the old bus move faster. Davies sat calmly on the seat across from me, hands in his lap. He kept giving me puzzled glances. "What is the hurry? There's no problem here. We made a bet, didn't we?"

His nonchalance made me want to scream, to grab him by the throat and strangle him. "You buried my husband!" I uttered the words through clenched teeth. I cried out as the bus hit a hard bump and my head hit the ceiling.

"He can breathe," Davies insisted. "I put air vents in the front and back."

"But it's *underground!*" I shrieked. "You buried him underground. How is he supposed to breathe underground?"

I glimpsed the two workers sitting in the back. They avoided my eyes, pretended to gaze into the blue-black darkness out the window. Kyle moved quickly to the aisle between Davies and me. "Let's not panic." He patted my shoulder. "I'm sure the coffin holds enough air to last your husband at least a few hours. We'll be there in time."

I grabbed his wrist. "But can you imagine what he's thinking?

His fright? He must be clawing at the lid. He must be screaming and clawing and pounding. He'll use up all the air." I turned to Davies. "You killed him! You *killed* him!"

Davies's face kept its vague smile.

The bus jolted to a hard stop. Out the window, I saw a stretch of bare ground, then the outlines of small graves in crooked rows, black against the inky, starless sky.

The driver opened the door and leaped out. The two workers moved silently past me, shovels in front of them. Davies made no move to get up. "I don't see what the fuss is about," he murmured. "We made a wager."

Kyle pulled Davies into the aisle and motioned him to the bus door. "Hurry, Clay. Show them where you buried that coffin. Stop arguing. Just hurry."

Kyle turned to me. "Maybe you should stay on the bus until we have the coffin up and know everything is okay."

"No way," I said. I hoisted myself up and shoved past him to the door. I stumbled to the ground, my eyes on the men climbing the low, sandy hill to the gravestones. A pale sliver of a moon drifted out from behind a cloud and sent a cold, silvery light over the rows of tiny graves.

The chill air felt heavy and damp. I shivered and wrapped my arms around myself as I jogged to catch up to Davies and the men. My shoes sank into the wet sand. I hugged myself tightly as if holding everything in, protecting myself from any horror ahead.

His white linen trousers fluttering in the steady wind, Davies motioned to the end of a row of graves. As he pointed again, his white hair flew up around his head. His eyes were wild in the silvery light.

*Crazy. Of course, he's crazy. Why did Denny want to do this?*

I'll never forget the sound of the shovels cutting into the wet sand. And then the soft thud of the sand clumps tossed to the side. Repeated as if in slow motion. Slow motion to me. Everyone appeared to be in slow motion.

"Denny? Can you hear me?"

The wind blew my words back into my face. I stepped between the men bent over their shovels, cupped my hands around my mouth, and screamed into the hole. "Can you hear me? Denny? Are you okay? Denny?"

No reply.

The only sounds were the grunts of the two men, digging deeper into the sand, and the rush of wind that swirled around us. Davies stood with his hands in his pockets, eyes on the deepening hole. Kyle had dropped to his knees beside the hole. Again, his lips moved as if he were talking to himself. Or was he praying?

I jumped at the sound of a shovel hitting something hard. One of the workers murmured something in Spanish. I lurched to the edge of the hole. Both shovels were sweeping sand off the top of the coffin.

"Denny? Denny? Can you hear me?"

Silence.

"Denny? Are you okay? Please tell me—are you okay?"

A gust of wind swirled sand back into the hole. Silence from the coffin. Silence. I was holding on to myself now, holding on tightly, the only way I could remain standing.

I stumbled back as the two men hoisted the coffin up from the hole. Clumps of wet sand clung to the sides and the top.

"Denny? Answer me! Denny! Why don't you answer?"

I glimpsed Davies on the other side of the hole. He was watching me, not the coffin, a blank expression on his face. No worry. No concern of any kind.

And then his caretaker stepped between the two workers. Kyle moved to the coffin, unlocked the latch, snapped it open, gripped the lid with both hands. He shut his eyes, as if he was praying. And then he shoved the lid open.

"Denny? Denny?"

And then I screamed.

The coffin was empty.

\*     \*     \*

Half an hour later, a sleek Gulfstream G650 took off into the night sky from the small mainland airport. Sy Wells, the man Ashli had known as Davies, settled back in a white leather seat and sipped his martini.

He hadn't had time to change. The stained sweater and mud-soaked pants cuffs seemed inappropriate in the pristine white-and-chrome luxury of the private jet. But he was more than willing to overlook it.

Sonny Clarke, who had played the part of Kyle Jeffrey, slumped in the chair across from Sy, his feet raised, a can of beer in one hand. In the row behind them, Johnny Angelini—aka Denny Sparano—had his eyes shut, hands gripped on the white chair arms. He wasn't a good flier.

Grinning, Sonny raised his beer can in a salute to Johnny. "She loved you, man. Did you see the look on her face? I thought she was going to drop into the empty coffin and just die."

"She wasn't bad," Johnny murmured. He snickered.

Sonny took a long drag on the beer can. "Next time I want to be the husband. Why does Johnny get all the extra benefits?"

"Because he's a stud," Sy replied. He swept a hand through his white hair and turned back to look at Johnny. "You okay?"

"I'll survive. Maybe."

Sonny reached across the aisle and bumped Johnny's shoulder. "Forget about airsickness. Think how much richer you are."

"This one was perfect," Sy said, twirling the martini glass. "She'll be searching for you for days, Johnny. I'll bet she's on the phone with the island police right now." He took a gentle sip. The plane jolted. He protected the glass with both hands. "She's sick with worry. Did you see how frantic she was?"

Sonny let out a whoop and raised his beer in another toast. "Johnny did his magic! He put a love spell on her!"

"It'll be days before she remembers she doesn't have the checks," Sy continued. "We'll be back in New York in three hours. And we'll have her check deposited and sent on its way to the account before she remembers Sonny took it."

"This one was cake," Johnny said. His sweaty hands left prints on the chair handles. A wave of nausea made his whole body tense up. *Sonny is right. Just think about all that money.*

Sy turned to Sonny. "Where are the checks? Let me see them."

Sonny reached for his shirt pocket. "She just handed them to me. It was hilarious. I said let me hold on to them, and she didn't say a word."

Sy laughed. "Two million dollars and she just handed it over? Well…we knew she wasn't too smart. I mean, she married Johnny—right?"

Sy laughed at his own joke. He took the checks from Sonny. And then his laughter stopped abruptly.

"Sonny, don't mess around. Give me the *real* checks."

Sonny blinked. He felt his shirt pocket. "Those are them, Sy. She handed them right to me. I saw they said *Chase Bank* at the top."

Sy's jaw clenched and his eyes bulged. He waved the checks in Sonny's face. "These aren't real. Look at them. *Look* at them!"

Sonny took the checks. He read the bank title in dignified black type across the top: *CHASE Your Tail Bank.*

"Hey! What the hell! Sy, they're both signed *Minnie Mouse.*"

Johnny groaned. He fumbled in the compartment at his side. "Is there a barf bag? Here comes my lunch."

Sy covered his face with both hands. "She was onto us. We've been conned."

Johnny's head was between his knees. He vomited like a volcano erupting.

"She got our two million," Sonny said. "Our seed money."

"Yeah," Sy murmured, his face still covered. "And now we got one more problem. How do we pay for this jet?"

# REMMY ROTHSTEIN
# TOES THE LINE
## (annotated)

## BY KARIN SLAUGHTER

DISPATCH: Okefenokee Swamp, Georgia
SUBJECT: Remmy Rothstein, "The Cajun Jew"
DATE: August 11, 2012
ATTEMPTED RECORD: Longest Tongue in the World (man)
WEATHER: 99 degrees with 89% humidity
ADJUDICATOR: Mindy Patel (badge #683290)

Dear Robert:

Again, I'd like to thank you for this assignment and your continued faith in me after the domino debacle. Not many Adjudicators would be able to survive the fallout (too soon?) from such a scandal, and your advocacy on my behalf is much appreciated. I promise you I'll do everything I can to earn my Senior Adjudicator badge back—no matter what it takes.

Now, as to my report:

I'm writing to you from the bottom right-hand quadrant of the state of Georgia, which offers a bucolic setting with the most delicate, birdlike mosquitoes. The swamp is a pleasant locale filled with many interesting characters, including the landlord of my B&B, Alexander Wooten (who looks remarkably like Delbert Jebediah Long[1]). Wooten is seemingly at my beck and call. Just last night, I woke to find him standing over my bed asking me if I needed a drink of water. You don't find service like that in New York City! Robert, thank you again for sending me to such a warm and welcoming place.

In fact, Wooten is not the exception to these friendly swamp people, but the rule. I'm not sure if I told you that I lost my bracelet on the drive down from Atlanta's Hartsfield-Jackson International Airport.[2] You can imagine my relief when a nice local boy found it under the driver's seat of my truck. I could hardly complain about the gas tank being empty after that! And I'm sure the scratches in the paint will be covered by my Amex card. Who wouldn't want a Confederate flag carved into their driver's-side door? Not this Punjabi! It's practically a sin not to show your pride down here. And the food is exquisite—I've never tasted blackened crawdads before. Yum! Thank you, again, for this wonderful opportunity. The World Record Adjudicator's first love has always been adventure.

Yours,
Mindy

PS: Just a note: I saw Kaitlyn on the *Today Show* this morning with Matt Lauer certifying the fewest pogo-stick jumps in under a minute. (Sorry, Biff![3]) She looked fantastic—I wish I had her looming height. Lauer was like a dwarf next to her (though certainly no Gul

---

1. Long skinned the most squirrels (1,238) in a one-hour period.
2. At 92,365,860 passengers a year, Hartsfield is the busiest airport by volume in the world.
3. Biff Hutchison, 39 jumps.

Mohammed[4]). Please tell Kaitlyn I said she looked fantastic in that plaid suit. She hardly looked overweight at all.

DISPATCH: Okefenokee Swamp, Georgia
SUBJECT: Remmy Rothstein, "The Cajun Jew"
DATE: August 12, 2012
ATTEMPTED RECORD: Longest Tongue in the World (man)
WEATHER: 101 degrees with 99% humidity
ADJUDICATOR: Mindy Patel (badge #683290)

Dear Robert:

As per the Manual of Adjudicator Conduct on the Road (rev), Rule #14, I spent more of the day getting a lay of the land and talking to people who might know Mr. Rothstein, our possible World Record Holder for Longest Tongue (man).

The Okefenokee Swamp, as you know, is the largest in North America; it is over 6,500 years old and formed on the edge of an ancient Atlantic coastal terrace. The name itself comes from the Cherokee word for "Land of the Trembling Earth," an obvious reference to the unstable peat "islands" that pass for land in the black waters. The swamp is approximately 438,000 acres and is home to many wading birds, amphibians, carnivorous plants, and American alligators (full list of native species and wildlife attached). The Honey Prairie Wildfire, which started in April of last year, has still only reached 65% containment and has left a swath of barren land in its wake. Amazingly, the wildlife seems to have thrived under these conditions, especially the mosquitoes. It's the burden of the Adjudicator to be extra wary of these flying beasts,[5] though

---

4. Mohammed, 22.5", is the shortest man ever recorded.
5. Excluding wars and accidents, mosquitoes have been responsible for 50% of all deaths since the Stone Age.

of course the locals find it hilarious when I swat at these creatures, which are capable of pinning down small animals. I wish I was exaggerating, but no one was laughing when that cat was taken away. Poor Squeamy.

Not many people appear to know Mr. Rothstein, though he seems to have lived in the area all of his life. On the Application for World Record Form 29(E), he listed his occupation as "certified VCR repairman" (a surprisingly popular occupation among our Record Holders [male]). Where locals seem reticent to discuss Mr. Rothstein, the subject of his mother is easily bandied about. By all accounts, she is a strong woman who raised two sons on her own during a time when these things were not done. For many years, the family seems to have held itself apart from the community, and more than one old-timer has described Mrs. Rothstein as the "Whore of the Oke." Thankfully, this is not a commonly uttered phrase (even down here, time seems to have inched forward, though one need only refer to the county census data to find that one in every three girls has experienced a pregnancy by the time she turns sixteen). Still, one can assume that the Rothstein family is no stranger to scandal (again, another attribute many of our Applicants [male] and Record Holders [male] share).

Prior to flying down here, my research led me to believe that all residents of the swamp ("Swampers") had been removed shortly after the cypress mining period initiated by the Hebard family (who could forget Oberlin Elton[6]?). You can imagine my surprise as I drove around the sandy Swamp Perimeter Road to find many Swampers still living in dilapidated shacks. No running water. No electricity but for the occasional diesel generator. Certainly not a lot of teeth!

---

6. In 1928, Elton was the oldest living man to find out that the Civil War had ended.

It is inside this swamp that Applicant Remmy Rothstein lives with his mother and older brother. By most accounts, Rothstein's family tree took root around the time of the Suwannee Canal[7] boondoggle. Others say the line goes back much farther. Embellishments seem to be a way of life down here, so should we indeed have a Record Breaker, a more firmly oriented timeline will of course have to be established.

Lastly, I understand the science division always has questions when World Records pertain to physical attributes or endurance and have taken a sample of the tannin-stained waters of the Okefenokee (a highly acidic substance that renders the shallow waters sparkling clear). Though I am no scientist, one could surely form a hypothesis that these waters could have led to the development of an elongated tongue. I know research continues on Stephen Taylor's[8] environment, but should Rothstein truly break the record, more research into his background and early diet is definitely indicated. But I'm getting ahead of myself!

The plan is to meet Rothstein at noon tomorrow.

Until then!
Mindy

(attachment: PlantsAnimalsOkefenokee.doc)

**DISPATCH:** Okefenokee Swamp, Georgia
**SUBJECT:** Remmy Rothstein, "The Cajun Jew"
**DATE:** August 13, 2012
**ATTEMPTED RECORD:** Longest Tongue in the World (man)
**WEATHER:** 106 degrees with 100% humidity
**ADJUDICATOR:** Mindy Patel (badge #683290)

---

7. The canal, meant to drain the swamp into the Gulf and Atlantic, respectively, was abandoned in the late nineteenth century.
8. Taylor's tongue measures 3.86" from the tip of his tongue to his top lip.

Dear Robert:

I'm really not certain what happened today, but I'll try to describe it as best I can:

Wooten, the helpful landlord of my B&B, gave me very good directions to Rothstein's meeting point, and I found it easily enough after a few hours of wandering around in the swamp. Did I mention that the air-conditioner in my rental truck is broken? Funny thing: it was fine on the way down, but after that kid took it for a joyride, it started blowing heat (and smelling, oddly, of boiled peanuts—a local delicacy). I took it to a mechanic (a nice lady who also owns the local restaurant) and was told that it would cost approximately $3,000 to repair.

After a few terse phone calls with the car rental company (note to Travel: it might be best in the future to steer clear of Jimmyz' Truck and Tractor Rental), it was made clear to me that no repairs were authorized (which I cannot argue with as, according to Jimmyz' rental agreement, which I had ample time to peruse while on hold, they are not responsible for any peanut-related mechanical failures, up to and including air-conditioning). Of course, all this means to me is that I have been forced to drive around in the heat.

And is it hot! I'm talking Al' Aziziyah[9] hot!

But I can hear your voice reminding me that it's about the potential Record Holder, not the Adjudicator, and certainly not about the fact that I have lost six pounds since yesterday (please tell Kaitlyn) and that no matter how hard I try to remain hydrated, I am well under my .28 gallons![10]

As I said at the top of the report, I set out first thing in the morning, when it was but a balmy 98 degrees, giving myself ample

9. Home of the highest shade temperature ever recorded, at 136°F (58°C).
10. The average person generates .28 gallons of urine a day.

time to make the noon rendezvous with Mr. Rothstein. I brought with me all the tools of verification: two rulers, a measuring tape, video recorder, tape recorder, and camera. I also took the liberty of bringing the Record Holder Certificate signed by Paolo Pergini, our esteemed leader, in case Mr. Rothstein, in fact, had broken the World Record.

As you know, per certification guidelines, Mr. Rothstein submitted via our website the proper paperwork as well as ample documentation of tongue length to be reviewed by our board of assessors in the New York office. Photos showed a metal ruler placed "tip to top" (tip of tongue to top lip) indicating Mr. Rothstein's tongue measured 3.9", a full .04" past the original world record. Between you and me, Robert, I was also hoping for a double record, as the photos showed what seemed to be an abnormally wide tongue, surely as wide if not wider than Sloot's.[11] I know as Adjudicators we're not supposed to get involved with our Subjects, but I feel like your knowing the level of my excitement going into this Adjudication will give you a deeper understanding of what happened next.

Thanks to Wooten's directions (which gave me a lovely side trip into Florida), I pulled up to Rothstein's dock at approximately 11:52 a.m. This dock was not a typical dock connected to a house, but rather a free-floating wooden structure onto which an airboat was moored. Obviously, one does not become an Adjudicator without a lust for adventure, but even I was a bit wary of this rusty contraption, which more closely resembled a cast-iron bathtub with a box fan strapped onto the back. And I do mean strapped on—we're talking enough bungee cords to make Alberto Reginni[12] nervous. Nevertheless, I strapped myself into one of the wooden chairs (with yet another bungee cord) and resigned myself to a ride deep into the swamplands.

---

11. Jay Sloot's tongue measures 3.1" at its maximum width.

12. Reginni is the record holder for most bungee cords (83) wrapped around his head.

My guide was not Mr. Rothstein, but his older brother, who is named Buell Rabinowitz. It is not just the unshared surname that leads me to believe Mr. Rothstein and Mr. Rabinowitz were sired by different fathers. Though it defies polite company to mention these things in public, I feel I must be completely truthful as an Adjudicator and reveal the facts: I have never seen an albino African American Jew before (possible record to explore for the Assessors' Office?).

For the most part, Buell spoke in the flowery Victorian parlance of the Swampers (this owing to little outside influence of the changing vernacular), only occasionally dipping into Yiddish and what I will describe as a folksy, backwoods slang. He was dressed in tan pants that were too short for his lanky, long leg (did I mention he only has one leg?) and a shirt that was obviously fashioned from a sack of flour.

Buell informed me that his people have lived in the swamp since July 5, 1742, when the ongoing War of Jenkins' Ear[13] forced them from Congregation Mickve Israel[14] in Savannah. I asked him about the Cajun part of the family, to which he answered (I felt sarcastically), "*Laissez les bons temps rouler.*" [15]

I asked him again about his brother. "Is Remmy..."

"A colored or a albino?" he finished.

"Well..." I said, but of course that's exactly what I'd been thinking.

"Nope. Remmy his own kinda special." He steered the boat away from a resting alligator, then navigated a slight turn through a forked cypress tree. "Do yaself a favor, gal. Don't say nothin' 'bout his har."

---

13. Started in 1731 when Spaniard captain Julio León Fandiño boarded the English *Rebecca* and cut off captain Robert Jenkins's ear with the behest to give the ear to the British House of Commons.

14. Organized in 1733, Congregation Mickve Israel, Savannah, is thought to be the third-oldest still-functioning congregation in the United States.

15. "Let the good times roll."

"What's that?" I asked, but he changed the subject, instead regaling me with a story about his great-great-grandpappy, a rabbi who fought in the Civil War.

This was to be a pattern with Buell, whom I found to be quite open about everything having to do with his past and family until I questioned him about his brother Remmy. On all topics Rothstein, Buell declined to answer, instead telling me that he had to be careful around this part of the swamp because "them alligators are meshugganeh."

Instead of focusing on Buell's ice-blue eyes, or the word "FLOUR" emblazoned on his narrow back, I found myself staring at the stump of his leg, onto which a poorly wrought, wooden prosthetic had been fashioned. It wasn't exactly a peg because it had a kind of shoe at the bottom—a badminton racket, really—but I feel that "peg" is the best descriptor as the racket was attached with duct tape. Buell explained to me that the soft ground of peat posed a problem for the peg (much like a high heel, I imagine—did I mention I've lost two pairs of shoes since I got here? Invoices attached). The racket seems to act as a snowshoe of sorts, and thanks to the duct tape, could be quickly removed in case he needs to run.

Run from what? you might be thinking. If only I'd considered the same question.

I can't tell you how long the airboat ride lasted. Frankly, the fumes from the gas engine seemed to be exhausting directly into my face. There was no muffler, per se, just a length of metal pipe with a sock taped onto the end. Watching the sock flop across the water cast something like a hypnotic spell, and I'm ashamed to say that I found myself nodding off. I must admit that I haven't been sleeping well at night. It was quite a relief knowing that Mr. Wooten would not be gently nudging me awake to offer me a backrub. (And come to think of it, I have the strange feeling that he was wearing a pair of my shoes last night, which is silly, because he's a size ten at least and he's told me on more than one occasion that red is not his color.)

But back to the swamp:

As I said, I'm not sure what time it was when I awoke, but we were deep into the swamp, large cypress trees weaving their fingers together in a canopy that blocked most of the light. I tried to look at my watch, but the LED had melted into a puddle that rolled around under the glass like pus in a blister.

I'm sorry to cut this short, Robert, but Mr. Wooten just came out from under my bed. He forgot to tell me that there's something else wrong with my car. I'll go ahead and send this off now as it's required by the Manual of Adjudicator Conduct on the Road (rev), Rule #22, to present a daily log.

More anon—
Mindy

(attachment: ShoeInvoice.pdf)


**DISPATCH:** Okefenokee Swamp, Georgia
**SUBJECT:** Remmy Rothstein, "The Cajun Jew"
**DATE:** August 14, 2012
**ATTEMPTED RECORD:** Longest Tongue in the World (man)
**WEATHER:** 104 degrees with 99% humidity
**ADJUDICATOR:** Mindy Patel (badge #683290)


Dear Robert:

Sorry for the abrupt ending yesterday, but I know what a stickler you are for rules, and you know that I am doing my utmost to be the best Adjudicator I can. As you often say, when life gives you lemons, the good Adjudicator verifies a World Record for Most Lemons in a Twenty-Four-Hour Period!

Regarding the car: I'm afraid it's another peanut-related incident, so not covered under the rental car agreement warranty. It seems that the transmission (which I noticed was slipping a bit when I made that U-turn in Florida) is gone. How a peanut got into the pistons is beyond me, but as Mr. Wooten says, "Them's what happens in the Swamp." Ah, what a character.

In reviewing my report from yesterday, I have to agree with you that it took way too many personal detours. I apologize for this and promise to rectify the situation beginning now.

Buell nudged me awake as the airboat slid up against another wooden dock. This one was attached to a piece of land, the ubiquitous peat, upon which stood a simple one-room shack. The wood was clapboard, browned with weather and age, or perhaps singed from the Honey Prairie Fire. There was a strange glass in all the windows—Coke-bottle green with a round center that bubbled out to the edges. Victorian, I imagine. The first person to come out of the front door (in fact the only door) was an old, stooped woman with quite a long beard (I know what you're thinking, and no—Vivian Wheeler[16] can rest easy). She kept her gnarled hands gripped together as she walked across the peat. I'm not sure if the ground was shaking or she was. She was quite old (though not Valentim[17] old) and I had to strain to hear what she said, which was "Welcome, darlin'."

Robert, you know that as an Adjudicator, I take my work very seriously, but I cannot lie to you and say that I was completely prepared for this case. As I mentioned yesterday, I'd brought all the proper tools needed to measure and document Mr. Rothstein's tongue, but it is with great shame that I admit I did not bring the one tool that would've been most useful in this situation, and that is a flashlight. This thought only occurred to me as I followed the woman into the shack. The green glass that I mentioned served to further filter the

---

16. Wheeler is the Record Holder for longest beard on a living person (female).

17. Maria Gomez Valentim is the oldest living person in the world.

light, so that when I entered the room, I could barely make out my surroundings.

As my eyes adjusted, I took in several things rather quickly. There was a small bedstead pushed into one corner, a quilt laid over a bare straw mattress. An otherwise clean fireplace was set with wood but, thankfully, there was no fire. Metal implements adorned the walls: pitchforks and axes serving as objets d'art. Strangely, there was a large—I would say at least 60"—plasma-screen television taking up one wall. The old woman patted the set as if it were a familiar, telling me, "A gift from Remmy."

And that is when I realized the other thing missing from the room: Mr. Rothstein.

"Is he here?" I asked.

"Give 'em time," she told me, pulling out a wooden stool I'd not noticed before. It was a three-legged stool, the other leg being currently used by Buell Rabinowitz, who at that moment clomped into the shack. He carried the badminton racket at his side, a piece of duct tape dragging the ground like a tail.

"Remmy always late," Buell said. He leaned against the fireplace. I noticed the ropey muscle underneath his homespun shirt. He glared openly at his mother.

The old woman carefully balanced herself against the wall to make up for the missing leg. She teetered a bit, glaring back at Buell as if this was his fault, before finally settling down.

And then there was silence.

Well, you don't send Adjudicators to Mrs. Dalton's School of Manners and Social Conversation for nothing!

I cleared my throat a few times, then politely asked, "Where is Mr. Rothstein?"

"Don't worry, gal," Buell told me. And then, thank God for my work certifying the World Record for the Most Yiddish Puns Told in a One-Hour Period,[18] because I completely understood him when he said, *"A falsheh matba'ieh farliert men nit."* [19]

The old woman reared up like an angry possum. "Don't you derogatory my Remmy!" she snapped. "You ungrateful *fagala*."[20]

*"Ku fartzer,"* [21] he shot back. (I blushed.)

*"Gai kukken afen yam."* [22] She waved him away like swatting a fly. Or maybe she was really swatting a fly. There were hundreds in the shack. I'd swallowed at least five since I walked in.

Buell could barely look me in the eye, but he apologized. "Sorry, Mama ain't never liked me much."

"Can you blame an old woman?" She ignored her son, kindly showing me a row of gums. "You a pretty girl. You married?"

I deflected that as easily as I did with my own mother. "You must be proud of Remmy for going after the World Record."

"Remmy my pride," the old woman told me. "Boychik over der"— she nodded toward Buell—"not so much."

Buell's fists clenched. The sprinkling of freckles showed under the sweat on his knuckles. The old woman tilted up her chin, dared him to come after her.

A chill went through me, and I gritted my teeth against the whimper that wanted to come out. Robert, you know I'm the daughter

---

18. 7.
19. "A bad penny always turns up."
20. Faggot.
21. "Cunt eater."
22. "Go shit in the ocean."

of Indian immigrants. The worst they ever did to me was tell me they were very disappointed I did not become a doctor like my two brothers or even a lawyer like my sister. This exchange between mother and son was shocking, like nothing I'd ever witnessed. And the language! Even during the great Domino Debacle, the worst Jimmy Butler managed to call me was a psycho bitch fuck. Granted, he was only nine years old at the time and hadn't slept for four days because he was setting up his domino display to try to achieve the record (believe me, to this day I still have nightmares about bumping into that table), but the point I am trying to make is that the hatred between the two people in that swamp shack was so thick I could've easily certified it as the Thickest Hatred in the World. And you know an Adjudicator never exaggerates about World Records.

Again, the old woman teetered on the stool as she settled the three legs back onto the floor. Buell flinched as she stood with a sweeping, almost threatening, motion. She went over to the fireplace and placed her hand on a wooden box I hadn't noticed before. It was quite lovely—cherrywood rubbed into a warm red, and small enough to fit in two hands.

Buell nervously eyed the box. "Mama, please. We got comp'ny."

She patted the box, and I could tell she took a dark delight in its contents. She told me, "Remmy a good boy. He never do know it, though. Always tryin' for things, never gettin' 'em. Bless his heart."

For just a moment, I felt a shock of panic. Was she telling me that Remmy was in the box? Had he passed away before I could verify his World Record?

And—I have to admit, there was another, more startling thought: had they killed him?

I know it's silly to have these dramatic, dark ideas, but Robert, you must understand that in this kind of setting, one cannot help but conjure up *Deliverance*-like atrocities. Indeed, for the first time since I landed in Atlanta and drove down to this backwater swamp, I felt the sweat dry on my skin. Dry? Nay, freeze. And then it crystallized to dry ice when next the old woman stabbed her finger into Buell's chest and said—

"You."

Buell flinched from the hard jabs.

"You's done got on my bad side today, ya freak."

His lips trembled. He begged, "Mama, please."

And she said

I'm sorry, Robert. Mr. Wooten has just come out from behind the shower curtain. He forgot to tell me that the sheriff wanted to talk to me.

Def. more tomorrow—
M.

DISPATCH: Waycross, Georgia
SUBJECT: Remmy Rothstein, "The Cajun Jew"
DATE: August 15, 2012
ATTEMPTED RECORD: Longest Tongue in the World (man)
WEATHER: 104 degrees with 98% humidity
ADJUDICATOR: Mindy Patel (badge #683290)

Dear Robert:

Greetings from jail! Please don't panic—it's just a misunderstanding about the car. Apparently, Jimmyz' filed a bench warrant over the truck. No big deal—really! There is absolutely no stigma here about being in jail (haha, the locals say if they're not in church, jail is where you can find them) and I've had many kind visitors. Until they found him in the storage closet, Mr. Wooten even kept me company. My God, that man has a lovely singing voice. I have to tell you, Robert, living in New York, you forget what a community is all about. But as to the jail thing—it's fine. Really. Of all the Adjudicators you have to worry about, I am not one of them!

So let me continue telling you the story of what happened the other day. Three days ago! I can't believe it's been that long since I've had a shower. Honestly, now that I've had air-conditioning and water on a consistent basis, I'm thinking much more clearly. It just goes to show you how hearty these Swampers really are.

As I was saying, the old woman was taunting Buell. There was a level of hatred coming off her like none I ever experienced in my life. She truly and unremorsefully seemed to despise him. I half expected her to take one of the axes off the wall and do something about it.

She said, "Today gone be the day, you don't watchit."

Then she put her hand on that cherrywood box. Now, macabre thoughts aside, it was a beautiful box, and probably very old (though not that[23]old). The carving was incredibly ornate, and certainly you could not fit the ashes of a grown man inside the thing.

She said, "You wanna see 'em, boychik?"

Obviously, something awful was inside, because Buell had backed away the moment the old woman took the box off the mantel. I felt a little trepidation myself as she stuck her thumbnail into the catch and started to open it.

But then there was a clatter outside, feet shuffling across boards. I looked out the front door and there stood on the front porch the

---

23. The Box of Hadrittah, unearthed in 1848, is believed to be the oldest wooden box in the world.

ugliest man I have ever seen. I know that the internal debate over whether to certify ugliness has been going on in the Assessors' Office for years, but one look at this man would tell you there is not an uglier creature walking the face of the earth.

So ugly was this man that even now I cannot find the words to describe him. Was he unclean? Remarkably so. Was he hideous? Without a doubt. Was he hairy? Yes—but only to a point.

His face was remarkably clean-shaven, not even showing a trace of a beard. In fact, the hairline was almost completely receded, though his dirty, kinky braid ran from the back of his head to his waist. Shirtless, he presented a bare chest. His back, on the other hand, showed a carpet of hair that glistened with sweat. Tendrils poked up from the waist of his pants, a trail of fur touching the center of his belly button and shooting out like rays from the sun. His legs were hairy. His arms were hairy. His ears were hairy. My fingers itched to grab my ruler, my camera, my notebook. Justin Shaw,[24] Anthony Victor,[25] Toshie Kawakami[26]—for the love of God, Douglas Williams![27]—why was this man bothering with his tongue? He was magnificently hirsute, a textbook study in localized hypertrichosis!

But his face. My God, his face. Everyone knows that symmetry equates with beauty—a certain distance between the eyes, a straight, perfectly aligned nose, a pair of sculptured lips: these are the gifts that God gives beautiful people.

God gave this man nothing.

His nose was squarely out of joint, zigging and zagging down his shovel of a face. His eyes were too far apart on his head, giving him

---

24. Longest arm hair measured.

25. Longest ear hair measured.

26. Longest eyebrow hair measured.

27. Longest nipple hair (male) measured.

the look of a perplexed minnow. And his mouth. It was as if the awfulness had drained down, settling into his lips, giving them the twisted, wet look of two broken hot dogs resting atop the dirty bun of his cleft chin.

The old woman beamed at him as if he were a god. "Dis my Remmy," she said, chest puffed out, hands proudly tucked into her hips.

Remmy seemed embarrassed by his mother's obvious affection. "Afternoon, cher," he told me, extending a long-fingered hand my way.

*Har,* I thought. Buell said not to say anything about his *har.*

I forced myself to shake Remmy's hand, to ignore the soft feel of hair on his palms, the feral odor coming off his hairy body. Robert, have I ever told you about the time my father took us camping? We left soon after setting up the tent because there was a bear in the area. We never saw the creature, but we could smell him—rotted meat, sweat, and dirty feet all rolled into a motley scent that made his presence known for miles.

That bear had nothing on Remmy Rothstein.

And with them both, I should've seen it coming.

**DISPATCH:** Atlanta Penitentiary, Georgia
**SUBJECT:** Remmy Rothstein, "The Cajun Jew"
**DATE:** August 16, 2012
**ATTEMPTED RECORD:** Longest Tongue in the World (man)
**WEATHER:** 106 degrees with 100% humidity
**ADJUDICATOR:** Mindy Patel (badge #683290)

Dear Robert:

Sorry for the abrupt ending to yesterday's email. There was a bit of a riot. I say a bit because it was only four of us, but you'd better believe that shiv came in handy. Lord, those country girls are strong!

Back to Remmy.

For all his unnatural odor, there was something sweet about Remmy Rothstein. Was it his eyes, which were dark and piercing, like staring into the muzzle of a Glock 19? Being honest, the touch of his hand sent a cha-chunk into my heart, and I swear it was like a shotgun being pumped. (Sorry for all the gun metaphors; this is how you talk in prison. Did I mention we're in prison now? The jail burned down.) Robert, I just have to tell you, if you didn't look at Remmy's face, or feel the prickly hair jutting out from his eyebrows, you'd swear to God he was George Clooney.

And the mouth on him! No, I'm not talking about the silky, soft hair on his tongue (though we'll get to that later). He was the sweetest talker I've ever met in my life. He said I was beautiful. He said I was dainty. He said those moles on my ass look like the face of God. God, Robert! Not balloon animals (though I understand given our Adjudication that day why balloon animals were on your mind).

Was it all true? Am I beautiful? Am I dainty? Who knows? Let's just say Remmy Rothstein made good use of his 57,782[28] times.

But I was not there to fall in love. I was there to Adjudicate a World Record, so I set about telling Mr. Rothstein the procedures for verifying his claim. He told me he understood the proccss, and we agreed that we would proceed. The proper paperwork was signed (attached) and both Buell and his mother acted as witness.

While he went down to the water to shave his tongue, I used an alcohol wipe to clean the two metal rulers, as well as the measuring tape. I put these all out on a cloth napkin, as instructed in the

---

28. The average person tells 57,782 lies in his or her lifetime.

Manual of Adjudicator Conduct (rev), then tested the batteries in my camera and video recorder.

Mind you, we had to do all this outside in the daylight, but that was fine. I was beginning to enjoy the outdoors by now, and such was the sweat on my skin that the mosquitoes could no longer find purchase. Lemons/lemonade!

Rebekkah joined me outside the cabin, the box in her hand. (Did I mention the old woman's name is Rebekkah? Thankfully, she's my cellmate. All those years on the three-legged stool have given her thighs of steel. Combine that with the beard and there is no end to what the ladies will do for her. I haven't had to wash my own laundry since I got here!)

Rebekkah stood by quietly, her eyes nervously going from me to Buell and back again. He leaned against the shack as he strapped back on his badminton racket, giving her equally beady looks. I kept hearing her earlier warning that he had gotten on her bad side today, but worrying about these two wasn't in my job description, so I let it go.

Big mistake.

By the time I had tested everything and taken out a fresh pen to write in my notebook, Remmy was back. The sun was peering behind him, and I could see the wifty loops of hair off his shoulders. He rubbed his hands together as he approached. Up close, I recognized the features from the photos he sent in to the Assessors' Office. The round, red lips. The gouge of the philtrum between his nose and mouth.

Buell hobbled over, unsteady on the peat. Rebekkah stood beside me.

I said, "All right, Mr. Rothstein. Show me your tongue."

Fuck me. Another riot. More later.

(attachment: Rothstein-Remmy.zip)

**DISPATCH:** Atlanta Penitentiary, Georgia
**SUBJECT:** Remmy Rothstein, "The Cajun Jew"
**DATE:** August 18, 2012
**ATTEMPTED RECORD:** Longest Tongue in the World (man)
**WEATHER:** HOT
**ADJUDICATOR:** Mindy Patel (inmate #4290-6632)

Dear Robert:

I can't say I was happy to see Rebekkah taken out of my cell. She's become quite a confidante over the last few days. Thankfully, it was after Shabbat. Did I tell you she's been teaching me the Kiddush? Anyway, it's only a week in solitary. I'm sure it'll go by fast.

As you now know from my earlier attachment, Mr. Rothstein's tongue was nowhere near the 3.9" to meet the standard for World's Longest Tongue. In fact, even the width was barely more than the 2.1" average. I couldn't fucking believe it. Three days in that hellhole of a swamp! Two nights of being shocked out of my sleep by some pervy freak leaning over my bed. Thirty-six hours of nonstop sweating. Untold numbers of peanuts shoved up my tailpipe and the fucker had lied the entire time.

I'm sorry for my language, Robert, but prison makes you hard.

And, I have to say, I let Remmy's lies get to me. I know Potential World Record Holders lie all the time. I know they fake photos and try to get one over on us. I know it's the Adjudicator's job to just simply say, "Thank you for trying," as they head out of town, but I screamed the biggest "WHAT THE FUCK?" ever heard in that swamp. We're talking Silbo Gomero[29] loud. I'm surprised you

---

29. Under ideal conditions, this whistled language is intelligible up to five miles away.

didn't hear it all the way up in New York (though I'm sure you were busy watching Diane Sawyer interview Kaitlyn about the Most Dogs in Fancy Dress[30] record. Really, Ms. Sawyer? This is news?).

But—Remmy. Poor Remmy of the average tongue. He was crestfallen, though surely he knew when he Photoshopped those pictures that there was no way his tongue was long enough. Did he think we'd just give it to him? Did he think that a record as important as the Longest Tongue in the World was something we would just rubber-stamp through the Assessors' Office? There are standards and practices. There are ethics. What was I supposed to do—give him the second-longest tongue? There's a girl in California[31] who might have a word or two to say about that!

I remember my first day of Adjudicator Academy when we were told that our integrity was on the line every day, that people depended on us to report the truth, the whole truth, and nothing but the truth. We're certifying World Records! We're telling one individual that he or she, above anyone else, is the best, the brightest, the gnarliest, the most pierced, the fattest, the oldest, the fartiest, the most reckless—of any other human being in the world. Our motto isn't just on our badges; it's on our hearts. This is what the Adjudicator takes on the road with him or her every single day: "For every record you give someone, there's another person who loses a record." Could I take away what might be Ms. Tapper's biggest claim to fame for the sake of a downtrodden Cajun Jew living in a South Georgia swamp?

Could I do that? COULD I?!?!

No, really—I'm asking, because he keeps calling me every day.

---

30. 426 dogs assembled in Dunedin, Florida.

31. Chanel Tapper holds the record for the longest tongue in the world (female).

DISPATCH: Atlanta Penitentiary, Georgia
SUBJECT: Remmy Rothstein, "The Cajun Jew"
DATE: August 19, 2012
ATTEMPTED RECORD: Longest Tongue in the World (man) DENIED
WEATHER: Look at the date. Look at the location. WTF do you think?
ADJUDICATOR: Mindy Patel (inmate #4290-6632)


Dear Robert:

Sorry. Lights out really does mean lights out here, and my lawyer says after the stabbing (long story) I need to be on my best behavior.

Re: our last—

I know what you're thinking. It's not the tongue, stupid. It's the integrity of the organization. It's honoring the Adjudicators before me, the ones after me. It's about the truth.

I believe this. I really do. Which is why I had to be honest with Remmy standing there in that swamp.

"It's not long enough."

That's all I said. It was like watching the air leave a balloon. His shoulders slumped. His head dropped. Even the hair on his arms lost some of its bouffantness. I have seen many a grown man cry, but never have I seen one so broken. My heart felt as if it was crumbling in my chest. I could practically feel his desolation, his loneliness. What did this man have other than his awful mother and freakish older brother? Sure, he was her pride and joy, but that's like being Hitler's favorite dog. At the end of the day, what does it really mean? What lasting impression has Remmy Rothstein left on the world other than the strands of hair he leaves in his wake?

I looked at Buell. I could tell he was thinking what I was thinking. He shook his head, but I couldn't heed his warning. Tentatively, I asked, "Mr. Rothstein, is there another record you might be interested in?"

Remmy was too devastated to understand the question. His voice cracked. "No, cher. I got nothin'."

Was there ever a bigger elephant in the room?

I looked at Buell again, thinking surely he would call attention to the fact that Remmy's back looked like a wall in Elvis's music room. Then I looked at Rebekkah, but she only sneered at me in the threatening way she'd sneered at Buell.

And I know what you're thinking—a good Adjudicator finds a Record no matter what—but you tell me this, Robert Putrovnik: how do you say to a guy, "No, your tongue isn't long enough, but Jesus Christ, let me smack a ruler against that nipple hair"? I was really at a loss standing there on that peat mound. There's nothing in the Adjudicator's Manual of Conduct on the Road (rev or otherwise) that tells you how to politely suggest that there might be another record to be had.

Because no one seemed to be even close to suggesting that 75% of Remmy Rothstein's body is covered with hair.

So I said what I could, which is, "I'm so sorry, Mr. Rothstein. Perhaps another time."

Rebekkah hissed at me. I'm not going to lie—she's kind of scary when she wants to be, and those thighs could strangle a python (trust me, if there was more time I'd tell you that story).

Buell was the only one who didn't seem bothered by this. As I said, he'd been silent at first, but maybe it took some time for him to process exactly what had happened. Remmy had lost. He'd lost big. And something told me that Buell saw Remmy's loss as his own gain.

A huge grin spread across Buell's face as this realization dawned. He spat on the ground and said, clear as a bell, "Shyster."

Now, I told you Rebekkah was old, but that doesn't mean she wasn't fast.

She said, "That's it," and grabbed an ax off the woodpile.

She bolted after Buell so quickly I could barely process what was happening. Buell saw it coming before I did. He took off, pegging his way across the peat, dropping into the shallow water like a lemming, then popping back up on another mound of peat. Rebekkah kept up fairly easily, dodging the sticks and mounds of dirt he threw back at her. I stood there speechless as I watched her catch up with him. She grabbed him by the back of the shirt and rolled him into the water like a hungry gator.

They both disappeared under the churning water. The last I saw of Buell was his stump sticking up in the air. It really was a stool leg. Some duct tape was still attached to the end. It waved like a flag in the wind.

**DISPATCH:** Atlanta Penitentiary, Georgia
**SUBJECT:** Remmy Rothstein, "The Machine"
**DATE:** August 20, 2012
**ATTEMPTED RECORD:** Hottest Fuck in the World
**WEATHER:** Does it matter, bitch? Really?
**ADJUDICATOR:** Mindy Patel (inmate #4290-6632)

Robert—

Sorry about leaving you hanging like that. I had to get up in a bitch's grill.

So—!!!

As Rebekkah and Buell disappeared under the water again and again, I looked at Remmy and screamed, "Oh my God, she's murdering him!"

He just shrugged and said, "She ain't never forgive him for being born with six toes."

???

Remmy shrugged. "Ain't no record," he told me, as if it wasn't common knowledge that you can't throw a rock without hitting a polydactyl.

"Six toes?!" I repeated. "That's why she hates him?"

"On each foot." He shook his head sadly. "My three nipples, she ain't got a problem with, but she been kvetchin' about them toes long as I 'member." Remmy gave me a knowing look. "Took off that one foot when he was nine. Been gunnin' for them others ever since." He stared out into the thrashing water. "Cain't pretend like this day ain't been a long time comin'."

My mouth opened and closed like a fish gasping on the shore.

THIS was what upset her? Not that her oldest son was an albino of indeterminate ethnic origin? Not that her youngest son had sprouted enough hair to cover at least two standard poodles? She lived in a swamp shack with no running water or electricity and, if I was guessing correctly, did her bathroom duty in a metal bucket whose contents, judging by the trail to the water, were dumped into the swamp every day.

SIX TOES CROSSED THE LINE?

But none of this seemed to matter to Remmy. He was obviously still focused on his World Record loss and not the sound of his mother drowning his brother in the tannin waters of the Okefenokee.

I said, "Shouldn't we—"

"It's the way of the swamp, cher." He shrugged one of his shoulders. The hair stirred in a sudden wind, sending strands into his mouth. He delicately pulled them out between his thumb and finger. His nails were greasy black, like a car mechanic who works nights in a coal mine.

He said, "I'm sorry I brought you all this way, cher. I thought I had a chance." Tears rolled down his soft cheeks, slid down his chest, then trickled along his happy trail[32] like water off a duck's back.

I couldn't help it, Robert. I told him, "There are probably other records you can break."

Only, I was talking about the hair and he thought I was talking about something else. Or maybe I *was* talking about something else. Who the hell knows? It was so damn hot. I hadn't slept in days. The exhaust from the boat was still in my lungs. The peanut smell from my car was clinging to me like a spicy Thai roll.

But here's the other thing, Robert—just to let you know, female Adjudicators have a special kind of hell we go through on the road. I'll admit it—I get lonely. Sometimes I'll hook up with a guy at the bar or in a gas station Arby's or, if I'm really lucky, a Chili's will have a Ladies' Night. I'm human, all right? But I never tell them what I do for a living because it invites the inevitable joke: "Bet I just broke some records, darlin'."

No, they did not. Most of the time, they couldn't break a two-year-old goat's hymen (though trust me, I'm sure some of them have tried).

But Remmy...oh, Remmy.

Why was I attracted to this man? He was filthy. Hairy. A genetic anomaly. Going by his Application Packet, he was functionally illiterate.

And yet...

I was drawn to him like a bucket to a well. I dropped down and down and down that dark wet shaft as I took him in—this cool drink of Cajun Jew water.

It's true (as you well know) that I've always had a thing for pathetic,

---

32. The line of hair between the pubis and navel.

broken men, but there was something more to it than that. When Remmy took off his pants, the coarse burlap sliding over his wavy hips, the hair on his legs parting across thick muscle...

My God, my God. You would not believe this man.

Actually, I've attached a photo so you can see for yourself. Let me tell you there are women in here who have paid up to FIFTEEN CIGA-RETTES to see this image, so consider this my early Christmas gift. And a final explanation as to why I've finally moved on from that night we adjudicated Most Modeling Balloon Sculptures Made in One Minute.[33] You told me to get over it, Robert. Well, here's your proof that I have certainly gotten over—and under, and round and round like a merry-go-round.

Next thing I knew, Remmy scooped me up like a fireman rescuing a person who is in a burning building and needs to be rescued. My fingers dug into the fur on his back, got caught in the curly rings growing like Spanish AstroTurf on his ass. I would say the earth moved, but it was the Okefenokee; the earth always moves. I've never loved a man so wildly, so passionately, so...frenziedly. My fingers ran madly through his hair. All of his hair. And sometimes my hair. I don't know where his started and mine began. It was like going to a different planet. A planet of love, or maybe this is what those furry[34] people feel like, because my God, I rocked that hairy man. I loved every inch of him. And he loved me. He even said it—

"I love you, cher," Remmy moaned—over and over. "I love you! I love you!" All the while pounding into me like an extended clip banging home into the butt of a nine-millimeter.

---

33. Thirteen sculptures in one minute: a bone, a bracelet, a crocodile, a dagger, a dachshund, a dog (no breed specified), a dragonfly, an elephant, a fish, a hat, a honeybee, an Indian headdress, and a sword.

34. People who dress up as animals to have sex.

I tell you this with all my heart, Robert:

Remmy was fully loaded, but when he pulled that trigger, I was the one who exploded.

(attachment: Rothstein_GIGANTOR.jpg)

DISPATCH: Atlanta Penitentiary, Georgia
SUBJECT: Remmy Rothstein, "the Shitard"
DATE: August 21, 2012
ATTEMPTED RECORD: World's Hairiest Liar (man)
WEATHER: Why would you think it changed?
ADJUDICATOR: Mindy Patel (inmate #4290-6632)

Sorry, Robert. Had to put the sheet up over the bars and take some me-time. By now you'll have downloaded that picture and understand why. Oh, Remmy. You bastard. You machine. I keep going back and forth between hating him and loving him and hating him all over again. I can't describe my mood, except to say I'm in the right place for it. Half of these bitches are on Prozac and the others stay doped up on lithium most of the time. Maybe I should be charging them more? I don't know. Decision for another day. Anyway, I have a story to tell:

After making love (four times) Remmy and I emerged from the shack. I was surprised to find that it was still daylight. And that I could walk (you looked at the picture, right?). I knew I needed to get back to the hotel room to file my report (though, as I said, you were the last thing on my mind).

Buell was nowhere to be found and Rebekkah was sitting off in the woods with that small cherry box in her lap (the case is all over the Atlanta news, but I wonder if it's made it to New York yet? If not, Google "ax" + "six toes" + "Mother"). I waved good-bye to Rebekkah, but I'm pretty sure she didn't see me. She didn't seem to see anything. You'd think she was a leprechaun with a pot of gold, the way she was clutching onto that box.

Remmy took me back to my truck in the airboat. He gently kissed my hand, then helped me up to the dock and then steadied me as I got used to firmer ground. He promised me that he would call. He promised me that we would see each other again. He made lots of promises, but I knew nothing would ever come of it. He wanted me for my Adjudication. I see that now. All the phone calls. All the letters. They're always about that damn World Record.

Tongue! Of all things, why did he pick the tongue? He could walk into any World Hair Record, easy-peasy. His ears alone are riddled with pokey, curly strands like pubic hair. And as for his pubic hair—hello, New Category! Trust me, I'm still pulling long hairs from places you don't even want to know about. That man is a shedder. And he could have ten World Records if he would just admit—

But no, it'll never happen. The only record Remmy Rothstein's tongue could break (at least one we could write about) is Most Lies Told in a Three-Hour Period. He lied about the length of his tongue. He lied about the width. He lied to get me out to the swamp and then he lied about loving me.

I tell you this with a heavy heart, Robert. The bastard isn't even Jewish.

DISPATCH: Atlanta Penitentiary, Georgia
SUBJECT: Remmy Rothstein, "Fuckwad"
DATE: August 22, 2012
ATTEMPTED RECORD: Shittiest Asshole
WEATHER: Seriously? Are you an idiot?
ADJUDICATOR: Mindy Patel (inmate #4290-6632)

Dear Robert:

What a crazy day! I met with my lawyer all morning. He thinks the best route vis-à-vis the stabbing charge (it wasn't me) is to get something on Rebekkah. She's getting out of solitary today, so I have to be quick about it.

I feel really bad about this because I think of Rebekkah as a friend. Well, as friend-like as you can get on the inside. We all know that the two rules of prison are (1) Don't run from the Po-Po and (2) Don't tell anybody anything you wouldn't tell the judge. I think being out of the swamp has made Rebekkah soften a bit. Not that she wouldn't have my back in a knife fight (thank God!), but she's so out of her element that she's clinging to the familiar, and in this case, that familiar is me. Let's face it—you don't find many Indian or Jewish cliques in prison (mostly because we're all in medical school. Haha).

But let's go back to Rebekkah, who I really do feel sorry for. She's been very depressed without Remmy (Buell—not so much). I finally got her to come clean about the whole World Record thing. It's as I suspected. Rebekkah used her Veterans Benefits to help Remmy get the tongue picture professionally Photoshopped (she fought in the Korean War—that's where she met Buell's father, "a goyim with the right amount of toes"). She and Remmy never in a million years thought that you'd send an actual Adjudicator to the deep, dark swamplands.

Frankly, neither did I, but that's a conversation for another day.

The thing is: remember I told you about that cherry box? The one that was on the mantel that Rebekkah was about to open in front of Buell? And then she had it in her lap after she (allegedly) chopped off his leg with an ax and (allegedly) drowned him?

Well, since I told the lawyer the same story as I'm telling you, he's thinking that there must be something in that box that Buell didn't want to see. If I can find out what's in there, then I can testify against Rebekkah in exchange for a get-out-of-jail-free card. Because, let's be honest, there are tons of snitches in jail—death row would be empty without them!—but if I could get that BOX and tell the judge and whoever would listen that Rebekkah showed it to me, that she trusted and confided in me...well, you see where this is going.

Your wife is a lawyer, right? She knows how these things work. Right?

The only thing is the box was returned to Remmy (Buell's closest relative who didn't [allegedly] kill him), and while Remmy loves his mama, there's only one thing that is more important to him than she is.

We see this every day in the field, Robert—people so desperate to be something, to have One Thing that they are Certifiably Better At than anyone else on the entire planet. They need that accomplishment. And we need them to succeed. Adjudicators are people, too. We need to know that there are Record Holders out there enjoying life to the fullest each and every day—and who gives them that magic, that life-altering designation that makes them somebody?

We do.

And we love them for it. We take pride in giving it to them. We mourn the loss when they lose it. I know you felt the same pain as I did when we heard that Lee Redmond[35] was in that accident. The loss wasn't just hers—it belonged to all of us. Remember it was me who saw you crying in the bathroom. It was me who helped comfort you during that awful time of need. Remember how much you

---

35. Before an automobile accident broke them, Redmond's fingernails, the longest in the world, measured a total length of 28' 4½".

laughed when I put that balloon animal on you? Oh, the smile on your face was worthy of a photograph. Several photographs. And because of that time we had together, I know you understand what it's like to want some poor soul who's been a loser all of their life to be a Winner.

So here's the thing, Robert: I need you to certify Remmy Rothstein as having the Longest Tongue in the World (man). As you know, my badge is suspended pending trial or I'd do it myself. I know this is a stretch to ask you, but I need to let you know, Robert, that I've been thinking about turning these correspondences into a book. My lawyer has already gotten me an agent (trust me, between the two of them, I'm not going to have that much money left) and she thinks she can get me a book deal in the mid–seven figures. And it can or cannot include the bit about our balloon animal sexcapades, and before you say no, please look at the attached picture, which I've also shared with my lawyer.

Peace,
Mindy

PS: We need to talk about Kaitlyn.

(attachment: Robert_BalloonOnPenis.jpg)


## FROM THE NEW YORK HEADQUARTERS OF THE WORLD RECORD HOLDERS' OFFICE OF ASSESSORS

Dear Mr. Rothstein:

Congratulations! You have been certified as having the Longest Tongue in the World (man)! From tip to top, your measurement of 3.9" has been Adjudicated as the World Record; thus, you may from here on out, or until the record is broken, call yourself a World Record Holder.

Holding a World Record is an Awesome Responsibility, Mr. Rothstein, and please be sure that your information, as well as supporting documentation, is contained in the World Record Holders' Assessors' Office vault in New York City. This information will be kept for your lifetime and will continue to stand so long as the Record is held.

Congratulations again, sir. You are literally One-Of-A-Kind!

*Paolo Pergini*

Paolo Pergini
President
World Record Holders Association, Corp.


**DISPATCH:** Two Egg, Florida
**SUBJECT:** Carol McGubberson
**DATE:** July 6, 2013
**ATTEMPTED RECORD:** Largest Nostril Opening (female)
**WEATHER:** 103 degrees, 100% humidity
**ADJUDICATOR:** Kaitlyn Poole (badge #363941)

Hi, Robert—

Two Egg is really lovely this time of year. People keep saying it's hot, but I say it's a wet heat. Makes all the difference. Woke up to 98 degrees but it feels like 110 and it's not even noon yet! No need to even take a shower! Saves lots of time!

As you know, I'm here to Adjudicate Mrs. McGubberson's Nostril, but I wanted to let you know that I saw Mindy's book at the airport bookstore. Not just the one in New York, but in Chicago, Fargo, Seattle, and finally Sarasota—every single airport where I had a layover on my flight to Florida. How crazy is that? Our Mindy a *New York Times* bestseller! Hello, Ms. Steel![36]

I have to admit that I actually bought a copy. I just couldn't resist. How many books has Elizabeth Gilbert[37] said she wished she'd written? Everyone on every plane seemed to be reading it, and I have to admit Mindy has been really good in all those television interviews. Though I never realized she's as short as Matt Lauer!

Seriously, though, I'm glad that she's doing so well. And you were so heartbroken that night in Knoxville when you found out she was leaving the firm. I'm so glad I was there to comfort you. And to do with you all the other magical things we did. Oh, don't worry, Robert, I'm not going to bring that up again! I'm moving on! Honest!

Anyhoo, long day tomorrow—Mrs. Gubberson lives six hours from the motel—so I should tuck myself into bed. Definitely the kind of place where you sleep with all your clothes on! I'm starting Mindy's book tonight and will let you know how it goes.

I have to say the title has me a little puzzled—TWELVE TOES IN A BOX?

I don't get it.

Kaitlyn

---

36. Danielle Steel holds the world record for most consecutive weeks on the *New York Times* bestseller list.

37. Author of *Eat, Pray, Love*.

# ABOUT THE AUTHORS

**Jan Burke's** bestselling books include *Disturbance*, *The Messenger*, and *Bones*, which won the Edgar for Best Novel. Her short stories have won the Agatha, the Macavity, and other awards.

She has a degree in history and loved doing the research for this story. She is currently at work on her next novel.

**Laura Lippman** is a *New York Times* bestseller who has published seventeen novels, a novella, and a collection of short stories. Her work, which includes the Tess Monaghan series and several stand-alone novels, has been published in more than twenty languages and has won multiple awards, including the Edgar. She lives in Baltimore and New Orleans.

**Libby Fischer Hellmann,** an award-winning Chicago crime fiction author, has published ten novels. Her most recent, *A Bitter Veil*, is set in revolutionary Iran, and was released in April 2012. "War Secrets" is a prequel to that novel.

Libby's other stand-alone thriller, *Set the Night on Fire* (2010), goes back, in part, to the late sixties in Chicago. She also writes two crime fiction series: one featuring Chicago PI Georgia Davis (three novels) and the four-novel Ellie Foreman series, which Libby describes as a cross between *Desperate Housewives* and *24*.

Libby has also published fifteen short stories in *Nice Girl Does Noir* and edited the acclaimed crime fiction anthology *Chicago Blues*. She has been nominated twice for the Anthony Award and once for the Agatha. All her work is available digitally.

Originally from Washington, DC, she has lived in Chicago for thirty years and claims they'll take her out of there feet-first.

More at her website: www.libbyhellmann.com.

**C. E. Lawrence** is the byline of a New York–based suspense writer, performer, composer, and prizewinning playwright and poet whose previous books have been praised as "lively..." (*Publishers Weekly*); "constantly absorbing..." (starred, *Kirkus Reviews*); and "superbly crafted prose" (*Boston Herald*). *Silent Screams, Silent Victim,* and *Silent Kills* are the first three books in her Lee Campbell thriller series. Her other work is published under the name of Carole Buggé. Titan Press recently reissued her first Sherlock Holmes novel, *The Star of India*.

Visit her online at http://celawrence.com.

**Joseph Finder** is the *New York Times* bestselling author of ten novels, whom the *Boston Globe* has called a "master of the modern thriller." His most recent book, *Buried Secrets*, the second to feature "private spy" Nick Heller, received the 2011 Strand Critics Award for Best Novel. His first novel, *The Moscow Club*, was named by *Publishers Weekly* one of the ten best spy novels of all time. *Killer Instinct* was named Best Novel of the Year by the International Thriller Writers, and *Paranoia* is in production as a major motion picture starring Liam Hemsworth, Harrison Ford, and Gary Oldman. His novel *High Crimes* became a hit movie starring Morgan Freeman and Ashley Judd. A *summa cum laude* graduate of Yale, Joe did graduate work at the Harvard Russian Research Center and is a member of the Council on Foreign Relations and the Association of Former Intelligence Officers. He lives in Boston and Cape Cod.

**James O. Born** is the award-winning author of five police thrillers and a number of short stories. He is a recipient of the Florida Book Award. In 2009 he won the Barry Award for a short story in the Mystery Writers of America anthology *The Blue Religion*. He was also named one of the twenty-one Most Intriguing Floridians by *Florida Monthly*.

Under the pen name James O'Neal, he has written two near-future thrillers that have received critical praise. *The Human Disguise* and *The Double Human* are published by Tor. They are a fusion of police procedural and urban fantasy.

**S. W. Hubbard's** most recent novel is *Another Man's Treasure*. She is also the author of three mystery novels set in the Adirondack Mountains: *Take the Bait, Swallow the Hook*, and *Blood Knot*. Her short stories have appeared in *Alfred Hitchcock Mystery Magazine* and the anthologies *Crimes by Moonlight* and *Adirondack Mysteries*. She lives in Morristown, New Jersey, where she teaches creative writing to enthusiastic teens and adults, and expository writing to reluctant college freshmen.

**Joseph Goodrich** is an alumnus of New Dramatists and an active member of Mystery Writers of America. His short story "Murder in the Sixth" appeared in the 2011 MWA anthology *The Rich and the Dead*, edited by Nelson DeMille. His plays have been produced across the United States and in Australia and are published by Samuel French, Playscripts, and Applause Books, among others. *Panic* was awarded the 2008 Edgar Award for Best Play. Joseph is the editor of *Blood Relations: The Selected Letters of Ellery Queen, 1947–1950* (Perfect Crime Books), and his nonfiction has appeared in Mystery Scene and Crimespree.

**R. T. Lawton** is a retired federal agent, a past member of the Mystery Writers of America board of directors, and a Derringer Award nominee for 2010 and 2011. He has published over eighty short stories, of which almost a third appeared in *Alfred Hitchcock Mystery Magazine*, where he has four ongoing series. Other publications include the anthology *Who Died in Here?*, the e-anthology *West Coast Crime Wave*, *Easyriders*, *Outlaw Biker*, and several mini-mysteries in *Woman's World* magazine. Four of his short story collections in e-book form are currently available at Amazon.com for the Kindle and at Smashwords.com for other e-book readers. You can also find him at http://tinyurl.com/rtlawton and blogging at www.sleuthsayers.org.

**Tom Rob Smith** was born in 1979 to a Swedish mother and an English father and was brought up in London, where he still lives. He graduated from Cambridge University in 2001 and spent a year in Italy on a creative writing scholarship. Tom has worked as a screenwriter for the past five years, including a six-month stint in Phnom Penh storylining Cambodia's first-ever soap. His first novel, *Child 44*, was long-listed for the 2008 Man Booker Prize, was short-listed for the Costa First Novel Award and the inaugural Desmond Elliott Prize, and won the Crime Writers' Association's Ian Fleming Steel Dagger Award for best adventure/thriller novel of 2008, and the American edition won Best Debut at the International Thriller Awards and Best Debut at the Strand Magazine Critics Awards.

Former model and world traveler—in her early days she drove overland from Europe to India and the Himalayas via the Silk Route—**Mary Anne Kelly** returned to hometown Richmond Hill, Queens, New York, to write. From *Park Lane South, Queens* to *Pack up the Moon*, her Claire Breslinsky series portrays in mystery the life she leads.

Now settled in Rockville Centre, Long Island, with her husband and son, Mary Anne composes fiction and writes songs from the grandfather chair in her kitchen. She is currently on location in Munich, researching her next novel.

**Tony Broadbent** is the author of a series of mystery novels about a Cockney cat burglar in austerity-ridden, black market–riddled postwar London who gets blackmailed into working for MI5.

The first novel in the series, *The Smoke*, received starred reviews and was named "one of the best first mystery novels of 2002." *Spectres in The Smoke*, the follow-up, received the Bruce Alexander Historical Mystery Award in 2006 and was proclaimed by *Booklist* "one of the best spy novels of the year." The third in the series, *Shadows in The Smoke*, was published in 2012. *Skylon in The Smoke* is next in the series.

Tony has written for newspapers, magazines, radio, television, and film and works as a consulting brand strategist and ideator. He was born in Windsor, England, and now lives with his American wife in Mill Valley, California.

**Steve Berry** is a *New York Times* and #1 internationally bestselling author who mixes action, history, secrets, conspiracies, and international settings into pulse-pounding contemporary thrillers. He is the creator of the Cotton Malone series, which started with *The Templar Legacy* and continued with *The Alexandria Link*, *The Venetian Betrayal*, *The Charlemagne Pursuit*, *The Emperor's Tomb*, *The Jefferson Key* and his latest, *The King's Deception*. He also has four stand-alone thrillers—*The Amber Room*, *The Romanov Prophecy*, *The Third Secret*, and his latest, *The Columbus Affair*—along with three e-book originals, *The Balkan Escape*, *The Devil's Gold*, and *The Admiral's Mark*. His books have been translated into forty languages and are sold in fifty-one countries worldwide. He lives in the historic city of St. Augustine, Florida. He and his wife, Elizabeth, founded History Matters, a nonprofit organization dedicated to preserving our heritage. To learn more about Steve, his books, and the foundation, visit www.steveberry.org.

After law school, **Angela Gerst** moved from New York to Massachusetts and over the years worked as a journalist, as a campaign consultant, in magazine sales, and in marketing. Long an admirer of Colette's fiction, she wrote "The Secret Life of Books" after devouring a collection of Colette's own short stories.

Her first novel, *A Crack in Everything*, a Susan Callisto mystery, won a starred review from Kirkus and praise from such disparate writers as Lisa Scottoline and John Barth. Angela is currently at work on the second novel in the Callisto mystery series. She and her husband live near Boston. Visit Angela, Susan Callisto, and Colette at angelagerst.com.

**Catherine Mambretti** learned at the University of Chicago that she wanted to write, not lecture about, fiction. Haunting the library stacks there, she discovered Kate Warne, the world's first female detective. Catherine knew, even before earning her PhD in literature, that she had to write about "The Very Private Detectress," a woman whose Civil War adventures included serving as the disguised Lincoln's bodyguard and capturing a cunning female Southern spy.

Catherine is the author of a short story collection, *The Evil That Men Do*, and *The Juror Hangs*, a novel inspired by jury duty at Cook County's notorious Criminal Courthouse. She is a Derringer Award nominee and the winner of a Textnovel.com Prize for *Chalk Ghost*, the novella that inspired her forthcoming novel, *Snow Ghost*. She is an active member of Mystery Writers of America and the Authors Guild. Visit her at www.ccmambretti.com.

**Stephen Ross** is a failed rock musician who turned to a life of crime. His short stories have appeared in *Ellery Queen Mystery Magazine*,

*Alfred Hitchcock Mystery Magazine,* and others. He has been nominated for an Edgar Award and a Derringer Award, and he was a 2010 Ellery Queen Readers Award finalist. Over the years, Stephen has lived in Auckland, London, and Frankfurt, but he currently resides on the beautiful Whangaparaoa Peninsula of New Zealand. He still writes and performs music, when no one is around, and he maintains a website at www.StephenRoss.net.

**Caroline and Charles Todd,** writing together as Charles Todd, are actually mother and son. Caroline lives in Delaware and Charles in North Carolina. They write best when not in the same room. Both travel to England to give their settings and their plots a firsthand realism. They are the authors of the Inspector Ian Rutledge Mysteries and the Bess Crawford Mystery Series, as well as many short stories.

Charles has been a corporate troubleshooter and holds a degree in business and communications. His favorite place is any beach, and his favorite team is Tar Heel basketball. He collects seashells from around the world, and he brakes for historical signs wherever he travels. A longtime *Columbo* fan, he is also a movie buff.

Caroline has degrees in history/literature and international relations. History has always been her first love and travel her second, although the Atlanta Braves are a close third. She collects bookmarks from the countries she visits, and shares Charles's love of books and movies.

**Jonathan Stone** does most of his writing on the commuter train between the Connecticut suburbs and Manhattan, where he is the creative director of a midtown advertising agency. His four published crime novels have all been optioned for film, and when you see the proverbial pigs overhead, you can trot over to your local multiplex to catch one of them.

"When I read the parameters for *The Mystery Box,* I thought of a manuscript I had on the shelf that would fit perfectly. One problem: my manuscript was a novella—at 34,000 words, almost five times too long. So for me, writing 'Hedge' was a protracted, rigorous lesson in editing. Having it chosen for the anthology probably confirms once again that less is more. On the other hand, if anyone wants me to expand the short story into a novel?...hey, I'm your guy."

A graduate of Yale, Jon is married, with a son in college and a daughter in high school.

**Katherine Neville** has been described as the female Umberto Eco, Alexandre Dumas, and Steven Spielberg. Her first swashbuckling adventure/quest novel, *The Eight*, was credited by *Publishers Weekly* with having "paved the way for books like *The Da Vinci Code*," and was recently voted, in a national poll by the noted Spanish journal *El País*, one of the top ten books of all time. Neville is the first author invited onto the board of the Smithsonian Institution Libraries; she also serves in the Monticello Cabinet of the Thomas Jefferson Foundation and is a regular cochair of the Authors Guild Foundation's annual fund-raiser. Her bestselling books (*New York Times, USA Today, Washington Post*) have been translated into forty languages and have pleased millions of readers around the world. She lives in Virginia; Washington, DC; and Santa Fe.

**R. L. (Robert Lawrence) Stine** is one of the bestselling children's authors in history. His Goosebumps series, along with such series as Fear Street, The Nightmare Room, Rotten School, and Mostly Ghostly, have sold nearly 400 million books in this country alone. And they have been translated into thirty-two languages.

His popular TV series, *R. L. Stine's The Haunting Hour*, is in its third season on the Hub TV network.

The year 2012 marked the twentieth anniversary of the Goosebumps book series, which comprises over 100 books. In the same year, R.L.'s hardcover horror novel for adults, *Red Rain*, was published by Touchstone Books.

## ABOUT THE AUTHORS

In 2011, R.L. was honored by the International Thriller Writers as ThrillerMaster at their annual banquet. R.L. lives in New York City with his wife, Jane, an editor and publisher, and their King Charles spaniel, Minnie.

**Karin Slaughter** has written twelve books that have sold a combined thirty million copies in thirty-two different languages. A longtime resident of Atlanta, she splits her time between the kitchen and the living room.